THE
FEAST
OF ANGELS

THE
FEAST
OF ANGELS

Denis R. Tougas

CITIOFBOOKS, INC.
3736 Eubank NE Suite A1
Albuquerque, NM 87111-3579
www.citiofbooks.com
Hotline: 1 (877) 389-2759
Fax: 1 (505) 930-7244

Ordering Information:

Quantity sales. Special discounts are available on quantity purchases by corporations, associations, and others. For details, contact the publisher at the address above.

Printed in the United States of America.

ISBN-13:   Softcover   979-8-89391-239-5

               eBook   979-8-89391-240-1

Library of Congress Control Number: 2024916195

TABLE OF CONTENTS

PROLOGUE

As it was in the beginning, so it shall be in the end. Days of change surrounded everyone. It happened in every nation of the Earth, none was exempt, for what was happening and what had already transpired was witnessed by all. No one had the foresight to see the obvious, except maybe the sages and the enlightened ones. The people of this planet were disappearing, not whole families at a time as one would assume, but as if they had courageously and boldly decided to escape under the cover of darkness, avoiding the winds of evil that encompassed them.

The missing were the chosen ones, selected out of families of every faith and denomination. There were criteria involved with their disappearances that had nothing to do with social status or monetary enlightenment, nor was there any political agenda tied to the selection. They disappeared from the slums of Bombay, the barrios of Mexico City and from the Russian elite to the New Guinea forests. Name the city of state, the country or continent, and it made no difference. People disappeared.

The date it all started was a date that had explicit implications to most, while it meant nothing to others. Explanations for some of the disappearances made it into a few of the local newspapers in various countries, stories loosely based on known facts about the individual, speculating as to where they may have gone or what they may have done.

For some time, just one or two from any given area were turned in to police departments as missing persons or as runaways in some cases, depending on age. No one was the least bit alarmed at first. The police wrote their reports, sent out bulletins, and chased fruitless leads. Some families even posted their own fliers, trying desperately to locate their loved ones, but to no avail, for they, the chosen, were never seen on this earth again.

It would be some time before anyone made the connection regarding the severity of the issue. As usual, with any change, they are not abrupt at first, just small numbers of people had vanished; likened to a child counting digits on his hand, one then two and so on until the magic number ten was achieved. Then it became larger numbers, more like counting the grains of sand you could pick up in your hand at the beach, the sheer number of grains when totaled in the tens of thousands. It then became a numbers game that rose exponentially.

Long before it got to that point though, some people demanded answers to the disappearances, but as usual, their pleas fell on deaf ears. The powers to be were reckless, more concerned about a solid bottom line than the welfare of one or two of their fellow men. The tabloids finally got wind of some of the rather unusual cases when they involved people of status and stature, making predictions that the disappearances were the result of alien abductions, serial killers, cults, slave rings and the like, but it was much more serious than that. How serious not one quite realized at first, nor even halfway through the process, for that matter. The abductions were unpredictable, for this is what they were termed to be.

At the height of the Crisis, which took some time to develop, theories began to abound, the foremost being why? The learned and the religious gathered as one, putting their animosities aside, as they attempted to solve the riddle, forwarding some concrete thoughts and ideas, hoping to soothe the masses from their growing paranoia. They even brought the latest technologies to bear. However, the situation would not rise to a furor for some time to come. When it began, no one and I mean no one, even bothered to look at the one constant that foretold this plague on humanity. A battle was being fought. Not in the sense of battles with visible armament, but a battle of a different sort, which did not really include the known forces of man against man? They were forces though, just the same.

The Learned though, were the ones that finally recognized what had transpired. They were the ones who finally figured it out, only to be branded as strange, insane or mad by the general populace. The answer was not received well, as they were hunted down like the purported witches of the middle ages. These were the fortunate though, who received the visions or dreams that, along with research, gave them an opportune piece of the puzzle that helped to put these pieces together. Then, the truth of the matter was finally revealed.

Many other changes were also happening at the same time -climate variations began in earnest: hurricanes, droughts and adverse weather conditions, more than ever recorded before. It even snowed in the Sahara and Gobi deserts. Unpredictability became the buzzword for most of the world's forecasters, for there were no prior records that even hinted of the seesaw weather patterns that happened now with increased regularity. Case in point - New York City in the middle of the dog days of summer recorded, a fetid ninety-eight degrees on August 5th, and the next day it snowed.

Hurricanes, tornados, and typhoons were on meteoric rise. As far back as records were kept, never before had so many been recorded at any other time in history, such catastrophic events became the norm. The planet shook and shuddered with a record number of earthquakes for which no one had an explanation. Finally, the politics of the situation heralded in all the naysayers.

The sign of the times was an old but wise saying as some people walked through the streets, squares and plazas holding the banners high and shouting, "Repent! The end is near!" So it was for some, for the maelstrom was building. The most popular books on the best sellers list became religious tomes for all the faiths.

Parties became all the rage once again, not cocktail parties as you would imagine, but Prayer parties - groups of people banding together, hoping to make some sense of an unexpected image. Religious attendance soared and the hierarchies of these religious beliefs were ecstatic. Their coffers swelled as people gave unselfishly so as they might be spared. The deed was an old but foolish one. The religious leaders though, were either mum or slow in telling the constituency otherwise. They let their flocks assume that what they did and thought was truth. In essence, nothing could be farther from it. So the story begins...

CHAPTER 1

An Early Disappearance

Milan, Italy

The Reverend Father Giuseppe Lorenzo rushed onto the train platform and made it onto the Metro just as the doors began to close, angling his body so as not be caught between them. He smiled to no one in particular and entered the inner platform at the end of the car. He saw his reflection in the mirror, unconsciously palming the back of his head in the process. The mirror hung on the wall at the end of the car, an attempt to appease the vanity of the Italian people. Conscious thought would dictate that women would use the mirror more than men to check their form and appearance, but the opposite was true.

He tried to scan the car upon entry in an effort to see if he was fortunate enough to spy an open seat as the tram began to move, jolting him backwards in the process. He braced himself, silently wishing he were a few inches taller than his five-foot four stature allowed. Standing on the toes of his black leather shoes, he was finally able to look over the shoulder of the man who had blocked his vision. Unfortunately, he was out of luck. The car was full, though he knew if he made his way into the confines of the car's interior, his collar would have afforded him a seat. This was an abuse of power in his mind, so he patiently waited to see if his fortunes might change. Maybe someone would get off at the next stop.

Luck was not with him today. No one got off at the next or subsequent stops, either. The Metro made several more stops as it headed south, with nowhere to sit, the landing area of the car filled to capacity. The priest stood still, packed in place, and resigned himself to being jostled about with everyone else standing alongside him this morning.

He occasionally looked out of the window of the tram to track its progress, having taken this route many times before. He knew the exact location of the car as it moved, the clacking wheels resonating a rhythmic beat that he felt through the soles of his shoes. The familiarity of his surroundings lulled his mind and he became preoccupied with other matters, which at this moment were of greater importance to him.

His intended destination was the Duomo of Milan, where he was to meet with an old childhood friend of his deceased father, his mentor Archbishop Robbia, the man solely responsible for his current occupation of choice.

Giuseppe glanced at his watch and knew that he was cutting it close. He was worried that he would not make Mass in time, an occasion that the all too busy Archbishop Robbia still liked to partake in with a measured degree of punctually. The powerful man gathered his close acquaintances and confidents together for this weekly rite and afterwards, over breakfast, discussed any subject of relevance that may have come up during the course of the previous week with which he needed assistance.

The train was running late, which was typical, though just this once he had hoped it would be on schedule. His only reason for taking a later train than he was normally accustomed to taking was the fact that this morning he had returned a rather urgent call from his sister concerning their ill mother as he ventured out toward the station.

The conversation ended up taking longer than he had expected, throwing him out of his normal routine. He could tell by his sister's all too panicked voice and its rapidity that it would take some time to calm her enough for her to speak with a measure of clarity. He had to stop on the sidewalk several times in order to maintain his cell phone reception while walking toward the train station as he attempted to calm her sudden anxiety. From what he surmised; she had just arrived at their childhood home. He must have just missed her. She had finally witnessed what he tried to futilely convey to her on the phone the evening before, which was the subject of their mother's sudden illness. Originally, he just wanted her to check in on their mother while he was at the Duomo, never imagining that his sister would become so distraught over the sight of their mother's sudden ailing condition.

That was the one thing he detested about his sister, Jole. As he listened to her prattle on incoherently, he wished she could, just once, take him at his word. She had one solemn rule; never believe a word he said, a true doubting Thomas if ever there was one. He was just a ten-block walk from the station and seriously debated whether he should return home. Still, passing on the required meeting really wasn't an option either.

He strove to keep the conversation brief and to the point or else Jole would go off on a tangent and belabor past grievances against him. Before he hung up, he specifically instructed his sister that if their mother's condition worsened, she should take her to the hospital and phone him immediately. He would meet her there.

As a matter of habit, Giuseppe spent one night a week visiting with his mother, an occasion he always looked forward to. Doing so afforded him a chance to spend some time with her, whom he always enjoyed, and the visits lessened the effect of his arduous travels from his current station in Rome.

The priest hoped to God that his mother would improve as quickly as she had fallen ill. He prayed silently for her as the train moved along, for she was still a young woman in most respects, in good health that belied her fifty-nine years. She still had the vitality and youthful appearance of a woman in her late thirties, so this sudden turn of events was totally unexpected.

The Metro had one more stop to make before it arrived at his destination. By the look of the situation on board the tram, he doubted anyone else could either embark or disembark the car, it was so packed. He just hoped that he would not be caught up in the center of the wave of humanity as it exited. He glanced at his watch once again and noted that he still had several minutes to spare, which calmed him considerably as the train slowed to his stop.

He was a punctual man as a matter of habit, which he felt redeemed some of his otherwise less than stalwart attributes somewhat. He knew one thing for sure - the human condition was rife with frailties, as he had come to know, both religious and otherwise, and he was no exception.

The train finally stopped at his destination and he was forced back into the reality of life as soon as the door opened, almost having to force his way out. He quickly moved up the stairs and out onto the piazza. There, he saw the beauty of the cathedral as he gained the top step, for it was right in front of him. He was biased, but he thought it was one of the most beautiful buildings in the entire world and never grew tired of looking at the multi-faceted structure with unuttered awe. Words really could not express his thoughts about the aged edifice, which offered him a sense of complete satisfaction and bolstered his religious might, for the building and its contents were works of art. He crossed the piazza with swift measure, the pigeons scattering out of the way as he walked straight for the front door of the church.

The only thing that he detested on his weekly sojourn was the giant television screen up and to his right, which loomed over the piazza and detracted his sense of sight. He stopped momentarily and shook his head at the sight of it. In this case, the old and the new did not mix and he secretly wished the screen would someday fall. "Sacrilegious," he muttered, looking away from the screen. He headed for the security checkpoint in front of the church. He hoped someone might address his comment so that he could once again expound on the indecency of the technological object, but no one did.

These were indeed trying times, he thought as he waited to be scanned by a metal detector before entering the church. While he realized the importance of the screening, as there were many factions about which sought to destroy great art works of the past, not only in the museums of the world but to historically relevant places such as this, but still wished it were not necessary.

Ensconced inside the cathedral was one of the most precious artifacts of the Roman Catholic Church itself - a nail from Christ's crucifixion. This in itself was singularly significant. Add to that the paintings and murals that adorned the walls of the building and the cathedral qualified as a museum in its own right. Giuseppe had acute knowledge of what it all meant too. He was a religious historian stationed in Rome, though his place of birth was North Milan.

The forty-year-old priest gained entrance to the church and hurried up the wide expanse of left side aisle, silently praying for forgiveness for his haste. He stopped briefly at the main altar to pay his humble respects and then moved behind the main altar to the private altar behind it, arriving within moments of the start of the service. He audibly sighed and nodded respectfully to Archbishop Robbia, and then took a seat as a serving participant.

After the service, as was expected, the Archbishop and eight of his closest allies gathered for a lunch on the church grounds. The luncheon consisted of customary Italian fare: cheese, meat, bread and wine. The archbishop usually reserved his comments until he had finished eating. He was content to listen to the varied comments about current events as his guests bantered back and forth around the old oaken table.

Giuseppe looked around the table of gathered men, remembering how he had been intimidated by this group when first asked to join them. At the time, he thought it not only an honor to be asked, but wondered why it was that he was chosen to join them. He later learned that his expertise in religious history had prompted his inclusion to the Archbishop's inner circle.

At the moment, several priests voiced their thoughts about the viability of the current Italian soccer team, while several others commented on current political affairs in Italy. Giuseppe was more worried about the anticipated failure of the olive crop again this year. A hard and unexpected freeze had killed off most of the olive crop in central Italy last year and another freeze was expected this year. Such events usually only happened once every twenty-five years or so, never two years in a row. This radical weather change deeply concerned him, and he discussed the economic impact of the situation with the priest seated to his right.

He stopped talking when the topic of conversation at the table shifted and focused on the raging turmoil in the Middle East. The din of voices rose and Giuseppe listened contently to the ensuing discussion but added no comment of his own. What started out being a good-natured discussion then became heated, as almost every one of the men seated at the table gave their own solution to the ongoing problem. Finally, after the octave of the room had risen high enough for him to finally take offense, the Archbishop held up his hand. The room grew silent at once, all faces turning quizzically toward the Archbishop.

"Father Lorenzo, you are the historian among us and silent up until now. What are your thoughts on the matter?" The archbishop attempted to stifle a burp in the process, which, Giuseppe saw amused some of the priests in the room, who began chuckling heartily.

Giuseppe had his own ideas about solving the problems that faced every nation with diverse religious and political backgrounds. "I believe every one of the nations that these learned gentlemen have previously mentioned ought to hire a historian and make them first council to all their leaders. For that matter, it should be a requirement for all nations of the world to do so," he commented, his voice void of any intonation.

"Father Lorenzo, you are evading the question in its entirety and raising your own banner in response to the question, are you not?" the Archbishop asked, his expression perturbed. His left hand gently strummed the table as if it were a piano.

"Not entirely," Giuseppe disagreed. "All of you gentlemen know that it was written that the twelve tribes of Israel will not unite until the end of days, so what is the point? There is no real solution to the problems in the Middle East as I see them, would you not agree?" He looked about the table for a note of encouragement on his behalf. His comments elicited a spate of protest from the ranks of knowledgeable men, most of them protesting the thought as evasive and voicing their own opinions in unison once again.

The rebuttal from the group to Giuseppe's statement was meant in part to impress Archbishop Robbia, whose name had recently been bantered about the Vatican as a likely candidate for the latest vacant position of Cardinal. He was a frontrunner for the position and most of hierarchy with inside connections knew he had access to the Pope's ear in regard to church's financial matters. Once inside the Sacred College of Cardinals, it was said that he would be a powerful force with which to be reckoned. No one even indirectly associated with the Vatican denied that.

Giuseppe knew that Archbishop Robbia would soon become a Cardinal, as it was a known historical premise that anyone likely to run the Duomo of Milan was assured the position in due time. He also knew that the men surrounding the Archbishop were currently posturing for position and not likely to back a lowly priest such as himself. Still, he thought to press his point anyway. Warding the continued comments off with his hands, he glanced around the room, begging silence with his eyes and then looked directly at the soon-to-be Cardinal.

The wiry man in the all-white gown raised his hand to silence his comrades once again. The Archbishop looked as if he were beginning to show his true age. Giuseppe could not be sure, thinking it might just be the lack of color contrast with the white linens he wore. He studied him closely; thin lips and whitened brows arched downward, reflecting a pensive mood. His black eyes glittered with interest though, almost as if he was asking the priest to spurn the intended mockery to his chosen profession.

Giuseppe grinned slightly as he spoke. "When Hitler invaded Russia during World War Two, the venture was doomed from the start. Napoleon, his predecessor in that very endeavor had failed before him in exactly the same manner as Caesar failed before him after passing the Rubicon. Had either of the latter two men enjoined a historical advisor on staff, the same mistakes would probably not have been made in succession." The priest paused to allow the information to sink in, his eyes still locked in contact with his mentor. "To cite another more recent account of my meaning, how was the United States supposed to win in Vietnam when the French could not? The British and the Russians could not win in Afghanistan and the Americans didn't either. Historical facts, gentlemen, all of it, and mistakes such as these could have easily been avoided as I previously mentioned."

The Archbishop smiled broadly, exposing widely spaced teeth in the process. "A point well taken, Father Lorenzo!" His hand stopped strumming and his palm was now turned upward, acknowledging the younger man's right of speech without further comment from his colleagues.

Bishop Alvito, however, had taken offence. As the second in command of this tightly knit group and the archbishop's closest advisor, his baritone voice boomed across the table, resounding off the walls of the small room in the process. The rotund man's face masked contempt, hardly believing what he had just heard. Giuseppe saw the infusion of red in the man's huge jowls as he shook his head in ghastly disbelief.

"What do you think we were referring to earlier, Giuseppe? During the last council of Bishops, the exact same subject was brought up and we all agreed that six of the twelve tribes are aligned for a distinct purpose, and that is the total annihilation of the Jewish state of Israel. This, by the way, is not new news. It's been going on for some time now. Had it not been for some brilliant diplomacy in the past by the Americans and sanctioned by the United Nations in the process for once, this exact scenario you so dearly quoted with aplomb would have already occurred!" Bishop Alvito's gaze bore into the younger man as he went in for the kill. "Please don't mistake everyone in the room as half-witted, as you apparently think we are."

The man then pointed his stubby index finger in Giuseppe's direction, which caused the young priest to sink into the chair.

"Furthermore, we may not have the advantage of your learned historical background, but our eyes and ears are not closed to our surroundings! Pray yours aren't when the time comes."

At that point, the only thing the priest could do was pray for intervention on his behalf. The jackals could smell his figurative blood in the room. The seat of his black trousers stuck to the wooden chair from a sudden cold sweat and he sat stunned, unable to utter an instant reply. He thought about how best to handle the situation without raising any further ire. The Archbishop finally looked down the table at his right-hand man in an effort to assuage his huge ego in some non-verbal way, which Giuseppe saw had an immediate effect on the irate bishop.

"It was never my intent to insult anyone's intelligence, nor was I being pomp about my profession," Giuseppe stated quietly. "If anyone in the room assumed as much…, you have my apology. In my position, part of the job in which I hold is to collect known facts that may be used to either enlighten or enable the hierarchy of this church to make wise decisions based on my research." He turned to the bishop and tipped his head. "Yes, Bishop Alvito, there is a unification of sorts with at least six of the tribes of Israel, though if I may correct an error in your last statement; it was the Egyptians, and with the aid of the Americans, who brokered the cease-fire you spoke about. If I may also say so, it will be the nations within the Middle East itself who will band together on their own accord without outside intervention, and then only out of sheer necessity." Giuseppe heard the audible sigh emitted from the lips of his tormentor, but it was the Archbishop who cleared the air.

"There are reasons why I bring all of you gentlemen here by my side, as each of you has your own specific talents." He pulled at his left earlobe as he gazed around the room. "I sometimes wish I could find one man who had all such talents combined in this room, but unfortunately for me, he has yet to be located. However, if I ever find such a man, I will know the meaning of true peace, for it is nearly impossible for a lone man to argue with himself."

Giuseppe noted that it was a rarity for the Archbishop to chastise the group as a whole. He also knew that the position of the man seated across from him came with demands he really could only assume to understand. The deterioration of world affairs had to add to the pressure on anyone unfortunate enough to sit in a position of high authority. The priest made no outward expression to the comment. Instead, he admired the Archbishop's innate abilities to quell a raging storm.

The Archbishop gazed into the faces of everyone seated around the table, so they would grasp his measure of sincerity as he spoke anew. "Gentlemen, forgiveness is a virtue in and of its own accord. Let us recognize the talents of each individual in the room and press on with the task at hand. We are at a crisis point here in Italy, and what I would really rather discuss at this meeting is the marked reduction in weekly attendance of Mass. We need to brainstorm here in an effort to come up with a way of heralding the lost and disenfranchised sheep back into the fold. Every one of you, I am sure, has their own ideas on how to achieve this. Short of a miracle or a divine revelation of some sort, which does not seem probable, something has to be done about this, which is what I would like to address today."

Giuseppe noticed that the Archbishop's face became veiled in earnestness, and his looks had taken on a chiseled form. His fingers once again drummed impatiently on the table for effect. "Monsignor Sforza, what is the precise percentage of practicing Catholics that actually attend mass each week?" Archbishop Robbia asked, without even looking at the man.

The priest sat straighter in his chair and a befuddled look crossed his face as he quickly made a sign of the cross. "Roughly about, and I am embarrassed to admit, twenty-five percent of the registered Catholics here in Italy attend mass each week."

"Good! So, what you are saying is that roughly seventy-five percent don't. What are your thoughts about why we have such a precipitous drop in weekly attendance?" the Archbishop asked, still strumming his fingers on the table for effect.

"Apathy?" Monsignor Sforza suggested, without conviction.

Giuseppe had noticed one thing about his mentor long ago, though he doubted that others in the room were as observant as he. Every time the archbishop liked or agreed with your answer, his fingers stopped tapping and direct eye contact was made. For some reason, if either because the man did not expound on his thoughts or possibly his reply was not the correct intended response, he continued to look down at his fingers as they tapped slightly lighter than usual on the table. Father Lorenzo silently prodded the monsignor on with his eyes, hoping he would continue as the elderly priest looked about the room for a united agreement to his thoughts on the matter. Giuseppe spoke up, breaking into the discussion knowing that he could very well be chastised for the move, coming to the aid of the elder advisor. The silence in the room loomed large.

"Excuse the intrusion," he said. "Our religion seems to be an institution in which the masses only turn when the conveniences of the world begin to wane. Take for instance the last worldwide recession, which started in 2008 and lasted well into middle of 2011. During that period, church attendance increased. Once that crisis passed, attendance fell once again. It's atypical of human nature, which as a rule only prays for divine intervention on their behalf when the chips are down. The morality of any nation is proportional to any crisis that it must endure, and the immorality of a nation increases with its good fortune and as a result, attendance decreases. This is not just happening here in Italy but seems to be a normal occurrence worldwide. This can be observed not only in the Catholic Church but also to all churches in general. What needs to happen here to change those numbers is to add new spark of enthusiasm to our church, which will affect our members in a positive way. This will drive attendance up, I believe, and I believe that Pope Alexander is trying to do just that. Maybe some sort of extraordinary action on our part is required for the numbers to change in any dramatic proportion."

The archbishop looked directly at Father Lorenzo. "Precisely!"

The word echoed through the room and the group as a whole began to expound on the question at hand. Both new and old ideas were bantered back and forth and Giuseppe knew he had left a marked impression on Archbishop Robbia once again. The resonance in the room began to escalate once again, and the priest wondered what could be derived from such a timeless question as blind faith and whether it could be restored once again in its original form. That hearkened back to the era of the infancy of the church. A trying time when the seeds of Christian faith had been planted and yet to sprout, when the Roman Catholic religion as a whole was persecuted for its unorthodox beliefs, its members tortured, maimed or killed for a belief that the savior had come once and will come again one day.

During the earliest days of the foundling church, Nero Claudius Caesar of Rome did more to advance the Catholic Church than he ever thought possible. His constant persecution of the early Christians did more to advance the religious cause than he realized at the time. Making martyrs out of the religious believers of this foundling ideology, advancing the cause of the new doctrine and spread the word throughout the Roman Empire as well.

Instead of stomping out the fires of fervor of this fledgling religion, as was the emperor's intent, it grew because of ongoing persecution. When the Roman Empire failed some time later, the only group left available to fill the political void was the Roman Catholic Church, as the empire looked toward the pope for its guidance and salvation from their duress.

Giuseppe knew this is what the church had taught him to do - to look for solutions solely based on known fact. However, as of late, he had begun to question many of the principles that were thought to be known fact.

The more Giuseppe researched into the background of the Bible and its ideology, which was the basis of the religion, the more he began to doubt some of its accuracy. He had a lot more questions about its authenticity than he had answers. These questions did not cause him to doubt his religious belief in any way, or the New Testament and its teachings.

It was the Old Testament, scripted by Hebrew scholars that bothered him most. He mostly thought that some of the text was not only translated improperly with a poor choice of words, but that some of the text suffered from misinterpreted facts. He would never go as far as to debunk the Hebrew tome as some scholars and scientists did, but he had his own doubts regarding the accuracy of its parts.

Every year, new facts were brought to the forefront questioning the validity of the Old Testament's accuracy. Researchers and religious scholars had found inconsistencies, just as he had. He spent much of his day trying to debunk most of these new findings as part of his job, with the world's greatest library at hand, in the Vatican City. It seemed like a never-ending project that kept him busy almost all of the time. He often wondered why the Catholic Church was so concerned about the inconsistencies in the Old Testament in the first place, being as it based its creed on the New Testament. He was also aware of his deep commitment to the truth, no matter what price he had to pay, be it time or his testament to his faith.

He wasn't complaining about the demands on his time, for there were days he believed he was just being tested to see if he really truly believed in what he purported to profess out loud. He believed everyone was tested every day of their lives in one form or another and his trials no different than any anyone else's. He knew it was Father Time that would test his beliefs, and no one person or misinterpreted fact in particular.

The current doctrine of the church relied on individuals such as him to offer unbiased interpretations of known facts, not to speculate on ideas that veered away from them for any reason. Yet he if nothing else, was a curious man, and coupled with his unaltered logic, was often left wondering every time he discovered a minute discrepancy of some sort or one was pointed out to him.

Still, anyone associated with this religion was taught to question neither dogma nor doctrine. This had brought him to the main altar of this cathedral numerous times in the past, to further contemplate his thoughts and actions. He prayed devoutly for a guiding hand in hopes of gaining answers to these complex questions. The truth to be known, even as a young man he often came here to contemplate his future. The confines of this particular cathedral seemed to have become his private sanctuary. He felt safe and secure here, within these walls. It really amounted to nothing more than that.

As he looked back on those early days, it seemed that fate had determined his lot in life long before he ever realized it. It would not be until much later when he finally met the then-Bishop Robbia for the first time that he would be told that he had been called. Being only a boy at the time, he had no idea what being 'called' meant. The bishop related that he was part of God's plan and that the hand of Jesus had reached down for him in particular. At the time, young Giuseppe was flattered by such talk, thinking that he may indeed be special. When his joyous family fostered the thought as well, young Giuseppe accepted the idea of becoming a priest as truth and embraced the idea wholeheartedly.

At the time, he had no idea what it meant to be a priest or even what the position entailed, but since his family had so vigorously encouraged the thought, it must be something worthwhile, he remembered. His only thought on the matter was that he had finally found the chosen occupation he had sought so rigorously. Never at the time thinking that just by sitting in a pew and gazing intently toward the main altar of this cathedral that he would receive a just reward right out of thin air.

Once he had finished with his pre-seminary studies and entered the seminary, he realized that very few were being 'called' and his graduating class consisted of just three men. It was a far cry from some of the former graduating classes, which had passed upwards of thirty young men at a time into this chosen profession. When he finally graduated the seminary and went on to complete his vows, he was so comfortable with the institution and its ways he really wanted for nothing else.

It was his minor in church history though, that ended up advancing him farther than he ever expected, for he felt when he graduated the seminary that he would be allocated to some obscure parish somewhere like his two other graduates had. They, like he, having to prove their mettle first by handling a small rural church before they advanced.

It was an unnoticed guiding hand that ended up benefiting him the most. He knew he'd been at the right place at the right time when he was assigned as an understudy to the Basilica archives. He spent quite some time cataloging ancient historical artifacts and was then assigned to the Vatican Library as part of his ongoing training. He never realized from the start that it was Archbishop Robbia who had used his influence to place him there in the first place.

The archbishop though, had had his own plans for young Giuseppe, whom he knew would only become useful to him once he'd obtained a good bit of knowledge on his own accord. This, Giuseppe discovered much later and quite by accident, for his mentor hardly wanted to use his standing in the church to unduly influence the young man's mind or prejudice his position.

The soon-to-be Cardinal had an inordinate sense of character and knew that one day Giuseppe would become a valuable asset not only to himself but to the church as well. He had sought out every one of the men seated here at his weekly roundtable, for he knew a good leader was not possible without high-quality advisors. This, his circle of eight as he liked to call them, encompassed all of his known weaknesses. Whenever he stumbled upon a problem that he could not solve, all he had to do was call any one of them and he would gain the answers he needed. The intent of the circle of eight was to use their knowledge to further his career. Still, he strove to impress his extensive knowledge on one man in particular in hopes that one day he may step into his exalted position, God willing that is, and that was the pope.

He was no fool though, for he knew that the appointment was not only a religious position, but a political one as well. He spent much of his day trying to impress the College of Cardinals as he did the pope himself, carefully laying the groundwork for his eventual rise to the premier position as head of the mighty Catholic Church.

Giuseppe was startled from his rumination by a faint buzzing on his right hip. He knew the Archbishop frowned upon any member likely to excuse themselves from these meetings to take outside calls, so he acknowledged the vibration with the flick of a switch. He thought about glancing down at the phone to see who had called him, but then thought otherwise. He glanced up and realized that the members in the room were looking at him, obviously waiting for some type of response. He deduced that the group as a whole had agreed on a way to answer the Archbishop's question and was waiting for him to agree in principle to the idea. He did, but then wondered how long it had been since he had retreated into his own little world. Luckily, no one seemed to have noticed the lapse, not even the Archbishop.

He then began to worry once again about his mother's condition and quickly glanced at his watch. He knew that the meetings never usually lasted longer than an hour once the meal was completed, as a rule, so he had no longer than ten minutes to wait before it ended. He could cull his curiosity for that long and bit his lip in an effort to quell his sudden anxiety. He looked at the Archbishop who seemed to be satisfied with the suggestions of the group, for he wore a faint smile, always a good sign.

The meeting broke up several minutes later and Giuseppe finally looked at his phone and saw a voice mail. He answered it promptly, recognizing his sister's voice. He hoped that a full recovery was in progress but was dismayed when he heard his sister's voice.

"The hospital, Giuseppe, as soon as you can!"

He hung up, immediately feeling panic rise. Stunned by his sister's frantic voice, he looked around the room as if he had misplaced something extremely valuable. He scanned his corner of the room and looked back toward the table. Men stood alongside, but Archbishop Robbia had already left the room. Giuseppe suddenly wished that he had not, for he felt an immediate urge to confide in him for some reason. He saw Monsignor Sforza walking toward him with a shuffling gait and assumed that he was intent on thanking him for his opportune intervention. The elder statesman spoke.

"You seem to be troubled, Father Lorenzo. Is there anything I can help you with?"

Giuseppe knew better than to voice any of his personal concerns with any of the seven other men in the room. It just was not a wise idea. "No, just distracted is all." He murmured his pardons and bowed slightly, acknowledging the man, and then stepped away, knowing the monsignor would be slightly baffled by the gesture. Still, he could not help it, and strove to keep his emotions in check, biting his lip once again.

He left the room several moments later and made his way into the cathedral proper, reminding himself to stop and give homage at the main altar before pressing his way back toward the door thorough which he'd entered. Never before had he swore an oath like he did then, and with utter piety. He hoped that his mother would benefit from that private conversation with the Lord. Turning and leaving the Sanctuary, he looked up high above the altar at the amber candle which denoted the presence of the sacred body of Christ transubstantiated into the consecrated wafers held within the confines of the vault upon the alter. He watched intently in hope that it might flicker just once, an answer to his silent plea. After several moments, he turned and left, hoping that the doctors at the hospital had the situation in hand.

All sort of things crossed his mind as he again traversed the piazza and made his way to the Metro. It had been quite some time since a crisis of any sort had arisen in his family, and for that, he was most grateful. The last time was several years ago when his younger sister Anna had been involved in an auto accident. This required several days in the hospital and about two months in a cast, her ankle and one arm fractured following a side impact with another vehicle. The resulting bone damage was something she still complained about to this day whenever the weather changed.

Giuseppe went to see the car after the accident and pronounced her quite fortunate to have gotten off that easily. She and her husband were currently living in Brussels, though at this particular moment in time he wished she were here by his side. He had always had a closer connection with his younger sister Anna than he had with his older sister, Jole.

Jole was the more serious of the two. She was also the one most likely to go off into deep fits of despair whenever any sort of problem arose that she could not readily solve. She was always looking for a deeper meaning to anything that occurred to her than was actually necessary. Everything in her life seemed to have tragic consequences. He was sure it all stemmed from her lifelong passion of reading and listening to famous operas, Verdi and the like. Life to her was no more than the act of emulating the quiet tragedies of the stage and it was evident in her character. This was the reason he felt that her murmured plea on the phone might be construed as nothing more than sister Jole taking provocative measures to heart once again.

When Giuseppe was younger and lacked patience, he sometimes rolled his eyes at Jole's grandstanding, which made her all the more irate. He remembered when they were children that Anna would laugh whenever he did that, sure that he was only doing it in order to encourage Jole to lighten up and take a more jovial outlook on life. However, the end result was usually opposite of his intent. Jole not only didn't take the hint, but pummeled him in the chest with her fists for his crass behavior. All he could do in response was to laugh at her childish antics. He knew whoever eventually took her for a bride would have their hands full, for she was always chastising both Anna and him for their lack of sincerity. He and Anna both thought that Jole enjoyed the attention more than either one of them did, though unlike Jole, Giuseppe knew exactly when to let down his guard and relax and when to bear down on the complexities of life.

He still remembered quite distinctly his mother berating him for taunting his older sister. He readily admitted that he was only doing so because she was so irascible. On rare occasions, when the bickering got to be too much for Donna, his mother, she sent Jole to her room. Her fake tears of rejection echoed through the house as a result. She was, and still is, a drama queen as far as he was concerned.

If his father happened to be home during one of these episodes, it was Giuseppe who ended up being punished. It was typical of most Italian families that the daughters were overprotected by their fathers, and their family was no different.

Anna, on the other hand, was similar to him in most respects, which is why they got along so well. At least that's how he remembered her when they were younger. It was almost a challenge between the two of them as to who could get Jole upset with the least amount of effort. As she aged however, Anna changed somewhat and became closer to her older sister.

Anna seemed to savor each and every minute of life. She was the type of girl who walked through life with a mischievous smile and always dressed as if she were headed for a social engagement. Her boundless charm naturally drew people close to her and she always had time to make polite conversation with them as a result. She had a way of understanding how to make ease of a situation. He realized that was why he felt he needed her at his side at this moment, just in case his mother's condition was a serious as Jole's intonation during her call made it seem.

He bought his ticket and boarded the Metro fortunate to secure a seat this time. He found a seat by the window and aimlessly gazed out of it with no specific intent as the train headed north, retracing its stops along the way. After some time, he had to look away. He had a pet peeve, Graffiti. A seemingly endless line of graffiti adorned almost every one of the buildings here in Milan and almost all of Italy for that matter, and it drove him to distraction. He was all for self-expression, but failed to see how anyone had the right to deface all these buildings with political sayings and with just about any other phrase, comment or graphic drawing you could imagine. Did the residents here in Milan have any pride left? He thought not. He never remembered it ever being this bad when he was a child. If his father had ever caught him doing anything like defacing a building, he was sure that he would not have been able to sit for a week. The moral decay of the family unit was evident in the expressions left on these walls.

He ignored the view and began to concentrate once again, becoming oblivious to his surroundings. He reflected on his current lot in life and thought himself a most fortunate man. There was really nothing that he wanted for, and nothing he needed. He had his work and the love of a good family. He missed his father at times, but he had been gone now for over six years and the man's memory seemed to blur as the years passed. Of course, when the family got together for the holidays, his presence raced to the forefront of his mind. His father was a mason by trade, a man who died tragically when the scaffold upon which he was working collapsed beneath him. At the time, none of his fellow workers could do anything to save him for all the mortar, bricks and tools stacked with him atop the scaffold fell on him when it gave way.

He thought that at the time of this unfortunate accident, his mother had nerves of steel, for nary a tear was shed during the three days that led up to his interment. At the time, Giuseppe thought that it was strange, for many of their friends and relatives wailed inconsolably with his passing. It was not until sometime later that he heard her sob for her loss and that was only when he happened to pass by her room late at night. He knew she missed him so. She never talked about him and only infrequently stated his name. This only occurred when he was sure that he had reminded her of her late husband in some uncanny way.

His father was a well-respected man lauded for his artistic talents. When he wasn't working as a mason, he could usually be found in the tiny workshop behind the house, carving one thing or another out of marble. He was a sculptor in his own right, and his statues became well known for their graceful lines and lifelike qualities. He became popular for creating carvings that adorned the yards of many of the citizens in Milan proper. People he never even knew came to the door asking, sometimes begging him to do a statue for them and price was usually no concern to them as his reputation grew.

An unfinished piece still sat in the little shop out back, his tools and his sketches still in the exact place he had left them, a reminder to all those close to him the he was really never that far away from them. Donna never ventured back to the workshop. Once, she stated to her son that it was too stark of a reminder to her, as she still thought that he was there busily working in the shop and would return when he had finished his latest creation.

Giuseppe loved his mother dearly, so her sometimes-odd habits were a quirk that he grew to ignore. He knew individuals had their own ways of dealing with the death of a loved one, so who was he to criticize?

He had a close bond with his mother for as long as he could remember. Not only was their relationship one in which they were at ease with one another, but also one close enough that they seemed to relate each other's feeling without even speaking a word. S o m e t i m e s, only a gesture or a look relayed their feelings on a matter that may have concerned them at the time. For the most part, his mother was good natured and loved to tease Giuseppe on occasion, only to see if she could get a dubious reaction out of him. The act was reciprocated at times and they would both get a good laugh knowing it was done intentionally. Sometimes this good-natured ribbing was done with the intent of altering a bad mood or steering a serious conversation. He guessed that was what he liked best about her.

She was a fine cook and continuously showed her affection toward him by placing the special dishes he had craved as a child before him every time he came to visit, even to this day, her way of telling him she loved him without ever having to verbalize it. Not that she ever forgot to say so whenever they parted, but it was just another example of how she doted on him as if he were her only child.

The phone rang once again and he rose out of the stupor of thought and answered it. "Bonjurno," he answered out of habit. A momentary hesitation from the caller on the other end made him think someone had reached the wrong number.

"Giuseppe?" Jole asked.

"Yes, this is he," he stated in such a manner so as to disarm his sister.

"Could you meet me in the lobby of the hospital when you arrive?" Jole asked, her voice firm and disapproving.

His sister's tone radically changed Giuseppe's mood. He felt as if a load had been lifted off his shoulders, knowing all too well that if his sister had spoken in a panicked manner that the worse was to be expected.

"Sure can, how is mother doing?" he asked with a measured amount of enthusiasm.

"She seems to be doing fine at the moment," Jole replied. "Not all of the tests are back but I should know more by the time you get here. How long do you think you'll be?"

"My best guess is about fifteen minutes."

"Good, I'll see you then."

Jole hung up the phone before he could ask about any of the tests that the hospital had done. A wave of relief passed though Giuseppe and a smile erupted onto his face. He felt as if his prayers had been answered and eased back into the chair, waiting patiently for the tram to slow. His disembarkation point was approaching, and from there he had just a scant twelve blocks to walk before he reached the front door of the hospital. At this point, he felt that God never turned his back on a sincere prayer, nor did He ever turn His back on those who were faithful to His word.

His mother was certainly that. She never missed Mass and tried to go to church each and every day if it was at all possible. The family as a rule abided by all of the church's teachings and all of the commandments, or at least he knew that his mother did. He would not call her saintly to her face, but that is what he thought privately. It was surely for those reasons that he felt so at ease in his position. He knew she was proud of him when he'd made his decision to become a priest. He could readily tell, for she beamed for days. "I'm walking on clouds," she had said. "There are two angels at my sides, holding me up amongst the clouds, allowing me to gaze down at all my blessings, and my greatest blessing of all is you. I am proud as I could ever be of you, my son."

His father said as much but not in such a flourished manner. Giuseppe remembered being embarrassed by all the attention poured onto him by friends, family and casual acquaintances when he had passed seminary. Now, when he looked back at the milestone in his life, he realized it was just their way of acknowledging his choice.

He arrived at the door of the hospital, and once inside gazed around the entry foyer looking for Jole. He didn't see her, but moments later the elevator door opened and there she stood.

"Ah, Giuseppe, perfect timing."

Jole wore a wry smile as she walked toward him with a purposeful stride. He knew if she were in a crowd, he could pick her haughty gait from a mile away. He had not seen her since the holidays, some three months ago, and though she looked unchanged, her demeanor was never predictable. "Hello, Jole, how good to see you." He gave her a big hug and a smile. Pushing back from the embrace, he noticed the unassuming look on her face, a change from the last time they met. "Has someone new entered your life, dear sister of mine?"

"Don't be rude, Giuseppe," she said. "Besides, that's none of your business, don't you think?"

"Maybe I'm just concerned about your welfare, is all I meant to say," he shrugged.

"That would be a first," she rapidly responded, a brief look of disdain accompanying the comment.

"Truce," he stated with empathy. "How's Mother doing? You know you scared me with your phone call this morning."

"Well then, join the club, she scared me as well. When I first arrived this morning, she was still in bed, which is as you know is in of itself an unusual event. Her color was grayish and she looked totally out of sorts. What scared me though was when she finally realized it was me and asked to go to the hospital!"

The look on her face was enough to tell Giuseppe that she was not exaggerating, not this time at least. "She actually asked to go to the hospital?"

"Yes, she did, and that's when I really became unglued," she confessed. "I guess I panicked a bit."

"Well, it's better to act on the side of precaution," he said. "How is she faring now?"

"I just left her a few moments ago. She's up in room 321. They just wheeled her back in the room after running a myriad of tests, though if you ask me whatever it was has probably passed, for she looks a lot better now," Jole stated with relief.

"Let's go up and see her," Giuseppe said. He wanted to see her immediately, for no other reason than to ease his own troubled mind.

"I have to stop at the nurse's station first," Jole said. "They were posting some of the test results and I want to check and see if any of them are negative."

"Yes, good idea. Still, I want to see for myself that what you say is true, that she's looking better, and if so, a load will be lifted, that's for sure." He pushed the button for the elevator and waited for the doors to open.

They arrived on the third floor some moments later. "Which way?" he asked his sister as she headed for the nurses' station directly in front of the elevator doors.

"That way," she said, pointing to the left.

Giuseppe moved down the hallway, counting off the rooms as he went. When he arrived at 321, he poked his head into the room but saw no one inside. There was but one bed in the small room and the door to the lavatory was ajar, so he knew no one was in there. He thought that perhaps he had made a mistake of some sort and headed back toward the nurses' station to verify the room number once again. His sister still stood there, looking through a sheaf of papers on a clipboard with pursed lips. He came up next to her so as not to startle her, noticing her intense concentration on the initial reports. "What room did you say she was in?" he asked when she finally took notice of him.

"Giuseppe, are you daft? I said 321," She sighed impatiently, rolling her eyes in the process.

"I was just in 321. There's no one in there. Is it possible that they took her out for more tests?" He was dumbfounded.

"I don't know," she said. "I'll ask the nurse." She looked down the hall for the nurse, but the hallway was empty.

"Maybe I made a mistake," he said. "I'll go back down and check the room once again." He returned to the room and entered, pausing just inside the doorway. Once more, he scanned the room and opened the door to the bathroom wide in the process. No one was in the room. Then a sudden, horrifying thought struck him and he rushed over to the far side of the bed just in case his mother had fallen out of it by accident. He felt relief that she wasn't lying hurt on the floor, but grew increasingly worried that he couldn't find her.

For some odd reason he felt compelled to examine the bed itself. The coverlet was neatly folded on the foot of the bed and the white sheet was slightly ruffled, as if someone had used the bed. In the center in the bed was the impression of a body. The slight impression reminded him of his mother's form in a way, though he could not be sure of it. After all, an impression was an impression. Then he noticed something strange in the concave impression of the pillow itself. A fine whitish-gray powder formed the profile of the impression. At first, he did not believe what he saw and began to carefully pull back the sheet to see if the powder continued down the length of the bed itself.

As he unfurled the sheet, he saw the hospital gown for the first time and reeled back. The fine powder wafted gently into the air, which startled him. Heart pounding, he finally conjured up the courage to touch the powder itself just to make sure his eyes were not deceiving him. He brought to powder that adhered to his index finger toward his face for closer examination, rolling the powder between his thumb and his index finger. A memory struck him as he did - something his mother had told him some time ago. He remembered her words to the tee. "I am an old soul Giuseppe, and when I leave this earth this time I will never return." He remembered the very conversation the two of them had been having. It regarded her thoughts as to why she thought the Hindus were right about reincarnation. At the time, he thought the comment odd, for it went against everything she had taught him about their religious beliefs in his youth. He brought the powder to his nose to smell, causing tears to stream down his face. The powder smelled of gardenias, his mother's favorite fragrance.

"Ashes to ashes, dust to dust…" he whispered, consumed with grief as he spoke. For some reason, one he could hardly comprehend, he knew his mother had been taken. It was just a feeling he had and nothing more, but he sensed the truth of it just as he still sensed his father's presence in the workshop behind their family home even to this day. He felt a sudden sense of abandonment and knew his mother had left the ash as a clue to her intent.

The priest had his own reasons to know this was the truth of the matter, though try as he may he was unable to convince his sister to believe in such unquestionable circumstances as he did himself. He hardly thought that Jole had the gift of faith anyway, so he said nothing further.

Jole insisted the hospital be completely searched, but to no avail. His mother Donna was never seen again. She became a missing person's case, which was filed and forgotten by the Milan Police Department.

The police told them that people disappeared all the time for various reasons, which was their standard reply in cases such as these. The missing invariably turned back up again when you least expected them, they said, but Giuseppe knew that sort of reasoning couldn't be further from the truth.

He felt as if something of dramatic proportions had begun. No one dies and immediately turns to ash. He trusted the Lord completely and knew when the time was right, He would reveal His plan, for what was happening to him and his family had yet to reveal the extent of its true nature.

One thing he was sure of; he knew it would change the context of humanity itself. The afflicted as well as the blessed would have to come to terms with these changes, changes that would not be readily accepted by any means.

CHAPTER 2

An Ominous Sighting

Central Egypt

He stood on the edge of the Nile, digging the toe of his right sandal gently into the cool, darkened sand of the riverbank. He watched as gentle eddies of the dark waters swirled as it passed him by, wondering with glee if Allah had meant all of this beauty just for him. He stood there for quite some time watching the noon sun glitter off the ripples of water, sparkling like polished white diamonds. He squinted, trying to catch all the deflected sunrays as they headed off in multi-directional paths. Every time a ripple of water peaked, its leading edge became intensely white for moments at a time, which fascinated him.

His face resembled weathered driftwood, the lines in his face permanently imbedded with black oils that no longer washed away. It gave his face the premise of wood grain but he never seemed to mind. Deeds were the measure of a man in this part of the world and much more important to him than mere looks.

The cool breeze off of the Nile felt good as he ruffled his tunic in an effort to dry his clammy skin underneath. He then reached up and scratched his coarse white beard where it protruded from underneath his lower chin. The eighty-year-old man then began to wonder why he was still here. His wife had died some twenty years earlier. Never would he have thought that he would have lived longer than she. Never as a young man, did he ever think he would reach such a stately age, for his life was one of toil and tumult. There had to be some reason why he was still alive, but he knew not why.

His name was Anhur the Minor, though usually no one ever addressed him using his entire name, least of all anyone he knew who recognized him by sight. He adjusted his turban, allowing the breeze to cool the matted mass of the white hair on top of his head as he sighed. His days seemed to consist of nothing more than idling away his time. At times, even he thought himself too feeble of both mind and body to do much more of anything else. Many a day, he didn't even venture away from his simple home. There was no real reason anymore to go too far astray, as his life's accomplishments were behind him now. He ebbed like the Nile River under the intense heat of the Egyptian summer.

He turned his back to the lifeblood of his beloved country and gazed toward the city in which he had inhabited his entire life, Asyut. The city lay a little over two hundred miles south of Cairo, considered one of the six oldest cities in the world, first settled during the time of the pharaohs at around 3100 B.C. At that time, Asyut was the thirteenth Nome or district of Upper Egypt, which at that time went by the name of Syut. It was a place of strategic importance, being the central location between the upper and lower Nomes of Egypt's then known districts. The original city now lay buried in ruins, partly by the ever-changing Libyan Desert. As was usually the case with ancient locations such as this, a newer version of the early city had long ago risen to take its place.

Asyut had grown in size and changed considerably since Anhur was a young man, though there were some areas of the city that remained as he remembered them from his youth. The market district was one of them, located in an area of the city that he once knew all too well, having worked there until he was unable to do so anymore. That had occurred about the time of his wife's passing, a time that had drastically stressed the fabric of his own life. He retrieved his prayer rug off of a nearby stone and then headed in that direction. Initially he thought about returning home but for some reason today he felt better than he had for some time. Every once in a while, the vigor of his early life returned, though less frequently as the years passed, and today seemed to be one of them. He thought about a route to take that would require the least exertion and finally coaxed his feet into action. The intense heat of the area sapped his energy more than ever, so as a rule he usually never ventured out this late in the day without reason.

He loved the open-air market. The sights, sounds and smells were a virile characteristic of the city itself. Its residents took their sustenance from the market stalls, as it was a center of commerce as well. It had always been the focal point of the city, ever since the earliest trade caravans began delivering their goods here. Before that, it had been the reed ships that plied the Nile, bringing their goods here as well. The market was also a central area of monetary exchange, and some traders he knew had become extremely wealthy on the currency exchange rates alone.

It was also once the end point for the Darb al Araba'in, the forty-day camel caravan trade route that linked Western Sudan's Dar Fur province with the city of Asyut. No one knew for sure who originated the route that was thought to be well over seven hundred years old. At one time, the road was a major slave transportation route up until the late 1800's, which ended up bringing untold wealth to the bustling area. The slaves were freely traded in the city for export to other areas of Egypt and to surrounding countries as well.

The market was also the place where all locally grown goods were taken, the products of the fertile valley in which they lived. The surrounding area and its fertile soil were consistently replenished by irrigation from the mighty Nile.

Wandering amongst the stalls of the market, Anhur saw few faces he recognized any more. Most of the stall owners that he had come to know so well in his youth had long since passed. A few owners that he recognized were still there and he stopped for several moments to greet them with words of encouragement or a faint smile in recognition for their longevity. One of them in particular had been trading goods for well over sixty years, seated in the exact same place Anhur always remembered him to be. This particular vendor never rose unless he was sure the sale of his goods had been consummated, and he had bartered from his seated position as long as Anhur could remember. He spent a bit more time with this particular merchant than he had allotted the others and asked about his family, and what was going on in their lives. He always hoped to obtain a bit of local gossip about the current political situation here in the city in which this vendor freely dealt. He often times wondered how these merchants could sit there day after day and watch life pass by in front of them without ever leaving the confines of their stalls. He thought he was most fortunate for having traveled as far as he had during his lifetime but like them, he had always returned to the comfort of the area he knew best.

After some time, he started to tire, yet he had made it only half way through the expansive market place. He began to retrace his steps as his thoughts turned toward home. All he thought about as he walked was the reassurance of his camel fur-lined bed and an afternoon nap.

He had some time ago given up any claim to ownership of his humble abode, passing it on in title and responsibility to his eldest heir. He had not been so easily convinced that he was no longer cognizant or coherent enough to handle the day-to-day operation of the house and finances and had passed the responsibility on begrudgingly, somewhat resigned to the fact that in the latter days of his life he felt more like a guest in the house he was born in.

Ramla, his daughter-in law, surely would be worried about his extended absence. He was sure he would be chastised for his wandering ways once he got back home. She was a good twenty years younger than his eldest son, Badru. She was his second wife, his first wife having passed during childbirth, a good woman of whom he had grown extremely fond. As he turned the corner of his street, he was greeted by his grandson, but it took several moments for him to recognize the boy, for he was standing amongst a group of youngsters in the center of the street. The boy moved toward him as he began to pass. "Sefu!" he exclaimed. He gently patted the eleven-year-old on the head in the process, his timeworn way of addressing his grandson growing extremely difficult as the lad had sprouted up like a papyrus reed, the makings of an adult becoming all too evident in his face.

"Mother sent me out looking for you. She feared that you had somehow lost your way," Sefu smiled.

His coal black eyes searched Anhur's face for some speck of truth in the matter. "Hardly," Anhur scoffed. "I feel better than I have been in quite awhile and went to the market to look around."

"You promised to take me there with you when you went."

"I will, I will," Anhur reassured him, trying to lessen the effect of his error. He saw the rejection in his grandson's face and tried to make amends. "Look, I brought you something I knew you would like."

What is it?" the boy asked, his voice almost pleading as disappointment gave way to excitement.

Anhur groped at the fold in his waistband and retrieved a small paper-wrapped package. He smiled as he handed it to the boy. "Don't you dare tell Ramla that I gave it to you? She would surely blame me for ruining your dinner. It is some of the best Baklava you will ever eat. Better than your mother's, but don't tell her I said so. She would kick me out of my own house if she heard I said that." He watched Sefu unwrap and stuff the entire square in his mouth before he even finished warning his grandson.

The act somehow reminded him of a starving man he once found wandering aimlessly in the desert, greedily eating and drinking without consequence to his actions. Anhur had to stop the man from overindulging, knowing that his stomach would pay the price. The man hardly listened to him; his need seemed so great, until he doubled over in pain and swore he was being poisoned by the kind hand of the Samaritan which had bestowed fortune upon him.

"I won't!" Sefu promised; his voice was muffled, minute pieces of the cake curling off his lips as he spoke.

"Good boy, never betray a trust," Anhur said as he watched the lad lick his fingers with delight. The boy was a mirror image of his father, which got him wondering about his eldest son, Badru, who did not seem to have the patience to take much interest in his own blood. He would pay the price for that one day that was for sure. The tie would not be as strong if father and son did not spend adequate time bonding.

He was sure that Badru relied on him to do his bidding when it came to teaching the lad in the ways of the world. Anhur was not sure he would live long enough to complete the task. He had tried talking to Badru, hoping he would take more of an interest in Sefu, but so far this advice to his son had gone unheeded. Instead of listening, he was affronted by his concerns.

"Nothing but the babblings of an old man who has spent too much time in the sun," Badru scoffed. "Your memory does not serve you well. You were never here when I needed your advice or you're mentoring for that matter!" Badru brutally chastised his father because he remembered him being home only sporadically during his own childhood.

The sting of the insult still rang in his ears even after all this time, as he remembered all too well spending time with each of his three boys whenever he was home. He had made a point of it. Anhur somehow got the feeling it was not out of disrespect that this son spoke, but rather Badru's thoughts of supposed neglect when he'd been Sefu's age, when Anhur was gone and away from home for weeks at a time. Then again, his son also constantly reminded him that his faculties were not what they used to be and that he was guilty of only selective memory whenever it suited him.

Whatever that had to do with his own responsibilities toward his own son, Anhur hardly thought pertinent. Anhur realized that as he grew older, things that once would have raised his ire, such as his son's evident lack of respect, seemed less pertinent to him now and had somehow lost its zeal. The insults his son spewed forth were no more than a mere inconvenience, like a fly that tries to enter one's mouth looking for moisture. Still, it hurt, and he had only been thinking about his grandson's welfare when he made the suggestion.

Anhur felt his grandson's hand encompass his own. He looked down at him, smiling in the process.

"Come Grandfather, it's time to go home. You look extremely tired all of a sudden."

"Yes, I suppose I am," he stated as they began to walk toward the house. "The next time I'm in the mood to wander, I'll take you to the market for sure. A promise is a promise and I won't forget." A bemused look crossed the young man's face, but Anhur would not disappoint him a second time, he didn't have the heart for it.

Anhur still could not get the thought of his eldest son's cutting remarks out of his mind. He thought for a moment about asking his grandson for his opinion on the matter, but knew what the answer would be before he even opened his mouth. He knew all too well that the boy would never intentionally hurt his feelings no matter what, for he knew that his grandson adored him. What was past was past and he could not change a thing about it. Only Allah knew if he had done right by his son.

He had been a buyer of foreign goods traded in the market in Asyut, a position that required him to travel past the far reaches of the Sahara desert to markets that the local venders deemed necessary to increase the variety of their goods in the city market.

Anhur followed the quadrants of the compass, north skirting the desert into Syria and the like, south through the desert into Sudan and points south as well and east into Israel. His most arduous travels were west into Tripoli, almost crossing the entire breadth of the Sahara desert. The desert covered most of northern Africa and encompassed an area of over three million square miles. Anhur likened the size to the continent of Australia. The width of the desert from west to east ranged about 3,000 miles from the Atlantic ocean to the Red Sea and from north to south about 1,200 miles. Anhur would have liked to say he could recognize different areas of the desert only by gazing at the topography, but that would be stretching the truth of the matter somewhat. In reality, he had only seen parts of the vast desert and knew it would take many lifetimes to achieve such a feat, even if it were possible.

In his early days, he usually traveled by camel along some of the shorter trade routes out of Asyut. It was an arduous journey by pack animal that traced its roots, back several thousand years. This however, was not his preferred method of travel, though he learned over time to appreciate his ancestor's mode of transportation.

On occasion, he still ventured out into the desert on the back of a borrowed camel, which was all but exchanged for trucks that could ply the once known camel caravan trails and bring back his ordered goods all in good time. The thing that most impressed him nowadays was the system of highways that traversed alongside the now desolate trails he knew so well. Though he knew some of the roads through the Sahara were yet to be completed, there being still a few stretches of road still traveled on sand.

The time that it took to bring goods to market had been radically shortened by these paved routes. Even now, some of the truck trade was again being replaced by cargo planes that were even more expedient. With that thought in mind, he knew that his son was right in saying the things that he did, but never in his mind did he ever think that his travels were of any consequence, especially when it came to the instruction of his own three sons.

Anhur winked at Sefu as they reached the front door, a sign that was meant only for his grandson. Sefu licked his upper lip in acknowledgement of the sign as if to say that their secret was safe within him, a minute smile evidently sealing the pact. Anhur again patted his grandson on the head.

They entered the house; Ramla scurried about the kitchen in an effort to replace the dishes of the delayed lunch onto the table from the warmer. Upon entering the kitchen, Anhur noticed she wore a distressed look on her face, detracting from her well-sculptured facial features. At first Anhur thought it was because he was late, but then he saw the irate look on Badru's face. His plate was clean and he sipped a Turkish coffee and looked at his watch all at the same time. He was late returning to his position at the ministry office and Anhur was sure it was all because he had made himself scarce. He had not really stated where he was off to this morning but hardly thought that he was required to do so. He thought he had informed Ramla that he was going out, but apparently had not. He could tell by the look on his son's face that he had better sharpen his wits, for a confrontation was brewing, somewhat like the pot still steeping coffee on the stove.

"Your bewilderment, Anhur, never ceases to amaze me," Badru scowled. "Must you be leashed like a cur in order to rein you in?"

Anhur scanned the room, intent on biting his tongue once again. He saw his grandson's upper lip quiver perceptively and Ramla's brows arch in anticipation of yet another power struggle unfolding around her. Anhur knew she felt sorry for him, but knew it was not her place to say anything in his defense. Women were not deemed worthy of any response unless directly asked to do so and she was not about to heighten her husband's ire another notch. She knew what the consequence of such an action would entail and dared not have the ire in the room directed her way. That and the fact their religious beliefs stressed that her husband was always right kept her silent, even if she believed her husband was wrong. She had been taught to have the utmost respect for her elders. The growing conflict between father and son had been building between the two men for quite some time and Ramla was hard pressed to do anything about it.

Anhur had heard her praying for peace in the household. Her chants to Allah had fallen on deaf ears and wondered when the entire situation would crest and then finally subside. The air was eerily electric as she stiffened and waited for Anhur to respond to the insult.

At first, Anhur was not going to respond, but the fact that his grandson stood in the room and the fact that Badru was seated in his chair, the chair that once exclusively belonged to him alone, fueled his fury. "Am I to even acknowledge such an insult with another?" Badru shrugged off the retort without reply. This gesture was taken as an admonishment, though Anhur was not finished. "I should think that the ministry director would hold you accountable for your rash behavior. Returning late to your exalted position does not bode well for your character." Anhur paused, a frown darkening his brow. "It seems to me that it would also serve you well to have some respect for your father, being as it was written for you to do so!" Anhur shook his head. "Tell me you are not above the rules which bind you, for Allah himself would have you cast asunder."

Badru's eyes widened with shock at the frank retort. He'd surprised his son by bringing the rules of religion to the forefront, something he'd never done before. Badru knew he'd crossed the line but dared to rebuff his father in spite of it.

"Allah commands the respect of those who are deemed worthy," he stated in a subdued manner. He glanced up at his father and then quickly lowered his eyes. He coughed lightly, and then rose to leave without waiting for further comment from his father. He brushed past Anhur and Sefu without a glance and left the house, slamming the door behind him.

"What has gotten into him?" Anhur asked Ramla. Ramla knew that she must answer, but tried to do so in such a way as to ease the lingering tension in the room. She thought for several moments about it but then apparently realized the direct approach was the only way to deal with the matter at hand.

"He needs your advice but is afraid to ask. That's all that I can say."

Anhur didn't know what to make of the statement as he slowly sat down. Sefu was seated at the table already and seemed oblivious to the entire exchange, intent on shoveling all the food he could into his mouth at one time, like that of deprived street urchin. Anhur pondered the statement for some time while he ate lightly. He noticed that Ramla had taken a seat across from him, hands folded neatly below her bosom. He was sure she sat there waiting patiently for him to respond in kind to her initial statement. He finally looked up from his plate. "Does it have anything to do with his position at the ministry?"

"I'm sure of it, though I'm not sure that I could tell you what it entails in its entirety. I have only been given bits of information concerning his plight and do not know all the details. I only know he was waiting patiently for your return. The longer he waited the angrier he got."

This in itself explained the reason for his son's comment about tying a rope around him, though he was sure that Badru could have been more tactful in his choice of words. Anhur had been sure that his son's behavior had been more of the same, exchanging barbs in order to usurp the last vestiges of his authority. For once, he felt bad about his cutting remarks and wished he had not said anything at all. "It must be political," Anhur said, again looking at Ramla for some sort of acknowledgement of his thoughts on the matter.

Ramla opened her hands freely and studied Anhur's face for several moments. "It would be better if you asked him yourself. All I know is that he is deeply troubled by his present predicament. I can tell by his extreme change of demeanor."

"That's fair enough," Anhur said as he watched her rise and leave her seat. She already had her back turned to him and had begun cleaning the small kitchen when he finally let the matter drop. He headed off to his room looking back momentarily only to see his grandson still eating ravenously. He shook his head, wondering where he put it all.

That evening after dinner, Anhur found his son alone in the small stone courtyard behind the house. He was seated on stone bench built for two, which Anhur's father had constructed when he was a child. He and his wife used to sit there on that same bench after dinner hoping to catch a cool breeze as evening developed. As a rule, Anhur never really ventured out into the courtyard much anymore, for the memories of laughter and love still lingered there even after all these years.

Badru sat on the bench, a cigarette in one hand and a cup of Turkish in the other. Anhur silently watched his son for some time from the doorway before he gathered the nerve to walk over and try to make amends, though, in his heart he was sure that it was his son who needed to make the first move in patching up their earlier disagreement. He knew his son well though and knew that his hard-headedness would surely be his downfall. He had been like that even as a child; nothing had changed even after all this time. He was a demanding man, impatient to the point of sheer nervousness. Anhur watched him staring intently at a lizard as it sat on the edge of the old stone well in the corner of the courtyard. He silently wondered what was so interesting about the common sight. He approached the bench and sat down before his son had even realized it, sure in his mind that Badru was in some sort of stupor. Anhur spoke softly at first so as not to startle his son. "I hear there are some concerns of yours which you would like to address?"

Badru turned quickly toward his father's voice, flicking the cigarette toward the well in the process in hopes that it would scare the immobile lizard off. The projectile missed its mark by several feet and the lizard never even flinched. He studied the old man's face for several moments before he responded. "I'm not sure that there is anything that you can do."

"Me either, but sometimes just talking a situation out helps to find an answer to a dilemma," Anhur said, scratching his right eyebrow.

"I suppose it does." Badru turned away from his father and stared down at his worn sandals. "The Coptic church has applied for a permit again to finish the restoration of their cathedral. This has caused uproar yet again from the Islamic leaders who have openly suggested or demanded that the building be torn down instead. I have spent my entire day fending off accusations from one side or another. The fundamentalists tell me if I don't red-tag the building that they will blow it up. The tensions between the two religions are stirred up every time an application is made. In the past, I have been somewhat successful in denying or delaying the permit process by requiring inane certifications. I am told to do this from my superiors, who I am sure are being instructed to do so by one of our religious leaders. You know who I'm talking about; no names need to be mentioned. I am caught in the middle. I have had people threaten my welfare and the welfare of our family. They have used our religious beliefs as a gilded sword trying to persuade me. I feel as if I am the focal point in the dispute, though it is really none of my concern. My job is to review the application, issue the permit and sign it. Never did I think that such an easy task would be such a political nightmare." Badru finished his coffee, setting the cup down between them in the process. "I don't suppose you remember what happened the last time this came up?"

"I'm afraid I do," Anhur admitted with some distress. He remembered the uproar all too well, though it was some ten or more years ago if he recalled correctly.

"I'm just a civil engineer. Never did I imagine when I took on this job that it would be so stressful. I'm just glad I wasn't around the last time this came up. It is no wonder the man quit!" Badru stated, finally looking over at his father. "But that's not the worst of it. Every time someone comes in and voices an objection to the permit, I have to file a report on the matter with the government. I've spent weeks writing reports-- no that's not completely true either... its closer to months." Badru stopped speaking when his father raised his hand. "You're talking about the Cathedral of St. Mark in Assiut, are you not? I thought that it was completed?" Anhur asked patiently, knowing all too well, what had transpired a decade ago. The uproar over the permit was all anyone talked about back then. It was thought at that time that divine revelation had assisted in finally getting the permit passed.

"Yes, I am," Badru admitted. "They have decided to do some more renovations to the site. I ran across the original construction permit just yesterday, or if I may say, it magically appeared on my desk when I arrived in the morning. As I scanned through it, I found that it took well over a year and a half to approve the initial permit for restoration, though when I originally scanned through it; it seemed that approval had been postponed indefinitely by the government. That was until a spiritual intervention of some sort took place. As you may remember, mystical lights in the shape of the Virgin Mary were said to have appeared along with illuminated spiritual doves above the cathedral." Badru paused. "The Coptic Church called it lights from heaven and they said the nightly appearance of Mary was a miracle. Though I actually did not see the lights myself, some of my friends said that they did and could not explain them. That was the only reason the permit finally got approved in the first place. It was because of the purported visions of Mary. I personally think the church staged the event. I really don't believe it was anything more than that!"

Anhur interjected a comment when his son paused to light another cigarette. "I saw the lights with my own eyes, and I have never been able to fully explain them. It did look like an apparition of some sort to me - that and the white doves that formed perfect circles was hard for me to rationalize or ignore for that matter. I found it hard to agree with the skeptics that stated it was trickery of some sort."

"You never mentioned this to me before," Badru stated in surprise.

"There are some mysteries about this life which are hard if not impossible to explain," Anhur sighed. "Besides, I had to see with my own eyes what all the uproar was about. I believe there was a reason for the sightings. Did you know that when Mary and Joseph fled Bethlehem with the infant Jesus, because of the writ of King Herod to kill the first-born of every family, the family fled here to Egypt and were said to have stopped overnight in Assiut during their journey, almost at the exact spot where the Coptic cathedral is located. It was written that an angel of God appeared to Joseph and advised them to leave."

How do you know all of this?" Badru demanded curtly, shaking his head disdainfully.

"What makes you think that I wouldn't know anything about it? Allah himself said that Jesus was a prophet."

"That's blasphemy!" Badru interjected with a note of finality to it.

"Hardly," Anhur stated with forceful authority. "Ours is not a religion of hate, bias or revenge. You have been influenced by your fundamentalist friends who have begun to sway your true thoughts on the nature of our Muslim religion." "No, I haven't!" Badru protested, hands flailing back and forth in denial.

Anhur sighed. He sensed the animosity between the two of them rising to the surface once again. "Then do what you must. Approve the permit and leave the consequences of your actions in Allah's hands, or roll over and abide by the fundamentalist right that tries to run this city and this country as well. The choice is yours." Anhur started to rise; the stone bench was suddenly not as comfortable as he once remembered it to be.

"Egypt is a Muslim state, what would you do?" Badru questioned, his tone sounding defeated as he watched his father readying himself to leave.

"Give me several days to contemplate the situation as I see it, and I'll give you my answer, fair enough?"

"Fair enough," Badru replied again flicking the cigarette butt in the direction of the well in hopes of startling the lazy lizard, which still had not moved even after all this time.

The next morning Anhur thought about his son's dilemma for some time, knowing it was an unenviable position in which to be cast. He was unsure of any way that would not lay the blame for the wrong decision directly at his own feet. If he advised Badru to approve the permit and the situation backfired, his son would be fired as a consequence and he surely would be blamed. If he advised him to deny the permit, the same exact situation may occur, though he knew well that Badru would be praised by the majority for continued oppression of the minority religions here in Egypt. He wished that in reality he knew nothing of his son's plight at all. He suddenly felt too old for all of this contemplation and hoped that the situation would right itself without the need of his input. He knew that was the easy way out but in reality, he was bound by blood and had to give his son sound advice in this situation. He knew that his son was truly depending on him for once. The only way to rationalize the problem clearly was with an uncluttered mind, and the only way to achieve that was to be alone and without worldly distractions. He finally got an idea of how to do just that. He would venture into the desert. He left the house and headed to see an old acquaintance.

Mussat and Anhur had been friends for more than forty years. Mussat had been a camel trader in the market for about that long as well. When Anhur started into his position as a buyer, the young man was about his age and working for his father at the time. Mussat, being the eldest son, inherited the business when his father passed on. Before that time though, whenever Anhur needed a camel, he would always go to the same trader, for he had heard that the father and son team were trustworthy and honest in their dealings. Anhur had learned to rely on them for initially he knew nothing about camels, or what to look for in a good one, so he had to trust someone. Mussat and his father had never given him a lame or sickened animal so he dealt exclusively with the two. Thus began a lasting relationship between the two men.

Anhur made good on his promise and took Sefu to the market with him. He procured a camel for several days and bought needed provisions. He was a bit apprehensive about going out into the desert alone at his age but knew it was the only way he could clear his mind sufficiently and allow for unadulterated thought. He knew that travel in the desert was always the best way to do just that. He planned to leave the next morning.

Anhur rose early and headed for the market square before the rest of the family rose. He had informed Badru of his plans the evening before, which were less than well received. Anhur had to endure some disparaging remarks from his son, who thought that the old man's journey into the desert was ill timed and insane in nature. Anhur never bothered to explain why he was going from that point on, figuring that his son would not readily understand his reasoning. He was not about to listen to Badru's continued warnings that he would become lost in the desert and the expense of hiring a helicopter to find him and pointing him back in the right direction would be at his expense. Anhur was growing weary of being compared to a petulant child based solely on Badru's thoughts of his own capabilities. The taxi dropped him off at the staging area where Anhur was surprised to see Mussat standing by two kneeling camels.

"I thought that I might ride along with you until we reached the edge of the desert," Mussat said a boyish grin. "I assumed that you would be heading west since it is by far the easiest way by which to leave the city." He paused. "That is, if you don't mind?"

Anhur was delighted. "Of course not, I believe that I would truly enjoy the company." He felt better about the whole idea, now that he had some companionship for at least part of his journey. His intent was to travel west, ten or fifteen miles into the desert, then turn around and head back. He planned to sleep in the desert for only one night and then return.

"I must admit that it has been quite some time since I have ridden one of my own camels," Mussat laughed. "They hardly have the comforts of a Mercedes!"

"I can guarantee you that, and I doubt that I have ever seen a camel with an air conditioning unit strapped to his back," Anhur deadpanned.

His friend Mussat began to laugh so loudly at the thought of his absurd remark that he was sure the man was about to cry.

"You have struck on a capital idea. Just think about how much my business would prosper if that were possible!" Mussat chuckled.

The laughter became contagious as Anhur thought about his meaningless statement. He began to laugh heartily as well at his own impish declaration. "I believe we will have a fortunate ride, my friend."

Anhur saw that all of his provisions were neatly stored and all that he was required to do was to mount the camel. He was not sure at first if he could mount the animal with ease due to its girth. His age was indeed a factor, though in years past this obstacle would have never been a problem.

"Here, let me help you," Mussat said as his friend's first attempt failed.

Anhur wondered how he was going to achieve this feat alone in the desert, refused his assistance, and tried again. The second attempt was an awkward success of sorts that almost sent him off the other side of the animal when he caught his leg in the folds of his tunic. After righting his torso, he commanded the camel to rise. The animal initially complained about the command, but then rose in one fluid motion once Mussat's camel had risen.

Nothing was said between the two men for some time as Anhur tried to find the least distasteful position in which to ride. After little more than a mile from where they left, he already felt his thighs and rump chaff from the movement of the animal. He began to see the incline that led out of the valley and onto the floor of the Sahara. The sandstone cliffs skirted the western edge of the city, known for their archeological treasures and history. There were many tombs within the cliffs, home to some of Asyut's earliest leaders. Some of the tombs had been uncovered and explored in their entirety though Anhur knew that many more were yet to be discovered. A city this old had many secrets that only required the expense of time and ambition in which to uncover them.

They began the incline into the rising sandstone cliffs and Anhur had to lean into a forward position to maintain his balance. He turned his head backward and spoke to Mussat for the first time. "Turn around and look at the expanse of our beautiful city." He said it objectively, noticing the background of the Nile River as it coursed its way through the valley below.

"It is truly a grand sight, and one in which I have not witnessed in quite some time," Mussat exclaimed. "Sometimes we lose track of what is truly pertinent and what isn't. I drive the streets of the city every day but never seem to notice my surroundings with any degree of clarity."

"You're not alone; most people fail to notice the subtle nuances of nature that surrounds them…" Anhur never finished expounding on his statement in its entirety but instead concentrated on the trail, which had begun to steepen considerably. His camel had slowed to a snail-like pace under its burden, its head now low to the ground. Faint groans of protest became audible to Anhur's ears as he coaxed the animal on. Anhur thought that it would take some time before they reached the top of the incline at this speed, but also knew there was no easier way to the desert floor without traversing the valley below them for more than a half a day.

Anhur and Mussat finally made the rise to the flattened plateau above the city, where they stopped and rested their camels for some time. After taking his time enjoying the view, Mussat finally spoke.

"In what direction shall we head, my friend?"

Anhur was a bit perplexed by the question. It was his understanding that his friend was only there to see him up the incline. He had no idea that he intended to be with him during the entire trip. "We must part here, I'm afraid. I must do this trip alone." He noticed a surprised look on Mussat's face.

"But I insist!" Mussat declared.

Anhur then began to wonder. "Be truthful with me my old friend. Did Badru put you up to this?"

"I cannot lie, he did. He fears that you will become disorientated in the desert and never find your way back, I'm afraid," Mussat said without conviction.

Anhur assumed that Mussat had agreed in principle to Badru's assessment, which perturbed him somewhat. "Trust me, I know exactly what I am doing and my son's fears are hardly of any consequence. This is something I had planned to do alone. Besides, you have a business to run," Anhur said solemnly.

Mussat tried to persuade Anhur in a half-hearted manner that his intentions were sincere. He could obviously see that his argument was fruitless, as Anhur's face felt, and probably looked, as lifeless as the desert itself. They had been friends long enough that Mussat knew that no argument would convince him otherwise and finally conceded to the old man's wishes.

"May Allah always be at your side."

"And yours as well, my friend," Anhur said as they parted. Anhur wheeled the camel around and headed west, steering the camel though the mire of sandstone scrabble in the process. It was some time before he turned back to see if he was being followed. He peered intently, scanning the barren landscape only to find that there was no one else in sight. He was alone for sure and wondered now if he had been too stubborn to accept the company on principle alone.

The full expanse of the sun beat down on him. Its position was at its zenith. Waves of radiant heat bounced off the sand and stone and left Anhur stifled. He tried not to think of how uncomfortable he had become but slowly plodded on into the desert. He had long forgotten how intense the heat could be out here, especially during the summer. The desert was an unforgiving place. A mistake out here would cost you your life; for there was no water available in the direction he was headed. He reached behind him to check the sidesaddles; there was enough water for a four-day ride, which put his mind at ease.

Anhur traveled for several miles before stopping to rest. The topography of the desert began to change. What once was a flat and stony desert plain beginning to change. Small mounds of sand began to leave a serrated design on the desert floor, the effect of the desert winds evident in the wavy patterns of the sand. He knew the farther he traveled west, the larger they would become. There were some areas of the desert in which these small mounds became so large that they resembled small mountains where a traveler would spend as much of his time rising vertically as he did traveling horizontally. Anhur was glad he was heading west. He had to contend with only the foothills of sand where he was headed. The sand did not pile high until the Libyan border in the direction he was headed.

Anhur quenched his thirst from a goatskin of now hot water and prodded his camel on. The animal was a swift runner after he gave the camel lead. He'd held the animal back from the start, afraid that it would go lame on the sandstone scrabble they had traversed. Now that they were on the sure footing of sand, the camel seemed to carry Anhur with the least bit of exertion. Anhur was sure the camel had been bred for racing, as he made swift time across the desert floor.

He loosened the reins and let the animal find its own pace, then began to think seriously about his son's predicament. The political climate in Egypt these days was a tenuous one. There were extreme factions that hoped to rewrite Egypt's policy of tolerance of its citizen's right to religious freedom of worship. Some headway had already been made in that direction with pressure from the Islamic fundamentalists. The Egyptian government now required the Coptic Church to file permits for any repair or renovation to their church structures. Badru had been right about that much.

Anhur was aware of the history of the church, which found its beginnings as successors to the ancient house of Ptah, a deity in Egyptian mythology. They claimed to be direct descendants as sons of the pharaohs. Egypt as a whole is a highly religious state and the Copts was a term used to differentiate themselves from the native Muslims. All ancient Egyptians seem to have the sense of the unity of God and His infinity, and the rounded cross, or Ankh, had been a known symbol for untold centuries. The conversion to Christianity with the coming of the apostle Saint Mark, who was considered its founder, seemed to be effortless due to the similarities in religious doctrine and the belief in a singular high deity. Coupled with that was the Christian belief that Christ was resurrected fell in line with the thoughts and science of embalming and the belief in the afterlife.

The apostle Mark spent much of his time in Alexandria converting people, but also sensed a danger in the new rule of faith. He quickly anointed a bishop, who went by the name of Ananias, along with several priests. Having returned several years later, he was surprised at the following they had procured. He spent some time there celebrating Easter mass with the group when word spread of his return. He was dragged out of the church by an angry mob of pagans and tethered to an ox and dragged about the streets until the mob was quelled and he was thrown in jail. An angel appeared to him during the course of the night to proclaim that his name had been written in the Book of Life. The following morning, he was again dragged through the streets until his body was broken and torn. The thought of the mob was to cremate his remains but a violent storm arose out of nowhere and the crowd dispersed. Some of his followers reclaimed the body and secretly entombed him underneath the altar of their first church. The heinous act cemented the faith of these early Christians and the religion grew.

The Coptic's felt that any unnecessary regulations were discriminatory to their right to practice their religion freely. Many of the faithful had started to move out of the country because of the constant persecutions and strife that had befallen them. Religious tolerance was but one of the many restrictions which befell a minority religion in a

Muslim state. Many of the Coptic Church's faithful lived in Asyut and as a result, the city had become a political hotbed for religious rights.

The friction between the Muslins and the Coptic's has gone on for centuries. Asyut was also the home of the Islamic fundamentalist group. A group called Al-Gama'a al Islamiyya, whose roots were traced back to its inception at Asyut University in 1973, was an offshoot of the Muslim brotherhood. Al-Gama'a mantra was to overthrow the Egyptian government and replace it with a fundamentalist Islamic regime. The only way they thought to advance their cause was with violence. It took quite some time before the Egyptian government was able to squash their advances and that was only after one presidential assassination and the later attempted assassination of another president. The group itself split in 1992, one side calling for the end of violence that had spread to murdering tourists as well as its own citizens.

The other side of the group continued its propensity for violence, which never seemed likely to abate, as they aligned themselves with Osama Bin Laden's Fatwa of Jihad against the United States. In the late 1990's there seemed to be a radical change within this group that suddenly reversed its policy of violence and hoped to reconcile itself with the Egyptian government for past misdeeds. It was not until after the September 11, 2001 attacks on the United States coupled with Egyptian pressure that the group traded its ideology of violence for one of peaceful co-existence.

Anhur knew that there were still some radical-minded extremists living in Asyut who still raised the specter of religious friction at times such as these. He had made it his business over the years to study both sides of this precarious problem. He took it upon himself to research the background and history of the Coptic Church and its beginnings for no other reason than his curiosity had bettered him. He found out from his research, to his surprise, that these people were a god-fearing and docile group, which followed the teachings of Jesus Christ. He had never publicly admitted that he had done the research for fear of retribution, but he loved Asyut and hoped to thoroughly understand the misgivings between the two religions.

He also knew that the worldwide perceptions of the teachings of Allah were being misconstrued as a religion of hatred and violence. Just the opposite was true, with a vast majority of the believers adhering to the teachings as one of peace and peaceful co-existence. The minority influx of extremists was changing the fabric of the Koran to suit their own needs - one of political power, hoping to squash any resistance to their own interpretations with intimidation and hostility.

Indirectly he blamed the Americans for enabling these groups with their insatiable thirst for oil. The oil found in abundance underneath the Sahara furnished them with the unlimited funds from the Middle Eastern countries, offering newfound riches to advance unjust causes for political might. He also blamed the Americans for interfering with the political processes of the Middle East if only to provide an uninterrupted flow of oil to their shores. This bullyboy attitude of democracy did not sit well with most Arabic nations and forcing one's opinions on others did not sit well with the free life thought of these desert inhabitants. This among other things fueled the fire of hate and mistrust, not only amongst the people in the region, but between the countries in the area as well. Anhur secretly wished that they had never found the oil to begin with. Life had been much simpler, he remembered as young man, without the newfound riches of oil.

Anhur knew that ever since 9/11 that the governments in the Middle East, especially here in Egypt, began to systematically bear down on extremists, hoping to turn the tables on the violent minority by restricting their ability to function. For this reason, he thought that it might be possible for his son to approve the permit without reprisal. He thought about this and other things as well as he journeyed deeper into the desert

The flat plain of the desert had been replaced with higher mounds of sand which now stood at about the height of ten feet. The expanse between the peaks of sand began to spread as well, being about a quarter mile apart. Anhur could not believe the distance his camel had taken him in one day. The sun began to settle into the horizon as the mounds of sand grew in height. He decided it would be advantageous to stop at one of the flattened peaks instead of settling down for the night in the growing valleys, which would warm more slowly the following day. He traveled on in hope of finding one with a suitable flat table to bed on. Onward he ventured, utilizing the last vestiges of sunlight to his advantage until he spotted a suitable bedding area two mounds distant.

When he arrived at the spot, he realized why the area looked so flattened. Before him lay a deep valley that was all-together different from the ones that he had just crossed - one much deeper and much wider than he had traversed all day. He decided that at the top of this high valley he would go no further and ordered his camel to stop. He then ordered the animal to kneel so that he could dismount and went about the business of making an orderly camp in the faint last order of the day. He fed the camel first and then spread his bedding near the animal in case it became spooked for whatever reason. He thought also that the animal would provide him with a small measure of heat during the coming night. It was a cloudless sky and he knew that the retained heat in the sand would dissipate quickly.

By the time he had finished his chores the dazzling spectacle of a star-lit sky filled the expanse above him. He finished his chores by starlight, arranging an evening meal of dates, figs and bread, which was set out before him. He had also laid out a flask of wine and goat cheese. Now there was nothing left to do except to gaze intently at the stars as he ate. He was positioned at the very edge of the valley so that he could look down into it. It was a very suitable perch for his needs and he felt supremely content.

He idled through his meal, enjoying the still evening air and starlit sky when he noticed a single star that was unusually brighter than the rest. He watched with interest for some time as it began to illuminate the sky with greater clarity. All of the other stars seemed to wane under its light and he swore it was streaking toward him. Knowing that it might by a comet, he watched it with some interest.

Anhur knew that shooting stars were not an unusual sight in the desert. He had once witnessed four of them in a single sitting. He hoped that the stars would entertain him once again with their white contrails as they streaked across the sky. The half-lit moon began to cross the sky as it etched its way toward its apex.

Anhur then noticed something about the star in comparison to the moon and frowned in confusion. The star seemed to outshine the very moon. This was indeed a strange occurrence, and one he had never before witnessed. It also seemed to come closer and closer to his fixed position, seemly headed right for him. He felt a tingle of fear.

He also knew there was nowhere for him to go to escape this oddity as he watched it grow more intense by the minute. Then he thought that possibly it was not a star at all but a meteor of some sort. He knew that if the meteor was large enough, it could impact the earth, causing cataclysmic destruction in its wake.

He wasn't sure what to make of the uncharacteristic event as he sat frozen in it's ever- widening spell. He discerned that the object was not a comet, for its light tail began to widen the closer it came. By now, the moonlight was totally obliterated by the light of the star.

Anhur knew that it would probably break up if it entered the atmosphere. He tried to ease his agitated nerves, convincing his mind that the situation would right itself prior to any imminent danger to his life and limb. He went back to his meal with nervous aplomb, praying that the star would veer off. The valley before him began to brighten, the light becoming intense enough for him to almost see across the valley floor's expanse.

The dark shadows of the desert began to dissipate before his eyes as the star illuminated the entire area. He looked skyward once again as the star streaked toward earth with lighting speed. The camel began to bray and spit all at the same time, trying desperately to rise and run. Anhur grabbed the animal by the reins and settled it back into a seated position, comforting it by stroking its face and addressing it with soothing commands to relax. His worst fear now was that the animal would scamper off, leaving him stranded here in the middle of the desert with no means of transport. It was a long walk back to Asyut and one he knew he could not make without the provisions secured within the sidesaddles of the camel.

Anhur entered a stage of intense mortification, knowing that an impact was imminent. It was all he could do to hold the camel at bay, as he now straddled his body across the animal's neck so that it could not get up on its own. He readied a knife from his belt to maim the camel just in case he could no longer hold it down. His hope was that the animal would not stray far if it were wounded. He knew just where to inflict the wound under the front foreleg to hobble it, but hoped it would not become necessary to do so.

Finally, the light grew so powerful his only recourse was to look away. He stared down into the valley below. The light had changed from a bright white to an intense blue. It was a blue of such concentration that he felt compelled to close his eyelids into an almost squinted position as he concentrated on the valley below him.

As he squinted and protected his eyes from the vaporous blue surroundings that encompassed him, he saw something that he hardly believed. On his side of the valley, he swore he saw what looked like legions of men. As he scanned across the valley floor, he saw figures on the other side as well. The site s reminded him of a battlefield, or at least that was what his mind told him he saw. He could not believe it. The blue light was so intense now that he was able to see wings on the man-figures nearest to him. Opposing them was what looked like legions of figures, though it was too far away to see them with detail. Far more were lined up on the opposite side of the valley than were lined up on this side. The light was so intense he could hardly see any longer and his eyes welled up with water, a natural defense the body used to protect the corneas.

Moments later the light crashed into the sand on the opposite side of the valley. Yet, he came to realize, moments later, that there had been no impact. The ground did not shudder, nor was there any sound at all. It took several moments for his eyes to adjust to the now darkened desert and he looked intently for some sign of the battlefield below him. Now there were not any figures or any sign that they had ever been there. All he saw was empty space.

Anhur knew he had seen something that would be hard if not impossible to explain. Only one strange thought seemed to enter his mind as he scanned the valley below.

"You have witnessed this and you must inform all others."

The statement seemed seared into his mind, and it was the only lasting imprint he had of what he had just witnessed. Anhur finally had sense enough to release the camel from his stranglehold and stood up for the first time. He peered intently over the edge of the valley to see if he could see any imprints in the sand that would verify what he had witnessed. There were only shadows from the night-lights in the sky, too dark to see what he had intended to see. He would have to wait until morning for his proof. Sunlight would not arrive quickly enough for him, for he knew now that he would not sleep a wink tonight.

Anhur pondered the meaning of the vision in the valley and likened it to the miraculous occurrence of the circle of doves that had hovered over the Cathedral of Saint Mark's in Asyut. There was no other logical explanation for the sighting. His only regret, as he sat there waiting for the sun, was that there were no other witnesses to the sighting. He now wished he had not been so stubborn and had invited his dear friend Mussat along.

Early the next morning, he rode along the sides of the valley looking for clues to back up what he had witnessed, but there were none. No imprints in the sand, or any other sign of life, for that matter. The one odd thing that occurred to him as he looked was a feeling of sorts, and a thought that he was traversing through a crowd of people not unlike that of the market square.

After some time, he scaled the opposite side of the valley and again headed west, looking for signs of the star's impact. Again, there was nothing to be found, and yet he knew what he had seen the night before and proceeded, crisscrossing the desert in a search pattern for any signs of impact that would confirm his lingering doubts.

Anhur finally turned around and headed home, convinced that he had searched the area thoroughly. His only fear was that one would believe him.

Upon his arrival home, which was almost midnight, he was surprised to see that his son, Badru was up waiting for him, a complete surprise, for he was so weary that he had hoped to just fall into bed. He noticed the look of concern, waves of creased lines on his son's face as he spoke.

"I thought for sure you were lost when you did not return earlier this evening," Badru said.

Anhur was glad his son still cared enough about him to show his concern, though he was not sure he had the strength at this time to explain what had happened to him out in the desert. "I appreciate your concern and only wish that I had the energy to tell you about my trip, but I am afraid I'm so tired that it will have to wait until the morning, if you don't mind?"

"It can wait," Badru said as he waved his father off to bed.

The next morning Anhur slept in late. He still felt tired even as he shuffled into the kitchen. He was surprised to see both Ramla and Badru seated at the kitchen table. Ramla rose immediately to serve him while Badru looked on.

"I'll have some coffee, Ramla, if you don't mind." Ramla knew it was an odd request, for Anhur never drank coffee anymore,

"Why of course," she smiled with unbridled enthusiasm.

Anhur turned and addressed his son. "You must approve the permit!"

The statement surprised Badru, knowing that this decision could cause painful repercussions to the entire family.

"Why?" he asked in disbelief.

Anhur sat for some time, sipping on his coffee. He finally noticed that his son had become visibly irritated by the silence, and it was then he began explaining in detail what had happened out in the desert. He could tell that his daughter-in-law readily believed him, but that his son did not. He could tell by his facial expressions and the occasional shake of his head. Badru had wanted to question him while the story was being told, but Anhur warded off the questions numerous times so that he would not be sidetracked.

After numerous questions and answers, Badru finally agreed in principle to approve the permit, agreeing with his father's logic for once, though he stated that he did so not because of the sighting in the desert but because his father had stated the obvious political motivations behind his arguments so convincingly.

It would be some time to come before he actually understood and believed that what his father had seen in the desert was indeed the truth. This was not because his father had ever lied to him in the past. Anhur had never been prone to telling tales either. Badru finally agreed with his father due to the fact that outside forces were at work. He had heard rumors that someone was trying to find a witness to what had truly occurred out in the desert on that day. When the two strangers finally found their door, Badru then knew for sure his father had told him the truth, and finally believed the farfetched story that his father had so futilely tried to convey to him.

CHAPTER 3

A Continuous Evaluation

Washington D.C.

Doctor Kyle Hanson arrived at his office, punctual as usual, eight sharp. As soon as he opened the door, he frowned, knowing that it must have been another eventful day on the opposite side of the world.

He swept his hand though his all too grey hair while standing in the threshold eyeing the stack of reports piled neatly in the center of his desk. He recalled having cleared his desk late last evening before he left and all these reports had to have been generated since then. As was his habit, he spent several moments scanning the room to see if anything was out of place. Satisfied that everything else was exactly the way he had left it, he entered the room and set his briefcase next to the desk. He removed his suit jacket, shook it gently and carefully placed it on the hall tree so that it would be wrinkle free when he had to don it once again. Kyle was sitting at his desk when the door slowly opened.

Amy Walker poked her head though the opening and casually surveyed his expression. The pert thirty–six-year-old blonde could tell what type of a day it was going to be just by studying his face and most likely already knew he was none too happy with the pile of reports she had meticulously placed in just the right place on his desk. He had demanded such precision from his days as a former Air Force Colonel, and did now from his staff as well.

"Care for some coffee," she asked with a smile. "It will jump start your day."

"Sure, thanks," he replied amicably, wondering momentarily what it would be like to be married to a woman as seemingly vivacious as his secretary seemed to be. He had pondered the exact same thought many times before. Was she always as cheerful as she seemed to be? She never seemed to have a down day, which suited him perfectly. No matter how he felt personally, her attitude was contagious and it was just about impossible to have a dismal day at the office as long as she was around.

He began to scan through the pile of reports knowing all too well that as of late, he needed more of his secretary's optimism in order for him to make it through the day unscathed. The anomalies in worldwide weather patterns seemed to be fluxing with increased regularity, and that worried him considerably.

Moments later the door opened once again, and Amy crossed the room and set the steaming cup next to the pile of papers on the desk. "There's a call waiting for you from the National Observatory, Line one, in case you'd like to field it?" she stated, smile still in place.

"No, not at this moment," he replied. "Take a message if you would, and I'll return it later." He needed to first address the pile of papers stacked in front of him.

"Sure thing, anything else that I can do for you?" she asked as she headed for the door.

"No, I don't think so…" He heard the door close silently behind her before he even finished addressing her. He shrugged his shoulders, though even after all these years was not used to the fact that someone felt free to leave his room without being properly excused.

Doctor Hanson eased back in his chair, prepared to scan and digest the reports. His computer-like mind and photographic memory would file all the useful information in those documents, as was a necessary evil of his job as the sitting director of the National Weather Service, an agency that incorporated and studied many facets of weather monitoring, data collection and forecasting.

It was an important position and part of the Department of Commerce subtitled as a divisional agency under The National Oceanographic and Atmospheric Administration. The primary function of the agency was to provide accurate weather forecasting throughout the continental United States and areas outside the United States as well, including but not limited to U.S. holdings and interests in foreign countries. Any weather-related activity which directly affected the well-being of its citizens and interests was closely monitored. Its current motto pretty much encompassed its true purpose, "Working to save lives."

The required data necessary for accurate forecasting was collected from over one thousand stations throughout the world. Some of the stations were shipside, while others were remote stations not readily inhabitable by weather service personnel. The most valuable analysis tools at their disposal, though, were satellite and radar scanning.

The agency kept meticulous records of variations in weather patterns, as well as comparative analysis records that dated back into the previous century. The Weather Service as of late had procured a pretty good track record in forecasting temperature variations throughout the globe, due to the increased accuracy of computer weather models as well as advanced satellite and radar tracking. Enough data was being collected now so that the computer models had grown more precise. Dr. Hanson also knew that accurate rainfall predictions were also improving.

The only real thorn in his side resulted from the task of accurately tracking and predicting the aspects of weather that people feared most, and which was the most expensive in terms of lost lives and property damage - violent storms such as hurricanes, typhoons, and tornadoes. There was just no way of predicting the damaging effects of these types of weather conditions with any degree of accuracy, with too many variables to reliably track and report their severity with any degree of certainty. Upper atmospheric conditions as well as ocean and surface temperature conditions played an integral part in the development of these storms. Take in the consideration the variability of wind as well as other factors such as surrounding high or low-pressure fronts and such data also played a part in determining deviations to these storms. Last but not least, when it came time to tracking and forecasting these storms, was their proximity to or over landmasses and their topography.

The agency was gaining a slightly better track record in this area, though not as good as he would like. Still, considerably better than say, ten years ago. He was thankful to all the amateur meteorologists here in the United States and abroad, who had risked life and limb to film these violent occurrences.

With the use of these films of violent storms and their effects, the agency was able to plot their unpredictable tendencies against an enhanced aspect of their side-scan radar. The computers of today could plot the magnitude as well as determine degree of risk for potential development, growth and destruction. The doctor knew there was plenty of room for improvement in this area, but it was only a matter of time for newer technologies to improve their current record.

Nevertheless, this aspect of the agency was the least of his problems with the essential position in which he found himself. He finished scanning the worldwide anomaly reports, wide variations off of the mean averages and concentrated on the graphs and charts in the back of each of the reports. He was just about finished when the intercom startled him.

"You have a director's staff meeting at ten," Amy's voice heralded.

He hated the intercom system and preferred Amy knock on the door, but she would never adhere to this policy, another throw back to his prior military protocol. Henceforth, he never bothered to acknowledge the message, which was his usual practice, and grew annoyed with the time restriction that now limited him. He quickly wrote copious notes on the report findings for further study. He dreaded this meeting for several reasons, and had conveniently forgotten about it until he was duly reminded.

It was the ongoing political climate that he abhorred the most, most specifically the global warming bandwagon the oval office wanted him to ride on. As far as he was concerned, all this talk of greenhouse gasses was nothing more than a political smokescreen set up by lobbyists to feed the coffers of the new "green" economy and the corporations that benefited by it. No one wanted to tell it like it is, but the math was simple. The earth was covered by three quarters water, which left a mere twenty-five percent delegated to land. Of this remaining twenty-five percent, only about ten percent of it was inhabited. It was true that carbon dioxide levels were up, but that was not the only reason for the warming. It was actually warmer three hundred years ago than it was right now without the increased usage of fossil fuels or the population statistics the data experts now had. No one wanted to listen to the truth in that aspect of the equation, and were too busy lining their pockets with ill-gotten gains.

The fear factor card was working well enough to foster what looked like a new a trillion- dollar industry, and top levels of government were thrilled by the prospect of an enhanced economy once again. He and many of his renowned colleagues knew the real reason for the increase in worldwide temperatures, but no one wanted to hear about it. After all, there were palms to grease, and a new way out of a worldwide monetary crisis.

It would take only a few good volcanic eruptions like Mount Etna and Mount Vesuvius to cast this planet into a deep freeze, which would take decades to get out of. That was only one of the ways this temporary warming might abate. The real reason was hopefully going to be addressed at this meeting, and this time he was not going to be put off by his ill- advised colleagues and their agenda. He continued to write notes until the last moment possible, then with a disgusted mutter, rose, donned his jacket and headed out of the office.

He strode out of his office, felt his face flush with annoyance and issued a staccato burst of requests to his secretary for reports and the like to be ready for his imminent return. He scurried out of the outer office and into the hallway, turned left and heading in the direction of the main conference room, before he realized that he'd left his valise behind. With another muttered oath, he retraced his steps, not surprised to find Amy standing in front of the office, his briefcase in hand as she smiled indulgently at him, hand extended.

"Thank you," he groused.

"Have fun, play nice and don't let the boys kick you around!"

He smiled sheepishly at her comment, turned abruptly on his heels and left without saying anything in response. At a calmer pace, he strolled down the hall, wondering if he was as transparent as he suddenly felt or if his secretary was merely much more perceptive than he gave her credit for. He was still mulling over that thought when he heard a salutatory voice to his right. He had not even noticed the Director of Oceanic and Atmospheric Research, Dr. Charles Palmer at his side, but recognized the voice at once and responded. "Charles, I feel like I'm heading into the final conflict for some unknown reason. Whatever happened to the time when logic was able to accurately determine a policy decision in this administration?"

"Kyle, I hate to say this, but it is just you and I and a handful of maverick scientists, as the Commerce Department liked to call them, still trying to get the majority of the less enlightened to listen. The entire NOAA has folded under the pressure except us. There have been threats issued from above the Commerce department to radically reduce funds to individual agencies within the NOAA if we don't come to some agreement and that anvil hanging over our heads has already claimed the Fisheries Department and Ocean Services. Unless that is, we all get on board the green machine in unison, I'm afraid even our jobs are in jeopardy. You know well that Dr. Edwards is behind this. None other than the NOAA'S Environmental Service director and your pal, who by the way I am sure, has the key to the executive washroom and an eye for the top job of the Commerce department."

Kyle stopped in mid-stride to turn and look directly at his friend, trying desperately not to concentrate on the man's childhood rosella scar in the process. The scar glared a deep red whenever the man became excitable, as he was now. He knew that at one time, a disease of some sort had emaciated the man and he had never fully recovered. Though Dr. Palmer was a lot younger than he was, one would never have guessed it.

"Let's get something straight here, Charlie," he snapped. "Dr. Edwards is not my pal. We have a working relationship and nothing more, Hell, I couldn't even tell you what kind of beer he drinks, but that's beside the point. I would barter with the devil himself if he could supply me with the necessary tools required to do my job with the utmost degree of efficiency. The way I look at it, anytime I can access his satellites as well as mine to garner information, so be it. Any bit of useful information I can use to prove our point I look for, and this talk about unification is utter nonsense. I hate like hell to cheer for something like CO_2 emissions that in my heart is not proven, like he thinks it is. So far as I can see, I have no inclination to rise above the rest like Dr. Edward wishes to. I just want the agency to use some common sense for once and not to go off half-cocked and ready to jump on the green monster's back just because a former democratic vice-president wrote a book, for god's sake!"

"Kyle, I don't think you understand," Palmer said with a trace of nervous anxiety riddling his voice. "They're expecting us to all agree on the issue, you know... like the three musketeers' motto, all for one, one for all." "Charlie, don't worry about a thing, just cover my back on this one. I have all the proof we need right here." Kyle patted his briefcase. "I'm going to prove once and for all that this global warming grandstanding is caused only in part by the rise of carbon dioxide and soot particles. A majority of it is caused by the increase in solar flares and the change in axis of the poles, as you and I have discussed in depth prior to this."

"But how in the world are you going to get Dr. Edwards to capitulate? He's already put all of his chips on the table and I doubt if he would change his mind no matter what you said or did. Besides, they already rejected the theory once before."

"I really don't think that is of any consequence here. Its majority rules, my friend. Besides, it will be your job to convince the other directors, get them to see the light, no pun intended."

"My job?" Palmer gasped. "You must be kidding! I'm a researcher, not a politician."

Kyle noted minute beads of sweat surfacing on his forehead. "That's exactly my point, and the reason why they'll listen to you. Up until now, and for the most part, you've been relatively silent on the matter, though privately you are in total agreement with the facts. Today is your day to shine," Kyle said, trying to ease his colleague's uneasiness with a measure of rectitude.

"I don't know," Dr. Palmer said flatly, shaking his head. "If the scientific arm of NASA can't impress the politics of the situation, how are we?"

A nervous twitch was now evident on the man's right temple, causing his eyebrow to arch. Kyle wasn't too sure at this point if he should have forewarned his friend until they were seated in the conference room. "Look, you'll do just fine. Just hit them with the facts and be yourself. You're the expert here. You'll knock them dead. Now let's go or we'll be late."

"That's a real easy thing for you to say, Kyle, but let's be realistic here. You're the orator out of this group, not me, but I'll give it a try if you say so."

They began to walk step for step down the hallway. "That's the spirit!" Kyle said triumphantly, opening his briefcase and removing his report, handing it his colleague without losing stride.

"What's this?" Parker asked in surprise. "This was a set up from the beginning, Kyle, wasn't it?"

Kyle said nothing, but wondered how Dr. Parker would fare, hoping he could succeed where he had failed. He knew the man's integrity within the group would be at stake, but he had no choice in the matter. They would both go down on this one otherwise. Most of the time he felt that he and Dr. Palmer were trying to move mountains when it came to convincing the group as a whole. "More ammunition to bolster our argument with," he explained. "It's a report I penned on the increased variations in the worldwide temperature model. There are areas on the lee side of the current global axis that are readily colder than they were only twenty years ago. The slant of the axis is much more pronounced than I even thought. This, coupled with your research on increase of solar flare activity, should at least give some pause to the current theory, don't you think?"

"Yeah, I guess… I just hope your right," Dr. Palmer replied as he carefully studied the report.

"By the way, don't let them snow you on the reason for the axis shift either. The earthquake in Chile in 2010 did little to change what had already occurred to begin with. That's just a rogue's way of explaining to the general public what some scientists were lax in understanding to begin with. You and I know the truth of the matter and it will prevail in the end; rest assured."

By the time the two men reached the conference room, both men had laid out a strategy that was both prudent and sound. The pep talk had bolstered Dr. Palmer's flagging ego and he was seemingly ready to take on the task at hand.

Sometime later, Kyle returned to his office all smiles. He could tell by the expression on Amy's face that she couldn't believe it. Such radical changes in his behavior were rare.

"I take it all went well for once?" she stated quizzically.

"Yes and no," he said politely, as he palmed down an invisible cowlick toward the back of his head as he spoke.

"Surely you won't leave me sitting here guessing what the end result was? Admit it. Your answer was vague at best."

"Well, I suppose it was. We got a reprieve of sorts, if you would call it that. Dr. Palmer and I were able to finally introduce enough solid evidence that the Commerce director took pause and suspended the vote on the entire measure, pending further investigation. Now the Commerce chief is asking for a more detailed analysis of our research for further study. I will say one thing that surprised me, and that was Dr. Palmer's oratory skills. I told him that he was going to lead the argument based on his research models and he took it to heart. Never before have I ever seen someone with such a convincing argument. I sat back in wonder, for I never dreamed he had it in him. You should have seen it; everyone in the room sat silently, mouths agape, hardly believing that such a meek looking man could explain the facts as convincingly well as he did. Score one for the home team. Maybe there's still a chance common sense might prevail after all."

"You mean academic minds may prevail after all!" she stated hopefully.

"That may be so," he responded.

With that, he drifted off into the realm of deep thought; until she broke the moment by handing him a small stack of phone notes. It had been an altogether busy morning, what with her collecting his requests and answering the phone. "The two messages on top are of a rather urgent nature, "she explained. "One of them is a second call from the National Observatory Office at Kitt Peak and the other is from the National Security Advisor, which is odd."

"Odd?" He ambled toward his office to return his calls. Flipping through the phone notes as he walked, he immediately recognized an old friend's name in the pile, who always gave just his initials as E.A. whenever he tried to reach anyone he knew well.

He decided to call him first at Kitt Peak in Arizona, being as this was his second call and he had a feeling that it may provide some insight into why the National Security Advisor, of all people, might want to talk to him. Kyle reached the secretary for the observatory and asked to be patched through to Dr. Ernest Alexander, a resident astrophysicist at the site.

There were a group of scientists from specialty fields all over the country that met at least quarterly to discuss a myriad of topics related to the continued study of the earth and what effect outside forces had on its inhabitants, an elite scientific group to which both Kyle and Ernest were members,

"Ernie, how are you doing?"

"Doing fine, Kyle, and you?"

"Hey, just fine, though the Commerce Department is giving me fits at the moment, but it's nothing that I can't handle."

"I know the feeling all too well."

"Something must be urgent for you to do me the honor of calling twice in the same day?"

"There is…? You know that one day you're going to have to make it down here and let me show you around with all the new equipment. You'd be impressed with what we have here. The entire observatory has been updated and we're now able to receive a constant data stream from the Hubble telescope in deep space, as well as our land-based telescopes."

"I will, Ernie."

"Promises, promises," Dr. Alexander chided. "Look, the reason I called is that we picked up an inconsistency last night that I thought might be of some interest to you."

"What do you mean by that?" Kyle asked, his pulse quickening with excitement. It would have to be something rare for the man to take time out of his schedule to phone repeatedly.

"Actually, at first we thought the Russians had launched some sort of Star War's laser, for we picked up a beam of constant light from outer space. Upon analysis with a photo-spectrometer, we found that it lies within the blue spectrum instead of the red, which immediately nixed that idea. That was later confirmed by NASA. Besides, there weren't any of their satellites in the general area of the intended trajectory."

"Where do you think the light beam came from, if not from a satellite?" Kyle asked.

"We think it came from the Pleiades system, but that's just conjecture at this point. We're still bantering about ideas and thought you could help, being as this was a subject you once wrote a paper on."

"Wow!" Kyle said, baffled by the possibilities. "Did it reach earth?"

"We believe it did. Actually, you're not going to believe this, but it seems to have a plotted location somewhere in the area of the Eastern Sahara Desert."

"Do you think it was a gamma blast of some sort?"

"Gamma ray maybe, but as of now we're not ruling anything out. We're still looking into it with more than a small degree of curiosity."

Kyle knew what that meant, but remained silent, waiting for his colleague to continue.

"Kyle, I'd like you to take a look at it if you would, and give me your opinion of what you think it might be. I sent it to you this morning via Codex; after you've had some time to study it, let me know what your thoughts are on the matter, will you?"

"Sure! One question though, how's the resolution?" Kyle asked, knowing that the Codex scrambled the pixels of a photo and then tied them to the computer's binary code for transfer, which still had bugs in it when it came to fine resolution photos.

"I think it's pretty darn good, if you asked me. Oh, by the way, the State Department has already been notified just in case the beam is some sort of threat of some kind."

There was a pause for several moments and Kyle wondered if they'd been disconnected. "Are you still there?"

"Look, they might ask you for an assessment once you've had time to study it. I told them that it happens all the time; it's just E.T. taking pot shots at us from deep space. That, I'm afraid, didn't go over too well. I'll tell you one thing, those boys up there in Washington just have no sense of humor," Dr. Anderson chuckled.

Kyle could tell by his friend's intonation that the remark had got him in deep shit once again. "I know, tell me about it. I wouldn't worry about it too much though. They're all sitting on pins and needles these days what with all the atmospheric and other changes we constantly remind them of, it's a wonder any of them has any sanity left. But then, you have to have lost all your marbles to be a politician to begin with. Add to that, having to deal with all the political turmoil in the first place. It's certainly a job I wouldn't tackle."

"Right you are once again, Kyle. Check back with me if you come up with anything. This one has us all puzzled."

Dr. Anderson hung up the phone before Kyle could even ask if the spy satellites had been relocated to scan the target area. He knew it would be tough trying to find an area that might have been disturbed by a possible light beam in the Sahara Desert. It was hard enough when they looked for meteor strikes, let alone try and find something like this.

Kyle then dialed the State Department number, feeling better about having dialed Kitt Peak to begin with. Now he wouldn't be totally in the dark when it came time to fielding some of their inane questions even though he was dying to get to the Codex machine to see the anomaly with his own eyes. He knew he could feign ignorance on this one, at least until he had time to look at it.

F.B.I. Headquarters Washington D.C.

After a recent promotion, Special Agent Raymond Willis was delighted to finally utilize his degree in Business and Computer Science. The college graduate signed on with the Federal Bureau of Investigation immediately after his commencement exercises from Baylor University, lured in part by the bureau's stature, and the thought of assisting citizens in their quest of protecting the American dream.

He passed the rigorous training at Quantico, Virginia with flying colors, graduating near the top of his class, proud of his accomplishment and knowing his two years in the armed services had aided him immensely. At the time, the twenty-six-year-old black man thought for sure he was invincible, armed with the tools of his newly found trade when his first assignment out of training camp landed him in the drug investigation division.

He was wounded just three days later, after his team was ambushed while merely investigating the purported location of the hierarchy of a Mexican cocaine trafficking ring in Atlanta, Georgia. The bullet fractured his left knee and he spent three months in rehabilitation before he was able to walk with some degree of efficiency. To this day, a slight limp was still evident in his step and his knee was a perfect barometer whenever the weather changed. His days as a field agent were over before they had started.

The unfortunate start with the Bureau had landed him behind a desk for a number of years until he was able to prove his executive skills by working his way through a number of various departments within the organization. He worked as diligently as humanly possible in hope of advancement. It was his organizational skills while working in the new National Crime Information Center in Clarksburg, West Virginia, that finally got him noticed by the hierarchy at the bureau.

He had been assigned to the NCIC assisting in the set-up of the new computerized data system, which was a tool used to assist federal, state and local authorities. The original programming of the system was flawed from the start, and a new program had to be installed in its place. It was in essence a computerized library of criminal records, wanted and missing persons, fugitives as well as felony records of every person in the United States. The computer also stored records on stolen guns, cars and license plates as well as other pertinent data useful in the identification of wanted felons. This included not only mug shots and fingerprints, but also other useful information such as scars, tattoos, and street names that would aide law enforcement officers in identifying known criminals. This information could be accessed instantaneously anywhere in the country.

Now, at forty-seven years old, he was given his first real chance to prove himself as an administrator for the Missing Person's division of the bureau, the type of position that he had longed for ever since he was injured.

Raymond wondered if he was ever going to find time to get to the stack of paperwork that lay scattered in front of him. It was a matter of priorities, he mumbled quietly; though for the life of him, he wondered how in the world the prior administer of his new-found position did anything with any degree of proficiency. The advancement and the raise didn't seem to be worth all the time he now had to spend here in front of this desk trying to sort out what should have been done to the bureau's standards to begin with. His days were long, sometimes lasting well into the late evening hours.

The phone was lit up like a Christmas tree and he was already mentally tired, though it wasn't yet nine o'clock. He began to question his own organizational skills and thought it might be easier to pull out every hair on his thinning grey-splotched pate than to organize the colossal mess that lay before him. He knew for sure he would never pass his initial evaluation unless he was able to get a handle on this mass of chaos and pass the upcoming audit.

Delegate - that's what he had to do - bring all his assistants and whip this Missing Persons Division into a well-oiled machine. This division lacked integrity he thought aimlessly, and at that point, the bureau's motto popped into his head: Fidelity, Bravery, and Integrity. He thought of the motto as if it were a jingle of some sort and began to hum the words, a well thought out verse that aped the acronym for the F.B.I.

At this point, he knew he was totally at his wits end as he left his desk and wandered toward the outer office to stretch his legs, his left knee throbbing with frustration. He wondered why he had eaten so much of his wife's spicy Jamaican cooking the night before as he popped an antacid and slowly chewed it as he opened the door to the outer office.

He noticed his secretary as soon as he opened the door. She was new to her job as well, immersed in as much paperwork as he was, trying to organize the office to her liking. She briefly looked up at him as he passed by and reminded him that Interpol was on hold. He had forgotten all about the call and wandered back into his office to answer it.

He assumed when he answered the phone that some European celebrity had gone missing once again, probably having a tryst with some nameless woman, and Interpol wanted the bureau's overseas branches to aid in the search. This would not be the first time something like this had happened and the man needed to be found before the press got wind of his absence and caused a public scandal in the process. He had already fielded several calls for assistance in cases such as these and assumed that was what the call was about.

Hell, he had enough problems right here in this country without having to assist other countries with their missing person's problem. Every year more than eight hundred thousand people went missing in this country alone, dreadful statistics to be sure.

Most of them, better than ninety percent, were later found to be unharmed, though that still left about eighty thousand people a year who seemed to vanish for one reason or another. The most appalling part of the latter number was that ten percent of these numbers were children. Eight thousand adolescents a year gone missing!

This is what the agency strove to reduce with the help of the international, state and local law enforcement agencies. Some headway was being made in that direction. Still, he was sickened any time a file on one of these youthful statistics passed in front of him. There was a myriad of reasons why children came up missing - parental abductions, mostly a result of painful divorces. Some of these children were whisked out of the county when the marriages involved foreign-held visas. A number of children were also taken when a woman who lost her own child and sought a ready replacement to ease her guilt.

The worst though, were the pedophiles, who wished to sate their lust for sexual abuse and murder by taking the innocent. These were the ones that called for swift action by all police agencies. Raymond tried not to dwell on these cases too long, for they sickened him as well as most decent god-fearing Americans. These were the cases that received the most press coverage and were sensationalized whenever possible by the media. Raymond thought this type of shock therapy should be banned, for it was always the perpetrator and never the victim who ended up immortalized.

He sat down in his chair and fielded the phone call from Interpol. He knew that the Agency had an intimate working arrangement with all international police agencies and it was his job to assist in any way possible. "Special Agent Willis here, how can I help you?" he said, more sharply than he intended.

"This is Ebon Martine, Paris bureau. I was wondering if we might get your cooperation on a very sensitive issue which has just been brought to our attention."

Agent Willis knew the caller, having spoken to him on several prior occasions. He felt sure his assumption about a missing celebrity would prove correct once more of the details had surfaced. "By all means, what can we do for you?" he replied, resisting the urge to grimace.

"I would like it if you called me back on a scrambled line, for not a word of this predicament must be leaked."

Agent Willis listened carefully to the number, which he quickly memorized and then hung up. He reconnected in one almost simultaneous manner and punched his administrative number into the phone and then selected the proper option. He waited several moments while a series of interconnected clicks finally gave him another dial tone. He then dialed the memorized number, knowing that within ten minutes the number would no longer function. There could never be enough security as far as the bureau was concerned, for way too many people tried on a daily basis to hack their way into the Agency computer networks and phone lines. Several seconds passed before the connection was made and he heard the familiar voice once again.

"Special Agent Willis, I hope once we have finished speaking that you will understand the reason why I have asked you to go to such a great length in securing this conversation. I cannot stress to you enough how much the matter is of an extremely sensitive nature and why we are in need of all of the resources you can muster."

This was the first time the agent had received such a stern warning about the content of a conversation. This piqued his interest and he was sure now that damaging information was forthcoming, "You have my word, Mr. Martine, I'm all ears. Let me know what it is and what you need and I'll be able to judge for myself the severity of the issue."

"All right then, but when I tell you the reason for the urgency, you will know why confidentiality is of the essence." He cleared his throat. "The Pope is missing."

"Excuse me? I don't think I heard you right. Would you repeat that?" Agent Willis said, flabbergasted by the thought. His heart leapt and his gaze automatically scanned the room, just in case.

"The Pope is missing. I cannot stress to you enough what the implications of this issue would be if anyone other than a select few know about this."

Agent Willis whistled low into the phone. "You're kidding right? I just saw him on television last night. He was in India dealing with the famine there. He was imploring the international community to come to their aid."

"A double, special agent Willis, No one can really tell the difference, not unless they know him on a personal basis, that is."

"How long has he been missing?"

"Just over thirty-six hours is our best guess, not long before he was scheduled to take the flight to India."

Raymond wondered why the State Department or the CIA had not been contacted instead. Then he remembered that it was the resources of the Bureau that were required. "You know that I will have to contact the Director on this matter before anything further can be done to assist you."

"We realize that. To further clarify why we contacted you instead of someone higher up, is that we believe from experience that there is a leak. Your State Department has a mole within its ranks and I don't want to chance another leak." He paused for several moments to emphasize the point. "I am sure you will agree with us that locating the Pope might be a most prudent avenue to take. That is our thought on the matter, and I hoped you would concur with that idea. What with multi-millions of the faithful, it would be a lot easier to find him than cause an international panic. Don't you think?"

"Sure… I'm sure you're right. I would hardly dare to think of the consequences if he wasn't found. There would be chaos in the streets of every major Christian country. Is it possible that he may have been kidnapped?"

"The issue of that possibility has already been explored, what with the pontiff's recent criticism of the Muslim leaders' lack of control over their fundamentalist factions. It's a plausible option. However, the Vatican State Police have informed us that the idea of someone raiding the Vatican and abducting someone out of the confines of its walls was a near impossibility. That… and no ransom has been demanded as of yet."

"But it has not been ruled out, am I correct in assuming as much?"

"Like I said earlier, we believe that it's a highly unlikely scenario."

Raymond wanted to be sure of the facts. "Have you any more detailed information on the matter, if kidnapping has already been ruled out?"

"All we have been told at this point was that the Pope retired for the evening and the next morning, when his aide came to awaken him, he was not in his room. A thorough search ensued from the Vatican security forces to no avail."

The new director now had a million questions which he was dying to ask and was not sure where to start, "Are you sure that he didn't secretly leave the premises without anyone knowing? It happens all too often when heads of state want to get away from their responsibilities for awhile."

"I'm afraid you don't quite understand!" Martine snapped with impatience. "What possible reason would the Head of the Roman Catholic Church have to want to escape his duties? Besides, we are talking about an eighty-year-old here, not a derelict politician with a penchant for variety!"

"Look, I don't want to come across as condescending, I just need all the information that you have at your disposal. I need some kind of tangible information that I might use in order that I might better be able to persuade my superiors of the urgency of the matter, in hopes of answering your call for immediate action."

"My apologies," Martine sighed. "We have already started a dossier on the issue, which I will send to you within the hour. I must stress though, that time is of the essence here."

"I realize that, and I'll see what we can do to assist in any way possible."

"That's all that can be expected, Chief Willis."

The line went dead and Raymond listened to the series of disconnections while he pondered the severity of the issue. It would be a matter of minutes before he finally hung up the phone, still feigning disbelief for some reason, looking at the black handset as if it were contaminated in some inordinate way.

He finally hung up the phone and redialed, requesting a private meeting with the Director. He addressed the severity of the issue with the appointment secretary without divulging the reason for the impromptu meeting. He was not sure what the Director's response might be to this development but knew that it was solely up to him to relay the sensitivity of the issue. For the life of him, he could not figure out how a head of state could disappear without anyone noticing. There had to be insider assistance in order for a man of that sort of stature to up and walk away without anyone noticing. This kind of news would be bigger than the kidnapping of renowned aviator Charles Lindbergh's baby in 1932 if it was leaked. When that occurred it had been an international sensation, but this would be a thousand times worse than that.

He sat back in his chair, gathering his thoughts and pondering the implications. Who would want to kidnap the Pope, and for what reason? Logically it didn't seem to be a likely scenario, and really didn't make any logical sense.

He quickly logged on to the computer and searched the Agency's database for that likelihood, looking for any known terrorist group or sect that might have expressed an interest in kidnapping the pope.

Having intimate knowledge of the F. B. I. computer network, he was able to tie it into the CIA network as well, and information streamed across the screen so fast he was unable to see anything more than a blur of letters. Within minutes, a list of possible group names was on his screen, along with their leaders and particulars. He printed a list and set it aside.

He then entered another set of criteria of known verbal threats against the pontiff and again waited for the information to compile, then printed it. When it was complete, he stacked it with the other list. He then thought it prudent to compile a complete Missing Person's query for known heads of state and prominent citizens. He wanted to be armed with the latest statistics before he met with his supervisor. He tapped some keys and the computer produced a graph the information for the last five years. He was surprised to see that there had been a minute but steady rise in the chart.

He was about to print that when he froze. He suddenly recalled an internet story he had read several months ago about a missing high-ranking Buddhist monk. He couldn't remember if the holy man had ever been found. He hit the print button and then redirected the computer to an inquiry on 'missing religious leaders' then sat back, staring intently at the screen,

"What the hell is going on here?" he muttered. His computer screen flashed red. Scrolling across the top of the scarlet screen were the words

CLASSIFIED! CLEARANCE REQUIRED!

A black box then appeared on the screen, flashing like an intermittent warning light. He entered his administrative code and waited for a response.

"Access Denied." The screen flashed briefly and then the computer default sounded "Goodbye!" and shut down.

The screen defaulted to the Agency screensaver. Raymond was flabbergasted by the action. He had worked on many of the agencies' computer programs and had never experienced a computer denial of his administrator access code before. Perhaps he had mistakenly entered the wrong number. "That's got to be it, just a mistake," he mumbled, then carefully reentered his administrative code once again. He got the same result. Frustrated by the denial, he threw his hands up in the air as if he was imploring the almighty to come to his aid.

"This is crazy!" He sat back in the chair in deep thought, his hands folded carefully across his chest, twirling his thumbs. He thought about the dilemma for several moments before he finally surmised that someone high up in the chain of command was blocking the information he had requested. He glanced at his watch, wondering if he had enough time to access the information though the "back door," a means of gaining entrance to the information by circumventing the security protocol. He lurched forward in his chair and hit the keyboard, fingers flying, trying to do just that. After ten exasperating minutes, he was denied access once again.

This time the terminal went dead.

He bolted out of the chair and strode into the outer office, charging his secretaries' desk in the process. He saw her startled look as she instinctively backed away, chair and all. "I didn't mean to scare you, but I need to use your computer right now!" He came around the desk before she could respond. He saw the fear in her eyes and was sure she thought he was not only certifiable but dangerous too. He slowed only long enough for her to rise out of her chair and leave the cubicle. "My computer crashed and I needed to use yours," he explained as he sat in the chair and wheeled it around like a bar stool, ending up in front of the screen before she could say a word. He prompted her terminal and the departmental logo appeared. "So, the system is not down," he muttered again. What the hell was going on?

He clicked on the icon for the internet and waited momentarily for it to boot, glancing at the woman who now warily leered back at him from a distance. He began to feel bad for her, knowing that he had never really established a rapport with her. He looked back at the screen and prompted the screen for news about a missing Buddhist monk. This brought up a link to the Washington Post, so he entered the news screen and read the initial and follow-up stories. The conclusion he made from the gleaned information was that the man had not yet been found. He exited the program and slowly rose from the chair. "I must apologize if I startled you," he said sincerely. Her face began to soften. "If it's not too much to ask, I need you to call a computer tech to look at my terminal. It seems to be on the blink." He relinquished her chair.

"Yes," she stammered. "I suppose I could do that for you."

He left her office, gathered up the newly printed documents, and stuffed them in a plain manila folder and then he headed out the door for his meeting with Arthur Bremmington, the Director of the Bureau. His knee throbbed from the stress and he felt himself limping.

The Director's receptionist was less than cordial. Other asking for his name, she said nothing to him at all, but slowly rose and gestured for him to step into the ante room. Raymond thought the reason for this was merely a way of conveying the importance of the man whom he was about to meet.

Other than seeing the man from a distance on occasion, Raymond had only spoken to the Director briefly when he was interviewed for the position. He was a bit nervous about his first professional encounter, not knowing what to expect. He had heard numerous stories about the man, but they were just stories, and some of them he found hard to believe. He ignored them and wrote them off as gossip from fellow workers envious of the position.

He sat in the anteroom for what seemed to be an inordinate amount of time. The room was drab in comparison to some of the lower-level director's offices he had previously seen. The room reminded him of a waiting room for a dental office. Two non-descriptive couches sat opposite one another with end tables at either side. Brass lamps on the end tables were a throwback to the late forties and the patina on the lamps was dulled to an olive-copper tone. He was sure that at one time the lamps had been used as sidebars on a large desk.

Above the couch across from him was the only picture in the entire room, a mural-sized oil painting of J. Edgar Hoover, the originator and first Director of the Bureau. The painting had a strange effect to it. At first, he couldn't figure out what it was about the painting that seemed so beguiling, so he rose and examined it closely, close enough to see the brush strokes on its surface. He backed away and then turned, looking back over his shoulder at it from a totally different perspective. He returned to his seat without looking away. Then he figured it out. No matter where you stood in the room, the eyes of J. Edgar Hoover watched you.

A few minutes later, the door opened and five men left without even giving him as much as a second glance. He didn't recognize any of them. Several minutes later, the director opened the door and welcomed him in. The inner office was radically different than the stark feel of the outer office. The room was totally white with all black furniture, accented by modernistic clear glass sculptures that adorned the furniture. The only color in the room came from two green frond palms, which stood like sentinels in the corners. Two heavy black leather chairs on either side of the desk offered seating. The director pointed for him to sit. Raymond did so, exceedingly nervous for some odd reason. He tried to settle his nerves by trying to figure out what the glass sculpture on the left side of the desk looked like, and could have sworn it reminded him of the Madonna with child, but could not be positive.

The director sat down and looked as if he was sizing up his new Assistant Director of Missing Persons. Two files laid in front of him, splayed open. Raymond assumed one of them was his. As for the other, he had no idea as to its contents.

"What can I do for you, Special Agent Willis?" the director said without the slightest hint of emotion in his voice.

Raymond hoped his choice of words would not fail him as he locked eyes with the man with a rather ruddy complexion for a man who sat indoors all day. His flaxen hair was coiffed in such a way that it almost looked air brushed. He belied his true age with almost boyish-like facial features. The only signs of age lines on his face were minute crow's feet emanating from the corners of his mouth. He was trim and fit, looking like he had just stepped out of the academy at fifty-eight. He cleared his throat. "It has been brought to my attention that a rather serious issue has surfaced about one of our world leaders. I was informed that this man has come up missing, and I have been asked to aid in any way possible. It's quite likely that if this man is not found, the ramifications could cause a world panic of sorts, Sir."

"Aren't you being a little extreme, Agent Willis? Or if you prefer, I would much rather address you by you first name, er... it is Ray, right?"

"Yes Sir, Ray it is, and I don't mind at all. Back to your question, and the answer is... no. I'm not being extreme, not in the least, Sir."

The director sat motionless and expressionless, though he did glance down at the fingernails of his left hand.

"Ray, so pray tell me, who is it, and what, if any information about this man do you already know and how did you come about this information?"

"I received a phone call from Interpol... from a liaison officer, Ebon Martine, who asked for assistance in locating the Pope of the Roman Catholic Church--" A bubble of laughter caught him off guard, but the director resumed his abrupt manner immediately.

"Special Agent Willis, you're joking, right?"

"I'm not, Sir."

"Did you verify your source, which I am sure you are aware, is standard Bureau policy?"

"I did, Sir."

"Go on then, excuse the interruption."

Agent Willis went about explaining in detail what had transpired up until this point without further interruption. He got to the part about the dossier from Interpol and handed it to the director, who began to peruse it while he continued. He omitted his bureau inquiry about missing religious leaders but did inform the director about the alarming increase in missing persons over the last twelve months. He informed the director of his research on known possible threats to the Pope and handed both documents over. He also started in on a summation of his own thoughts as to whether the case could be a kidnapping or just a missing person request.

The director finished reading the documents and looked up when he finished speaking.

"Very thorough work, Special Agent Willis," the director offered.

"Thank you, Sir," Raymond replied.

"Does anyone else know anything about this?" the director asked.

"No, Sir."

"Well done then, please leave the matter in my hands and I'll make sure that Interpol has all the resources that it needs."

The five men who had previously left the office reentered and made their way to either side of the director's chair. Raymond knew something was up but not sure what, and felt intimidated by the five men in identical black suits. The director spoke once again.

"You swore an oath of fidelity when you signed on with the Bureau, and as your record shows, you have upheld the code up until this point and your file has been spotless up until today. It is my wish that you do not divulge any of the information about the Pope that you have come to know. I cannot stress enough the implication of repercussions you may suffer because of any error on your part. Do no more research into this case and act as if you knew nothing about it to begin with. Is that clear, Special Agent Willis?"

The statement was made with such forceful verve that there was no mistaking his intent. "Yes, Sir," Raymond responded, though he now knew that there were forces higher than the Director who were also privy to his information. He also knew why the computer terminal had frozen; there was no doubt about that now.

"In the meantime, Assistant Director Willis, it is my wish that you accompany these men, who I have no doubt, wish to question you in minute detail about what you know about this issue."

"They are not with the bureau, are they?"

"You're very perceptive Assistant Director Willis. Actually, they are with the NSA and they would like to have a word with you, and your full co-operation is mandatory."

Raymond knew that his livelihood and his position with the Bureau were at stake by the way the director had used his rank twice to preface his commands. There was no doubt that he would be terminated in more ways than one if he refused to cooperate. He knew about some of the tactics the Bureau used to eliminate a problem and in his mind's eye could see his body floating down the Potomac and out to sea. "I guess there's no choice in the matter," he sighed.

"No, no choice at all!"

Several days later, Raymond read the headlines in the Washington Post:

THE POPE IS DEAD!

The byline to the story read that the Pontiff had died in his sleep as a result of overexertion from his trip to India. Raymond wondered if, by chance, the Pope had in truth been abducted and killed. He feared for his own life and was lax in coming forward with what he knew to be the truth for fear of the consequences. He had been forewarned. He took the threat seriously.

CHAPTER 4

Questionable Circumstances

Vatican City

Father Giuseppe Lorenzo was shocked by the sudden death of the pope, as was the rest of the world. He knew at least one hundred thousand or more of the faithful would soon flock into the Vatican in hopes of getting a final glimpse of such a well-respected and much-loved leader. Though the pope's tenure had been short - a mere twenty-two months - his impact had been felt by all. Pope Alexander had done much in the way of advancing the true nature of the Catholic religion with his pious and forthright ways. Historically, no one had done more to advance the true intent of Christ's teachings and he was surely the best loved of his long line of predecessors as the representatives of Christ's church in Rome.

No one had done more to aid the sick and hungry, the infirm and maligned than he had. He had spoken daily on matters of social injustices, implored nations of the world to seek out and stop any and all prejudices against mankind. He had utilized his podium like Roman soldiers had once wielded their swords, lashing out in defense of all. The glint of the sword's polished blade represented his fiery passion for all life.

He had also prompted the wealthy nations of the world not to turn a blind eye to the increasing starvation and calamity that had befallen many of the less than fortunate nations on this planet. He led by example, empting the coffers of the Catholic Church in an effort to relieve world hunger that had beset many. Food though, was just part of the problem as he saw it; the lack of potable water was another problem that he sought to overcome as well.

He had prayed aloud daily for Muslim, Buddhist, Jew and Christian alike to lay down their weapons and work together in an effort to ease the growing debacle of failed crops and erratic changes in weather as well as depleting resources in the sea which threatened mankind's very existence.

He had also done much in the way of realigning all Christians to reunite them into a single cohesive unit. On behalf of his churches past injustices, he confessed the fallacies of the church in an effort to induce reconciliation. He was well aware of the facts behind most of the reasons for their initial splintering; some of his earlier predecessors were less than forthright and honest in their direction of the church and its true intent. He sought to bring together the Orthodox Christians as well as the Lutheran and Anglican, Methodist and others into one fold in an effort not only to stem the rising tide of cynicism and mistrust which had riddled the land, but to utilize the Christian faith as one in an all-out battle against the sins of mankind.

He had even coined his own phrase whenever he began a speech. "Satan is no friend of ours!" It was rallying point upon which he exposed the injustices of friend and foe alike. There was not an issue that the holy man would not touch, be it family life, social mores and obligations or any of the seven deadly sins.

It had taken some time before Giuseppe had realized that the Pontiff had utilized an ongoing theme in his sermons. Each day of the week, one of the seven deadly sins was expounded upon in his daily sermons to the rest of the world. Somewhere in the text of each and every speech, one of the seven deadly sins was mentioned. To the Pope, these cardinal sins were the basis for man's eventual downfall.

Giuseppe knew the Pope had been accused by many religious and social leaders as a man who barnstormed countries in an effort to foster his own agenda of religious right and might, though nothing though could be farther from the truth. He'd been a man of true purpose.

The priest had been fortunate enough to meet his revered leader, though it had occurred quite by accident. He had been rambling through the aisles of the Vatican Library early one morning, replacing a religious tome which had been left out on one of the tables the night before to its rightful place, when he happened to cross paths with the Pope. He had never known the holy man ever to visit the library before. The proper procedure, as he knew it, was to send any book the Pope might request to his personal secretary, who would then place the book on his desk for his review. The pope, who was an avid reader, would sometimes request ten or more books at a time.

Giuseppe had been told that he read them from cover to cover. How true this was, he was not sure, for it could have been that the messenger who conveyed the books to the pope's secretary merely trying to make him feel good about the prompt attention Father Lorenzo paid to the Pope's wishes. He knew for a fact that it was just not religious books that the Pope read, but books on many subjects, as well as periodicals and daily newspapers from all over the world. This man could read, write, and speak in at least six languages that he was aware of.

Giuseppe recalled with vivid clarity his meeting with the Pontiff. He was startled by the chance encounter as he nearly ran into him while scurrying though the aisles. He stopped abruptly and at first was baffled by the sight. He then realized what he was supposed to do, bow deeply and kissed the ring on the Pope's proffered right hand. He remained in a prostrate state for some time before the pontiff spoke.

"Rise my son, your deeds will be remembered."

"My apologies," Giuseppe stated sincerely as he looked into his eyes. There was something about this man which impressed a level of sanctity which he hardly thought could be achieved by man. That was the feeling he derived from the encounter. He was awed by the accidental meeting but also at a complete loss for words, bowing once again and letting the man pass rather than making a complete fool out of himself.

Now, in retrospect, he wished he'd had the courage to say something to the Pope. The only reason being was that the holy man was now dead and he wished there might have been some sort of enlightening antidote that he may have had the chance to pass on. To this day, he still felt a bit idiotic regarding his mute behavior, for he usually was never at a loss for words.

The *Sede Vacante* or Vacant See had commenced with an announcement early that morning, that there was no leader at the helm of the Church. The College of Cardinals had hurriedly assembled to carry out the *Ordo Exsquiarum Romani Pontificis,* the order for burial and the appointment of a successor to the pontiff, planning the funeral rites in accordance to specific determined guidelines.

Pope Alexander had specified a burial date of no longer than five days after his demise, a request that the college had to adhere to in his *Universi Dominica Gregis,* a request written by Pope Alexander just several months before. It could be best compared to a last will of sorts, regarding the pope's religious preferences.

The mood throughout Vatican City and the rest of the world was somber. Giuseppe felt a sense of overwhelming gloom wherever he went. He, for one, was completely out of sorts by the loss and sensed that anyone he met reacted in much the same way. There was a lot of confusion and questions about how a man who seemed so fit and active had just slipped away in his sleep with no apparent sign of distress.

By the end of the first day, the rumors and innuendo's regarding his untimely demise had spread as rampantly as a wildfire. How much truth was interlaced with conjecture at this point was hard to determine, for there were many theories as to the pontiff's death, which were nothing more than just that - theories. The worldwide news media got wind of the death almost instantly and were partly to blame for some of this chaos. They camped out around every known entrance to Vatican in hopes of finding someone to substantiate some of the implied rumors that they themselves had started. Giuseppe likened them to a pack of hungry wolves laying in wait for an unsuspecting lamb to pass.

Everyone inside the Vatican wished to avoid the melee at the entrances and were forced to utilize some of the secret passageways that lay beneath the walls of the Vatican itself. Almost all of the church's hierarchy made their way into Vatican through these secret passageways, which at any other time would have been both blocked and sealed off or locked and guarded.

Giuseppe had misjudged the popularity of the fallen pope. The first day of scheduled viewing, which would last for four days, over one hundred thousand mourning patrons tried to storm Vatican when the doors opened. At least another hundred thousand and maybe more had held a constant prayer vigil outside the walls, waiting patiently though they did not try to enter. Not since the death of John Paul II, who was extremely popular as well, had so many people been so affected by the loss of a papal leader. Nineteen people were trampled to death and another hundred of so seriously injured because of the initial surge, and it was all the Vatican City police could do using crowd control tactics to prevent the number of casualties from being higher than they actually were.

There had been a private showing the day before for all of the Catholic Church's selected witnesses and Cardinal Robbia had been one on them. Rumor had it that it was a closed casket viewing. Now, on the initial day of public showing, the rumor proved to be truth. Giuseppe wondered if the pope had specifically asked for it to be that way, and could only presume that he had.

Throngs who streamed by the closed casket in the viewing hall in the Apostolic Palace clamored their objections to this first ever occurrence. They wanted to see the pope with their own eyes in an effort to put some closure to the stunning event. The level of protest was so high that some of the guards protecting the casket thought that the windows of the hall would explode from the tumultuous din. An extra line of security had to be established for fear that the crowd may storm the cordoned off area and physically try to pry the casket lid open.

The protests of indignation were just as loud outside after leaving the hall itself. No one at the Vatican was quite sure how to react to such a physical show of dismay. Some of the benches in the courtyard that led away from the viewing hall had been smashed into unrecognizable little pieces. Anything the crowd could pry loose now became fair game in venting their anger towards the officials responsible for the closed casket. The word of this unusual occurrence electrified the crowd outside of the Vatican. Throngs of disenchanted people began to riot outside the walls. Those who did not participate in the rioting wailed uncontrollably and the fervor could be heard from miles away. A panicked call for assistance went out to all available police to come to the aid of Vatican City Police, who were in essence, Swiss guards.

The City of Rome sent in all the officers they could spare in an effort to quell the rising turmoil. The melee quickly grew so widespread that it spilled onto the streets of Rome and the Italian government had to step in, dispatching troops in an effort to restore order.

Even though it was no longer safe, thousands upon thousands more flocked into the city. It was soon estimated that close to a million people tried to flood into the city on the second day following the announcement of the Pope's death. It was all public officials could do to stave off the waves of humanity. All public transportation had been halted but it did no good, for people walked in streams toward the Vatican and no one could stop them. Police lines and roadblocks seemed to be nothing more than a mere inconvenience to the burgeoning crowds. Finally, it was deemed safer for the public officials to remove the barriers and defend the entrances to the Vatican itself.

Even more astounding results to the unexpected fervor happened the third day following the Pope's death, when Muslim leaders of the world fell just short of calling the man a prophet for all men, something that Allah had once said himself about Jesus. This was totally unexpected.

Some Muslims even began to make their way toward the Vatican to bear witness to the occurrence, not because they believed in the man's religion, but just because he had garnered so much respect and gave it as well. This was due to the fact that when Pope Alexander first rose to power, he had extended an olive branch to the Muslim faith. He knew that there were many similarities between the two religions that could not be ignored, and also knew that many of the teachings in the Koran and the Bible were almost interchangeable.

On that third day, the casket was removed from the Apostolic Palace and placed in a secure area. In its place was put a life size picture of the man taken while he had been consoling an abandoned child on the streets of Maputo in Mozambique.

The press tried desperately to find the abandoned boy to add notoriety to the story, but the boy who had been put in an orphanage, under the orders of the pope, had died a year earlier, never recovering from the ravages of malnutrition. Still, the press took pictures of the orphanage and interviewed its director in an effort to sensationalize the story. The grave of the orphan was the endpoint of an enduring human rights story about a Pope who cared for all.

Giuseppe didn't know what to make of the reasoning behind the closed casket in the first place; he thought that the Pope might have requested it. He had his own ideas though. He thought about his mother's disappearance. He surmised that the Pope had vanished in the exact same manner as his mother had. He had no possible way of knowing whether this was the reason behind the closed casket, but theorized how the Vatican could display a body that no longer existed. He remembered vividly that there would be nothing but fine ash left coving the sheets where the body of his mother once lay. Now, were it possible for him to speak to the Pope's aide or gain entrance to his apartment, he might have been able to prove his theory. He knew though, that the apartment of the Pope had been sealed off and his ability to question the Pope's aide or secretary to prove his theory right was not a likely prospect. What with all the mass of confusion within the Vatican, he knew that now was certainly not the time to go nosing around and asking off-the-wall questions to the aides or anyone else. Suspicions would only increase.

At the appropriate time, he knew that the former Archbishop Robbia could aid him in the search of the truth. Just ten months ago, he had attended the ordination of the new Cardinal of Milan. As he had predicted, the man had been nominated by the pope and approved by the Sacred College of Cardinals. The swift approval was conveyed by all members of the elite group and by the Pope himself, who had eagerly awaited the final vote. There was no doubt as to whether the Pope would give his blessing to the newly formed cardinal, for he was already an integral part of the hierarchy.

Ever since Cardinal Robbia had been elected, a visible power shift had occurred within the College of Cardinals. Some of the Cardinals who did not agree to the new policy changes of Pope Alexander were soon shunned. The policies that were being lobbied into enactment by the new Cardinal and a majority of the Sacred College was seen as act to aligned themselves behind the new driving force of thought, for Pope Alexander.

The church as everyone knew it had to change with the times, the reasoning being that it must adapt or be left behind. Just as Pope John the Twenty-Third had done in the early nineteen-sixties with his Second Vatican Council, change had to come about once again. It had been over fifty years since the last major change in church policy. The Pope had used Cardinal Robbia as a front man in his efforts to bring about this change. He had picked the right man through whom he could do his bidding. The cardinal was thoroughly knowledgeable about the inner workings of the church. Prior to his eventual election, he had already impressed most of his future allies. Cardinal Robbia, being an extremely educated man, also knew how to use the power of persuasion to achieve what was deemed necessary. He was an astute study of human character, lobbied each of the Cardinals for their ideas on specific matters, and made friends of each and every one of them. He also used the ear of the Pope to exchange favors for votes. Being as he was just about assured the position as financial secretary, he used this power to his advantage, dictating to any opponents of upcoming policy changes.

These adversaries to change were warned of the future need to increase their contributions in their districts for the good of all. Some conservative Cardinals, opposed to change, believed that this was nothing more than a veiled blackmail attempt. Cardinal Robbia had in his hand an edict from the pope, who politely turned a blind eye to the strong-arm tactics.

On the fourth day of the funeral rite, the speculation of Pope Alexander's death was turned over to a tribunal in an effort to calm the sea of protest. The authorities hoped that an inquisition into his death might quell the crowds and restore order in the city. This seemed to work a dual-fold purpose, for the media then shifted its attention away from the dead Pope and began to speculate as to who might readily be able to fill his shoes. This was one tall order, as no one was likely to fill it effortlessly.

Once this had occurred, Giuseppe was glad to see some assimilation of order restored in the city even if the waves of humanity had not left the city proper, and would not likely do so until the burial. He knew the outpouring of love for the deceased man would fade with time and wondered, as did everyone else, who might be appointed his successor.

He did not think it likely that his mentor Cardinal Robbia would be appointed, solely because of his lack of tenure. Nevertheless, you could never really be sure. A conclave had yet to be established. The College of Cardinals had assumed power over all church functions once Pope Alexander died and it was this same college that would sequester themselves until a majority was achieved by secret ballot, electing a new successor to the position. Once elected the new candidate had the right of refusal, but generally speaking, acceptance was usually a foregone conclusion once the candidate was formally asked by the Dean of Cardinals.

On the afternoon of the fourth day, Giuseppe received a note from Cardinal Robbia. In the note, he was asked if they might meet later that evening. He sent along his reply, looking forward to meeting with the Cardinal, who he knew was privy to much more detailed information about all that had transpired then Giuseppe could gather. He was not sure what the meeting might entail, as the note only stated a time and a place in which to meet. Giuseppe thought that the meeting was a private one, but was surprised upon his arrival that all of the circle of eight were in attendance.

He was almost the last to arrive as the Cardinal, seated at the head of a conference table, idly chatted with Bishop Alvito, seated at his right. The Cardinal motioned to the empty chair to his left for Giuseppe. After greetings were exchanged, Cardinal Robbia returned to his conversation with Bishop Alvito. The two men spoke in a whisper and Giuseppe couldn't readily discern the content of their discussion. He sat patiently waiting for the meeting to start.

It commenced shortly afterward as the last of the counselors to the Cardinal arrived. Then an eloquent prayer was recited by the Cardinal, who asked Jesus to take pity on the soul of his departed servant Pope Alexander and implored Him to let the light of wisdom flood down on those who were about to steer the course of His church here on earth.

Giuseppe, impressed by the sincerity of the appeal, felt as if the prayer would surely lift the blanket of despair from the sad course of events that had befallen the church. He looked around the table, wondering if those seated with him felt the same way as he prayed silently for an intervention of some sort to take place. The Cardinal then lifted his head and spoke.

"I have asked you all here today under these sad circumstances to ask if you might assist me in my quest to seek the election for the newly appointed Pope. I ask Bishop Alvito to be my secretary during the conclave and Giuseppe to be my servant. It is my hope that until all the cardinal's are sequestered, that each and every one of you might use your influence to lobby on my behalf. It is perhaps a daunting chore, but I need all the time you can muster. It is my belief that I am eminently qualified to continue with the changes that Pope Alexander started. He and I saw eye to eye when it came to the needed changes necessary to continue doing Jesus' work. "

A murmur of approval circulated around the table. Each and every one of his councilors voiced their approval, as did Giuseppe, though shocked by the fact that he was being asked to be Cardinal Robbia's servant at the conclave. It was an honor he would readily accept under any circumstances, though he secretly wished he had been asked prior to the meeting in order to mask the surprised confusion, which he was sure, had momentarily clouded his face. The only thing that truly worried him about the request was the fact that he would have to spend all that time in close quarters with Bishop Alvito, a man he really could not stomach. Boisterous, was not a strong enough word in which to describe the man.

The position as servant was one that required him to pass along notes to other sequestered Cardinals, as well as ballots to the Dean of Cardinals, so he knew he would not be as confined to quarters as the position of secretary. He would also be responsible for supplying food for the two men, cooking it if asked to do so, a task for which he held no claim or degree of proficiency. These days it was not a requirement to do so, for a complete cafeteria was at their disposal. If relegated to cooking chores, he knew that the rancor of criticism on Bishop Alvito's part might rise to crescendo proportions in that regard. This he based on observation alone, for as time progressed, the man seemed to expand with it as well. He knew he would be praying for a swift and decisive vote for the next Cardinal to rise to the papacy for that reason alone.

Cardinal Robbia continued speaking at length, laying out a sure strategy that he hoped all the men in the room might use. He fielded questions submitted by men and the meeting took on the air of a pep rally. With high expectations, the meeting was adjourned after about an hour. Before Giuseppe had a chance to rise out of his seat, he felt a hand on his shoulder, and the cardinal silently indicated that he should stay seated until everyone else had left. He wondered what might be required of him while he patiently waited for the room to clear.

"If you don't mind, Father Lorenzo, instead of campaigning on my behalf, I have a special assignment for you that may require the use of your many talents."

"Why of course, your Excellency, what have you got?" Giuseppe asked, wondering what was so important that it couldn't be said in the presence of the others.

"Some rather disturbing news has crossed my desk which I have not had time to attend to. It concerns what, in scientific terms, constitutes an anomaly. This occurred about a week ago in the Egyptian desert, and investigated by the scientific community in depth. As yet, they have no explanation as to its origin."

Giuseppe, intrigued by the possibilities, inadvertently cut off the Cardinal, interjecting a question. "What kind of anomaly was it, if I may ask?"

"Patience, my son, is a virtue that you need to practice," he gently admonished. "Let me finish before you interrupt."

Chastised for his curiosity, Giuseppe merely nodded acceptance to his error.

"It seems that there was some sort of light projected from the heavens onto the desert. The anomaly seems to have left no trace on the desert floor and the scientists have already ruled out any type of laser. We have secretly sent two people to investigate the matter in hopes of finding a witness to the event. To date, they have not found anyone. They, however, are still searching as we speak." Cardinal Robbia paused briefly to take a sip of water from his glass, which sat in front of him.

Giuseppe had to bit his lip to keep quiet, not daring to interrupt again despite his impatience.

"I would like for you to see if there is any religious significance to this type of anomaly and report back to me if you find anything. Specifically, what I'm looking for are any references to light."

"Could it have been a meteorite?" Giuseppe asked, thinking about the last book in the Bible.

"From what I have been told, that has been ruled out. NASA has a new orbiting satellite that does just that. It searches the solar system for meteorites and asteroids most likely to affect the planet."

"Would you mind if I had a copy of this report? I am sure it would aide me immensely."

"No, not at all. I'll have someone deliver it to your quarter's today. By the way, congratulations on your degree. I am a bit confused about what title I should use to address you. Should I be addressing you as Doctor or should I use Monsignor?"

Giuseppe was surprised by the declaration; he had just received his doctorate in historical studies at the university but had not informed his mentor of such. He also knew at this moment that he had been promoted from Father to Monsignor. "I'm honored on both counts, but how did you know about the degree?" he asked, dipping his head in deference.

The Cardinal smiled broadly. "My son, there is not much that concerns you that I do not know of. I long ago made a promise to your father to watch out for and guide you, but you have earned the title as Monsignor on your own volition with exemplary servitude to the Lord. Be proud of your accomplishments, as am I."

Giuseppe felt his face flood with heat. "Thank you for the compliment, though I'm sure it will take quite some time before I'm used to my new title. I'll look into the matter of this anomaly at once. I realize your time is precious, but I have a small favor to ask from you."

Cardinal Robbia could hardly refuse any request his protégé might have. "Go ahead and ask," though he glanced at his watch as he spoke.

"That is if you have the time," Giuseppe said. Cardinal Robbia nodded. "I was wondering if you might give me any information that you have on Pope Alexander's death."

"If I can, I will," the Cardinal stated.

He sounded reluctant. "Did Pope Alexander request a closed casket ceremony, which historically, has never been done before?" Giuseppe respectfully asked.

"I can't answer that right now because I am not sure."

Giuseppe felt as if his mentor was holding back, an intuition on his part. "Do you know what caused his death?" he pressed, seeking the truth. He noticed the Cardinal's his hand began to strum the table, that old, familiar gesture that, accompanied a look of annoyance that forewarned him that his request would not readily be fulfilled.

"Let's just say that he died under questionable circumstances and leave it at that, shall we?'

"Did they happen to use the silver hammer on Pope Alexander's head?" Giuseppe asked. The use of the hammer was a historical tradition last used in the sixties, when Pope John the Twenty-Third passed. It was a symbolic and practical gesture meant to bear witness to the pope's death. Giuseppe had never witnessed the account first hand and wondered how hard the silver hammer, struck three times, tapped on the deceased Pope's forehead in order to assure that death had truly transpired. His thought behind the question would assure his initial hunch that there was no head in which to strike.

Cardinal Robbia sat mum, strumming his finger rapidly on the table and did not even acknowledge the question. He pressed the issue, knowing even as he did so that it might strain their relationship for the first time. "Excuse my forwardness. Normally, I wouldn't pry into matters you don't wish to divulge, but I have a personal reason for asking," he said somberly. The room was silent for several moments as the Cardinal's face flushed. Giuseppe knew he had overstepped his boundaries on this one, for he had never seen the Cardinal give him such a taciturn look.

"Not now," he sharply retorted. His expression softened a moment later. "Maybe later, I have not had the chance to put my dear friend to rest as of yet."

I'm so sorry," Giuseppe said sheepishly, as the relationship between the two men had never entered his mind. The priesthood was like a fraternity of sorts where enduring bonds were formed early on, usually when their formal seminary studies required the constant interaction of thoughts and ideas. Giuseppe should have known better, for the two men had graduated at the same time from the same seminary. They had worked so well as a team for change.

"Apology accepted, the Cardinal said, rising and putting a slightly trembling hand on the younger priest's shoulder. "Now, if there is nothing further to discuss, I have another meeting to attend."

"No, nothing else that is pressing at the moment," Giuseppe replied. He knew that when the time came, the Cardinal would answer his questions at length, so he just had to be patient. He watched the man leave the room, unanswered questions still preying on his mind.

He had recently heard of other circumstantial deaths that mirrored the pope's and had been researching the possible cause. He had a vague idea of why these deaths had happened, but couldn't prove it as of yet. His original theory about his mother's death had long since been discounted as he continued to search for answers.

He returned to the Vatican library in an effort to thwart off his sense of pessimism and began to research the Cardinal's request. With over a million books to use as reliable resources, he knew he had his work cut out for him to narrow down the sizable reference material into a number of books he thought likely to contain a reference to a blue-white light emanating from the heavens. He worked on the request well into the night. This was not unusual for him to do when it came to research, but he knew on this particular evening that it would cost him, for he had to rise early to aid in the preparations for the funeral.

As he prepared to retire, he prayed that the two agents for the church, now in Egypt, would soon find a witness to the event, which would make his research somewhat less complicated. Recently, he and several of his colleagues had completed cataloguing the entire Vatican library onto a computer program, which made the research somewhat less tedious. Still, if he had more concrete information he might know where to look in a more expeditious manner.

The day of the funeral brought leading dignitaries and religious leaders to the Vatican from all over the world. Never before had so many dignitaries gathered in one location. The scene outside St. Peter's

Basilica resembled the United Nations to a great extent. As part of the fallen pope's wishes, a religious leader from every faith had been chosen and asked to take part in the Funeral Mass. This was the first time that this had occurred. The standard protocol was for just Eastern Orthodox bishops to assist in the requiem mass. There had been a heated debate over this change, as some Church leaders were appalled by the break in tradition. They'd tried to suppress the request, citing it as a breach in steeped tradition. The apostolic constitution had to be read and reread several times in order for this unlikelihood to finally be agreed upon. Still, more than a few Cardinals abstained from voting on principle alone, even though the former pope had specified this request in a quest for religious unity.

Even more provocative than that, the entire event, from the funeral mass to the final procession, was broadcast in its entirety around the world. This was another first. Up until this time, only select parts of the funeral were aired to the general public. This was part of the sweeping changes Pope Alexander had initiated in an effort to educate those interested in the inner workings of the faith. The body of Pope Alexander was transported to the Grotto beneath St. Peter's Basilica, where the final preparations for internment took place.

Monsignor Giuseppe Lorenzo noticed nothing out of the ordinary in either the rite or the procession, having witnessed the same ceremony twenty-two months earlier when Pope Benedict XVI was laid to rest.

*   *   *

Florence Rinna was once again disgusted with her inability to say no.

She sat heavily in the chair of her assigned first-class seat headed for Rome and let out an audible sigh. Once again, she had let the senior editor of the Washington Post talk her into an assignment for which she had no interest. His only argument for assigning her to the task was that she spoke fluent Italian. "Who better qualified do I have around here to cover the death of a deceased Italian pope than a member of my own staff fluent in the Italian language? Flo, I really don't want to hear another word about it. Get on that plane this afternoon or else!" he'd said in no uncertain terms.

"But I'm already am on assignment," Flo argued. "Do you expect me to just drop everything and run over to Rome? Send someone else. I'm telling you, if the story I'm working on is as good as it seems to be, it will be front page news for weeks to come."

"I don't care. Get out of my office and onto that plane!" the editor stated pointing to the door as he spoke, his face was the color of good claret as Flo opened her mouth to protest once again.

"Not another word, do you hear me?"

The finality of his last statement left her no option if she wanted to collect a paycheck at the end of the month. She bolted out of his office in a huff, showing her displeasure in his decision. The two had locked horns on job assignments in the past, though she usually understood the practically of his requests, it didn't mean she had to readily agree to them. She had been an editor of her college newspaper and had a good idea of what his position entailed. However, she was tenacious if nothing else and once she had fixed her efforts on something; she wanted to see it through to its completion. There would be hell to pay if anyone got between her and her intended goal. She was a focused individual who would dog any type of assignment until she completed it.

She also knew that when she had first applied for the job as an investigative reporter, it hadn't been her credentials that the senior editor looked at. He was more enamored with her cleavage than the list of accomplishments and letters of recommendation that lay before him. She thought she might have to remove a tissue out of her purse to wipe the drool off of his chin. As a third-generation Italian residing stateside, she still held all the charms of a typical Roman woman; jet-black hair, sculptured facial features and an olive compaction were just some of her assets. A looker was what she was called, and no one seemed to see anything beyond that, which made her mad as hell.

Flo had been less than pleased with the man when they first met, for exactly that reason. Once she proved that she had beauty and brains as well as attributes that scared most men off, they had reached an understanding with each other. It was her independent nature that left most men despondent and gave the editor fits. Trying to tame the lioness was no easy chore. She was resolute, yet extremely sociable.

That's not to say she didn't use her striking looks on occasion to get what she wanted, information or otherwise. She knew most women in her position did so. She could charm almost any man into submission, if need be, but it was not her usual mode of operation. Over the years, she had come to terms with her exquisite looks and at thirty-two relied on her intelligence instead.

She sat back in the easy chair and kicked off her shoes, looking about the cabin in an effort to see if she recognized anyone on board who might be flying with her today. After all, her circle of friends and acquaintances was large. She was interrupted by the flight attendant, asking if there if there was anything she might need to make her flight a bit more comfortable. This prompt attention irritated her somewhat, not because the attendant was doing her job, but because of the fact that she knew that there were going to be thousands of reporters in Rome covering the story, all of them in direct competition, vying for an exclusive story in which to bolster their careers.

She had her story already and knew that in her absence it would be passed on after she had done all of the initial legwork. Once again, someone else would reap the benefits of her labor. She grew despondent and gave the flight attendant a staid reply to her inquiry. She watched the young woman slowly back away and suddenly felt bad about the way she had acted. She was usually never rude, but realized that she must have come across as a hoity bitch by the look on the woman's face. She immediately excused herself and struck up a conversation with the woman in an effort to make amends. With her apology accepted, the two women spoke for some time before the attendant excused herself to aid another passenger.

She thought about the assignment for several moments and wondered what she was going to do in Rome for five days. She knew what these assignments entailed and was sure that her editor would probably get more information off of the AP wires than he was about to get from her. Still, she consciously made a promise to herself to do what she could to create a unique angle to pique interest among readers of her newspaper.

The publication, like most others around the United States, had fallen on hard times, and subscriptions were down considerably after falling prey to the internet. No one was about to pay for something they could get free. The world of reporting the news was rapidly changing; instant access to stories from sources all over the world directly affected competition here in the states. Newspapers with marginal subscription base couldn't sustain the losses and were folding in alarming numbers. Flo was conscious of these facts and always tried her best to deliver provocative and interesting stories, although she knew that this wasn't always enough. Many of the larger papers had merged in an effort to cut costs. The Washington Post had survived so far, but who knew what the near future might bring with the instant streaming of information that telecommunications brought to hand-held electronics?

Lately, Flo felt as if she were encompassed in a whirlwind. It seemed to her that natural calamities around the world were on the rise. These were the stories making front-page copy daily. This trend of depressing news made her feel unsure of the future. Intuitively, she felt that an endpoint of some kind was nearing but it was nothing that she could put her finger on. Nevertheless, she felt as if the entire world's population was pulsating under the stress of continuous calamity.

Cultural animosity was on the rise. It seemed to her that in between wars, threats and innuendo between nations and secular groups that the planet was splitting at its seams. The level of trust between nations was fading, and more border skirmishes were reported. The Korean situation was about to explode into an all-out war once again. The situation in Korea was the largest ongoing threat to date, with the North now having full nuclear capability. The threat was real. She wondered what type of intervention might be needed to extinguish the fires of anguish, which seemed to erupt on an almost continuous basis. She knew that the United States could not play policeman any longer, for the economy was in a shambles and the days of wearing a shiny badge of the enforcer were numbered.

The stars and stripes were becoming more tarnished by the day as other nations watched and waited for the last Goliath to fall. Some nations waited in anticipation for the demise. On the other hand, there was no one left to take its place and she knew when that happened, mass chaos would ensue. This much she was sure of.

Still, she held out hope that having lived in one of the greatest nations in the world that no matter how bad it got, the people of this nation would still fare a lot better than the rest. Immigration into this country was still at an all-time high, which seemed to support her thoughts about the matter. She knew, whatever the outcome, that this nation could still retreat and protect its own borders in the process. The economy was continually undermined and jobs were hard to come by, but this was the result of the meltdown in late 2008 and the Dow Jones trends had looked like a sine wave ever since. Wall Street had been in a shambles ever since, and people around the world wondered whether we would ever pull out of the continuing recession they were mired in.

Ironically, she once did a feature story in late 2010 about a soapbox preacher, who went by the name of Jeremiah, after the prophet. He carried his soap box, which in actuality was a plastic milk case, to the entrance of the exchange on Wall Street every morning to quote scripture and to announce to anyone who would stop and listen, his favorite quote, also written on a placard in blood red letters. *"Repent, the end is coming sooner than you think!"*

Though these were not poignant words per se, as they had been repeated constantly throughout the ages, yet he bore them like a badge of courage. Every day the stock market was open, he was seen perched on his box wearing only threadbare clothing, seemly impervious to any adverse weather conditions that befell him. It seemed that his message was what provided him his barrier against the elements, which surprised many of those who passed by him on a daily basis.

The customary response to his message was to mock and spit at his proclamations. Some even tore and grabbed at his clothes, trying to knock him off of his lowly platform in the process. No one wanted or cared to hear anything he had to say in the beginning, and some brokers had called the police on a regular basis to have the "public nuisance" removed from the entrance to the stock exchange.

Now, in early 2012, passersby stopped to listen to him in awe. Crowds of people gathered and for all intents and purposes blocked the entire street, much to the chagrin of the brokers and analysts who tried to gain entrance to their once famed establishment.

Flo knew for a fact that even some of these brokers stopped on occasion to listen to what the man had to say. She thought it likely that in some ways Jeremiah had influenced their thinking about their past practices of pomp and avarice, as a few unlikely policy changes had recently been enacted, indirectly related to Jeremiah's message of doom.

Flo had gotten close to the preacher and knew he was sincere in his intent. On occasion, she wrote about him, keeping the reading public updated on the man, and her stories had received wide acclaim. She remembered talking to him, and noted that he had repeatedly stated that a war was raging. When he said "them," she was not sure what he meant. Recently, after his popularity had grown exponentially, she had interviewed him again, rather surprised that his message was essentially the same. *The war rages on*, he insisted, though no wars of major significance were ongoing at this time. The war in Afghanistan was winding down and she wondered what in the world the sometimes-incoherent man was even talking about.

The plane landed in Rome, where Flo would spend the next five days trying to chase down an exclusive. Her morning routine consisted of going to the Office of Press Relations for the Vatican, only to receive a handout, what she considered second-hand or day-old news items. For the better part of the day, she tried to chase down high-ranking officials within the Vatican itself, but to no avail. She was either ignored or politely passed over to a secretary of some sort, who ran interference for them. By the end of the day, she had nothing to show for her efforts except that she was worn to a frazzle, collapsing in bed in hopes of a better day tomorrow. She was running out of time and felt intense pressure building. She must perform or else! The little voice inside of her egged her on. She knew when she returned to Washington empty-handed what her editor would say to her. She was no failure, that was for sure, but she couldn't let that sort of thing happen to her. She was way too smart for that.

By the third day, when she realized that any exclusive information was almost impossible to obtain, she switched tactics. She began to interview the myriads of pilgrims who had journeyed from afar to witness the historical event. She did profiles in hopes of gauging the true impact of the fallen pontiff. On the morning of the fourth day, she was receiving praise from her editor for her insight. If there was anything she could do well, it was getting complete strangers to open up and give her their life story. He told her to continue sending these stories, for they were well received. This praise seemed to ease her into a sense of complacency and she began to relax a bit; taking in the sights Rome had to offer. It was the home of her grandparents, and a place she had last seen when she was a child of ten. She hardly remembered any of her past experiences in Rome and was taken anew by her surroundings.

On the day of the funeral, she was able to get close enough to proceedings to take in the entire scope of events. As a non-practicing Catholic, she was nevertheless impressed by the ceremonial rites, having never witnessed them first-hand. The press was allowed close proximity to the proceedings and she stood daunted by the solemnity, which left a lasting impression on her, one she hardly thought possible.

*   *   *

Monsignor Giuseppe Lorenzo left the proceedings after the casket was transported to St. Peter's Basilica, knowing that he would soon be sequestered with the conclave, which occurred the day following the burial of a fallen pope. He knew that he would be tied up in research for Cardinal Robbia until that time and felt that now was the best time for him to leave. He was hungry and hankering for some of his deceased mother's Milan-style cooking. There was only one restaurant in Rome that even came close to her cooking. The owners of the establishment formally lived in Milan and had migrated south, hoping to bring a diverse fare to the area. The restaurant was a success among the locals, and Giuseppe frequented the place whenever he felt homesick.

As he walked through the streets on the way to the eatery, he was amazed by the number of people milling about the streets. Never before had he seen so many people occupying the sidewalks. He almost had to muscle his way through, sidestepping the masses in route. He finally made it to the restaurant, only to be turned away and told to come back in an hour when a table would be made available to him, seeing as he was a regular at the eatery.

An hour later, he was ushered in to wait in line for the next available table. He could tell the attending waitress was less than enthused by another patron languishing in the doorway awaiting a table. She spoke to him briefly, explaining that the priest would be seated with another single for the sake of expediency, nodding her head in the direction of a woman standing nearby. The waitress impatiently waited for his expected objection, shifting her weight from side to side, her body language denoting that she had better things to do than wait for a prolonged decision on his part. He noticed that the waitress looked toward the woman briefly once again in case she might voice an objection of her own.

Giuseppe glanced in the direction of the younger woman standing several feet away and voiced no objection, nodding his head in approval. He glanced back toward his dinner date and thought that she was amazingly beautiful. He smiled briefly. The woman had witnessed the exchange and looked at him with surprisingly purposeful eyes.

From his perspective, the priest thought that it might be a pleasant diversion to have a dinner partner for once, and he really needed someone to talk to. Good conversation always seemed to compliment a meal, somewhat like a good glass of wine. He flushed at his good fortune. Normally he didn't react in this way, but then again, he usually didn't have this type of opportunity presented to him either. There was something about her that struck him amicably. He was not particularly daunted by her extraordinary appearance, and there seemed to be something about her resolute looks that dared inquisition.

Flo examined her dinner partner from head to toe while he turned back toward the waitress. Although he was a bit shorter than she was, she noticed he had an almost boyish charm about him. She guessed him to be in his mid-forties, though he could have been a bit younger, as his hair still retained its natural color, black like night. His slight figure made his garb appear a size or two too large for him. When he turned toward her once again, she was completely disarmed by his smile even before his rather bashful introduction.

She waited patiently for him to say something in order to gauge her original assessment. When he finally did, she could hardly understand him at all, he spoke so fast and fluently. She wished he would slow down a bit so that she might understand him better, but was afraid of insulting him. She thought her reasoning for that might have something to do with the white collar he wore around his neck and the fact that she had never dined with a priest before.

She vaguely made out his words and then realized he was asking if she had any objection to dining with him. She replied in Italian that there was none. She saw the change in expression on his face the moment she spoke. She had been found out instantly as a foreigner who only looked native. She was sure it was her South Jersey accent that gave her away. She wondered momentarily if he might reject her once he found that out, but he smiled in a most pleasant manner once again.

To her surprise, he switched to English and tried to carry on a conversation. This, unfortunately, was not working out so well, which caused her to laugh momentarily. She then asked him to switch back to Italian, though at a much slower pace. He was polite and responded with his apologies and began to speak in a slow but deliberate manner. She had assumed the man to be a local parish priest but was surprised by his introduction as an assistant curator to the Vatican library. She smiled immensely and noted that it was his honest looking expressions in return that disarmed her completely. She felt an instant trust with this priest for some reason, the kind of trust that only a lengthy amount of time procures. For some reason, she knew this was going to be a dinner she wouldn't soon forget.

They spoke in generalities while waiting for the table, and he asked why she had come to Rome, assuming at first that she had come on pilgrimage with everyone else who milled around outside. Once she informed him, she was a reporter for the Washington Post, the mood between them changed slightly. She sensed that he began to cloister his thoughts and sought to alter the mood to her advantage. "You have nothing to fear, I'm not looking for a story, though I do have a question to ask that I am sure you might be able to answer," she said, thinking about the sea of red vestments she had seen earlier in the day.

"I thought that all priests who worked in the Vatican wore red?"

"You aren't Catholic," he replied. "Or else you would know that red is the vestment colors of a cardinal. The only other time these red vestments are worn is during the funeral of a pope. It is a centuries old tradition." He looked away momentarily.

He seemed nonplussed regarding her faux pas. "I'm sorry, but I'm afraid I am... Catholic, I mean." She ventured a tentative smile. "Though as of late, I'm afraid that some of our steeped religious traditions have eluded me." She felt herself blush. "It's just a lapse on my part, I'm afraid.

He looked at her but he said nothing. His lack of response didn't sit well with her, and she almost felt like she was being chastised by the silence. She grew oddly irate with him for a moment. "What are you anyway? You're just not an assistant curator at the Vatican library. You're a historian of some kind, aren't you?" she asked. It was her turn to put him on the defensive.

"Right you are," she said.

He appeared rattled by her astuteness.

"I have a Doctorate in Historical Religious Studies from the University of Rome," he said, his tone almost apologetic manner.

"I don't see why you're ashamed of such a commendable achievement."

"I'm not," he smiled. "It's just that I find it hard to accept compliments. We usually set our own goals in life, and not for the benefit of others." He spoke the words so softly that she almost couldn't make out the words. She thought to change the subject and asked him why he frequented this particular restaurant. They were seated at their table before he had a chance to answer the question.

"The food here reminds me of my mother's cooking."

"All of their dishes or just certain ones in particular?' she asked, noticing he appeared more relaxed.

"There are various styles of cooking which are native to particular areas in Italy," he explained. "Having hailed from Milan, this restaurant is the only one here in Rome that I know of that cooks native dishes like my mother made for me when I was growing up."

"Is she still alive?" she asked, hoping he would expound on his background.

"No, she isn't, why do you ask?" he said quietly.

She noticed the flash of pain that crossed his face and sought to excuse the private intrusion. "I'm sorry, when did she pass?"

"Some time ago, I'm afraid, though I still miss her dearly," he said, looking down at his hands.

She noticed his voice falter. "How did she die? May I ask or am I being too inquisitive?" He finally looked up. "No, not really, let's just say she died under questionable circumstances."

"You know, holding your emotions at bay are no way to come to terms with your bereavement. Sometimes it's better to confide in someone," she said. "It helps in the healing process to talk about a loss."

"Is it that obvious…? I suppose you're right. I probably need to at some point in time." He sighed. "Though it's hardly appropriate to do so with someone you've just met, don't you think?"

"No, not at all, knowing that we will probably never meet again, why would you think otherwise?"

"Are you sure you want to hear about it?"

"Why, of course I would."

The waitress finally made it to their table and she deferred the ordering to him. He did so without even looking at the menu. After the waitress left, she prodded him on. "Please continue, I really want to know a bit more about your mother. And if you would start at the beginning, from your fondest childhood memories, so that I might get some idea of her."

He smiled ever so briefly and began to tell her about his mother and the effect she'd had on his life. He only stopped on occasion to nibble on a breadstick and sip some table wine. The one-sided conversation continued until the main course arrived, and he finally stopped to eat. "I must be boring you to tears," he said with a small smile.

"Hardly, I can tell that it's helping, I can tell by the change in your demeanor. Please go on."

"You're right, it is helping and if you don't mind, I will."

He continued with his story up until the part of his mother's mysterious disappearance. Suddenly Flo thought that the din of the other patron's voices faded into obscurity as she concentrated on what he was saying. She sat on the edge of her chair, hardly believing what she heard. She shook her head in disbelief. He had no reason to lie about anything, she thought. He had not done so beforehand as far as she could tell. He was a priest, so why would he lie about his own mother's death? She listened intently but was anxious to interrupt. She was vexed by the story, having never heard of such a thing like this before.

He stopped shortly. "I noticed your reaction to the circumstances which precluded her death. Does that bother you?"

"Yes, it does, but no more than it seems to bother you," she replied honestly. "Please continue." She tried in vain to mask her true feeling for the sake of the developing story. She thought silently what kind of mileage she might get out of this story, which was one-hundred times better than the story she left behind to come here.

When he finally finished, she could hardly contain herself and fired off a barrage of questions. "Are you sure that's how your mother died?"

"Yes, of course I am."

"And you're telling me there was nothing on the bed but a fine ash?"

"Yes."

"Has anyone ever explained to you what might have happened to your mother in scientific terms? I've never heard anything like this before!"

"No."

"Do you not think that in of itself is strange?"

"Yes."

"Who did you talk to in that regard?"

"Anyone, who would listen,"

"Meaning who?" She knew she was grilling him but couldn't help it.

"The police, the scientific community, they all thought I was crazy, and even I began to think so."

"You seem sane to me. In your gut, what do you think the reason was for her disappearance?"

"A divine intervention is my thought on the matter."

"Why do you think that? Isn't divine intervention the hand of God interceding into the affairs of man?"

"Yes and no," he mused. "It depends on the perspective one derives from such an intervention."

"As to whether or not you believe in miracles or the like?"

"Possibly…"

"Can you prove it?" Flo could tell he was visibly shaken by the questions, and she knew he must feel as if she were testing his resolve.

"It's nothing that I can prove as of yet," he shrugged. "I'm still looking into it."

"What do you mean by that?"

"I'm researching the possibilities."

"Have you had any luck in that regard as of yet?"

"No."

"Do you know of any other cases that might mirror your mother's death?"

He leaned a little closer and spoke abruptly. "Yes, I think it may also have happened to Pope Alexander."

The moment he said the words, his eyes widened and she could tell that he wished to immediately take back his words.

"What?" She spoke louder than she expected and her voice carried across the small dining room. Heads turned to look disapprovingly at her. She felt the heat of a flush creep upward and almost felt like crawling under the table. The distasteful looks were now turned toward the priest, as if he had assaulted her in some way. She quickly tried to diffuse the situation. "Well, tell your sister congratulations on her impending arrival! A baby is always a true blessing!" After her words traveled across the room, the diners quickly lost interest.

"I have to admit one thing, you are quick," he said sheepishly. "I really have no proof that what happened to my mother also happened to the pope, but something that I feel in my gut to be a matter of fact." He looked at her with a stern expression. "I would not repeat this if I were you. The Vatican would deny it even if it were true."

"I won't if you promise me that if you find out its true, you'll tell me and me alone."

"What are you going to do if it's true?"

"The same thing you're doing... research," she whispered.

"Will you print it?"

"Eventually, the world has to know, don't you think?"

"Yes, they do, but promise me one thing. Whatever happens, my name will never be mentioned."

"I promise!" she assured him. "Let me ask you one last question, though I don't want you to get the wrong impression. You have been resolute in your thoughts of your mother's disappearance. Is that solely based on your unwavering belief in the Creed, or would you think the same if you were not wearing the white collar that defines you?"

Monsignor Lorenzo sat back in his chair, frowning in thought and the question's implications for several moments before he answered.

"It's not a question of my religious belief here, which is undeniable. It's more of a question of if I truly believe this to be part of something larger, and I believe it is."

"That's a terrifying prospect, if you ask me. If you find that your intuition was right about the pope as well. Will you call me at this number?" she asked, sliding her business card across the table. It lay untouched for some time as he contemplated the ramifications of picking it up. She could tell what he was doing by the dissolution in his face. Finally, he picked it up and slipped it into his vest pocket, and she tried to reassure him. "If you're the least bit worried about the confidentiality of any future story I may write, I'll be sure to leave any reference of your family name obscured."

"For some reason, I know you will." He wrote his cell number on a napkin and handed it to her. "Call me if you find out anything. This has been eating at me for quite some time." When Flo tried to get up, her knees felt wobbly and her head suddenly ached, but for the life of her could hardly begin to feel how this priest must feel. He reached out to assist her, grabbing her by the arm. She felt his sweaty palms against the bare skin of her arm. She was so taken by his predicament that she had to stifle back tears, an involuntary reaction to be sure, but present nonetheless. After they had parted ways, she wondered why she felt so affected by this man and felt foolish for allowing her emotions to get away from her. Her usual defensive armor had been pierced by a man with a white collar, a highly unlikely reaction indeed.

CHAPTER 5

Monumental Disasters

The Philippine Islands:

"The ring of fire is a term scientist's use for the line of volcanoes that stretch across the Pacific Ocean," said Professor Chin Lei. "It is an area of the Pacific that encompasses the entire Philippine chain of islands, which is its midpoint and one of its most active areas. It stretches north to the eastern coast of Russia, encompassing the Japanese Islands in the process. It follows an arc line south, taking in the entire Indonesian chain of islands before it bends backwards and ends just south of New Zealand. This line of volcanoes, if traced on a map, is the actual location where the earth's tectonic plates are in continual friction with one another.

"To the east of the Philippine islands is an area aptly called the Philippine Trench, where the ocean is some thirty-four thousand feet deep? In this area of the ocean, plates of the earth's crust are continually forced under one another by a process known to scientists as subduction. The crashing of tectonic plates in of itself is not a rare occurrence, as it is a continual process that is usually slow and sometimes hard to recognize. This area is about the most active area on the planet. The shifting of the plates here is almost a continual process. Scientists and geologists recognize that it is hard to gauge the reaction between the plates with that depth of water above them, but the effects of the crushing forces are felt elsewhere.

"This reaction between plates or breach if you will causes magma from deep under the earth's crust to seep upward and outward at these weak points, which forms volcanoes. I would like you to compare these volcanoes to a similar application. A safety valve on a boiler relieves excess pressure to keep it from exploding, and this is why we have eruptions from time to time. Now, keep in mind that there are exceptions to any rule, and not all volcanoes form at the plate lines. The Hawaiian Islands are one such exception. These volcanic islands are the result of a weakness in the center of one of the Pacific plates. Now let's get back to the ring of Fire. As I explained earlier, the midpoint of this ring is centered near the Philippine islands. The most active volcano to date in the region is the Mayon volcano, which has erupted more than thirty times since the late 1700s.

"It sits on the Bicol peninsula on southeastern Luzon Island. The reason for the activity within the Mayon volcano is rather easy to explain. It's a direct result of the forces of interaction between these plates. The last eruption of any major proportion occurred in late 2009. Any questions?"

Professor Lei scanned the room, frowning with consternation. Usually, one or two of the ablest of his students asked questions, but today there were none. "All right then, class is dismissed." Students scrambled out of their seats. "Remember that all of my lecture material is subject to a pop quiz! Spend some of your free time reviewing tectonic plates, volcanoes and magma shift as it relates to polar shifting." Professor Lei heard the groans of protests as his students filed out of the room and gazed about momentarily to see if there were any stragglers. For once, no one had lingered.

That was the odd thing about his American students in comparison to his Chinese counterparts, he thought. American students didn't really ask a lot of questions, but seemed to grasp the information readily, whereas his Chinese students tended to display a show of hands with a bit less hesitance. With a sigh, he quickly filed his notes in his briefcase and headed for the door, happy it was his last class of the day.

Lei was the premiere geologist on the planet, having won a Nobel Prize for his papers on the subject of shifting tectonic plates and its effect on global climatology. He was on loan to the University of California at Berkeley as part of a cultural and educational exchange program with the Chinese government. He held a teaching position at the University of Shanghai, though the change of scenery here in America was something that he grown to admire. The northern California climate suited him as, and his sinuses were under control for once, a condition he blamed on the cold and humid Chinese winters and, to a lesser extent, his exposure to volcanic ash.

When he was not teaching, he could be found pursuing his continual research on the study of volcanoes. During his fifty-three-year tenure here on earth, he had scaled or studied just about every known dormant or active aboveground volcano around the world. A childhood fascination that had grown into a full-time career, he still never lost his desire to learn more. Even though he was considered one of the best geologists in the world to date, he felt that one could ever know enough, and as a result, his life study continued.

Little did he realize when he walked out of the room that one of the largest displays of volcanic activity the modern world would witness had just begun. Having finished his class schedule for the day, Professor Lei had nearly arrived at the faculty quarters the college had provided for him when his cell phone rang. He thought this to be a most unfortunate circumstance just before he had even inserted his key in the door lock of his third-floor apartment. He fumbled for the phone, caught in a fold of his suit coat pocket. At first, he thought about letting it ring until he entered as he fumbled with the door key and the untangled phone, his house key falling to the floor in the process.

Thinking it was only an invite to one of the many colleges social functions these American professors adhered to on a regular basis; he thought to let the phone call go to voicemail. Then he thought that it might be his wife and answered it without glancing at the screen as he entered his darkened foyer.

He recognized the voice on the other end of the line. The caller was Doctor Hans Larson, who at this moment was stationed in Manila monitoring the seismographic conditions of the islands. At first, he could not make out what the man said, as the connection was sporadic due to his location. All he could make out was, "Twenty-thousand or more fear--" He quickly crossing the living room of his apartment and headed toward the balcony. He again fumbled with the latch of the sliding glass door, hoping that the connection was still made.

"Repeat that Hans, you were breaking up," he said as he pulled open the sliding door and heard the man's voice return.

"Utter chaos, professor, you have to get out here any way you can."

The professor heard the edge in the man's voice. "Start over from the beginning. I missed almost everything you said."

"White Island in New Zealand has blown its top and the percussion has caused Mayon to flow once again," Hans repeated. "This time there seems to be repercussions all the way up the fault line. The initial reports out of New Zealand indicate twenty thousand or more dead."

"Impossible!" Lei uttered. "I was just there last year and there was no indication to lead me to believe it was so unstable." He felt flustered by the news and scratched his bald pate in consternation.

"Believe it! We have a hell of a show going on down here!" Hans said.

Professor Lei stood momentarily shocked and dismayed by the news. The message was daunting and he said nothing for several moments, sure the death toll was going to be much higher than that. If Mayon had blown, causalities would be closer to fifty or sixty thousand. What surprised him the most though, was the area around New Zealand had been relatively stable for quite some time and was an area that had worried him the least. The latest set of data from the area proved that. Seismographic charts showed just about a straight line, indicating little or no variations. "What do your charts look like there? Can you stream them to me?"

"Sure can," Hans said. "They're all over the place. I'm not sure if it's due to Mayon erupting, or possibly a chain reaction occurring down the line. What do you think?"

"I won't know until I see the data," Lei said. "If you can relay a message to all posts along the line and ask them to send on their latest data, I'd appreciate it. Can you do that?"

"As we speak. Wait...wait a minute, I just received a report from Japan. It seems Sakurajimi has exploded again as well. Hell, it's starting to look like the whole ring is about to erupt. You need to get here and see this for yourself, Professor Lei."

"I'll get there as soon as I can," Lei said, growing impatient with the fact that he was on one side of the world and all of the action was centered on the other side. "Send me any information or reports that have been generated and any documentation of first-hand or eye-witness accounts."

"Will do."

"Look, I'm going to try and have a look at White Island before I arrive in Manila," he said. "That may help me get a better idea about what's going on."

"I don't know about that," Hans warned. "There's a pall of ash over the area, air space is restricted, and visibility is just about zero. It looks like the Icelandic eruption of 2010. The only way you could get on the North island would be to fly into Christchurch on the South island, even the Wellington airport is closed off on the southern tip of the North island, no where to land."

"I'll get there somehow. I have to see it for myself in order to judge the severity of the situation."

"Suit yourself and lots of luck--"

The phone went dead before he could reply. He was sure the warning system was up by now and turned on the television while he made preparations to leave; hoping some of the early news of the catastrophe was on the air. He was afraid that pressure beneath the plates was just starting to build instead of ebbing.

He was not really surprised by the eruptions of Mayon and Sakurajimi; they were ongoing situations that, according to his prior research, were just relieving magma pressure below the shifting plates. What surprised him the most was that he figured the Indonesian islands would be the next hot spot. The readings and the earthquakes seemed to be steadily on the rise and he was just waiting for another Krakatau.

Krakatau was one of the largest explosions ever to have occurred in the area. Near the end of August 1883, the island exploded. The blast was heard over 3,000 miles away, and caused tsunamis over one-hundred feet tall. Most of the 36,000 killed died of drowning from the wave, though several thousand died from hot ash, which spread over a 25-mile area. The volcano acted up once again in the late 1920s.

Professor Lei knew the area was overdue and that was the area he had monitored the closest.

Professor Lei left the apartment and headed for his office in the Science building, where he could readily access the data sent to him. He received the report some time later,

On the north island of New Zealand in the Bay of Plenty, an area named as so when explorer Captain Cook first sailed there and named it for its abundance of fish, laid a submerged volcano with just its peak exposed above the water. The peak formed an island that went by the name of White Island.

The bay lay on the north end of the island is in close proximity to the country's largest city, Auckland, whose only protection from a volcanic eruption was a peninsula that made up the west side of the bay. The effect of the island's explosion was immediate. It had been rumbling since the late 1990s, sending out low-intensity signals ever since. Professor Lei wondered where they had gotten their ill-found information while he read on.

The explosion of the island caused the water from the bay to form a huge wave, which breached the peninsula and sent water over the city, immediately killing thousands of city dwellers. Thousands more were swept out to sea. Hot ash and lava spewed thousands of feet into the air from the exposed opening, covering the entire north end of the island in no time at all. The water surged south, covering the town of Opotiki in a matter of moments. Residents never knew what hit them. The impact also set off a chain reaction in the resort town of Rotorua.

The town was known for its volcanic mud baths, which actually sat within the rim of an adjacent volcano. On a regular basis, small areas of the town's landscape sank, exposing the residents to the ancient cone's past activity. The residents of Rotorua would laugh at their sinking landscape in the past, warning new real estate owners that there was no guarantee that they wouldn't be purchasing an eventual hole in the ground. This time, half of the town sank immediately, and the Tudor Towers bathhouse, a landmark, sunk slowly out of sight. Survivors said it was like watching the Titanic slowly slip between the waves. In their case, instead of a surge of air after the ship sank, a surge of ash plumed over the gaping hole in the landscape where the building once stood.

The impact of the explosion of White Island was felt as far away as Sydney, Australia.

Below the wire story was a hand-scribbled note:

The shock impacted the Tectonic plate line heading north even more. The entire ring of fire shaken by the emerging volcano caused the Mayon volcano in the Philippines to erupt once again. This caused the entire plate line to move momentarily and yet another volcano erupted in the Sea of Japan. I am awaiting results from the area north of Japan. Eastern USSR has not reported yet.

Professor Lei suspected as much, and after reading the note and studying the charts, knew he had to leave posthaste. He left the office in a hurry, charts in hand, and reading material for the flight over. He had just started to pack his bags for the trip when the phone rang once again. He answered it on the first ring, thinking there was more bad news in store from the Philippines.

"Professor Lei, this Dr. Charles Parker. I'm sure you've heard the news by now, but I just wanted to touch base with you and get your initial thoughts about the eruptions. Bad business this is."

The director of Oceanic and Atmospheric Research knew the man well. They had been having conversations from time to time whenever the need warranted it. The scientific community was a tight knit group when it came to analysis and dissection of problems when they arose, unlike the politicians who, whenever they got together for a summit on global conditions turned it into a circus of sorts with their own specific agenda in mind. None of them readily agreed to anything if it came to concessions or cost money.

"Charles," Lei acknowledged. "Yes, yes, it is quite severe from what I have been told. I have had only time to look at the data briefly, and am packing to leave as we speak. I want to get a firsthand look at the situation before I can judge how bad it really is."

"Look, Professor Lei, maybe we can help," Parker suggested. "I have already been in contact with NASA and they're redirecting their EOS to encompass the entire Pacific area of concern. Terra is beginning to change the direction of its orbit and in no time at all we'll be able to get a good look at exactly what happened."

Professor Lei knew exactly what the man was talking about. The Earth Observing Spacecraft was part of the NASA program dedicated to observation of climate and other natural conditions, quite unlike the spy satellites major countries were able to launch. Its design functions were completely different. It could zoom in like a spy satellite but did not have close range capabilities. It went under an acronym MTPE, or Mission To Planet Earth and was used as an observation tool to analyze changing conditions on earth from space. Professor Lei grew excited by the offer. "Yes, that would be much appreciated. I have a favor to ask if you don't mind," he said, stroking his moustache as he thought about the satellite's capabilities.

"Sure, no problem, what do you need?"

"I was wondering if you might take a succession of photographs along the length of the fault plate from New Zealand all the way north to the East Coast of the U.S.S.R. Do you have the capability to make a continual scroll?"

"No problem, what time sequences do you want it in?" Dr. Parker asked

"In one hour sequences, if you don't mind," Professor Lei replied. "And could you zoom in on White Island and give me a view of the damage as well? It would help me immensely to be able to see the severity of the damage from above."

"Better than that," Charles said. "We can plug in the coordinates and give you a continuous scan of the fault line if you would rather have that in real time. You wouldn't even have to deal with dated material. How does that sound?"

"That sounds even better, if you ask me."

"Look, the reason I called was to get your thoughts on what you think the overall effect on the region might be. Dr. Hanson with the National Weather Service and I are worried about the effects of the ash plume as it relates to the change in weather conditions. We've done some initial computer analysis on the change in weather conditions and were wondering what your thoughts were on the matter."

"Well, there will be some change even if the area stabilizes, though I'm not sure that we've seen the last of the eruptions."

"What do you mean by that?"

"Think of the entire plate line as hardened piece of stretched piano wire. If I pluck it in the middle, it oscillates in both directions, lessening the impact of me striking it in the middle. But if I take the same wire and grab it at the end and then do the same thing, the energy will move back and forth several times before it dissipates at the other end of the wire. In this case, the Mayan and Sakurajimi volcanoes erupt with it, while the wire is already oscillating and it is then magnified once again. My thought is this will cause more volcanoes to erupt because of this continued oscillation. What we're talking about here is just the volcanic eruptions we can see above the water. What is happening below the surface of the Pacific is hard to judge."

"You can't be serious," Charles said. "Never mind the devastation it would cause to the area, but any more simultaneous eruptions would change the weather patterns throughout the world. The light refraction caused by the ash would do exactly what Dr. Hanson and I have been warning the government about. The sun's rays would be deflected back into space, cooling the surface of the planet. As a net result, we will be thrown into a deep freeze for sure."

"I agree, though I am hoping that there is enough cushioning material between the two plates to absorb the shock."

"I hope you're right. If not, we're all in trouble!"

"That's an understatement," Lei agreed. "Look, I'll keep you posted, but first I have a plane to catch. Once I get a handle on the situation, I will know how bad it might get. Send that streaming information to the Philippines, will you?"

"Sure will, and by the way, best of luck. If you need anything let us know, will you?"

Dr. Parker hung up the phone, wondering why everything was topsy-turvy as of late. Never before had such conditions been so erratic. As a rule, there were fifty to sixty active volcanoes throughout the world at any one given time during the year. Usually, thirty or more volcanoes became active while the other thirty went dormant. This year there were more than one-hundred active volcanoes at the same time. He wondered about the reasons behind the increase but had no answers He thought about the Mayan calendar, and for a brief moment wondered if the end of days were truly upon them, as they predicted. Here it was, the 20th of April. If what the Mayans had predicted was true, the 21st of December was closing in on humanity faster than anyone truly realized.

Still, he was a realist and was more concerned by the changes as it affected day-to-day life than dealing in abstract terms. He left the speculation to others who basked in the realm of uncertainty. He was too pragmatic to be caught up in the recent wave of sensationalism that had seemed to have taken over the country. The countdown to the end was scaring a lot of people out of their wits and he knew the closer to the date they got, the worse things would seem. He likened it to the computer scare during the change of the century. Everyone had predicted a massive shutdown of communications and commerce. The result was hardly what everyone had predicted. In essence, other than a few minor glitches, nothing of any major consequence had happened. It was a major let down to the ones who had predicted a doomsday of sorts.

Dr. Parker dialed the phone to relay his findings to Dr. Hanson. This situation, if it got worse, would require constant monitoring on their part.

Professor Lei made it to Christchurch by early morning of the next day, and the time change had him reeling. Passing the date line had inverted his body clock and he was dead tired, not having the luxury of an in-flight nap due to the amount of data he had to peruse. He knew he had to fight his exhaustion however, for it was more important for him to see the damage the volcano had done to the area than to waste a moment more of time hoping for a nap. He was greeted at the airport by an Australian bush pilot waiting to fly him around White Island and the surrounding area, arrangements that had been set up by the United Nations in advance of his arrival.

As one of the directors of the WWW or World Weather Watch, he knew that soon enough his colleagues who belonged to the ICSU, or International Council of Scientific Unions, would be clamoring for his perspective. The call from Dr. Parker with reference to his learned colleague, Dr. Hanson, was actually the first of many he could anticipate. The two men were involved with the Global Atmospheric Research Program known as GARP and like most joint scientific endeavors, were found under the umbrella of changing worldwide environmental issues.

The flight on the Cessna 182 north toward Bay of Plenty was for the most part uneventful; they were on a flight line for White Island until they reached Rotorua. Once they got near the city, air turbulence became unpredictable. The pilot, whose name was Tom, let out a whoop of glee while the plane rose and fell due to the temperature differential of layered air currents. Professor Lei was not prepared for what happened next as the pilot pushed the wheel forward and dove.

"Hold on Mate," Tom hollered. "We're in for it!" The look on his face said it all as he bore down on the city like he was piloting an acrobatic two-winged barnstormer.

Professor Lei's eyes locked on the altimeter as he watched the gauge leave 4,000 feet and rapidly spun backward until it reached 500. There, the plane leveled off while he clung rigid and white-knuckled to his seat. He stared ruefully at the pilot for several moments, expressing his disdain for the man's actions. All he got for his complaints was a hearty laugh in return.

"She'll do better at this altitude!" Tom promised.

Professor Lei looked out the window and began to survey the damage to the city as they flew over. The initial reports on the area did it no justice. The damage was more extensive than he imagined. The shock from the eruption had undermined the ancient cone, causing part of it to collapse. "Fly around the rim one time, if you would?" he commanded and was too preoccupied to register the pilot's response. The plane began to turn in exacting proportion to the rim of the old volcano. From what he could ascertain, the shock wave from the adjacent volcano had to be quite severe. Part of the fallen cone was smoldering. He figured as much, but had to be sure, as there was a distinct possibility that the ancient volcano might erupt too. After completing the three-hundred sixty-degree rotation, he felt assured of one thing - the Rotorua vent posed no extended threat yet. They were now headed straight for the White Island tragedy.

"Bring us in as close as you can," he quietly requested, watching huge clouds of steam and ash rise into his vision.

"Hold on, Mate!" the pilot stated as the plane dove for the wave tops of the bay.

Professor Lei knew that was where the most stable air existed, though he also knew the funnel effect was drawing the water-cooled air up into the plume. This was an extremely dangerous maneuver, but a necessary one just the same. By the looks of it, the island had about tripled in size and the flowing red-hot lava looked ominous. The island had also doubled in height as the lava spewed forth in every direction. The pilot abruptly turned and began to circle the plume in an ever-widening circle in an effort to stabilize the plane. Professor Lei was able to see the forming cone of the volcano with heart-wrenching clarity, and felt the heat of the plume through the skin of the metal plane. "Too close!" he hollered without looking at the pilot, his vision concentrated on the amount of lava flow, a good indication of the possible duration of the eruption.

On the backside of the original island, it was possible to see the direction of the initial blast, which had blown out into the Pacific Ocean instead of toward land. This in itself had saved thousands of lives, though this did not bode well for the plate line, as the explosion seemed on a parallel line with it. They were now away from the lee side of the wind and the plane began to shake erratically. One of the wheels of the plane momentarily touched a choppy wave top, and the resulting spray of water covered the windscreen like a steamy vapor. He looked at the pilot momentarily, wondering why they had ventured so close to the plume. "Get us out of here! Your way to close!" he screamed. The plane suddenly veered away and out to sea and then settled once more. Chin Lei could finally see the fading fear in the bush pilot's face and announced that he had seen enough. It was much too dangerous to go any further into the directional hot air currents caused from the volcano. They had already risked their lives for a look at the west side of the emerging island.

By the time Professor Lei arrived in Manila, he had obtained enough information at the monitoring station to deduce a rational theory for the subsequent eruptions - plate shift shock. That is what had caused the Mayon and other volcanoes to erupt. His original theory had proven correct, and it was the only viable explanation he could offer.

As in late 2009, some 50,000 natives had been evacuated away from the Mayon volcano for safety's sake. The problem was, as he saw it, was that there was no real way of safely predicting the outcome to the ongoing situation. The Mayon had to naturally vent pressure in order to relieve the stress of two colliding plates, and only God had control of that. How severe the situation might get was just about anyone's guess. He had another problem as well. It was almost impossible to predict the duration of the situation due to the White Island explosion.

The subsequent eruptions on the Indonesian island of Sumatra several weeks later had the entire scientific community wondering what in the world was going on and how were they to stop the cataclysm that had reached new and staggering proportions. A closed-door emergency meeting of the scientific union came up with several suggestions, but only one of them had any merit, according to Professor Lei. That was deep- core drilling into the seam of the diverging plates in order to cause the formation of an underwater volcano. This costly remedy would in fact lessen the impact of airborne pollutants on the atmosphere. The time frame though, was almost unrealistic when it came to an immediate solution. There was only one ship capable of doing this and it was located in the Arctic sea at the moment. An effort of this caliber had never been tried before, though it was theoretically possible. No one had tried to drill through the entire mantle of the earth, and the professor's only fear was that there would not be a drill of any size large enough to do what naturally occurred when the plates parted long enough for the magma to rise naturally. It was then suggested that a series of holes placed within close proximity might do the trick. This procedure, if it proved successful, could be used in other parts of the world as well. Still, he worried about the time factor. The longer it took to relieve the ongoing pressure, the more apt other volcanoes might erupt. Professor Lei, never a naysayer, agreed to the proposal in principle. Where to drill was the real question at hand. This was left up to him and several of his colleagues, though he thought the entire situation would hardly be remedied by their efforts alone!

*   *   *

Dr. Kyle Hanson rigorously prepared for another meeting of International Council of Scientific Unions in Stockholm, Sweden. He and most of his colleagues would attend and hopefully come up with some sound strategy. The world press clamored for answers to another calamity that had befallen the earth, and had forced the meeting of minds in search of a reason why such a disaster like the ruin of New Zealand might have happened to begin with. Still reeling from the Haitian disaster in early 2010 and the devastation in Honduras in 2011, the press took this latest misfortune to the *nth* degree, clamoring for answers that were not available.

Professor Chin Lei had inadvertently set the press clamoring for his head on a platter when he'd stated, in regards to the ring of fire, this *might just be the start of it all.*

Dr. Hanson knew there was no such thing as good news these days when it involved the weather and worried privately if and when it would all end. He knew weather patterns and calamities were cyclical in nature, but it was oftentimes impossible to convince people otherwise. Some scientists were using the current data to project when the planet would eventually just cease to exist. Dr. Hanson worried that grandstanding tactics such as this, used by some to make a name for themselves, would only exacerbate an already excitable press.

He prepared a catastrophe line, similar in many respects to a time line, in hopes of showing the constant progression of disaster. He had done this for years at the National Weather Service, though it was only a reference guide for his own personal use. His original intent on doing so was solely based on his desire to track minute changes in an area's weather patterns. He thought of one day of writing a paper on the subject to present to his learned colleagues. He actually had to spread the last ten or so years out so that he could fit all the data on the line in a concise manner. He was explicitly instructed by the president of the ICSU to add a mortality chart to his findings, though, the doctor thought it was against his principles to add a loss of life progression to the catastrophe line because it felt to him as if it was an insensitive data point.

He had to admit one thing ever since the hurricane Katrina fiasco in 2005 - things had radically changed for the good. Gone were the days of a country such as the United States refusing aid because of their supposed status. The then President Bush had refused any foreign aid for pride's sake. Many of the failed policies of disaster relief had been revamped as instantaneous response teams were formed to close in on major catastrophes with lightning speed. There would be no more lives lost due to apathy on the singular part by a nation due to its ethnic population. Consequent disasters were answered immediately and effectively by all nations. The Haitian earthquake was an exemplary example of nations working hand in hand to relieve the suffering of humanity due to unusual occurrences. This unfortunate occurrence, a major earthquake in the capital city of Port o' Prince, became the model for all later calamities. Some twenty-eight days after the initial and subsequent shocks, rescue crews had successfully removed the last entrapped victim, which stated unequivocally that the combined rescue attempt was undoubtedly successful.

Dr. Hanson continued to work on the time-line in order to be ready for the upcoming meeting. He decided that a bar graph might better explain the exponential rise in disasters that had continued unabated since the turn of the century. There was little he could do to mask facts that denied logic. The current trends indicated that the rise in catastrophic events was doubling by the year. This was something even he had not expected. Now some of his colleagues were sending out stern warnings that every fault line on the planet was subject to earthquake activity. To a certain extent, this was true.

He found that he had little time to study the mystic light over the Sahara. To date, he had taken all pertinent information he had accrued to Dr. Allen Heisenberg at Massachusetts Institute of Technology for further study. He had ascertained that it was no lightning strike, as the projection line was perfectly straight. Lightning strikes grew jagged as they traversed the lower atmosphere. He really wasn't sure what this was, but it was something he had never seen before. If anyone could tell what the light was, it would be Dr. Heisenberg, as he was the leading expert on light and light refraction. He had the equipment to analyze the light to a greater degree than anyone else he knew, and the doctor had promised to get back with him as soon as he had found out anything of pertinent value.

CHAPTER 6

A Conscious Election

Ablack wisp of smoke rose intermittently into the sky above the Sistine Chapel. Every puff hung in the air as if suspended, slow to dissipate in the windless, cool late morning air. This was the first official signal to the public that denoted the start of the conclave. The first vote had been taken and no one had been elected by simple majority.

The conclave's origins dated back to 1271, when it took over two years and nine months to elect Pope Gregory X. Local church officials had grown weary of the extended procrastination of the then ranking electors and brought them all together in an effort to force a vote. They even went as far as threatening to starve them, giving them just bread and water until the process of appointing the new titular head of the church was accomplished.

Over the years through trial and error, the system had continually improved. Present-day rituals for the pope's election are, as with most elections, designed to expedite the process.

Earlier that morning, the College of Cardinals had gathered one last time in the Sistine Chapel as a group to pray for divine guidance in electing one from amongst them, and to listen to the chanted Litany of Saints. One of their numbers soon would emerge as the new pope, the spiritual leader of the church here on earth. The college had listened to a sermon of guidance once in the morning and once again in the afternoon the day prior to the first ballot. They gathered this morning to participate in a Mass that marked the start of the conclave in Saint Peter's basilica. Each one of this elite group would soon be sequestered and the process of election would begin. The rules regarding the protocol of the election ceremony were strictly adhered to once the signal of announcement was given. This was denoted as well to the occupants within the chapel by the ringing of bells.

Many of the cardinals looked about the room in an effort to ascertain a level of agreement as to who might be selected as their next pontiff. Some, if not many, in the room scanned the well-known faces of probable few leading contenders for the position and some looked in Cardinal Robbia's direction. He smiled demurely and felt good about their vote of confidence. He noticed however, that just as many occupants in the room looked toward Cardinal Edmond Piazorra. He was the Sicilian cardinal whose steadfast and unwavering commitment to the church's historical past and present policies was unquestioned. The seventy-two-year-old cardinal was well respected among his peers and even Cardinal Robbia felt he would be an apt pick to secede his friend, Pope Alexander. Whether he would continue with the needed changes begun by the fallen pope were something else to be seen. In the past, some of the new changes that had been proposed did not sit well with him. He always had an eloquent way of arguing his position, which hardly denied his intent. Most of the time the opponents to his views listened to his orations with rapt attention and in the end, he was able to win convincing arguments based on his position without even raising his voice. Most of those who ended up agreeing with his position did so without realizing why they had. Most of the cardinals agreed that he was a wise and logical man. Cardinal Robbia had summed the cardinal up as a wise and unquestionable council to many. This was all good and well at preserving the status quo of the church, but he was not so sure that the man would be able to continue with the needed changes required of the next pope. Such a man had to have enough conviction to propel the church well into the twenty-first century.

The entire world was in flux as far as Cardinal Robbia was concerned, and they needed to see a stable but continually changing church on which many had come to rely on. It wasn't merely the Catholic Church affected by the election. It was much more than that. The sphere of influence had long since left the confines of christened Catholics alone and now many of those who were not even believers looked upon the pontiff for guidance though these most trying of times. The ability to intervene in hotly debated political situations required someone who was able to see changes in advance, someone who had ability and might be thought of as proactive instead of reactive. Cardinal Robbia thought on that point alone was where Cardinal Piazorra's weakness lay. He didn't have the ability to deal with sensitive issues that were an integral part of the position of pope on which this church relied.

It had been a past and present fact that many of the world's leaders had come to the door of the pontiff seeking council. This had been true for quite some time. It was felt that it was the exalted leader's duty to provide sound advice in such a way that precluded questioning. It was also the duty of the pope to uphold the rights of meek and sometimes disenfranchised populations. The position required the pope to uphold the rights of all for greater good. This was a daunting task in and of itself, which required not only wisdom and clarity, but also the need for pragmatism and stanch perseverance. It also required one of the more critical aspects of church dogma itself, and that was enlightenment from the Holy Spirit, though this fact was one that normally did not find its way into the equation for public debate. It was a truth nonetheless, considered to be of vast importance to every one of the cardinals here in the room. Each of the likely candidates would be scrutinized on that aspect as well.

Cardinal Robbia could think of just one other person in the room, other than himself, who had the required and eminent qualifications to carry on the task at hand, and that was the Cardinal from the Archdiocese of New York, Stanislaw Czerwinski. He was a second-generation Pole whose family had immigrated to the United States at the beginning of the Second World War. He was a knowledgeable man who had all of the necessary requirements to suitably fill the position. The only detriment to the likelihood of his election was that he resided in the states. Never had a resident outside of Italy, except for the Polish Pope John Paul, ever been seriously considered for the position. It was highly unlikely that the College of Cardinals would break tradition and do so.

Cardinal Robbia knew there would be certain advantages to election of an American, and that would of course be a greater unification of the church itself in regard to the sometimes-troublesome church in the United States. Certain policies were less than enthusiastically welcomed when it came to the church there. Electing Czerwinski would cement a bridge between the Atlantic Ocean with greater adherence to these policies on the part of the American church. Still, Cardinal Robbia discounted the man all together in his mind. The odds were just too great for an American cardinal to succeed.

There was just one other variable in the equation that he felt might bar his way to the title, and that was a dark horse. There were several likely candidates for that position, someone with the wherewithal to voice his likely qualities to the group. Cardinal Robbia was not sure how much individual effort was brought forth in that regard, and was much too focused on winning the election to pay much attention to a probable dark horse candidate.

Instead, he relied on his closest councilor and newly appointed Archbishop Alvito. He had assigned the man the task of assessing all probable candidates, including those who had an outside chance of winning the vote of the College of Cardinals. He hadn't had a chance to speak with him as of late, but had waited until they were sequestered to get his opinion on the matter.

Now, with the first ballot tallied and the results posted, there appeared two front-runners for the title - Cardinal Piazorra and himself. He felt honored by the first posting and saw that the vote was about even, with as many votes, to a lesser extent, cast in minor proportions to other candidates. Cardinal Robbia felt relieved that his dark horse thoughts were for naught. The American Cardinal was a distant third.

He knew that whatever the outcome, it was left in God's hands at this point and he waited patiently for the second ballot to be cast this evening. He hoped that they would make a conscious effort to choose from among himself and Pizzorra the man who would, and could, continue with the changes initiated by Pope Alexander. If such were the case, he felt sure of the election.

Cardinal Robbia and Monsignor Giuseppe Lorenzo had taken lunch in the Cardinal's cramped quarters within the Sistine Chapel. This was simply an example of how the cardinal was in essence a pious man who required little nourishment and demanded even less from his surroundings. Giuseppe figured were it centuries earlier, he would probably have enjoyed the seclusion of a monastery high atop a mountain and would have been perfectly happy to wear the brown woolen garb of a monk and enjoyed quiet isolation. The fact that he could make do without the creature comforts of life in this day and age told its own story about the man's character. Giuseppe stood at the small table as he watched the cardinal point to the seat opposite him. "Where's Archbishop Alvito?"

"He's gone to the cafeteria for lunch," The cardinal said.

Giuseppe saw the direct result of this comment in his mind's eye. Many things had changed in regard to these conclaves. The rules eased significantly as long as no verbal contact was made between the sequestered parties. He knew now why he had been asked to fetch just two trays of food. He knew Archbishop Alvito would be piling his plate many times over before the end of lunch today. He smiled, thinking the Archbishop would have been better served if there were a cart route between the kitchen and their quarters. "I see." Cardinal Robbia was quick to grasp his comment and had a good laugh as well. "I must talk to him one day. He loves his food, and you can't say he doesn't, but it does almost border on gluttony to me." It was said in such a deadpan manner that the two men could not help but laugh at the man's weakness.

The unbridled laughter seemed to ease the cardinal's state of mind and he leaned back in his chair with a satisfied nod.

"Let me ask you, Giuseppe, have you made any progress in your research on the assignment that I gave you?"

Giuseppe noticed the look of deep concern that crossed the Cardinal's face and he hoped that what he had to say might ease the sudden tension lines he saw. "Yes and no, which I am sure you'll find as a vague answer." He paused to collect his thoughts. "Please let me explain. Without the benefit of an eyewitness account, I'm looking at a varied amount of information. I was hoping that you might have found the key for a more specific and defined search on my part?"

The cardinal frowned, which Giuseppe interpreted as a no. He shrugged and continued. "Well then, that being the case, and without a witness to the event, and now knowing that the light was not natural by any means, I looked strictly for scriptural connotations at first, from the shining star that had led the Magi to the birth place of Jesus all the way through into the book of Revelations."

"So what did you find?" the cardinal causally asked.

"Well, we could spend our entire day talking about the meaning of light in the context of Christianity. Foremost, I think the light represents the divine light of God, which in this case, I am not sure applies. Historically, from the third century on, lights or candles were burned to illuminate the faithful during times of worship. They took on a symbolic meaning as a result, in which light began to take on a different meaning as the believers of Christianity were not worshiping in the dark but rather it was the light of Christ, which upheld their belief. This though, is not what I really think the light means in this case, either. It is not true in its symbolic form here, anyway. I began to think along the lines of the early painters who depicted a streak of white oil as light in their paintings as a transposed message on canvas. Somewhat similar, I suppose, to the likeness on the hand of God with streaks of white emitting from his fingertips, sending a message to the writhing masses below. I followed this line of thought for quite some time, thinking a message of some sort had been conveyed, the recipient, as you so indicated, yet to be found. So, until we find this person, I'm leaving this as the most viable option to date." Giuseppe noticed no discernable change in the cardinal's demeanor and pressed on. "There were other avenues I pursued as well, as I will not limit my research to anything that I feel might be a tangible explanation for the unnatural light. First, though, I took the liberty of contacting parties involved in the discernment of the oddity. I hope you don't mind, for it is necessary to be precise."

"No, not at all, I know you must do what you feel is necessary, and I expect no less," the cardinal stated matter of factly.

"I looked into the actual area where this took place as well, tracing the volumes upon volumes of books with reference to that area of the desert. I came up with some past and recent facts which I pursued under guise of unexplainable lights."

"Such as...?" the cardinal asked.

"The appearance of angels is one such reference; a bright light usually precedes the intervention of an angel to relay a message upon mankind."

"That is a possibility; it has been recorded many times in the past. Do you think that's what happened here?"

"Possibly, but I'm just not that sure at this point." He watched the cardinal's expression deflate once again. "There is yet another interesting fact that I found as it pertains to unexplainable lights, and it deals with a purported miracle the Coptic Church has proclaimed as it deals with the town of Asyut, Egypt. This is an area of Egypt where Mary, Joseph and baby Jesus fled to during their escape from King Herod. I don't know how much time you have to deal in such matters, so please let me know if you already know what I'm talking about."

"Vaguely," Cardinal Robbia nodded. "I remember reading something about it some time ago that pertained to the purported claims of the Coptic Church, but my memory eludes me at this moment. We do not proclaim miracles readily. It takes time and proof before we recognize them, as you well know."

"Well then, there is a possibility here as well. The Coptic Church, when trying to rebuild the church in Asyut, ran into stiff opposition from the state of Egypt and Muslim extremists. Apparently, a vision of the Virgin Mary appeared and aided in the approval of the rebuilding permit." The monsignor continued to fill in the details of the events as they unfolded during that time, and then paused as Cardinal Robbia digested the information.

"Interesting, to say the least," he finally spoke. "Do you think there may be some relevance here as it pertains to the blue light in the desert?"

"It is an avenue that I have not had time to thoroughly explore, but one which is another possible explanation to the dilemma. I must admit that this is a daunting task and I am not about to leave any stone unturned in this matter. It would be invaluable to me if we could find more clues to the source of the light, as I might be able to further isolate my research."

"I realize what a task it is, now that we have had a chance to talk. I just wish I had more resources available to assist you, but until then I'm afraid you'll have to go solo on this one for awhile."

"There is one other avenue here, which I will assure you I'm researching as well."

The cardinal drummed his fingers on the table in an effort to control his growing frustration. "Which is?"

"The Fatima letters," Giuseppe said flatly, hoping that he would not be chastised for revealing his thoughts on the matter.

"In what regard? Why would you say that?"

"I will say that this may be a long shot, but I am, if nothing else, thorough. All references to any sort of light were considered, even with this avenue, so if I may go out on a limb here for a moment, let me explain myself." He scratched his head and looked away from his mentor in an effort to quell the rising sound of the ever-tapping fingers before him. "In regard to the all-too-secret third letter, which has until recently, has been locked away until a reasonable explanation for its existence could be found."

"Be careful here, Giuseppe," Cardinal Robbia warned with a frown. "You know that they used to kill people for sedition, and topics such as these are usually left to our skeptics, not our learned advisors."

"I am, as you say, careful but thorough, though you surely must admit that the policy of our predecessors was one in which they would rather cloak the truth instead of explaining it honestly to the masses." Giuseppe scanned the cardinal's face in such a way as to ascertain his objection. "I, for one, do not feel the explanation for the letter's content was at all truthful. I find it hard to believe that the Blessed Virgin Mary would send such a simplistic message. It is naive to say that the true intent of the letter could be so easily explained away as the attempted assassination of a pope. If so, why did our predecessors keep it hidden all those years without revealing its content? That pat explanation may easily convince the uninformed masses, but I find it hard to swallow."

"So be it as it may, that is the church's position on the matter. You are not the one who dictates policy here, as I recall."

"No, I'm not, and at times I think I should be more conscious of that reality. The Church should spend more time obtaining the true order of facts that are not so easily swept under the carpet. Don't you think?"

"Look, I cannot be held personally responsible for the digressions of my predecessors. I can only deal with what comes across my desk. No more, no less."

"I would never think otherwise," Giuseppe said. "Maybe we can save this discussion for another day. When doing research, you learn to question all sources and information before coming to a logical conclusion about anything, your Eminence." His use of the title had the desired effect that Giuseppe had hoped for. The term of rank had always been used by his father whenever he dealt with his childhood friend, and he saw the Cardinal smile.

"Your father warned me long ago of your sometimes single-minded purpose in the pursuit of truth," Cardinal Robbia said. "I had at one time thought that you were being ostentatious, for at times I find it hard to follow your chain of thought. This is probably due to the fact that you are extremely intelligent or plain pig-headed... I'm not quite sure which." The cardinal began to laugh, though almost as soon as he began, he stopped. "Let us meet again, for my mind is preoccupied with other matters at the moment."

"Of course, of course, there is a lot to absorb when it entails research. You cannot be expected to have it all sink in at a moment's notice. How about the same time tomorrow? Lunch, once again?"

"Splendid!"

That evening the black smoke curled upwards toward the heavens once again, ballots were burned and the results tallied. Monsignor Giuseppe Lorenzo wondered how many people knew a chemical was added to the paper to get it to burn black or white. There was still about an even vote between the two front-runners, and to a lesser extent, the third-place finisher, as were all other contenders, were dropped from the ballot. At one time, a two-thirds majority was required for an election, though that rule had been changed in 2006 when a simple majority was required. This simplified the voting process and prevented a deadlock.

Apparently, Cardinal Robbia felt better about the second vote than the first, realizing he had not lost any ground. That translated into only one thing, and that was that needed changes to church policy might continue if he were elected. He was hoping this would be the case, but either way would try to continue carrying the banner of his fallen friend, Pope Alexander. He knew if he lost, it would be for a good reason and that was, in his mind, the will of God. He would staunchly support his rival no matter what, win or lose.

The next morning the results were even somewhat better, and Cardinal Robbia had taken a slim lead over Cardinal Piazorra. He appeared elated by the news and when he met with Giuseppe for lunch that day, he was in good spirits. Giuseppe had all the intentions of taking over where he had left off the day before, but the decided to take advantage of the situation. "Your Eminence, first off I'd like to say that I feel that you will win and want to be the first to congratulate you."

"Aren't you being a bit presumptuous in that respect, Giuseppe?"

"Hardly," Giuseppe smiled, "My father would be proud, were he here today."

Cardinal Robbia gazed into the younger man's face, "I just know he is looking down upon us at this moment and is just as proud of me as you seem to be."

"I am," Giuseppe nodded. "After all, it's not every day that you have a Pope as a mentor."

"Nor do we sometimes have the likeness of a childhood friend at our side. There are days when I still think about your father with fond childhood recollection. You remind me of him every time I see you, which is a good thing. When your father came to me one day and made me vow if anything ever happened to him that I would take care of you, I was of course flattered. Never did I expect what happened to him might have been a premonition when he first suggested it, though I swore on the Bible that I would take care of you. As children, your father and I always challenged one another. Arturo was a very talented man and I admired his ability to create art from a simple stone." He nodded somberly. "When he made me swear to watch over you, he chose his words carefully to convey what he wanted me to do. I remember to this day what he told me. 'Like I mold stone into statue, do the same for my son, and mold his character'. I have always done as he had wished, whether you realized it or not."

Giuseppe felt surprise by the man's words and listened with rapt attention.

"I have done so, sometimes in clandestine ways that you never noticed. Years ago, when you used to come to the Duomo of Milan to sit and wonder, it was I, through the acolyte, who first kindled the idea of you becoming a priest in your mind. I had instructed the acolyte, now Reverend Chanter, that every time he saw you, he was to approach you and instill the thought in your mind. Your father knew about this long in advance of his death. That's why, when you first mentioned your calling to him, he was not surprised."

Giuseppe recalled the event and nodded in agreement. It was as if his father had anticipated his words before they'd been spoken.

"Don't get the wrong idea though" Cardinal Robbia continued. "You were never forced to accept your calling. It was only when I became sure of it myself that I finally suggested it during our first meeting. For the most part, I let the seminarians find and promote your strong points; I had no hand in that. It was something you achieved, using your own volition. There were times though, that I did use my influence to keep you close at hand, getting you your post here at the Vatican as I waited patiently for you to hone your skills. What better place could there be than right here at the most extensive library in the whole world? The century's worth of knowledge here at one's fingertips. I must admit that I had ulterior motives, for I was in need of someone with exactly your capabilities. I'm not afraid to admit it. Yes, I believe my friend Arturo is looking down upon us at this moment with admiration of us both."

Giuseppe didn't know what to say. He had never fully realized that he had been so thoroughly influenced by this man, and his admiration for him abounded once again, a compliment to the cardinal's character and judgment. He became melancholy. "I miss both my parents at times. It is during those quiet and sometimes obscure moments that I reflect on their influence in my life, as you just have. However, there's something that's been troubling me for quite some time, and I never could quite bring myself to the point of discussing it with you. I feel that I might never again have the chance, so now would be as good a time as any."

"Well, I don't know about that," Cardinal Robbia said. "You know I'll always be there if you need me. What is it that you think I can help you with?"

"It's about my Mother's death. Please let me clarify that. It isn't the fact that she's dead, but how she died that bothers me most. If you will grant me some leeway here, I'll explain." Giuseppe went on to explain the un-natural circumstances of his mother's death in detail. He watched the change in expression on the cardinal's face as his face drained of color until his skin took on an unhealthy hue of gray. The cardinal sat immobile. When he had finished, he held his mentor's comment off with a raised hand in an effort to quell his mentor's words. "I was wondering all along, and please be perfectly honest with me, for this matter is important to me. Did the same thing happen to Pope Alexander as well?"

The Cardinal mulled the question over for several moments. "Do you really need to know?" he finally asked.

"I realize that you don't have to tell me and feel no obligation in that regard. I also know, like my father, that he was also a dear friend of yours. Though you must realize why I ask this of you. It's not only for my benefit that I ask. There is something else at play here that I have yet to understand. With that in mind, I'll let you decide whether you should tell me or not. I just feel that it is of vast importance that I know."

The cardinal was slow to speak. "When I first entered his quarters, called there by his aide, I could never have believed that he would up and just walk away from his responsibilities. That was not his way. He took pleasure in his position as head of the church. How would he walk away without anyone noticing anyway? At first, we thought that he had been kidnapped, but then I saw the clothes he was wearing still on the bed as he had worn them. It wasn't until I saw his ring lying next to the articles of clothing that I noticed the dust, as you did with your mother. How can you explain something as unusual as that to anyone? This is why you yourself have been slow to admit to it. After an exhaustive search ended with no result, we then fashioned a cover story for his disappearance. We had the dust analyzed and found it to resemble the dust produced by cremation. This is when we pronounced him dead in his sleep. We dared not divulge the true circumstance of his death, sure in our minds that panic would ensue. Realistically, you just don't have a head of state just disappear, so we did the next best - and only thing we could do - without raising any suspicions." He paused and eyed Giuseppe. "How did you know?"

"The closed casket was the most obvious clue to me."

"Swear to me one thing," Cardinal Robbia insisted. "You must not let a word of this get out. There are but a select few who know the truth of the matter."

"I swear, though I must ask one more question... do you have any idea as to why?"

"No, none at all, and until we can figure that out, no one will ever know what really happened as far as the church is concerned."

"I'm not so sure that's wise, though I may be able to help. There might be some viable reason for the disappearance, and I've been looking into this as well." He was interrupted when Archbishop Alvito returned from lunch. Amazingly, he'd managed to keep his vestments stain-free for once.

Archbishop Alvito apparently noticed the discerning look on the cardinal's face and stared at the two men as if trying to analyze what was transpiring between them. "Is there something the matter?" he finally asked, scowling at Giuseppe.

The cardinal was quick to reply. "No, it's nothing that should concern you."

"Huh," he stated and headed for the desk, where he sat heavily in the chair.

Cardinal Robbia nodded to Giuseppe and then left the room. Giuseppe sat for quite some time after the cardinal got up, pondering the implications of the similar deaths, wondering if he should tell the reporter what he knew. If he was any judge of character at all, he knew that his slip of the tongue had already started the ball rolling downhill and it was pointless not to tell her. She would find out on her own anyway. He finally decided to think about the entire situation for several days before making up his mind.

That evening a pillar of white smoke rose out of the window of the Sistine Chapel. A joyous cheer rose from outside the chapel as murmurs of approval were heard on the inside. Cardinal Robbia sat in his chair for several moments in stunned disbelief as attending cardinal's rose to greet the new head of the church. The Dean of Cardinals stood patiently before the crowded room of his compatriots, waiting to ask the crucial question, as was the tradition.

"Do you accept the position as head of the Roman Catholic Church, Cardinal Robbia?" he finally asked.

Cardinal Robbia had not even realized that the Dean had made his way to the front of the room. He answered as if his mind were in a fog, though his voice remained strong and true. "Yes, I do."

The Dean of Cardinals smiled. "And by which name do you wish to be called?"

The bells of Saint Peter's Basilica began to ring even before he had a chance to respond. He heard the loud peals and the exited response from the courtyard of the building outside of the chapel once again.

"Romanus the Second!" Following his announcement, the room went silent, for no one seemed to recall the name ever being used before.

Later, after hearing the chosen name, Monsignor Giuseppe Lorenzo had to look it up in order to attach some significance to the title. The name had belonged to an obscure ninth- century pope whose reign lasted just barely over four months. He was thought to be disposed by opposition forces to the church at the time. Little was truly known about the man or what, if any, contribution he had made to the church. There were but a few lines in reference to him at the time by a historian named Frodoard writing about how the man had first become a monk. Some later scholars would interpret that as a derogatory term, silenced by his adversaries.

Giuseppe thought otherwise in regard to voiced opinions about why the cardinal picked the name in the first place. He realized that Cardinal Robbia took the name solely on the implication of the name and not it's slight, though both references suited him in any case. He was sure that Cardinal Robbia had given great thought to the name, though he knew not many people would be able to decipher his reason why. No one was allowed to challenge the name anyway; it was solely a discretionary pick. He thought about the name for some time and realized it conveyed a strong sense of character, much like the Romans and their empire had conveyed to the rest of the known world during their tenure. It came across in exactly the same way as his best friend's choice of the name Pope Alexander had - conquerors one and all.

Giuseppe was elated on one hand by the election, and despondent on the other. He had a strong sense of foreboding for various reasons. For one, he had ascertained that the deaths of both Pope Alexander and his mother were no coincidence at all. This was preying on him like a festering wound as he puzzled though the implications. Secondly, he felt that the newly installed Pope was about to follow in the footsteps of his chosen namesake. He thought the name Cardinal Robbia had chosen was an omen of sorts, and that the cardinal's future days was numbered. He thought of the name, Romanus in terms of a historical misstep, defining the repetition of failed tactics or campaigns, doomed to failure from the start. He just wished that his mentor had consulted him prior to his selection.

A sense of total dread closed in on him in that respect, but he had no way of truly explaining how he felt other than to think there was no real reason to fear unknown and dark corners of a room except that one's mind sometimes compelled one to think of the worst possible scenario hidden in darkened corners. He buried those thoughts in his research, hoping to find answers to ease his troubled mind.

CHAPTER 7

The Web of Distortion

Florence Rinna boarded the plane for Washington without thinking twice about the implications. Her editor had phoned her and told her to stay on for the ordination of the new pope, but she ignored his directive entirely, thinking that she had been gone long enough. Her headstrong attitude about what he thought and what she thought were good cover for the newspaper was about to clash once again. Besides, she had good reason to return early; she had the story of a lifetime brewing on the back burner and somehow felt that there was a cover up of some sort that needed to be exposed, somewhat similar to the old Watergate scandal, which was required textbook reading for any novice reporter to this day.

Besides, she was a writer for the Washington Post, not the Catholic Digest. She mulled over the ramifications of the priest's story several times and recalled with vivid clarity his exact words. She knew the priest was telling the truth, for his body language had said as much about the story as his actual words had. Her only concern in the whole matter was convincing her editor to give her free reign in the investigation without divulging her source or the true severity of the issue. She was sure she could protect her source, but not so sure how much depth of explanation might be required to explain the circumstances. She thought if things worked out for the worse, she could take a leave of absence and pursue the story as a freelance reporter, not unlike what she had done for a time prior to signing on with the Post. The only drawback to that scenario was the lack of extensive resources the paper had to offer. In the end, she thought she might have enough clout to convince her editor, David McCloud, otherwise.

Later the following day, she sat in the chair opposite of him listening to him rant and rave. "How long are you going to carry on about this already?" she asked.

"As long as it takes for you to follow a directive!" he shouted. "If everyone on this staff did as they pleased, we'd never get this paper out in a timely fashion."

"All right then," she stated contritely. "I'll write your story for you and you can get it in the evening edition." Her words had little effect on his still dour expression.

"It's not the same," he grumbled. "Besides, the story should have run yesterday as a follow up to your human-interest pieces, which would have been the prudent thing to do."

"This is getting a bit tiring here," she sighed. "It's not like it cost you anything, since the return flight was already paid for." She paused and tried a new tact. "Do you think Pope Alexander is the only religious leader to have recently passed away? Just about an hour ago, a leading theologian connected with one of the Islamic Universities in Cairo was said to be kidnapped and feared dead. Do you want me to get on the plane and get that story as well?" She saw the surprised look on his face, surmising he knew nothing about the latest wire story. She did not feel, after learning this latest information, that these disappearances were not isolated incidents, nor were they exclusive to the Catholic Church.

"No!"

She studied his face for some time to judge the extent of his ire, but it seemed to have faded somewhat. He looked away momentarily, a measure of discomfort noticeable, his forehead creased. He began to toy with his pen, which lay on the table, a sure sign to her of his fading conviction. "Look, I found out something while I was in Rome which is not only baffling but strange as well," she said, further trying to mollify him. "I'm sure that it would make headline news for weeks. If I could be given some leeway here, I need some time to do some investigation on my own."

"Why would I want to do that?" he demanded. "Moments ago, I thought the only way you could be taught to follow the rules here was to give you unpaid leave and let you think about your precarious position here."

Flo saw that his piqued look still prevailed, and knew by the tone of his voice she would have to be careful, though she was sure he was just throwing his weight around. She had been in this position many times before and knew she had just gained an edge. "Well, I guess that's up to you, but I know one thing, and that is if what I have found ends up having as much substance as it appears to have, you'll have to stand in line and bid for an exclusive like everyone else. It's your call."

"Damn it, Flo, this had better be good or else you'll be out on the street looking in. You better realize that. Now what have you got?"

She knew she had him now and smiled amicably. Still, she refrained from gloating over her victory, knowing he would probably get pissed off once again as a result. "You have to keep an open mind here to realize what I've stumbled upon. It's nothing short of remarkable. It seems that people have been disappearing. I know what you're going to say, it happens all the time, I can tell by the look on your face, but bear with me here. This is not about people who just up and walk away from their lives for whatever reason, it's more than that. It's deeper than that, and borders on the realm of unbelievable circumstances not unlike a science fiction movie." She could see he was intrigued. He'd leaned forward in his chair.

"What exactly are we talking about here?" he asked.

"Have you ever seen the movie 'The Invasion of the Body Snatchers?" By his facial expression, she could tell he had, but he said nothing, afraid to admit to it. "Well, this is similar in nature as I see it. Let me refresh our memory... if you remember in the beginning of the movie, alien mold spores had made their way to earth, where they planted themselves and grew as pods. These pods then transformed humans by copying their bodies while they slept, transforming the entire planet of humans into aliens as a net result. Their old bodies withered away as a result of the transformation."

He smiled and shook his head. "You're kidding me, right? Is this your way of getting back in my good graces, by telling me some farfetched story in hopes that I might be dumb enough to believe it?"

Flo grew irate. She was dead serious and now felt he was making a game out of this. "Look David, I said it was similar just so that you might get the idea in your head on how farfetched reality may have crossed the line into science fiction. Be serious for a moment here until I can explain what I meant to say to begin with. If I had told you outright, you would have thrown me right out of the office for wasting your time. Now be quiet and listen for a moment."

Flo had to reach into her reserves to quell her rising fury as she saw the child-like smirk on his face. She somehow felt he was getting some sick sense of pleasure out of all of this, thinking she had lost her mind all of a sudden. "Look, just sit there and listen. You can judge the story on its own merits when I'm done."

He sighed, looked at the ceiling momentarily, and then sat back in his chair for effect. He mumbled his agreement and she related the story almost verbatim from what the priest had told her. When she finished, she could tell he was a bit unsettled by it. His hands were crossed at his chest, and his body language denoted disbelief.

"Who's your source? In all my days, I've never heard such a farfetched yarn."

"A priest!" she responded.

"Did I hear you right? A priest? You must be kidding!"

"No, I'm not and you should know me well enough by now. I would have discounted the story myself if I thought someone was just pulling my leg. This is a very reputable source with everything to lose and nothing to gain by telling me something like this." She could tell he finally began to believe her, for his growing look of trepidation said it all. "Not only that, but this priest seems to believe what happened to his mother also happened to the pope, which might be the reason for the closed casket at the funeral. That's why I got on the plane and came back here. I would hardly want to compromise a story such as this by relaying it to you over the phone. You yourself have told me how the government monitors calls, especially from overseas." She watched him intently for several moments, gauging him.

"These changes everything," David said, "You did the right thing in coming back. See what you can find out and get back to me as soon as you can. I want to know what you find out when you find it out. Is that understood?"

"Frankly, there's too much at stake here for me to do otherwise."

"I agree."

Flo left the room unencumbered by thoughts of her editor breathing down her neck, having escaped the noose once again. Her mood elevated and she smiled as if she'd just received a Pulitzer, a lifelong goal she had yet to attain. Maybe, she thought; if this story is half of what she thought it might entail, she might achieve that goal yet.

She was on her cellphone before she reached her cubicle in the central office, which she liked to call The Social Club - too many reporters with too much time on their hands, doing too little, bent on nosing into one another's private business. She heard his voice on the end of the line. "Trey, I have a favor to ask, if you don't mind?"

"Go ahead shoot, what do you have?"

She heard his deep baritone voice soothing her ears. This guy had asked her out several times in the past, and while she liked him, could not bring herself to make the first move toward what she felt might be a budding relationship. She felt funny about crossing the line of commitment once again, having been burned before by men who felt she was just a pretty package, and easily conquered. Privately, she talked to her girlfriends about him. Of course, when she did, they cajoled her for her hesitant stance, offering her all the staid and expected responses of how her body clock was already seemly winding down. Time was her enemy. She filed those collective opinions away, but every once in a while, they'd resurface to try and spurn her into action once again. "Trey, I need you to dig up all you can on missing persons, and don't be selective either. Look worldwide. Facts and figures, progressions, famous or otherwise, and I need this as soon as you have time."

"Gotcha, what else do you need?"

"Along the same lines, I also need what you can find out about lost, missing or presumed dead political and religious leaders of all faiths in... let's say the last thirty-six months?"

"Is that all?" he asked playfully.

She knew this was a tall order on its own, and dared not ask any more of him now. She knew he had his hands full as a software engineer for a research and development firm. He never really told her what type of research he did, though she thought it was somehow related to a government project of a clandestine nature. He was always evasive about his work whenever she asked, so she had quit asking some time ago, content now just to get the information she needed without asking obvious questions on how it was obtained.

"Look, I owe you one," she said. "I know, I know, but then you always say that and never come through." He chuckled.

"I'm going to wear you down sooner or later. You know that, as well as I do."

"Maybe the next time you ask it may be different, who knows? I wouldn't stop trying if I were you."

"Never will," he said. "I'll get back to you, this afternoon at the latest."

She heard the note of optimism in his voice as he signed off, knowing that he would do his best to call her as he promised he would. She stopped at her desk, hung her suit jacket on her chair, and phoned the research department. She asked for just about the same type of material and hung up, then headed down to records to see what see could dig up on her own.

Several hours later, sitting in her cubicle thinking about the entire situation, the phone rang. From her caller I.D, she knew it was Trey. "Hold on a minute, I want to put you on screen." The newspaper office had the latest technology, enabling her to put him on screen as if he sat across from at her desk, without the now outdated mounted webcam camera. It was possible now to just look at the screen and get an instantaneous picture streamed via internet. The ability of a screen to see in as well as out was not new, but only recently had been approved for public use. "I got you now, go ahead." She saw the concerned look on his face as he spoke.

"I think you stuck your foot in it this time," he said, scoffing.

"How so? I didn't think what I asked was that big of a deal."

"The data you required on missing people wasn't, that's routine and a matter of public information. The other though, was a bit of a tangled mess."

"Why do you say that?"

"Looks like to me that someone is blocking any access to the information you asked for regarding missing religious and political leaders."

"Do you mean as in Homeland Security? Why would they do that?" she frowned. She could see him toying with her, hoping she would guess. He shook his head and began playing charades on screen.

"I'll give you a hint here. It's the agency that first introduced the nine famous words you never say on the telephone for fear of reprisal."

"The FBI?" She could tell by his rotating index finger pointed skyward that it was probably the wrong answer. "Who then?" she asked, frustrated. Come on now; grab the golden ring for once. From what I had to do to get what you wanted, it's the least you can do. Play along here. It only gets better once you guess."

"Well, it's not the CIA. They're finally doing their appointed task for once, gathering intelligence instead of sequestering it."

"Right you are," he nodded. "It's much higher than them. You're familiar with the name, not their intent. "

She suddenly smiled. "Not the NSA?" she said facetiously.

"Bingo, none other than the National Security Agency, you get the ring this time. The home of mega computers, satellites, and encryption games, fighting a war in cyberspace, the final frontier for arm chair generals."

"Why do you think it's them?"

"Because, they're the only ones with a computer big enough to do exactly that; monitor and block all other computers in the world. I've never seen the computer but they call it Big Mac, or the Whopper or some ridiculous name like that. Its sole purpose is to snoop on other computers."

"Snoop? I never knew that. Why in the world…?" She was aghast.

"They have a system which is commonly referred to as a High Policing Unit. Like with phones lines, they can monitor and store any I.P. address that tries to look up blocked or secure information, accidentally or otherwise. If you bother to look for internet information on the NSA, they'll monitor you as well. The computer is an advanced model of the ones the police commonly use to monitor child porn sites. Bang on one of those sites long enough and you'll see what I mean. In no time at all, there'll be a knock at your door with a private invitation to see the judge."

"So why don't they just block the porn sites then?"

"How else would you catch a rat if you left no bait out?"

"Wait a minute. I thought everything on the web that's posted is free game?"

"It is in some respects, but secured information or blocked information is usually encrypted and hard to retrieve. If there's something that they don't want you to see, you won't. It's there, it's just not visible and certainly not accessible on an everyday, run of the mill laptop. We're talking about national security here."

Baffled, Flo wondered out loud. "Why in the world would they want to hide information on missing religious leaders?"

"I don't know, but then you asked for the information, I didn't."

"How did you get it if no one else can?"

"Leave that one alone, Florence," he warned. "The only thing that you should concern yourself with here is why? Maybe I can help in that regard. I have a friend of a friend, so to speak, who might just be able to get you some more information. I called him today, and he got you an appointment with the missing person's director of the FBI. Maybe he can help you."

"That would be a great help."

"One more thing, you're going to need help if you think you can go up against the NSA without any repercussions. Remember, they have free reign and are an independent agency, titled under the Defense Department, using high-ranking military leaders. They answer basically only to the Commander in Chief. Then again, I'm sure the president really doesn't know what they do all of the time, either. What's this all about anyway?"

She thought about the implications for several seconds before answering. "Leave that one alone, Trey," she aped him with a smile. "I hope you covered your tracks?"

"Always, I never leave a computer cookie uneaten," he mused.

"Thanks, Trey, but you know something? You have a weird sense of humor."

"So they say."

The screen went blank moments later. Flo knew the information that Trey had retrieved would come the next day via independent courier, as he didn't trust the UPS either. She remembered him telling her that the ability to read mail without opening the seal was old hat. Trey was a good resource, she thought, but sometimes she wondered why he was so overly cautious.

Early the next morning, the phone rang. It was her editor, wondering what, if anything, she had found out, and requested that she meet him in his office for an update. Flo reluctantly agreed.

"What have you come up with? Knowing you, you're probably deeply mired in the mud on this one already."

"Actually, I am," she agreed. "It seems there are some issues involved which I am sure might interest you."

"Go on."

"I did some research and it seems as if there's a cover up of some sort that reaches into the highest levels of government. It seems the NSA is involved. Why, I'm not sure, though I presume it is to keep the public from panicking is my guess. They have just about locked out any inquiries into some of the information I need." She heard his low whistle but continued. "I've been looking over the statistics on missing persons, which seems to be incrementally increasing, both domestically and abroad."

"We have to be sure the NSA is involved before we go sticking our necks out. They don't think too kindly about the press mentioning their name to begin with."

"I know, David, no lecture is necessary. I've heard it all before and wouldn't dream of compromising our integrity." She knew him well enough to know what he was about to say.

"Have you heard from the priest yet? I would like some sort of verification in that sphere, before we proceed."

"No, actually I have not. I've been too busy to even think about calling him. I'm trying to verify the story from my end. I have an appointment with the FBI after lunch in hopes that they may provide some insight into the reasoning why the government might want to cover up a slew of missing persons. That in itself is strange."

"I agree."

"I just don't think this story is limited to known personalities, though it makes the facts more transparent if it was. Do you remember the feature story I did some time ago about the soapbox preacher named Jeremiah the prophet, who preached on Wall Street?" Though the video feed, she saw him nod his head in acknowledgement. "Well, three days ago, he came up missing and I never considered him anymore than a self-taught preacher. He would hardly qualify as a known person if it weren't for the publicity, he received from us and the New York Times. He told me that he used to be a dishwasher prior to taking up his calling. In my mind, he is just an ordinary citizen like the priest's mother... no more, no less."

"Your point...?" David asked.

"Well, isn't it the position of the government to protect its citizens from harm's way? If we had a serial killer running around snatching up people, every law enforcement agency, including the FBI, would be brought to bear in order to bring the man to justice. I would hardly think the agencies that be would want to just ignore the facts here. From what I've heard from a friend of mine who collaborated on the story with me, no one in New York City is the least bit concerned about his disappearance."

"You have a point there, speaking of which, if you intend to go up against the NSA, you're going to need help. There are legal ramifications to consider. We might want to think this through very carefully before we go up against the powers to be."

"Look, I'm not foolish enough to think otherwise. There may be another way around that stumbling block, which I'm still working on. In the interim, I'm going to fly up to New York and try and find out what happened to the preacher. I interviewed him in his walk-up tenement, a dismal hovel he shared with five other men. I'm sure they could give me some insight into his whereabouts. That is… if he's still alive. I should be back tomorrow morning."

She noticed the editor's frown, assuming she was off on a wild goose chase, though he made no remark. "Look, it's not likely the preacher is off on holiday. I had to give him twenty dollars just for food while I was there. My thought is, if I can verify the priest's story with one of my own, all the better."

"Suit yourself," David shrugged.

*   *   *

Ushered into Raymond Willis's office by his secretary, Flo wondered about the working relationship between the two of them. Her introduction to the assistant director had been less than cordial. The assistant director rose to greet her, his large hand encompassing hers almost within his palm. He looked to be around six-three and well built. She could tell by his muscular bulges even through his suit coat. He looked good for his age, about mid-forties judging by the whitening edges of his sideburns. He had a well-rounded yet studious face accented by black plastic eyeglasses.

"Call me Ray, if you don't mind," he invited with a smile. "I try to keep things informal around here. What can I do for you Ms. Rinna…? Washington Post, right?"

"Yes, call me Flo," she smiled in return. "I know you're busy so I won't take up much of your time. I'm doing a feature story on a missing preacher in New York City. I'm wondering what, if any, role the FBI plays when it comes to looking for missing persons." She watched him intently as he thoughtfully prepared his answer.

"New York City you say? I can't say that I have had any paperwork from a missing preacher come across my desk. Then again, it may be too early for that yet."

"What do you mean by that?" she asked, feigning ignorance.

He smiled briefly. "Well, the local authorities usually hold off beginning an actual investigation on a missing person's case for about twenty-four hours. Nine times out of ten the person usually returns. These are known statistics I'm quoting here. Sometimes, if they suspect foul play, they may act sooner. Usually though, they wait the proscribed period before they act at all. In a city as large as New York, it's easy to get lost; that and the fact that in the NYPD the process of informing and organizing an all-out search is sometimes a complicated affair."

"Would it be expedited sooner if it were a lost or missing child?" she asked, playing him ever so adroitly.

"Why, of course it would. Missing children always get prompt attention, even on the local level."

"So when do you, the FBI, get involved in a case such as the missing preacher?"

"Oh, that's easy enough to answer," He said. "Usually, it's when the local authorities deem it's necessary to do so. We provide a level of expertise that most local authorities aren't trained for."

"I'm not so sure I follow you here. Let me put a theoretical scenario together here so that I might understand you better. Let's just say that the preacher and the mayor both can up missing at the same time. Would it be more likely that the mayor, who has recognition, might get quicker attention than the preacher, who is hardly known at all?"

"That's probable," Willis admitted. "But then again, we're not running around looking for every person that comes up missing without being asked to do so."

"Now let me ask this," Flo broached. "What if someone comes up missing while they are overseas and not under the jurisdiction of the local authorities? What then? Do you get involved?"

"Of course we do, it's our job to try and protect all of our citizens no matter where they are."

"Does the FBI have agents in the field overseas?"

"Yes, we do," Wills nodded. "They're spread across the globe in strategic locations."

"Who would ultimately ask you to search for a missing person overseas were that the case?" She noticed a flash of wariness building in his sudden tensing. She didn't have much more time.

Willis frowned. "The State Department usually gives final approval but it's the foreign consulate in behest of the missing person's family which starts the process. I thought we were asking about a missing preacher in New York City?"

"We are," she assured him. "I just want to fully understand the process, is all? The more I know, the more I'm less likely to misinform the general public. Besides, it would give the average citizen a better understanding about the role the FBI plays in protecting their rights and shines a positive light on the bureau in the process, don't you think?"

"Yes, I agree," he said. "I'd like to read this story when you get done with it."

"You can be sure of that," she said, then returned to her questions. "Do you also extend the same courtesy to foreign governments as well?" A look of confusion crossed his features and she hurried to explain. "The reason I ask is that the preacher happens to be French National, not an American citizen, is what I'm told."

"Of course, we would, Ms. Rinna," Willis stated. "If we were asked, but in this case it's usually at the discretion of the State Department."

"Oh, I see, so the State Department works hand in hand with foreign governments looking for their citizens, but would do so trying to gain favor from the foreign government in exchange, am I right in assuming that?"

"Something like that I suppose, though I'm not exactly sure how it works, to tell you the truth."

"Would the State Department be more likely to agree to ask you to search for an average citizen, or let's say someone important like the Pope?" Flo noticed a nervous pall fall over the man. His eyes quickly darted from side to side and his hands began to shake ever so slightly. "Did I say something wrong?" she asked curiously. At that moment, she knew that he knew something about the situation.

"Who sent you here?" He quietly demanded, sitting upright in his chair.

Game point, Flo thought as she rose to leave, wondering if he would let her. She rose from her chair and stepped to the door. She had her hand on the door handle and turned it as she spoke. "Maybe we can continue this conversation at a later date," she suggested, staring him in the eye. "I might have overstayed my welcome." With that, she turned and left the room, passing though the outer office before he could utter a reply.

As she left the F.B.I office, thankful she hadn't been detained at the door, she phoned her editor to warn him. She hailed a taxi and a moment later it pulled up to the curb. With a sense of growing unease, she knew she would need protection and help on this one.

"To the airport please, and put your foot into it if you don't mind!" As the taxi pulled away, she saw Raymond Willis and several other men appear outside the entrance to the building scanning in every direction. She left unnoticed.

When Flo arrived in New York City, the sun had already set. She decided against walking into the bowels of the city this late at night without an escort. There were a lot of things she would do, but tempting fate was not one of them. Besides, with all that had transpired, she felt bone tired and had to have some downtime to sort through her thoughts. She booked a room in a second-rate hotel under an assumed name; making it harder for the F.B.I. to find her if they were looking for her. She paid cash and stopped using her cell phone. Trey had taught her well. She silently wished that he were there by her side to afford her some of his expertise. The next morning, she picked up a wire transfer from her editor and bought a change of clothes, something more suitable and less likely to bring attention to her figure. She called Trey on a borrowed cell phone and asked his opinion on the whole matter concerning the F.B.I. and he concurred that they knew about the situation, as well as the State Department and the NSA. His only insight into the situation was that the NSA was most likely pulling the strings on the other policing agencies. Proof of that would be hard to come by, if not totally impossible. He also stated that the men in black would be the ones looking for her in the end. She agreed with his logical assessment.

"It's better to leave the rest of the bureaucracy in the dark and concentrate on plugging the holes in the dike. I believe you have become a liability, unless you can prove otherwise," he said somewhat sardonically. "You won't smoke them out on this one, and not a court in the land would allow you to hide your source. I'd hide in plain sight if I were you."

"I am, but I might need more of your help if you can provide it?"

"Anytime, just call me if you need help, I would never refuse a call from a lady in distress," he said before he hung up the phone.

She made it to the six-story walkup around eleven. Any earlier would have been fruitless, as the preacher's roommates would not have been up any earlier than that. She noticed one of them sitting on the stoop, dazed and confused by the bright sunlight awash in his face. "I'm looking for the prophet Jeremiah," she said to him. "Is he in?" All she got in reply was a blank look of astonishment. For several moments, she stood waiting patiently before she decided that it was useless to repeat the question. She remembered the apartment was on the fifth floor and resigned her self to trudge up the steps and into the building. She wondered how the men drunk with sorrow found their way up to the place in the middle of the night to begin with. It had to be radar homing, for the dark hallways of the building seemed to absorb even the minimal light of day. It was depressing enough to let yourself be caught in the alcoholic web of despair, she thought, but this place only added to it. She wondered momentarily if she should have bought a flashlight to see her way up.

She was quite out of sorts by the time she reached the door of the apartment. She found it ajar, but she dared not enter unannounced. A faint chill rose up her spine as she rapped loudly on the door molding, announcing her presence.

The door swung open, catching her by surprise. The movement of air reeked of old men and she did her best to hide her sudden expression of disdain. She recognized the face before her instantly, trying vainly to remember the name associated with it. She knew if she could remember it would make the visit less obtrusive. Finally, she gave up and spoke. "I'm looking for Jeremiah the prophet. Is he here?" she asked reluctantly.

"Whoever's there, Martin, send them away!"

The voice came from behind the greeter, from a darkened corner of the room. She ignored the voice and spoke to the man standing at the door ogling her. "Martin, I heard that Jeremiah was missing. I don't know if you remember me, but I was here some time ago. I'm concerned about him." She noticed a faint glimmer of recognition as he spoke.

"You're that reporter lady?" she heard the man at the door whisper, studying his face. She noticed the watery eyes and running nose of his face from the dimly lit hallway, and the way his head bobbled from side to side as he spoke, as if it were too heavy for his narrow neck.

"Aren't you going to invite me in?" she stated cautiously. "Martin, I'm Florence Rinna, if you remember, from the Washington Post."

"Er...a ...yes. Come on in if you must. Though I must warn you, he isn't here."

She noticed him looking back into the room as he whispered once again.

"Frank might get upset, me letting you in this early, but I guess it's all right. You knowing the preacher and all."

He stepped aside and she gained entrance into the small living room. She remembered the layout of the apartment; a small, cluttered living room, one bedroom and a small efficiency kitchen. She noticed Frank laying on an uncovered mattress in the corner of the living room, a dim lamp to her left the only light in the room. It cast a shadow onto the supine man as he rolled over to look at her. She felt the hair rise at the back of her neck. She didn't know this man and analyzed any possible threat.

"Don't pay him any attention, he's harmless. He's new anyway and hasn't got much say here as far as I'm concerned, always in a foul mood, that one is."

Flo noticed that Martin had found enough voice for the prone man to hear and he rolled over in disgust.

"They come and go here. The only requirement is the ability to feed the kitty, if you know what I mean."

She nodded her understanding. "Where is Jeremiah? Do you know? I must speak with him."

"I don't know where he is," Martin replied. "To be honest, the last time I saw him was about four days ago. We bunk together in the back room," he said as he thumbed the direction of the room over his shoulder. "I woke up that morning, looked at his sleeping bag and he was gone. Funny thing though, he left his Bible and lectern behind. I just don't know what to make of it. He never goes out with them." He suddenly shuddered and then he began to cough at the same time. "You wouldn't happen to have a cigarette on you, would you?"

"No, I don't smoke."

"Too bad for me, I guess. I woke up dreaming of one this morning."

Flo understood. "I might be able to help you out, though if you don't mind, I'd like to look at his things first. They might give me a clue to his whereabouts."

"Sure thing," he said, offering a toothless smile.

He stepped aside and once more thumbed the direction of the bedroom, following her at a distance as she walked. Once she entered the room, she saw the plastic milk case in one corner of the room. A cardboard box sat beside it; the content of the preacher's life whittled down to a twelve by sixteen container. A worn and tattered Bible sat next to the bare mattress. A sleeping bag was positioned over it, fully extended. She stepped to the box, knelt down and began to rummage through it, Martin's voice behind her.

"Bad luck to rummage through a man's things like that, thought I'd let you know."

"I won't take anything. I just want to see if he left any clues to his whereabouts is all." Flo was spooked by the comment but tried to ignore it. There was nothing of any value in the box; a few odds and ends and some tattered clothing, but nothing that told her anything pertinent as to his whereabouts.

She went to the edge of the bed and kneeled once again, picking up the bible in the process. She fanned the pages looking for a slip of paper or anything that might be useful. It was while she was doing that when, out of the corner of her eye, she saw minute specks of dust begin to float upward from the bed. Startled, she dropped the Bible to the floor, which caused a small plume of dust to rise from the head of the mattress. She inhaled sharply, startled, but knew she had to know for sure. She pulled back the unzipped flap of the sleeping bag and began to tremble as she saw the outline of the neck of a shirt underneath. She straightened. The situation was exactly as the priest had described.

She had startled Martin by her sudden move and heard a yelp of surprise as she headed out of the room, pushing past him in the process. Shaking uncontrollably, she paused as she reached the door. It was all she could do to remove a twenty from her purse and hand it to Martin without a word. She never looked back, scampering for the stairs before the event could overwhelm her.

She was down the stairs and bursting into the light of day before she could even breathe steadily, hastily making her way up the street, when she reached the corner she stopped and studied her surroundings, confused and in need of a respite to get her thoughts together. She made her way into a diner and sat down, never realizing that she had ordered anything until it was placed in front of her. The reality of the entire situation began to sink in and she felt drained by it all. Believing the priest and witnessing such an occurrence were two different things. Flo absentmindedly sipped on her coffee, trying to shake off a stupor of discontent and sadness. *Pull yourself together* she kept repeating, over and over. *This will drive you crazy if you don't put it in proper perspective. You're a reporter; just do your job here.*

After about ten minutes, she realized that she had wanted to find the preacher in much the same way the priest had found his mother, the finality of proof being self-evident. She had her collaboration, and a likely reason to continue her investigation. She thought about the ramifications of her story for a long time. Mass chaos would ensue, but sooner or later, someone would notice the obvious. Wouldn't they?

Flo realized another thing as well as she sat there; the government was responsible for the cover-up, but not the disappearances. She felt the NSA was looking for the reason as well as she was. Something or someone else was responsible for the actual disappearances; logically, what would be the benefit of the government doing away with a common street bum? She knew what the tabloids would do with this type of information, and she could see the headlines in her mind's eye and it read, *'Aliens abduct the Pope.'*

She felt the situation had not started in this country to begin with and it wouldn't end here either, troubled by a nagging question. *Why was this happening to begin with?* There was no answer, not yet anyway.

*   *   *

Anhur the Minor had not left his home, nor had he slept for more than two continuous hours in over six weeks. Ever since the sighting in the desert, he often woke awash with sweat, mumbling the words, *'You must bear witness,'* over and over again. He originally thought that he must convey the message, but his quandary became, to whom? Who would believe the babblings of an old man anyway? Who even cared to know? This indecisiveness led to lethargy as he lay abed, voluntarily confined in his room.

He knew that he had been given a vision as well as having been visited by an angel. The Islamic religion was quite specific in that regard. Angels were created from light by God and were the link between God and man. They also served as a recorder of man's deeds. Man is the responsible caretaker of earth. Yet despite knowing all this and being taught humans are superior to angels, Anhur still took the coward's path. He hated himself for his weakness and found himself on his prayer rug more often than not, praying and pleading with Allah to give him the strength to complete the task or else provide him with the strength to pass his burdens along with the aid of a honed scimitar.

Misfortune had rained down on his family ever since the sighting. His son Badru had approved the construction permit on the Coptic Cathedral and had lost his job as a result. Surprisingly, he did not blame Anhur for the loss of income. If nothing else, they had actually grown closer. His grandson Sefu had broken his arm while out playing in the streets, and Ramla fretted constantly over the child, fearing the arm might fester and have to be removed, the litany of her discontent audible even to Anhur behind closed doors.

She wailed constantly about Anhur's condition, for his presumed immobility, pleading in Allah's name for him to find the resolve to once again rise. Anhur wondered if all of this adversity was just a coincidence or a direct result of him not giving testament to what he saw.

Then, one evening, he had slept through the entire night. Once awake, he thought at last the curse of misfortune had been lifted. He made it to the breakfast table and sat in his chair with the rest of the family just as he heard a knock on the door. Anhur feared the worst as Badru rose slowly to answer it. He noticed an apprehensive look of wonder on his son's face. Before Badru could open the door, the knock became impatient. Anhur trembled. No one knocked and expected admittance at this time of day. It is much too early for visitors or for bill collectors for that matter. He heard his name being called and answered. He rose, bidding Ramla and Sefu to remain seated. As he approached the door, he found himself looking over his son's shoulder to find a partially obstructed view of two men dressed in the garb of Bedouins. The interesting part about this was that the two men were not Bedouins at all, but foreigners dressed in camouflage to protect their identities.

"Step aside Badru, I must see their faces," he whispered slowly. At that moment, it all began to make sense to him. He'd needed a full night's rest so that his mind would be clear. "Please, Badru, move out of the threshold and let these two men enter."

"But father, you have no idea who these men are," Badru warned.

"But I believe I do. Please go and tell your wife we will be having coffee in the courtyard and then meet us there," he calmly stated. His son hesitated for several seconds before he reluctantly obeyed.

Once seated at opposite ends of the stone table in the courtyard, Anhur spoke. "How long have to been looking for me?"

The elder of the two men spoke. "For quite some time, I'm afraid. Better than a month, I'd say."

Anhur noticed that the man's dialect was perfect and wondered why his speech bore no hint of an accent. "If I may ask, how did you find me?"

"A camel trader told us."

"Where are you from and who sent you?"

"Actually, I was born in Lebanon," the man replied easily. "I spent a good deal of time in France when I was a boy. I studied at the university in Cairo, so I am quite familiar with Egypt, having spent my free time during breaks traveling, getting to know the country a little better than most, I suppose. As far as who sent me, let's just say for the moment that a religious concern has brought me to your door."

Anhur, impressed by the mannerisms of the man, conceded. "I suppose I should just let you ask the questions from here on in? I know why you're here."

Badru, who sat next to him, started to object. Anhur placed his hand over his son's, muting the objection. "Badru," he said. "I must do this for the both of us." This seemed to appease his son somewhat and they continued. Anhur noticed the man remove a small tape recorder from inside his belt.

"If you don't mind, I need to tape this so that I can transcribe it later."

Anhur nodded in approval.

They were interrupted at this point as Ramla brought a platter of coffee and pastries and set them on the bench, leaving without saying a word. The elder man continued after the pause. "Were you out in the desert and did you see a flash of light while you were out there?"

"Yes, I did," Anhur stated emphatically. The man's face light up with relief as he spoke. "Start at the beginning and tell me everything you saw and did while you were there." Anhur repeated the same story he had related to his son some six weeks prior. All the while he spoke; he saw the looks of anxiety and, at times, almost disbelief in his account from the two strangers.

At the end of his account, the elder man just said one word. "Amazing!"

"Is there anything else?" Anhur asked, relieved that his burden had been finally lifted.

"This is what we needed to know," the elder man said. "As a matter of fact, it is more than we expected to hear. Would you be opposed to traveling out of Egypt to repeat this story again to a group of my associates?"

"Let me think about that," Anhur said quietly. "Look… I don't think you understand what I mean here," he tried to explain. "You're what many would consider a visionary. I really don't think you realize what that means, but once this gets out, I believe your safety might be jeopardized. There are many adverse forces of evil that would like to silence you for what you have seen. We can provide you with safe haven. I don't think you really have a choice in the matter. I'm just being polite."

Anhur had never considered the ramifications of the sighting. What moments ago felt like the aura of relief now turned to near panic once he fully understood. "What about my family? I am sure they are in jeopardy as well…what am I going to do?"

"We can make arrangements for their safety as well. As far as staying here in Asyut, I don't think that it's possible any longer. I hope you understand that."

Anhur mulled the proposition over and looked at his son for approval. "What do you think, Badru?" He saw the look of despair in his son's face and waited for his thoughts on the matter.

"What do you want me to say?" Badru finally spoke. "I agree with the man. Besides, there is nothing left here anyway. I can't find a job and feared even before this that we were no longer safe here. I just wish I hadn't been put in this position to begin with, but maybe it's for the best. You told me yourself to trust in Allah. Maybe all of this happened for a reason, Father."

"I agree," Anhur nodded. "So be it then." He turned toward the strangers. "We trust you will look after our needs."

"You have made the only correct decision possible," the man said.

CHAPTER 8

An Unlikely Union

Monsignor Giuseppe Lorenzo was summoned by the pope less than two weeks after his ordination, awed by the invitation. He made his way to the appointment having never set foot in the office of a pope; it would be an honorable occasion, considering all the venerable men who had occupied the office prior to this date.

The Pope was seated at his desk pouring over a stack of papers when he was ushered in by the secretary. The pope looked up momentarily and gestured him to be seated while he spoke briefly with the secretary, handing him another stack of papers off to his right. It somehow reminded the Monsignor of a teacher grading papers. He looked around the room with a measure of awe, taking in all the minute details. Somehow, his mentor seemed to read his mind.

"Sometimes I'm amazed as well when I look around, wondering how one strives to reach such an exulted position as this one. I have been in this room on many prior occasions, but it is an altogether different perspective from this side of the desk. I never gave it much thought until now, seeing your face painted with childish wonderment."

Giuseppe chuckled. "Is it that obvious?" he questioned.

"Quite."

The priest chuckled once more. "I'll keep that in mind the next time you invite me here. I must admit though, that it may take several visits before I'm completely comfortable with my surroundings." He noticed a change in the Pope's demeanor and sobered. "What is it that you wanted to see me about?"

"Actually, I summoned you here in reference to our last conversation, where you explained your thoughts on the possible explanations for the strange light in the desert. This is not a trivial matter to me; let me assure you of that. If my memory serves me, you left me with your idea that what you thought had occurred was somehow related to a sign or a message of some sort, if I recall. Am I not correct?"

The pope noticed Giuseppe's nod and opened the center drawer of the desk, pulling out a folder. He handed it to the priest.

"This may assist you in your research. It seems our agents have found a witness to the occurrence. From what I have read, an oracle has once more revealed some ancient scripture. This may take some time for you to read, though I must warn you in advance not to let this document out of your sight. I have only read the summary page, but you will find a dossier on the man as well as exacting detail on his experience."

The monsignor scanned the file. "This is good news and will undoubtedly make my job a little easier."

"I believe it will. Now I hate to be rude, but it has been an eventful morning once again and you must excuse me. When you have finished reading it, do what you feel is necessary to either validate this story or dismiss it, but please get back to me when you have reached your decision on the matter."

The Monsignor rose and left the room, happy to learn that his assignment had just taken on a new light, which eventually might make his search for answers easier. He took the file to his quarters and was half way through his perusal of the document when his phone rang. So engrossed in the written account, he almost let it go unanswered. When he finally caught the voice, he felt surprised. "Ms. Rinna, how good to hear from you."

"Monsignor Lorenzo, I have to talk to you," she carefully stated.

"But I believe you are. Please go ahead." He heard a sigh of frustration on the other end of the line and regretted his lighthearted banter. "Is there anything the matter?"

"Yes… I need to talk to you in person," she said.

"But that is impossible," he stammered. "You're in America, Washington D.C. if I remember."

"No, I'm not. I'm here in Rome and I have to talk to you today if I can."

"I'm afraid that's out of the question," he said, wondering at her haste. "I'm very busy today and cannot possibly break away."

"How about sometime tomorrow?" she asked.

"Possibly, but I'm afraid it probably wouldn't be until late afternoon"

"That will be fine."

He gave her instructions on where to meet and hung up wondering what was so urgent.

The following day the two met in the Piazza Navona. Giuseppe waited patiently for the reporter to arrive. When Flo hurried toward their meeting place, she noticed him admiring the Bernini sculpture of the Four Rivers nearby. She smiled in apology as she approached, nearly out of breath. "Sorry I'm late… I'd make a lame excuse for my tardiness but you probably wouldn't believe it anyway. It's one of my bad habits, I must admit." She looked at him and then at the statue. Thankfully, he was being non-judgmental and dismissed the comment entirely.

He spoke softly. "Beautiful, isn't it? My father had a picture of this sculpture in his workshop. He said it inspired him to become more adventurous in his work. 'Expand your horizons and you can create great works of art', he would say as he worked his passions into a piece of stone."

She turned toward him. "Monsignor Lorenzo, I don't remember you telling me that your father was a sculptor, or at least it has escaped my memory. I would like to see some of his work sometime."

"You just might if you ever get to Milan. He once told me that we had come here to Rome when I was younger, though I vaguely recall when. We spent days here in the city just looking at the sculptures in the piazzas. He was inspired by the masters; it showed in some of his later work."

She turned back toward the sculpture with a sense of wonderment. "Who wouldn't be? These sculptures are treasured the world over, and once you see one of these you never seem to forget it. It gets imprinted in your mind, so to speak."

"I know what you mean," he agreed. "I am wondering, if you might be hungry, there is a restaurant several blocks away that serves the best pizza in town. If you're interested, that is? The restaurants here in the piazza are touristy anyway and a bit expensive for my taste."

"Sure, lead the way." She thought he felt somewhat uncomfortable escorting her through the streets of Rome with the white collar of his betrothed around his neck. She was not about to make him feel awkward and spoke in generalities as they made their way toward the restaurant. She could tell by his voice that he became more relaxed as they walked, much to her relief.

Once seated in a booth in the far corner of the restaurant and with their order taken, Flo steered the conversation toward her final encounter with Jeremiah the prophet, the soapbox preacher. She proceeded to relate the story in exacting detail. When she got to the part of finding the remains of the body, she noticed him cringe appreciably. "Look, I don't mean to bring up bad memories, but you had to know. When I saw with my own eyes what you had told me about your mother, I couldn't help but think of the anguish you went through. This man was not even a relative of mine and I was still shocked even though I knew what to look for. I can hardly begin to think what you must have gone through." She noticed the sheen in his eyes long before he spoke.

"Trust me; I have been trying to put the whole matter in perspective ever since we last spoke."

"Let me just say that there is more to this story than even you or I know."

"What do you mean by that?" he asked.

"Look…. I don't really want to pry and you're not obligated to tell me, but the facts seem obvious. Your hunch about what happened to the pope seems to be true. From what I found out; it seems that you weren't the only one to question the strange circumstances of his death. There seems to be knowledge of the affair within the highest reaches of our own government." She saw the shocked look on his face as she related the story of the FBI to him in its entirety When she had finished, she had to ask. "You won't deny what happened to the pope then?"

"Of course not, at least not to you, anyway."

She saw a measure of sincerity as he spoke once again.

"If what you say is true, then you have placed yourself in jeopardy, and you cannot deny it. Your federal agencies, if they're the least bit concerned about keeping a cover on this thing, will be looking for you. Am I right?"

"It's a possibility," she agreed, not wanting to voice her concern for the quandary she was in.

"I suppose you're checked into one of our hotels," he mused, raising an eyebrow at her. "If so, it is only a matter of time before they track you down and silence you for your knowledge. Am I right?"

"It's a possibility."

"There is a former nunnery here, close to the Vatican, where you can find refuge from prying eyes," he offered. "No one will have the faintest idea where you are. It's an updated building with all of the amenities but none of the exposure. I would feel a lot better if you stayed there. Please accept my offer. It is as I say, a safe haven; no one will be able to track you there."

She thought about the proposition for several moments before she accepted, not sure how well she had covered her tracks and how far the government might go to find her. "I have to ask you one thing. What do you think is the reason for all of this?"

He chose his words carefully. "I have a vague idea as of yesterday, but I am not totally sure as of yet. When I return, we will talk about it in further detail. But for now, I would feel a lot better if you just took me up on my offer and let it go at that."

Flo felt the inklings of irritation stroke her ire. She felt her face flush, not about to be coddled into thinking she was some piece of rare jewelry that needed to be safely ensconced in its hiding place until its owner decided to remove it and gaze adoringly at it. "Where are you going?" she asked, trying to keep her tone even. She could tell by his reaction that he intended to initiate some sort of damage control.

"I'm headed to Cairo in the morning and hope to be back in a few days."

"What for?" she asked

"It's official church business," he stated.

"That's a staid response, considering you're a priest assigned to the Vatican." Flo once again smelled a story brewing.

"I suppose you're right," he acquiesced.

Flo was not about to be put off. "I'm going with you." He opened his mouth to object, but she hurried to explain her reasoning. "I've never been to Egypt and you said yourself that I may not be safe walking the streets of Rome alone. If you think that I'm just going to hole up in that nunnery until you get back, you're only fooling yourself. With everything that I've just explained, and in complete honesty, I might add, the least you could do is be honest with me. Look.... even before I left the States, I had a feeling the true story behind all these disappearances lies somewhere other than there. It's the reason why I once again came to Europe to begin with. Besides, your English is terrible, and you'll need an interpreter. Now come clean and tell me why you're going to Cairo."

She had cornered him once again and he seemed to have no recourse, by the sheepish look she saw on his face.

"Are you always this demanding Ms. Rinna?"

"When I need to be, I am." She gave him a stern look to bolster the thought.

"The church, as a habit, is required to check into every purported religious oddity that might occur. Take for instance the recent spate of events the press has dubbed, *'The Tears of the Virgin Mary.'* I am sure you have read about them; statues of the Virgin Mary shedding supposed tears of blood. These religious oddities have to be individually authenticated by the church. They seem to have increased radically throughout the world's churches in the last several weeks or so. Some have said this is a direct result of the passing of Pope Alexander, though I find that to be an unlikely explanation."

"How do you go about authenticating something like that? Aren't you just supposed to believe in all matters of faith without question? That's what I was taught in religion class."

"You're treading a fine line here between what the hierarchy believes are miracles and what it doles out to its faithful. The question of infallibility of the church's teachings will undoubtedly arise, which is a different matter altogether. Let me answer your first question before you go off on a tangent, You Americans are known for your compound questions that seem to have no relative connection."

"Sorry," she said once she realized she had. "Go on… the statues?"

"It's an altogether complex process," he began. "Actually, we first try and get a sample of the tears and have them analyzed to see what type of compound it is. In the past, it has been identified as paint and or chemicals of some sort. Usually there is a zealot behind these sorts of occurrences. If we think there is some sort of valid occurrence, we try also to date the sighting and take witness reports. We will also try and do a DNA analysis if we think it is real blood, a tool that has become quite effective. We also look into the reasoning behind these sorts of anomalies. One of our researchers will look for visible proof as well. What I mean by that is that they will get first hand eye witness accounts of their own as documentation."

Flo's interest piqued. "So what did you find out? Is it real blood?"

"Our initial reports indicate that it might be, though we don't have enough researchers to cover all the actual occurrences, I'm afraid."

"And the DNA reports? Is the blood the same?"

"You really never miss a beat, Ms. Rinna," the Monsignor smiled. "I guess that is why they hired you to do what you seem to know best."

"Well, the answer is…? And don't suppose once again to take me down the road of enlightenment and leave me hanging." She knew he was being evasive once again. "Look, if you and I are going to work together, we have to be brutally honest with one another. How else are we going to sort through all of these dilemmas without abject truth and clarity? Don't suppose for a moment that you are going to try and solve this problem on your own. If that were the truth of the matter, you would have already done so. Two heads are better than one and you need me here, so don't deny it. Answer the question without reservation for once!"

"Whew," the Monsignor whistled, shaking his head. "You are strong willed, if I may say so, Ms. Rinna. But, to answer your question, yes, the DNA is the same."

"So what you're telling me is the tears of blood are presumably the same in Manila as they are in Rome. How can that be? Is it possible that one person, a zealot as you say, is responsible for what, ten... twenty different occurrences? How many is it really, Monsignor?"

"There are thirty-eight cases to be precise; within the realm of the Catholic Church."

"I presume in thirty-eight different countries as well?"

"How did you know?"

"An educated guess, you and I both know that it is near impossible for one person to accomplish such a feat within a fixed moment of time. Then you say only in churches of the Roman Catholic faith, but how many more are there?"

"We can only presume at the time, but maybe hundreds of them, of all different religious denominations."

"I hope the church doesn't view this as only an *'oddity'* if I might quote you here. I would like to think this falls into the realm of something more like another intercession of some sort with a message for the masses."

"That is possible, but a bit farfetched at this point."

"Now, please talk to me about this most fortunate act of God if ever there was one, which occurs conveniently within our midst," Flo pressed. "I'll bet the church is happy about that, talk about bolstering religious attendance and throwing in a miracle or two while the world is at its wits end over unprecedented social and economic calamity. Then you have the perfect recipe for unqualified belief. You could tell them the world had flattened itself once again and they would probably believe you."

"You're being a little dramatic here, are you not, Ms. Rinna?"

She sat mum, her hands folded across her chest and looked at him.

"I see what you mean though."

"I should hope so!" she finally said. "If it's that obvious to me, what do you think... that others won't see the obvious as well?"

"I agree that it could be construed as a set up, a combined effort to convince the masses," he admitted. "But let me assure you that you are wrong about your final assumption. This has the church baffled and we have come to realize the effect of this recent development as a sign from God or, if I might be more precise, Mary, who is the matron of the planet."

She noticed that he made the sign of the cross rapidly when he had finished. "It has to be a sign and if what you say is true... look, don't question my faith as well as yours. Mine is not as strong, but it's getting there. So is that is why we're going to Cairo, to look at a statue?"

"No, not exactly, though there is one there in Cairo which we could look at if you like."

"I succinctly remember being taught about the weeping Madonna while in parochial school," Flo stated. "This is nothing new, though if my memory serves me right, there never were multiple occurrences at the same time. What did the church conclude the first time this happened?"

"They didn't."

"Don't you think that's odd?"

"Look, Ms. Rinna, we could banter back and forth on this issue all evening and still have no concrete answers." He sighed and started to rise. "There is plenty to do and little time to do it in. We must leave so that I can get you clearance for the flight tomorrow; it's a private Vatican jet and I might add that it is an early flight. I'll need your passport and I need to arrange for someone to retrieve your luggage from your hotel and set you up in the nunnery."

Flo sat for several moments and reveled at her persuasive abilities once again. Her editor was a pushover next to this priest, who she was sure, was going to deny her request to assist him. It wasn't until the last moment that she felt she had decisively convinced him that he needed her. It was nothing he said, but the way he looked at her in the end that told her what she surmised had to happen to begin with. She didn't know exactly why they were going to Cairo, but at this point, it didn't really matter. "Well then let's go there doesn't seem to be a moment to lose, is there?"

*   *   *

The flight to Cairo was uneventful; the Lear jet made the trip almost effortless. There was not much conversation between them however, which seemed surprising to her. He thumbed through a file of papers, which he seemed intent on studying in private, but did not reveal the contents of it to her. She had asked about them, but had been politely rebuffed. She noticed the papal seal on the folder, which told her that it was something of a sensitive issue to the church. Two Vatican security police escorted and traveled with them on the trip. She did find out that it was standard procedure for them to do so as bodyguards of the pope. They were less than informative when she spoke with them in regard to the true nature of the visit, and after a time had drifted off to sleep, bored with the secrecy and lack of interaction. She knew she would find out soon enough and was content with that thought.

The touchdown at the airport in Cairo startled her awake. She looked out the window to see a car waiting for them on the tarmac. In a matter of moments, the two of them were traversing the streets of Cairo. Barely awake, Flo didn't know what to expect, having never been here before. She was surprised by the view. After several minutes the Monsignor spoke.

"I must apologize if I seemed preoccupied on the plane," he explained. "I was not avoiding you on purpose, but I didn't want to tell you anything that might have compromised this situation. You can never be too sure, especially in times such as these."

She looked at him quizzically. "What on earth do you mean by that?"

"Someone might eavesdrop on our conversation."

Flo thought about what he said for several moments before replying. "I thought for sure that the Vatican would scrutinize the background of its own employees?"

"It does, but temptation is a potent enticement, and all you have to do is look at one prime example - Judas Iscariot - who sold his soul and betrayed Christ for twenty gold pieces."

"I see what you mean," she admitted, then turned to look out the window. "Where are we going anyway?" The car slowed, its horn blaring, warning a man walking with a donkey to move aside. She heard it bray as the man whipped its flank in an attempt to steer it to the side of the street.

"The church has access to accommodations here in the city. The man driving the car, Antonio, is one of our agents. Antonio used to live in Beirut and is fluent in English and French and knows the local language well. He's stationed here at the moment, keeping a watchful eye on a family you'll meet tomorrow. It's eldest member a visionary of sorts, who I must interview in order to collaborate the testimonial I read on the plane."

"A visionary? You mean like Juan Diego, who had a vision of the Virgin Mary in Mexico City, around the 1500s if I'm not mistaken?"

"I'm impressed, Ms. Rinna," the Monsignor smiled. "Actually, it was 1531 to be precise. You really know more than you reveal. In actuality, it is something similar in nature, I'm supposing. There have been many visionaries throughout church history, and the church does its best to try and authenticate these visions if at all possible. Still, at times it seems that the church drags its feet on issues such as these. Our Lady of Guadeloupe is a prime example of this. But, it's always best to err on the side of caution in these matters, for sometimes they have an immense impact. I know the church had been lax when it came to Juan Diego, but then again, change within this institution has always been that way. He's now a canonized saint, as you well know, so the situation has righted itself. It only took about 470 years to do so, but that was due to the ongoing conflict that arose over the lack of authentication to his vision, which is our sole purpose for this visit. In the interim, if you'd like to see the weeping statue of the Virgin Mary, we could do that. I would like to see it. It's always better isn't it, to witness something such as this? It defines its existence, wouldn't you say?"

Flo readily agreed to the suggestion as he translated his intent to the driver, but she was also intrigued about the vision. She noted the closed look on the Monsignor's face, but could not help it. Her all too curious nature sallied forth once again. "Tell me about the vision," she quietly pleaded. She noticed no reaction to her question for several moments as the priest seemed to be lost in deep thought. She was altogether disappointed by his delayed answer. "All in due time, Ms. Rinna."

"You have a knack for being evasive, Monsignor Lorenzo," She stated with ill-concealed disappointment. Inwardly, she fumed at the purported slight on her intelligence once again.

"So I'm told, but we all have our own faults, don't we?"

She could have run with the comment but instead decided to act as if she had not heard it. He wouldn't have paid attention anyway, she noticed, lost once again in deep thought.

The car came to an abrupt halt within a block of St. Mary's church, a Coptic Cathedral in the suburb of Zaytoun. She leaned forward to see the street completely blocked with a mass of people milling about. The driver spoke while he dialed the phone. "Can't go any further than this unless you want to risk walking, though the way you're dressed that's not a wise decision," Antonio spoke to her, his eyes on hers in the rearview mirror. "It's frowned upon to show any exposed flesh around here and that skirt of yours will get you into trouble, I can assure you of that. You'll be heckled by the men and they'll act like a pack of jackals toward you, I'm afraid. There is a back way into the cathedral which will be safer for all parties concerned."

Moments later she heard him conversing on the phone. The car reversed and they headed behind the building through a narrow alleyway. When they got to the other side, they approached a gate. Several men waited to let them inside the perimeter. The guard scanned the vehicle and signaled for the gate to be opened. They pulled up alongside the church, where Flo saw a long line of people waiting to enter. The driver turned back toward them. "You'll be escorted in through this door. It's much safer this way. I'll be waiting here for you when you get out."

Flo interpreted the statement in Italian to the Monsignor, who she figured had caught the gist of the entire conversation anyway. Once inside, they were permitted a close examination of the statue. Flo felt awestruck by what she saw, and it sobered her. The red liquid from the inside edge of the statue's eyes had coursed down Mary's face to the midpoint of the statue, where it seemed to have congealed and turned a pasty brown. She could actually smell the metallic odor of blood and had no doubt that it was. The monsignor actually stepped closer to the statue to examine it but she held back, fearful to the point of actually feeling her knees wobble underneath her. Afraid to speak, she watched the priest as he studied the icon. The sight made her nervous as she had the sudden urge to scratch her scalp in numerous locations. She bit her lower lip to stave off the urge. To take her mind off of her discomfort, she removed a pen and paper and began to take furious notes on what she saw. She stopped for several moments and began to formulate the story in her mind as to what she needed to say and began to once again to write. By the time the monsignor had completed his examination, she had written about half of the story that she intended to send to her editor. She felt the monsignor's presence next to her, momentarily distracting her, though she continued to write at a feverish pace.

`"What do think?" he asked.

His words completely broke her concentration, for she had to answer. She looked at him and spoke her voice full of serenity. "There are mysteries for which there are no words in which to describe them."

"But you seem to be doing just that."

"Hardly, I… I try and express an unbiased viewpoint, though in this case it seems to be an emotional response; emotion seems to always get us reporters in trouble." He only nodded his agreement. "Let's go, if you don't mind. I can finish this later." She placed the pad and pen back into her purse.

They started to retreat from the apse and despite her attempt to appear calm and unaffected; she knew she'd failed as he turned toward her with a frown of concern.

"You seem to be troubled by what you have seen. I can tell you seem to have lost your sense of verve."

"I believe I have, but it's not what you think it is. It's not what my eyes have seen as much as it's the reason why it's happening. That's what bothers me most."

"In both the Old and New Testaments of the Bible there were numerous signs cited within its text," the monsignor said. "It's whether or not we heed this warning that is the more important question here, don't you think?"

"Individually or as a whole" she murmured. "I know what you're driving at, but it's sometimes hard to keep an open mind to all this, especially when one bears witness, which is what I meant to say. How do you cope?"

"You're asking me how I keep the proper perspective. The only way I know how is to gather any information I can and the sum of all the parts, which will sometimes lead me, or you, to the answer you're looking for. I have to step away from time to time in order not to become too deeply involved in the details and focus on the entire picture." He paused briefly and shrugged. "When it is no longer possible to do that, I resort to meditation. That is what I do, and it is not necessarily applicable to every situation. Every individual has their own way of dealing with problems that sometimes have no real obvious answers. We can fret and stress if we choose or we can think issues out in a logical manner. Fretting is the easy way out; the second part requires some effort. Many wish to take the easy way. You're a lot smarter than you give yourself credit for. Just step away if you wish, and then turn back to it with an objective purpose and your sense of logic will ensue."

Flo felt a rush of emotions, amazed by his wisdom and insight. "If I may ask, how old are you?"

"Forty-two," he said.

"Hard to believe," she admitted.

As they drove away from the church, Flo looked back at the edifice with a profound sense of wonder. She said nothing more the rest of the trip until they got to their quarters, lost in quiet contemplation.

She was brought out of her reverie as the vehicle stopped in front of a pair of iron gates, though Flo had no idea where they were. She could see what looked like a large courtyard through the crack as the doors slowly opened.

She looked from side to side only to see what only could be described as a non-descriptive street. There were no trees or even a sidewalk. Houses were packed together, forming what looked like one continuous building from one end of the block to the other, broken only by color schemes at various intervals. Most were a sandy beige, somewhat faded by constant exposure to the sun. The faded areas took on a pink hue in the fading light. Off to one side of the gates she saw a faint reminder of an arched door, the walled-in area unevenly mortared in. On the rest of the buildings on this side of the street, the pedestrian walk- through was still intact, painted in contrasting colors to the unit's exterior.

The gates opened far enough for her to get an unobstructed view; it looked like an oasis inside. The date and fig trees that lined the sides of the courtyard hung heavily with fruit and seemed to droop over in honor of a fountain, which made up the focal point of the courtyard. Interspersed between these trees were giant palms casting intermittent shade in which stone benches and tables were placed. A slight wind rustled the leaves of the palms, interspersed light painting the pink and red bougainvillea, which hung off the courtyard walls, with a fusion of color.

"Wow!" she exclaimed. "We're staying here? Who would have ever even guessed it was so beautiful from the building's exterior." The car pulled off to the left side of the front wall, leaving her view unobstructed once again. Her mood completely altered. "I can't readily believe the church proclaims to be broke with properties such as these?"

The Monsignor balked in protest. "No offense, Ms. Rinna, but once again you wish to incite an altercation of some sort out of me with an uninformed remark such as this. I will not banter back and forth with the misinformed. Busy yourself with the task at hand, which is why we are here."

She demurely apologized for the purported slight as the driver opened her door.

The priest acknowledged the apology with a faint smile. "There's no harm done if none was intended, Ms. Rinna."

The priest exited his side of the vehicle and the driver set about familiarizing the two of them to their surroundings, pointing out various locations. "Straight ahead in the center of the back wall is a fully stocked kitchen. Please feel free to help yourself. To the left of the kitchen is the dining room; to the right is the living room. The sides of the compounds are all bedrooms." he turned to her. "Ms. Rinna your room is center left, and Monsignor Lorenzo, yours is center right. I have taken steps to ensure everything is in order. There is a maid and cooks, so if there is anything you need, just ask." He then turned to remove luggage from the trunk of the car. "Follow me Ms. Rinna," he instructed. "Monsignor Lorenzo, I'll be back for your luggage in a moment."

On the way to her room, the servant's quarters were pointed out as reference. Flo was still smarting from her lapse in etiquette with the monsignor, hoping to make amends. She thanked the agent for his assistance and he left her cases on the bed, smiled and left, closing the door behind him.

The room was sparse in decor but sufficient with a double bed and an en-suite bath, the fixtures old but sparkling clean. With the door closed, the air conditioner droned in a most peculiar way. It was neither soothing nor irritating, but she found the noise bothersome to her heightened senses. The room was sufficiently cooled enough to chill her skin. She shivered and then wondered if it was just her state of mind that had caused her to shake involuntarily. With all that had transpired already today, she wondered if her body was merely reacting to all that she had experienced. She freshened up, then with a sigh lay atop of the bed, staring up at the plaster ceiling. Before she knew it, she fell fast asleep.

She was startled awake about an hour later, clammy and irritated, having once again dreamed of her mother's face awash in blood. She had not had this dream for quite some time, but realized it had been brought on by the sight of the statue of the Virgin Mary.

When Florence was seven years old, she and one of her older brothers had accompanied their mother to the supermarket. While en-route they were involved in a traffic accident. Her mother and her brother were in the front seat, but she was strapped into a child seat on the rear passenger side of the car. Her mother, who was not strapped in, hit her forehead on the top of the steering wheel upon impact. She had been a woman short in stature, barely able to see clearly over it. Florence recalled the sight of her mother as she watched her through the rear-view mirror. She heard the moan of pain and then witnessed her panic, eyes wide with fear as she tried to see if her children had been hurt. She had been able to look over at her brother, but could not turn her head toward Florence due to her injury. The impact had split the skin of her forehead and blood streamed out of the wound in copious amounts. Florence felt helpless and all she could do at the time was cry, shocked by the sight of so much blood. Her mother died several days later from blunt force trauma. It had taken Florence years to recover. She had experienced the dream sporadically, well into her early twenties, until they finally subsided.

Flo bolted up out of bed and tried to shower away the memory, hoping the cool water might once again stifle her recurring anxiety. She dressed and quickly left the room without drying her hair. The lasting effects of the dream caused the walls of the room to close in on her and she had to get out. Once outside, she noticed the courtyard was empty. No one stirred at all. She literally felt as if she was totally alone and desperately wanted any sort of company to distract her. She ambled into the kitchen, retrieved a cola and a glass, and then looked into the dining and living rooms for any signs of life. Again, not a sound was to be heard. She made her way into the courtyard once again and sat at a table underneath one of the huge palms. A warm, intermittent and brisk breeze seemed to settle her once again and she began to finish writing the story of the Virgin while it was still fresh in her mind. She had just about finished when she heard approaching footsteps on the finely pebbled courtyard. She never bothered to look up, intent on penning the last line of the story on paper.

Monsignor Lorenzo approached the table cautiously so as not to startle the woman. He noticed that her hair was not coiffed but blew across her face, concealing its features. It was longer than he had supposed reaching almost to the table as she bent over. He failed to see how she could even write with the obstruction, but her flowing hair didn't seem to bother her. For the first time he noticed she was left-handed, as the pen in her hand was turned in what looked like a most uncomfortable position, bent back away from her wrist. Her hand skated across the page in a fluid motion and hesitant to bother her, he almost turned to walk away. He was concerned about what had happened earlier and wanted to make amends. He straddled the stone seat opposite of her and said nothing, waiting for her to finish. He noticed the glass of cola was untouched and had warmed, for there was no evidence of moisture either on the glass or the can itself. He almost rose to get her a fresh one when she finally looked up.

"I must apologize for my rude behavior this afternoon," he said quickly before she could speak. "All I can say is that I was a bit out of sorts and under a lot of pressure, as you will soon find out."

"It is I who should apologize," she said. "The comment was uncalled for and I hope you will forgive me. It was tactless and rude." She brushed her hair away from her face with one hand, holding onto the loose paper with the other. "We Jersey girls are sometimes boisterous with not only our mannerisms but our comments as well. We run off at the mouth at times, but it's just our way of expressing ourselves and nothing more. I'm sure you probably don't understand that, but if you lived there for some time, you'd see what I mean. Trust me, not too many people are able to get the upper hand or push us around, but when they do it becomes admirable, if you know what I mean?"

He chuckled at her honesty. "You're something someone like me takes some time getting used to. I believe it's probably an admirable characteristic in some respects, and at least you're not afraid to speak your mind." For the first time he truly noticed the beauty of her face. She wore no make-up to highlight her facial features and the natural radiance of her features was unmasked. He felt suddenly uncomfortable and tried to disguise it. "Back in Rome, I had my reservations about asking you along. But you were right about me in several respects. My English isn't all that good, as you have noticed, and I am in dire need of concise translation. You also made another valid point when you said two heads are better than one. In this case, however, it is your ability to question my thoughts and ideas that seems to have made the most sense. We -and I do mean you and I - hopefully might be able to solve this riddle if we can work together. There's a lot at stake here and the only reason I have not even informed you earlier is I thought that I could use an unbiased interpretation of the facts as I know them. I felt that telling you anything in advance might pollute your thoughts... and I need that perspective." She reached out to touch his hand. He felt her light touch on the back of his hand as she spoke, and her hair had spilled back over her face in the process.

"I'll do whatever you need me to do, for I can see that you're troubled by what you know. I can see it in your face at this very moment. I also want to thank you for the compliment, and I expect no more. Whatever it is we are about to embark upon, trust me... I won't let you down, I... I need you to know that."

He felt her touch dissipate, as did his fears of her fealty. "Good," he nodded. "We have made arrangements to have the visionary come here tomorrow instead of us traveling across Cairo to talk to him. Antoine will get him in the morning and bring him here around ten. In the meantime, enough talk. I'm hungry and was hoping you might join me?"

"Sure," she said, and began to gather up her papers.

"Would you like me to wire that story for you?" he asked. "I'm sure Antoine could do that if I asked."

"That would be appreciated," she said.

He rose from the bench and waited as she wrote the address on a cover page, still amazed by the agility of her left hand.

"My editor will certainly be surprised," she said, smiling. "I haven't talked to him for about four days now, ever since I left him instructions on where to find the remains of Jeremiah the prophet for verification of my story."

She told him that she hadn't spoken to any of her friends eitherl, fearful that they might get implicated in the search for her. She was sure the NSA was still trying to track her down to question her or silence her, she was not sure which. The only plausible recourse she had was to expose the story and the NSA. The only reason she had not really started to write that column yet, she said, was because she was not sure where the story would take her.

The next morning at a quarter to ten, the gates to the courtyard began to open. Monsignor Lorenzo and Flo had just finished their breakfast and were sipping Turkish coffee, casually bantering back and forth about any subject that came to mind. Flo could see in the priest's face that he had not slept much the night before, but dared not ask why. She figured if nothing else the Turkish coffee would wake him, for you could stand a spoon in the dense liquid. It was so strong that she had to add sugar in heaps to mask the acidic and bitterly potent taste. Her nerves tingled as a result.

When the car door opened, Flo saw the man the priest identified as Anhur the minor slowly extract himself out of the rear of the vehicle. He slowly shuffled toward them, Antoine at his side, as if he was there to support him if he happened to fall. Flo was instantly conscious of his facial features. They appeared hewn from grainy stone, his beard the prominent feature of his face, snow white and unkempt. However, it was his eyes that caught her attention and mesmerized her at the same instant. She wished she could take him aside and talk to him privately, for he exuded wisdom, or at least that was her initial impression of him as they waited to be introduced. She knew her wish would not be fulfilled. She had been forewarned of custom and knew that unless he directly addressed her, she could say nothing to him. She was mindful of that as they were introduced. He merely acknowledged her presence with a slight bow of the head and nothing more.

They made their way into the living room and closed the door for privacy. One of the living room tables had been set up for refreshments which surprised Flo, who had witnessed an empty table only moments before. There had been some discussion earlier as to the effectiveness of language barriers; they were so seated so the nothing would be lost in interpretation as Antoine explained the predicament of translation to their aged guest. He explained that the monsignor would ask questions in Italian, and Flo would translate them into English. Antoine would translate the English into Anhur's language, and vice versa. Flo knew that this meeting would last for some time because of the circumstances. She waited for her cue from Monsignor Lorenzo. If he wanted to ask a question directly to Antoine, Flo was there if there was anything lost in the English translation, requesting her services.

She noticed the priest had removed a sheaf of papers from the briefcase he had carried at his side. He asked Anhur to begin his story at the start, without leaving out any of the detail. Though she understood nothing the man said in Arabic she was impressed by his body language. His hands periodically rose and fell and his expression of thought was evident in his face. The translation of the three languages did not seem to cause much confusion at this point, but they did take an inordinate amount of time. Anhur was not interrupted by the priest until he got to the point where he described his encampment for the night in the desert. Antoine translated as best he could, and Flo listened with rapt attention.

"Could you find this spot once again if you had to?" the priest asked him.

"I think so," Anhur replied.

"Now this is of utmost importance," Monsignor said slowly. "Please describe in detail when you first saw the light and what you originally thought it was."

"I really didn't know what it was at first; I thought it was a shooting star or a meteorite of some sort. When you have spent as much time in the desert as I have, you begin to ignore these common occurrences. Shooting stars and meteorites are commonplace in the desert, as there is no artificial light to obscure them. There were days out in the desert when I could see shooting stars streak across the entire heavens. On rare occasions, I would see more than one."

"What changed your mind about your initial assessment?"

"Probably the fact that it seemed headed straight for me," Anhur shrugged. "I became scared I guess, and there was nowhere to hide out in the open desert like that. When my camel spooked, I knew the light was headed right for me."

"When you first noticed it and this is critically important, did you notice it change color in any way?"

"No," Anhur said.

Flo watched a wave of relief cross over the priest's face.

"Describe to the best of your ability the color that you saw. Had you ever seen this type of color before?"

Flo did not fully recognize the question's importance.

"Blue-white," Anhur stated, nodding. "And it was intensely bright in nature. It cast a blue aura over the desert floor and it hurt my eyes. I remember at first that I began to blink almost continuously until my eyes adjusted. I have never in my eighty or so years ever seen anything like it in the desert before."

"Could you identify the color once again if you saw it?"

"I believe so, it's hard to forget," Anhur said.

"Once your eyes had adjusted to the blue light, was it then that you were able to see down into the valley?"

"Yes, but I would have never seen the armies had the camel not tried to rear up and run. I had to hold it down.'

Armies? Flo thought. What armies? Though she wanted to break in on the conversation at this point, she dared not. Her mind raced. She noticed the monsignor staring at her because of her apparent lapse. He repeated the question. "Describe what you thought you saw in detail once again if you can. I am especially interested in any description you might have about any of the individual soldiers on either side of the battlefield."

Flo's mind swam as she translated the question.

Anhur gave concise detail of the battlefield and its combatants.

"Is that what you saw or what you thought you saw?" the monsignor persisted. "Are you sure? I have to know."

She noticed ire in Anhur's face when the question was translated and he answered once again. "It is not what I thought I saw but what I did see," he rumbled. "Let us make this perfectly clear here, though my vision was obscured by the dispersed light on the far side of the field, I clearly saw my side of the fight... in vivid detail I might add!"

Flo translated the priest's apologies for his slight of character and asked if the man might continue, which he did.

"The best way to describe this battle would be opposing colors of black and white, except that it was bathed in iridescent blue."

"Just black and white?" the priest asked.

"No, they were the predominant colors, but there were other colors as well, but they were almost muted by the blue light."

"Did you actually see the opposing sides in battle or were they just in a state of confrontation?"

"An actual battle was taking place in the depths of the valley, from what I saw."

"Who seemed to be winning?"

"The dark side, or so I thought when I witnessed them engaged in battle. There were a lot more white bodies on the desert floor than black and there seemed to be more black soldiers than white."

Flo noticed that Anhur had become completely somber.

"Why had you not mentioned this before when Antoine asked?" the priest asked.

"He never asked," Anhur replied. "He just recorded what I could remember is all. I seem to be able to remember more, now that you ask. I have no reason to hide what I truthfully saw."

"When did the angel speak to you?" the priest asked. "It was an angel, wasn't it?"

Flo reeled at the question and could hardly translate at this point. She felt sure her ears had just deceived her. She looked at the priest for several moments before he nodded for her to go ahead. She turned to Antoine and translated the question.

"It is the most beautiful thing I have ever seen in my life; I can tell you that, and it was also the ugliest thing I have ever encountered. I know that sounds contradictive but it is the only way I know to describe it. Nothing will and has ever compared to it in any way. It was not until the blue light started to fade that I saw it anyway. When it first appeared in the faded light, it completely startled me. Its eyes were another thing I remember vividly... they looked like hollowed-out sockets of dark light. It looked to me as if I had proffered my hand, I could have swept it through the angel without obstruction."

Flo bit on her lip hard enough to draw blood in an effort to keep from reeling. Her mind then seemed to wander, trying to block out the truth. Objectivity was a must in this situation, she told herself, and bore down on her lip once again and licked the blood away with her tongue.

"Anhur, do you believe in angels as the Koran so states?"

"Yes, but not as you think," Anhur replied. "We believe that angels were put on earth to serve man. An angel according to Mohammed is ranked below man."

Flo saw the priest nod his head in agreement before he spoke again. "How did the angel speak to you? With its lips or did it just somehow transmit the message?"

"I believe it was transmitted, now that you mentioned it. I can't recall ever seeing its lips move."

"What was your reaction to this image as it conveyed this message?"

"I hate to admit it, but I was scared to death. I turned away from the angel as it started to speak. I would have run but I was holding the camel down at the time."

"Repeat to me once again exactly what the angel said, word for word. This is extremely important."

Flo noticed the priest had highlighted part of the page he was looking at. She was sure now that he referred to Anhur's original transcript of accounts.

"You have witnessed the truth and must tell all others," Anhur said in a deflated voice. Flo could see him visibly tire.

"But there seems to be a discrepancy in this account. Before, you said, *'You have witnessed this and must tell all others.'* Which is it?"

"You have witnessed the truth," Anhur repeated.

Flo bit her lip once again as she heard the statement corrected. She saw the fixation in the priest's face, a dour sense of foreboding is what it looked like to her.

"What did the soldiers look like, to the best of your knowledge? The ones that you could see, that is?"

"They had human characteristics; a head and hands and feet, though it is possible that it was only a shadow form of the human shape that I saw."

"Did you happen to see any animals or the like?"

"Oh yes I did, there was a form of some sort across the valley that was not human by any means, it was much too large to be human," Anhur explained, his gestures animated. "It was larger than a horse or a camel, but what it was, was not that clear to me. On my side of the field, I could clearly see horses of some sort. The riders looked like angels as well."

Flo could hear the priest take a deep breath and suddenly exhale. She was sure it was his way of settling his conscious mind.

"At any time did you hear any noise from the battle?'

"No," Anhur said faintly.

Flo saw the man's lids grow heavy and his chin wobbled toward his chest. The interview had sapped his energy. She looked at her watch and was surprised to see that three hours had passed already.

"Did you hear anything at all, music or the like, horns or proclamations?"

She asked the question, but Antoine literally had to force the answer out of the exhausted Anhur, whose reply was slurred and almost incoherent.

"Not that I can recall right now."

Flo finally spoke to the priest, the first time she even had tried to interject her feelings into the interview. "He needs to lie down," she said. "You know as well as I do that fatigue can slant one's memory. Let him be, and we can continue at some other point." She saw the priest give her a troubled look but he nodded in agreement.

"Maybe we can continue after dinner, if that is all right with Anhur?" he asked.

She translated the request and got a nod of approval from the visionary, who was then quietly escorted out of the room by the agent. Flo finally had a chance to speak freely and she took advantage of it. "Is he telling the truth? I find the story hard to believe."

"I don't know for sure yet."

"Is he describing what I think he is?" she said with doubt.

"It seems to be to be, I mean, I'm not quite sure yet, but that's why we're here."

She noticed that he shook his head in wonder. "Monsignor Lorenzo, have you ever run across anything like this before?"

"No."

"What are your instincts telling you? Do you believe the man?"

"I'm thinking that he may be telling the truth," he sighed, sweeping a hand over his eyes. "You heard him. What do you think?"

"I have my doubts, but if this is a true story…" She shook her head. "Look, this is scaring the shit out of me-- sorry - true or otherwise. Why now? And for what reason?" She saw that he was in no condition to answer either, for his eye lids had grown heavy and his face pallid. Flo got up and looked down at the priest. "It might be a wise idea if you took a nap too, Monsignor Lorenzo."

"I think I will," he said. With a heavy sigh, he got up and left the room.

Flo watched him leave, shoulders slumped and his body arched over like a fraught laborer. She felt sorry for the man, knowing just part of the burden he presumably had been carrying around. She had a million questions to ask but they would have to wait for another time. Flo went to her room and jotted down some of the essential points of the interview, still numb from the revelation.

*   *   *

Several hours later, Flo was again seated at the table in the courtyard, writing. She looked up when she heard a door open. She saw the monsignor crossing the courtyard in her direction and rose to get him some coffee. She had left her notes on the table and found him reading them upon her return.

"Your attention to detail is quite commendable," he complimented. "But you know I can't permit you to publish this interview. Not yet, anyway. I am sure once the facts are verified and I get permission from the pope, maybe you might be allowed to send this off."

Flo watched him intently for several seconds as he set the papers back on the table. "I know; it's just a habit I have of writing while everything is fresh in my memory." She sat down and passed a cup of coffee in his direction. "I have a question to ask which you did not cover during the interview." He reached for the coffee, took a sip and grimaced, then nodded toward her. "Is it possible that Anhur was hallucinating? I read somewhere that the intense heat from the desert can sometimes overheat the brain, creating acute distress of the sort that can bring on delirious images."

"Good point," the priest agreed. "I'll ask when we resume."

"I was thinking a man of his age is also probably prone to memory lapses. Is it possible that he's just substituting something in his mind, something maybe that he may have read?"

"I don't think so," the priest shook his head. "He seems to have all of his faculties intact. He may have read something similar to this in the Koran, which I will look up, but I doubt that it is in there. But this is not a coincidence, from what he has said. This frankly resembles the first verse of the first chapter of Mark in the New Testament."

She hung on his words. "So, are you going to make me look it up, or are you going to be nice enough to tell me?"

He smiled. "*Behold I send my angel before your face who shall prepare the way before you. A voice of one crying in the desert, Prepare the way of the lord; make straight his paths.*"

"Amazing!" she said. "It sure sounds like an accurate description of events to me. It's either one of two things...either he has read the New Testament or he has truly seen what has been written, what, two thousand years ago?"

"My thoughts exactly," Giuseppe agreed. "What else do you think I should ask him that I might have missed?"

"Nothing that I can think of offhand, though I have a question to ask of you which I hope you can answer. I thought that all angels had wings, but in Anhur's description, they were either omitted or did not exist."

"No one really knows for sure if angels do have wings," the priest answered. "There have been various references in books that seem to lean toward that as a viable description. Though I might add, there was supposedly a depiction of a winged being on the cover of the arc of the covenant. Most times, angels are never described fully in religious text. The word itself is a derivative of the Greek word *Angelos,* which is the same or similar to the Hebrew word *Mal'akh,* which means messenger."

"Messenger… humm… do you think that a message such as this might also be impressed into dreams? I'm not looking at the religious context here, just what you personally think. Let me clarify that… I know there are numerous references in the Bible to visions or dreams and an entire book if I recall, in the New Testament. I just wonder if he may have fallen asleep and when he woke, he just remembered the dream."

"That's another good point," the priest acknowledged. "I will ask him that as well."

Flo noticed him rubbing his chin with the cleft of his hand as he receded deep in thought. She wanted to get up and take a walk. All of this information was making her despondent once again, for obvious reasons, and she began to play with her hair, spinning it around her index finger in an effort to quell her rising anxiety. She finally decided to get up when his stupor vanished.

"There's one other thing before you leave," he said slowly. "I intend to go with Anhur and Antoine into the desert to see if he can find the exact same spot that this supposedly occurred. It's a requirement that I do so. I also hope that revisiting the location might further jar Anhur's memory. I am wondering if you want to come along. We have rented a four-wheel drive land cruiser. They sometimes jostle you about, so be forewarned it's going to be a very rough ride. It's your choice; you don't have to come if you don't want to."

"That might be fun," she said elusively, as she silently wondered if she was being intentionally omitted from the investigation. "Though renting a dune buggy might be even better," she suggested. At his look of puzzlement, she explained. "You know… an open body frame with a souped-up Volkswagen engine in back, big balloon tires, roll bar, no roof… that's what we use in the States to traverse shifting sands and rough terrain." She laughed, knowing the priest didn't have a clue what she was even talking about. She could tell by the confused look on his face as she began to walk away.

After dinner, there was a short meeting once again, and Monsignor Lorenzo asked the questions that he and Flo had discussed. They ascertained several things. Anhur reiterated that he was tired but had not fallen asleep, nor had he slept much at all after the vision. Did he think he was overheated by the sun's exposure? He scoffed at the thought, telling them he knew the difference after all his years in the desert. The suggestion that he had read the New Testament book of Mark was something that the Monsignor handled well, yet still drew the man's ire. He quoted the Koran in this case, where no man of faith other than a Muslim could pass judgment upon him. He did concede that he was well aware of the religious tome, but had not read its pages. It was only word of mouth that had made him somewhat familiar with some of its passages. The priest convinced him to assist them in their investigation of his story and he agreed to go in the morning with them once again, sure in his mind that he knew exactly where all this had occurred so that the truth of the matter might be substantiated once and for all.

The next morning Flo was startled awake by a knock on the door. She was told through the door that they were leaving in ten minutes, and if she wanted to come along, she had better hurry. She looked at her watch and groaned. It wasn't yet five. She bolted out of bed and pulled back her hair, tying it with a piece of red cloth so that her hair fell to the sides of her head and landed on her shoulders. She was glad she'd had the presence of mind to lay out her clothes the night before. She quickly dressed and threw her toiletries into her purse. She gazed into the mirror as she brushed her teeth and saw the reflection of a worn woman. She tried to rub the fatigue lines from around her eyes in an effort to look somewhat presentable, then heard the eager knock once again and called out. "Just a minute, I'm coming!"

When she finally opened the door, it wasn't quite daybreak, an azure haze glowed just over the wall of the courtyard and wondered why the rush. She could barely make out three forms standing by the car. Being late was one thing, but being rushed was another. She heard Antoine's voice from across the way.

"Yallah, Yallah!"

She could almost guess what it meant in Arabic. When she got to the car, she saw the snicker on Anhur's face, as he seemed to enjoy seeing her run. Antoine and Anhur laughed at her apparent distress, though Monsignor Lorenzo said nothing, nor was there any sign of contempt on his face. He handed her a cup of coffee, appearing as blurry-eyed as she felt.

"What's the hurry?" she asked. "It's not even light yet." She said trying to ignore her rising anger at the two men's continued laughter.

"We have to drive to the airport, which is across town, if you remember. There's a private plane reserved to take us to Asyut. From there we travel into the desert by land rover. By the time we get where we need to be, it will be the heat of the day. It gets scorching hot in the Sahara," he warned. "I checked and it will be close to 46 degrees today, Ms. Rinna."

"Can you wait a moment longer while I get my jacket?" she asked, turning to hurry back to her room.

The priest began to chuckle, which started the two other men doing the same once again. "That's Celsius, not Fahrenheit, Ms. Rinna, around about … close to 120 degrees as you Americans read it. I doubt you will need that jacket after all."

Flo felt foolish for the lapse and climbed into the back of the car without saying another word. The priest sat beside her. She nudged his arm once he settled in. "It's much closer to 115 than 120," she impishly corrected him. "Your calculations were a bit off."

"I figured you had to get the last word in, so I fudged the results for your benefit," he smiled in return.

When she next looked over after pondering his retort, he was already nodding off. The trip to the airport was uneventful, nothing but vendors setting up shop en route. The streets were barren of pedestrians this early. When they pulled into the airport, the car stopped at an old hanger. They all got out, and Antoine retrieved some gear from the trunk and led the way. An old plane parked in front, which Flo thought had seen better days. The shell of the plane looked as if it had been sandblasted. She looked around for the pilot but no one seemed to be milling about. "Who's flying this thing?" The question hung in the air for some time as she watched Antoine load their gear into the plane.

"I am!" Antoine finally remarked.

"Are you qualified?" Flo asked, not entirely tongue in cheek. "Because I have my doubts about this plane and its ability to fly, if you ask me, it should have been scrapped years ago."

"It's a Beechcraft," Antoine grinned. "It looks a bit rough I must admit, but it's dependable."

She let out an indiscernible objection and looked toward the monsignor for support. He shrugged her comment off without hesitation.

"I'm sure it's perfectly safe, Ms. Rinna," he soothed. "Besides, I am sure Antoine here is eminently qualified."

She felt the heat begin to rise off of the tarmac as the sun began to wash over the plane and knew her objections had fallen on deaf ears once again. "How do you get into this contraption anyway?" she dejectedly asked Antoine. He chuckled once again at her predicament and she was definitely beginning to dislike the man for his condescending attitude. She was pissed now, and saw the step on the edge of the wing and mounted it without assistance. She turned and rebelliously glared at him while the rest of them followed her into the cramped interior of the plane.

When she was seated, the sun's heat on the skin of the plane had already turned the cabin compartment into an oven. With the doors closed, she smelled Anhur's overpowering scent. She reached into her purse and removed her perfume, then spritzed a plume into the air in an effort to mask the smell. The spray encompassed the small compartment and Antoine looked back at her.

"Nice, " he commented. "What is it, anyway?"

He was trying to make amends for his rude behavior, so she hesitantly decided to answer him only after the priest looked her way. "It's apropos for our little jaunt today," she said smugly. "It's called Safari!" Antoine chuckled at her double entendre as the engine roared to life, but his retort was lost in the roar of the engines. Flo could have cared less what he had said anyway, she was sure it wasn't anything more than a cutting remark.

After the plane took off, it followed the Nile River toward their destination. Out of Flo's side of the plane the expanse of the twisting river looked inviting. It looked as if there was nothing but desert on either side of the river. Occasionally, she spied a small town nestled among its banks, which at least provided her with a visual diversion. As they started to descend into Asyut, the view of the approaching city became clear. It was larger than she thought it to be. As they banked across the Nile and back, she plainly saw the residents in the streets. It looked as if the city had been strategically located, with rising cliffs affording protection to the city below. She was sure that on occasion the winds that strafed the desert had carried sand with it, etching the sandstone cliffs into the serrated shapes she saw from the air. The plane banked once again and then landed rather roughly on the runway, the wheels skipping and howling as the wings oscillated from tip to tip. She briefly saw the windsock next to the tower gyrating in the stiff breeze and had her answer for the rough landing. It was not as if she wasn't going to take advantage of the moment before it passed. "Nice landing, Antoine! We'll have to try that again sometime," she sarcastically stated. She only heard a mumbled reply as the plane rolled to a stop.

After loading the gear into the land rover, stopping for breakfast and provisions, then headed out into the desert. They traveled parallel to the cliffs above Asyut for some time before turning west, heading into the desert. Flo noticed a discerning look on the priest's face. The two of them sat in the back seat as Anhur instructed Antoine, pointing as they drove, his face glued to the windshield.

"A penny for your thoughts?" she asked, turning to the priest.

"What does that mean?"

She reworded the statement, knowing the man had no idea, once again, what she had meant. She suddenly felt tired of trying to explain her American colloquialisms to the Italian. "You seem worried," she said simply. "What's on your mind, Monsignor?"

"Well, many things actually, but what concerns me the most is what we'll do if Anhur cannot find the exact spot of this occurrence."

"You have to trust Anhur on that point. He seems to have spent his life out here, so I'm sure he knows where he's going."

"I hope you are right," he said.

"I personally don't believe or want to believe all of this for some reason. Are you sure you know what's going on here?"

"I think I do. I believe the lambs are being led to the slaughter!" he said, chuckling nervously at his intended pun.

Flo was not amused but interpreted the sidebar remark. "I realize, Monsignor, that you're trying to focus on the entire picture, but you only have part of canvas to work with here. The rest is covered up; let it unfold before you before you rush to conclusions on what it looks like. For all we know, like I said earlier, he may have been dreaming and is afraid to admit it."

"What scares me is if he's telling the truth," the monsignor admitted. "I liked it better when you thought he was delusional. The whole episode was easier to dismiss that way."

"Monsignor, let's change the subject," she suggested. "If you don't, it will consume you before you know it."

He reluctantly agreed. She thought to tell him her life story to distract him while they traveled deeper into the Sahara. "My grandparents moved to the United States when my father was a little boy. They disembarked the ship on Ellis Island, which was a staging area for new immigrants. He never really moved far from that spot. He settled in Elizabeth, New Jersey, which was just a stone's throw from Staten Island, New York. You are familiar with the location of New York City, are you not?" He nodded. "The reason he moved to Elizabeth at the time was the availability of jobs and the ethnic Italian community which strived there. He got a job as a longshoreman unloading cargo ships and became involved in local politics within the Italian sphere of influence. He ran unsuccessfully for city council three times and my grandfather says the only reason he never won was not that he wasn't well liked, though my father had a slightly different interpretation of his political aspirations. My father always chidingly says it was his, 'not so good-a English,' that cost him the elections, sort of like yours."

The priest began to laugh at his own shortcomings, which was good therapy. She continued. "He never got elected, but spent the rest of his life there in Elizabeth, content to raise his three sons with a bit more understanding of more than just the language. My father is the oldest of the three brothers and the only one who is still alive. He always referred to his upbringing as being 'ruled by the rod,' but he would always smile after he said it so you know he got away with a lot more than he ever led us to believe." She smiled at the memory. "Anyway, after my dad finished high school, my grandfather got him a job unloading cargo ships. He ended up marrying a girl he met at a church social. My grandfather instantly approved of the union, for unbeknownst to my father; he had dealings with *her* father in the past and knew him to be honest and hard working. They were a stout and devout Italian immigrant family that was not unlike our own. My two older siblings were born in Elizabeth, but I was not. I was born in the town of Salem, New Jersey, which is southeast of Philadelphia. I was the baby of the family if you will, when my mother started on her change of life."

She glanced at the monsignor. He appeared to be listening, so she continued, hoping to keep his mind from wandering to other fears. Besides, the talking eased her lingering nervousness.

"The reason we moved to Salem was that the city of Elizabeth began to fall on hard times, the economy soured and the city started to erode as a result. My dad, who was upset by the loss of core values, rising crime rates and apathy in the city, realized that the area was becoming a risky place in which to raise his family. Couple that with the fact that the shipping industry had stagnated, when the economy soured. He was used to working long hours at the docks, and when they cut his hours in half, he found life in the city to be too expensive and decided to pack up and move to Salem. Why they chose Salem, I'll never know. I believe it was the rural charm that lured them there, at least that's what my father said." She shrugged. "My mother has her own version of the story saying, *it's was like tossing a coin into murky waters,* she'd say, *'you never knew where it's going to land because you couldn't see it'* I believe there was an analogy in the quote, though I never fully understood it. Then again, you would have to know my mother to really understand her approach to logic. I, myself believe she just hated change of any sort and it was her way of expressing it.

"Anyway, five years after our family moved there I was born. I am the first and only girl the family has ever had to that point." Flo stopped momentarily, thrilled that her Italian was progressing so well. The flow of the language had returned to her, for her hands were flying back and forth emphasizing connotations like a maestro leads an orchestra. "My grandmother was still alive at the time of my birth, and she chastised my mother severely when she saw me for the first time, telling my mother, *'There was not enough spice in the meatballs.'* Now you take that any way you want; the implication is the same. For the longest time I never knew if my grandmother was talking about my father's manhood or my mother's cooking."

Flo had the priest in stitches over that one, and tears of hilarity streamed down his cheeks in the process. She could not help herself either as she laughed with him. It was a true story she always liked to repeat.

"Stop, already," he gasped.

I can't, we're just getting started here." He laughed once again at the story. She waited for him to settle before she began again. "Well... you had to know my grandmother; she could be wicked at times. Now where was I? So, by the time I was born, my mother had had enough raising two boys and had thrown all the old rules and regulations pertaining to child-rearing out the window and pretty much let me do as I pleased. My father, who was thrilled about having a daughter, not only guarded over me but spoiled me rotten," she admitted. "I pretty much got anything a girl could ask for, within the limits of the family budget that is."

"I can relate to that!" he said. "All Italian women are spoiled, if you ask me."

"Well, it's just because we were enabled to do so," she replied. "So, I grew up in a small town, and it wasn't that I didn't enjoy it at the time, it's just that I knew there was more of life that I wanted than a small town could provide. I took up writing at the urging of my journalism teacher, which was one of my favorite classes in high school. My English teacher assisted in my choice, and she urged me on because of my ability to write. I entered college and joined a sorority and my sorority sisters aided me almost as much as my drive to succeed did. Being as I had no sisters at home, I found the experience to be quite refreshing. I have made many friendships that have endured to this day. I still attend our semi-annual meetings whenever I'm in town." She turned to him and winked. "It's also an excellent networking tool that I use whenever the need arises. It's reciprocal as well; I do what I can to help them within my sphere of influence."

"I can believe that."

Suddenly, the Land Rover slowed to a stop. She heard Anhur's excited voice, which was translated.

"He thinks it's here, Monsignor," she told him. "He says he must get out and look around, but he's sure it's nearby, this is where the valley starts."

"Ask him how he knows for sure it is here," the priest queried.

The front passenger door opened and Flo immediately grew clammy as the stifling hot desert air entered the car. She watched as Anhur began to walk away, talking loudly as he did. He was quite a distance away before she thought to ask Antoine what he had said.

"He says there is a large stone which protrudes out of the sand somewhere near the rim of the valley and when he finds it, he can prove this was the site because he buried something near its base."

Flo and the priest exchanged a glance before they got out to aid in the search. "I thought he was making it all up, that the sun had addled him, but now I believe him somehow," she said as the Monsignor's mood seemed to once again darken.

"We better go and help him find the rock," he replied, his voice full of doubt. "Take your hat and some water. I hope we find it before were scorched alive."

By the time they left the vehicle and got ready to look for the stone, Monsignor Lorenzo noticed that Anhur was so far away he was barely visible.

"Antoine, I think you had better follow him in the car," he said, still looking his way so as not to lose sight of the fading figure. The heat off the sand rose in waves, distorting the man's figure even more. "If you find the stone he seeks, come and get us. We will follow the rim of the valley in the opposite direction."

Flo translated his wishes and he watched the agent get back in the car and slowly drive off. He turned to Flo and noticed she had taken the red headband out of her hair, unfolded it and covered her head with it. She was having difficulty fitting her hat atop her head. "If you wet it down with some water, I guarantee the hat will fit better and you'll be cooler as a result." He helped her do just that and after she adjusted her sunglasses, they started walking.

"I'll bet I must be a sight?"

He looked over and smiled briefly. "You look a bit different from what I'm used to, but I'm sure it doesn't matter out here as long as it works."

They had walked for quite a distance before either one of them spoke, Monsignor Lorenzo content to listen to the faint wind as it passed out of the valley. There really was nothing to see except for the ripples of sand on the desert floor. The sun was too intense to look up for any length of time and he used the contour of the valley edge as a guide.

"I have a question to ask, if you don't mind talking?" she asked.

He nodded.

"If we do find the rock, and there is something buried there which proves he was here, how are you going to validate his vision other than take his word for it?"

"It's a good question, and I don't know that we can." He noticed her looking at him.

"We? What do you mean by that?"

"I meant to say the church."

"I get a sneaking suspicion by your tone that the church has known about this for quite some time," she muttered.

"Not just the church I'm afraid to say, but also the scientific community. They originally asked us to look into this to see if there was some sort of religious significance to the light that Anhur saw. It seems that they saw it first from space, beaming here in the desert. We were asked to reference the light. I have been researching its implications for quite some time."

"How long have you known?" she exclaimed.

"Six weeks," he replied. They continued to walk as the stillness of the desert closed in on them once again. Giuseppe looked over on occasion and saw her mulling something over in her mind. He was afraid to ask her what she was thinking about. After some time, she spoke.

"If the light could be replicated somehow it might... and I mean.... it just might be possible that anyone could be able to see what Anhur had seen. Does that seem plausible to you?"

"I had never even given that a thought. What a brilliant idea!" he said, looking at her with awe.

"If it is something that could be done, would it not validate the story?"

"Of course it would, it would be proof positive, though, like you, I'm not sure it could be replicated. Only a scientist would know for sure. I will look into the matter when we get back to Rome."

They once again walked in silence for some time. Giuseppe was impressed by the woman's insight into solving a problem that he had spent the last couple of days wondering about. "Ms. Rinna, I have a question to ask, but it's rather personal in nature and you really don't have to answer me if you'd rather not. I was wondering, as seemly intelligent as you are and with so much to offer, why is it that you have never married?"

She looked over at him for several moments as if scrutinizing his request. He thought that she would not reply, for she looked away once again before she spoke in a measured voice.

"I realize this may seem odd to you, and it's not as if I have never been asked. I have been in what you might term the state of love several times in my life," she answered slowly. "Still, in every case an act of betrayal stunned my ability to make the commitment like you have. You, as far as I can tell, have totally committed yourself to the church and everything it stands for. I can tell by not only your attitude, but the zeal in which you attack any task that is asked of you. I believe if you were asked to lay down your life for these beliefs, you would do so without question. With that in mind, I have done so also. I will tell you this though, true love is an evasive thing for many people; unlike you; I have hardened myself when it comes to total commitment only because I have been seared in the past. I will tell you this, Monsignor, I am wary of true commitment only because I believe it might not be an achievable goal for me. Have I ruled out the possibility? No, I haven't, but there are no such things as shining knights and chivalry. I'm past that illusionary part on my life, and as you said to me earlier, we all have faults, don't we?"

"I suppose we do," he agreed. "There is no such thing as perfection when it comes to human frailties," he said.

"I would like to add one thing if I might, which I feel is necessary in order for you to understand a bit more about me. Happiness is a state of mind that is not necessarily achieved through someone else. It comes from within ourselves, and can never be interjected by anyone or anything. I know plenty of couples who thought just that. Thinking rather foolishly; that when they married, they would achieve true bliss. You know as well as I that this is not the case. There are many singles that are in a continual state of elation, and it's not because they are influenced by anyone else. That is the fallacy of uniting with someone who strives to achieve what some people's mantras never truly have. They end up dragging you into their web of sorrow. Stifling your existence to the point where you are essentially not happy either and this is sometimes a slow and unconscious decline." She shrugged. "If the affected party is lucky early enough, they're able to throw off these shackles and leave the bad situation behind them. If not, the situation becomes tenuous for the rest of their lives with only the thought that *hope* instills change."

He noticed she had stopped walking and he did as well.

"Don't get me wrong here," she continued. "I've not given up on the concept of marriage, but I have yet to find the man who can convince me to take the walk." She smiled. "When he comes along, I'll know it, but until then I'll just patiently wait until I find him.

He'll be something like this rock here to me, seemingly illusive…, yet potentially obtainable."

Giuseppe had been so preoccupied by her proclamation that he had not even noticed the stone that loomed a foot or so above the sand in front of him. He looked around for traces of human activity but there were none. After six weeks, the sand had become totally windswept.

"I wonder if this is it?" she said, pointing down at the rock.

"There is only one way to find out." He reached in his back pocket and retrieved a radiophone. "The nice thing about this little gadget is that it beams off of the satellite and back to whomever you need to talk to. Though I am sure you are aware of its function." He dialed it and handed it to her. "Tell Antoine we might have found what we were looking for." She did, and then they both sat on the rock and waited. It was their only place of refuge, though it was almost too hot to bear. After some time, he watched the vehicle approach. He rose as it arrived. Antoine and Anhur climbed out and then Anhur hurried to the place Flo pointed. They waited impatiently for the old man to acknowledge their find. He went up to the rock and dug out an area in its cleft. Giuseppe noticed him pull out a strand of beads and hoist them into the air, proclaiming them the worry beads that belonged to his son. With that done, Giuseppe walked to the back of the Land Rover and retrieved the bag that Antoine had been toting all the while. He unzipped the case as Flo watched him.

"What have you got there?" she asked.

"A GPS," he said simply. "I know you'll recognize it. Once I get a fix on this location, we can use it for future reference. There is no need for us to linger once I have confirmed our exact location." He paused. "As far as I am concerned, the beads have confirmed Anhur's story and there is no reason to stay in the desert any longer."

Anhur had wandered over to the edge of the valley and the group joined him for several moments. Giuseppe carefully scanned the valley for some sign of the apocalypse, but he knew there would be none. He talked for several minutes to the man, gesturing for him to determine the exact position of the battle as he saw it. The old man became retrospective; the priest saw it in his face. Flo translated.

"Why me?" the old man asked no one in particular. "For weeks now, I have been asking myself that same question over and over and cannot come up with a viable answer." Giuseppe shrugged his shoulders and thought about the question for several moments. "I suppose you were meant to see this all along. All I can say is it was Mohammed's wish, that you did so, and in some respects I'm glad you did." The priest watched a wry smile cross the old man's face.

"I had always wondered until now why it was that I had lived this long," Anhur said solemnly.

CHAPTER 9

Startling Revelations

Rome, Italy

Seated in the Vatican library, a stack of open books in front of her, Flo wondered if she had the strength to read them. She was still slightly fatigued from the trip to Cairo, and having just gotten off the phone with David McCloud, her editor, she was frazzled as well. She wondered if she could even concentrate long enough to absorb the material in front of her.

In her absence, there had been several turns of events that she had not foreseen. The seven-year-old son of a junior senator from the state of Colorado had come up missing and was presumed to have been kidnapped, even though no ransom had been demanded. A nationwide manhunt had ensued but to no avail. Coupled with the disappearance of wife of a Belgian diplomat, the news had caused a sensational uproar. Not a trace of either of the victims had been found though the search continued.

Her editor, who possibly knew what had happened to them, and had her story on the preacher, had decided to print it, only because he could authenticate the story with credible evidence. He had samples of the powered remains, some of which he kept and verified through an independent laboratory as the particle remains of a human.

He did not edit Flo's story in any way, but printed in its entirety, which included her accusations that the government was covering up known facts about the increasing rise in missing persons. This set off a chain of events that resulted in the Justice Department subpoenaing her and her editor to reveal their knowledge of the story. Flo, of course, knew nothing about the subpoena; the bailiff of the court didn't have any better luck finding her than the NSA had.

Flo knew now that she had covered her tracks relatively well, for there was no way the Justice Department would have gotten involved unless told to do so by the National Security Agency. The only thing that had kept the editor of the Post out of jail at this point was that he turned over all documentation relating to the missing preacher and had proclaimed in a press interview that the highly esteemed NSA was behind an abject cover-up, which had been going on for an extended period of time.

Most of the press at the other papers were finally able to put two and two together with these facts and had surmised that the exact same thing had happened to the son of the Colorado senator. That and the fact that the Washington Post had been holding the story for some time now steered public sentiment toward a probable senate investigation into the matter. The people demanded it. The NSA was quick to hide under the shield of immunity provided under the Homeland Security Act and told investigative reporters hunting for some clarity on the breaking story that they would stand mum under the act when subpoenaed, and that it was in the public's interest that they do so. This had all happened in the five days since she left.

The editor of the Post knew that he wasn't out of the woods by any means because the following day, he had boldly printed Flo's story on the Weeping Madonna of Cairo. He was sure he would be subpoenaed once again for withholding information on her whereabouts. With the second article though, the government finally knew approximately where his reporter was, but this was a chance he had been willing to take. The story was too compelling to do otherwise. The editor thought that this particular piece was the best she had ever written. As government agents in Cairo searched for her in vain, he knew from her call the previous evening that she was back in Rome before they had even begun looking for her.

Luckily for him though, he knew how to work the system to his advantage. The throng of public sentiment about Flo's missing person's article was so compelling that people began to fear their own safety.

Literally thousands of people had come forward with missing loved ones, demanding answers to their own personal dilemmas.

The story of the preacher debuted worldwide because of the uproar and caused the same type of reaction to occur. Soon, people harangued the governments of every nation in the world, asking if the same thing that had happened to the preacher in America had also happened to their loved ones in their respective countries.

She still heard his words ringing in her ears almost an hour later. "Your name is the buzzword here in Washington," he'd said. "Better than that though; I would say you have garnered national attention and praise as well for your astute insight and concise description. This is great publicity for the paper, if you know what I mean! Circulation numbers have skyrocketed. All the major players in the national television media market have been calling non-stop ever since the story broke... CNN, Meet the Press, Good Morning America, you name it, this is great!" he had related, ecstatic at the results of her hard work. "They're all trying to scoop an exclusive interview out of you. Of course, I only told them you were out of town on assignment, but I'm sure they're looking for you. Watch your back!"

Flo heard him guffaw, and by this time was furious with her editor. She said nothing in response.

"Are you still there? Ha…your name is likened to the popular old puzzle *Where's Waldo*. But in this case, it's *Where's Flo*? Not to worry though, I'm not about to give my ace investigative reporter up. Just continue to send me your stories," he urged. "The rest of the nation's periodicals are playing catch up on this one."

Flo couldn't control herself any longer and let out slurry of epitaphs over his comments, hoping that no one eavesdropped on her conversation. He laughed in her ear.

"Now I hope you don't want me to quote you on your answer to your call to fame?"

"Hardly!" she hissed. "You haven't got a clue on what's really happening here, do you?"

"It doesn't really matter at this point!" he exclaimed. "Pound for pound, you're worth your weight in gold if I can just keep the Justice Department at bay."

"You'll be lucky if they don't lock you up and throw away the key. There was a reason why I told you to hold the story in the first place!"

"When and if they find the powdered remains of the senator's son, there will be less of a reason to come looking for you. The way I look at it, I did you a favor, and this is the thanks I get?"

"You're sick...sick, sick, David, you know that, don't you?" She hung up the phone without letting him reply.

She was still upset about her editor's feigned ignorance an hour later, when she finally decided to lift the first heavy book up and set it in front of her. She wanted to run and hide somewhere, empty her mind of the entire situation. She secretly wished she had made another career choice other than this one. She felt intense pressure building in her temples and now had some idea of what it was like to try to solve the unsolvable. Never in her childhood dreams did she ever think she would be caught up in such a predicament as this. Now, she momentarily longed for the mundane life of a simple housewife in Salem, New Jersey. She felt like screaming, but instead bolstered her resolve with a few moments of quiet meditation before she resumed.

As she set the book in front of her, which she figured had to weigh close to ten pounds, she was immediately struck by the intricate detail of the book's leather cover. She opened it to the first page and saw that along either side of the centered script was a border of intricately colored ink drawings that seemed to tell a story as you looked down the page. She had never seen anything quite like it. The paper on which the text was written was course and thick; it was another thing she hadn't encountered before. She was still trying to discern the pictorial on the left side of the page when she was interrupted. Lost in thought, she had not heard anyone entering the room.

Monsignor Lorenzo spoke. "I noticed you were intrigued by the calligraphy of the text. Handle it with care if you would, that Bible is over five hundred years old. I believe it was done by Trappist monks in France, though I'm not one hundred percent sure."

Flo lifted her hands from the paper in dismay.

"I thought that the ancient text might give you a better feel for the subject matter. I have taken the trouble to bookmark the passages that I feel are relevant to our situation. If you feel uncomfortable handling the old book, let me know and I can get you a recent edition. The text is still the same in both editions."

"No…, no, this will do, just fine. It's a rare treat to be able to peruse something this old. Though I highly doubt I will get through all of these books today." She smiled as she glanced at the bookmarked stack of books in front of her.

"No matter," he shrugged. "Like we discussed earlier, I need your unbiased opinion on this. You already have made my job easier because of your intuitive insight. I'll leave you be for now and hope to discuss the subject matter later after you've had a chance to read."

"Fair enough," she said and went back to studying the drawings before she started reading. She randomly paged through the text and noticed that the pages were all formatted exactly the same. The only bookmark was near the end of the book earmarking Revelations 12; it took her several moments for her eyes to get used to the hand scripted text as she started to read:

"And a great sign appeared in heaven: A woman clothed with the sun and the moon under her feet and on her head a crown of twelve stars. And being with child, she cried travailing in birth: and was in pain to be delivered. And there was another sign in heaven. And behold a great red dragon, having seven heads and ten horns and on his heads seven diadems. And his tail drew the third part of the stars of heaven and cast them to earth. And the dragon stood before the woman who was ready to be delivered: that, when she should be delivered, he might devour her son. And she brought forth a man child, who was to rule all nations with an iron rod. And her son was taken up to God and his throne. And the women fled into the wilderness, where she had a place prepared by God, that there they should feed her, a thousand two hundred sixty days. And there was a great battle in heaven; Michael and his angels fought with the dragon, and the dragon fought, and his angels. And they prevailed not: neither was their place found any more in heaven. And that great dragon was cast out, that old serpent, who is called the devil and Satan, who seduces the

whole world. And he was cast unto the earth: and his angels were thrown down with him. And I heard a loud voice in heaven, saying: Now has come salvation and strength and the kingdom of our God and the power of his Christ: because the accuser of our brethren is cast forth, who accused them before our God day and night. And they overcame him by the blood of the Lamb and by the word of the testimony: and they loved not their lives unto death. Therefore, rejoice O heavens, and you that dwell therein. Woe to the earth and to the sea, because the devil has come down unto you, having great wrath, knowing that he has but a short time. And when the dragon saw that he was cast unto the earth, he persecuted the woman who brought forth the man child. And there were given to the woman two wings of a great eagle, that she might fly into the desert, unto her place, where she is nourished for a time and times, and half a time, from the face of the serpent. And the serpent cast out of his mouth, after the woman, water, as it were a river: that he might cause her to be carried away by the river. And the earth helped the woman: and the earth opened her mouth and swallowed up the river which the dragon cast out of his mouth. And the dragon was angry against the woman: and went to make war with the rest of her seed, who keep the commandments of God and have the testimony of Jesus Christ. And he stood upon the sand of the sea."

When she finished reading, she flipped three pages back and began to study the drawings along the sides of the script in earnest. Her thoughts were swimming, her mind reeling and racing at the same time. She was so enthralled in thought that she did not notice the Monsignor reenter the room and carefully stack the rest of the books off to one side as he patiently waited for her to recover her thoughts. When she finally looked up and saw him, she was startled, for she thought she was alone.

"I didn't mean to startle you," he apologized. "But I got to thinking this is one of the least understood books in the entire Bible and thought it foolish of me to leave. No one usually reads it through without getting lost in interpretation. I would like to know your thoughts on the subject, if you don't mind?"

"To be brutally honest with you, I can't say that I've ever read this before, or at least I don't remember having read it," Flo replied. "I know that you're probably going to say that I'm a lax Catholic, but this is the type of text that's usually left to the scholars like yourself, is it not? Though now that I have read it, I know why you have been so troubled by Anhur's vision."

"There is no need for excuses, Ms. Rinna," the Monsignor said. "Not many people spend the time to read it at all. It's a book of future prediction and I'm sure you are right in your observation."

Flo noticed that he was choosing his words carefully.

"There are only a handful of people that even know about this vision or revelation if you will; Anhur and his family, Antoine and his assistant, the pope, and you and I. No one else even has the slightest inkling what is going on here. One thing I would like to do is to disseminate the entire passage word for word. Not that I haven't read it at least a dozen times in the last few days, but when we get done collaborating its true meaning, I believe we will get a better understanding of Anhur's vision."

"But I'm not sure I can help," Flo frowned.

"That's where you are completely mistaken, Ms. Rinna," the Monsignor disagreed. "You already have done more to bolster the thought and idea of this situation than you truly understand. I have made several discreet inquiries about your idea of replicating the blue light, and hopefully something can be built that will enable us to see what Anhur saw. Whether this works or not remains to be seen, but my hope is that it does. This will convince the world and all parties concerned that the story you are about to write will be both convincing and true."

"Me? I…I'm not sure that I can do that. I'm not sure I have the ability to give this story the depth required." She was suddenly frustrated and it showed in her brunt denial.

"Of course, you can, Ms. Rinna, of course you can," the Monsignor assured her. "Why do you think you sought me out to begin with? You have been sent to aid me in solving this riddle. You're not unlike an angel yourself in some respects, you know. A good one too, I might add. Do not question your ability at this late juncture. That is all I can say at this moment, for I need your help."

Flo flushed once again. "What do you want me to say?"

"That question needs no response, Ms. Rinna. You will do what is right and what comes naturally to you. You will write this story and write it well, I dare say."

She noticed him looking at his watch for the first time.

"Look, we have a meeting with Pope Romanus in a half hour. Maybe when we're finished, we can come back here and sort some of this out."

"You're kidding, right?" She suddenly became self-conscious of her appearance and sought to press the invisible wrinkles in her blouse sleeves with her palms.

"Not at all, Ms. Rinna, not at all! I would never kid you. There is too much at stake here for me to do otherwise."

"This is something that I never expected to happen to me," she tittered. "Hobnobbing with a religious head of state! God only knows what my dear deceased mother would have said had she known about this!"

Monsignor Lorenzo only smiled at the declaration as he rose from his chair, waiting for her to do so as well.

As they were escorted into the office of the pope, Florence suddenly grew weak-kneed. She saw the pope rise out of his chair to greet them and proffer his hand. She suddenly realized she had to kiss the fisherman's ring, a sign of fealty. Once she straightened from doing so, she heard him speak to her in perfect English.

"So good to finally meet you, Ms. Rinna," he smiled. "I have heard nothing but good things said on your behalf."

He swiftly changed language and speaking in Italian, bade them to have a seat. Florence was suddenly overwhelmed and could hardly find the words to respond to the compliment, only nodding in agreement. Monsignor Lorenzo, as if on cue, took over the conversation. "Ms Rinna has been invaluable in regards to my investigation and I would still be floundering about if it hadn't been for her."

"I see," the pontiff said, smiling at Flo in the process. "What were the consequences of your trip to Cairo, Giuseppe?"

"It looks like to me that the visionary Anhur's story seems to be true as far as I can see. Though some of my colleagues would, I dare to say, argue that the story is bizarre and unlikely."

"Don't keep me in suspense," the pope admonished."Give me some insight if you don't mind. I have been patiently waiting to learn what you have discovered."

For the next half-hour or so, Flo sat quietly while the facts as she had witnessed them were presented in a concise and thorough manner by the Monsignor. From time-to-time Flo noted the show of concern on the pope's face. When the monsignor finished the pope asked several questions.

"Can you independently verify the story in any way?"

"We are working on that aspect."

"What, if anything, might you propose we do at present?" the pope asked.

"My thought is that we nothing as of yet, your Eminence. Once we have sorted through the details, I want your permission to let Ms. Rinna write the story on what we have discovered, once we have had a chance to sort through all the pertinent facts, that is. The benefits of exposing the details would be advantageous to both the church and masses of faithful."

Flo saw the pope frown at the suggestion as Monsignor Lorenzo tried to reinforce the idea. "All I can hope to do at this point is make you aware that I feel this will be advantageous," Monsignor Lorenzo continued. "The final decision, I know, rests on your shoulders and I do not wish to bias your decision in any way."

The pope frowned once again.

"I am merely suggesting this as a viable option, Your Excellency. Please do not close your mind to this suggestion. Once you read my reasons for this suggestion, it is my hope that you will eventually agree that this is the prudent thing to do. I hope to have a detailed report of our findings available to you within the next day or so, and you will then better understand my reasoning behind my suggested request."

Flo was disappointed that the priest had not yet convinced the pontiff regarding publication of their findings. Were she given the chance to speak, she felt that she could have made a stronger argument. She noticed the Pope turn in his chair to look at her, and then noticed an appreciable change in his demeanor when he spoke.

"If I end up agreeing with Giuseppe's advice, all I ask is that you use a skillful hand, Ms. Rinna."

"I'll certainly try to do my best," she responded. He stood and offered her his ring finger once again.

"Now if you will excuse me, I'd like to spend several moments in private with Giuseppe, if you don't mind."

Flo walked out of the office unescorted and waited in the outer office.

"Monsignor Lorenzo," the pope abruptly stated." Don't you think you are being a bit presumptuous when it comes to letting this story become public knowledge? You know that I would have to have full agreement from the College of Cardinals before you are permitted to allow Ms. Rinna to publish this. You had better be absolutely sure of your facts, for the political ramifications have worldwide implications. I am sure I don't have to remind you of that. Never mind that our religious hierarchy has been debating this very subject for decades!"

The Monsignor knew he was being chastised and sought to ease the pontiff's mind. "I would never do anything that would jeopardize the sanctity of this institution, nor would I ever think of circumventing your authority in any way. I am merely a lowly servant of yours, who knows my limitations. I will leave this decision in your capable hands, as you know that I will obey any decision you choose to make. I, however can't stress enough the apparent validity of this visionary and will present to you cited evidence as proof. You be the judge when it comes to what you are to do with the unenviable truth in this matter. I will say one thing though, and that is that I firmly believe that this visionary saw what he saw for a reason. This reason is as complex as the sighting. Like the scriptures denote, I believe that a revelation of some sort is near." Monsignor Lorenzo had bowed his head in respect. "Once again, let me express my sincere apologies, your Eminence, if you thought otherwise of my pious intent." The pope gently laid his hand on his head and he felt the pope's thumb make the sign of the cross on his forehead. He heard the mumbled prayer for enlightenment on both their parts and mumbled a sincere amen when he had finished.

"I trust you like a son and have no doubt of your sincerity or your intent, never think otherwise. I would just like you to keep in mind at all times that there are underlying forces that seek to destroy this institution and its teachings and we must and will persevere no matter what."

"I am aware of that possibility," the Monsignor flatly stated.

*   *   *

Flo noticed a look of concern etched on the priest's face when they met in the outer office minutes later. She was still beaming from her meeting with the pope, even though she hoped that it would have been under less tenuous circumstances. Flo was perplexed and had to ask. "Why do I get the distinct feeling you have a closer relationship with the pope than you have led me to believe? Be truthful here, he did use your first name in addressing you, did he not?"

"Yes, he did, and maybe I should explain our relationship so that you will understand my position a little bit better." They entered the courtyard in front of St. Peter's Basilica as they made their way back towards the library. "It probably would be best if we stopped here and had a seat, as this may take some time." He paused a moment and then turned to look at her. "I am part of his advisory staff, the circle of eight as we are called…" He then went into detail, explaining to her how his career had been advanced by the current Pontiff. When he finished the story an hour later, Flo had a better grasp of the man and his calling.

"Have you ever had any doubts about your vocation, being as you were practically hand- selected for your career without your knowledge?"

"I never gave it too much thought, but now that you ask, I would tend to answer no, I have no doubts at all. When we all have a trying day, we usually question our own motives in life and because I wear a collar, it doesn't mean I am no different than you or anyone else is, if that makes it any clearer to you."

"It does."

"What do you say to some lunch?" the Monsignor suddenly asked, completely changing the subject. "I believe the cafeteria is still open." He glanced at his watch. "We could use a break, don't you think?"

She readily agreed. After lunch they walked toward to library, Flo had regained her zeal to carry on. When they were seated at the table, the Monsignor asked her a question.

"How much have you read?"

"Just Revelation Twelve so far. I had hoped to re-read it once again."

"Please do and continue on into thirteen, as there is more. I'm going to leave you for a bit so that you can concentrate on the material. I have some things to do that require my immediate attention, but I'll return in an hour or so if you don't mind?"

"No, I don't mind at all." Flo watched him as he left, once again thinking how intelligent he was. It was his demeanor though, that struck a chord with her; he seemed to be the gentlest man she had ever recalled knowing and could not believe how he dealt with the intense pressure so easily.

She began to read Revelation 13:

"And I saw a beast coming up out the sea, having seven heads and ten horns: and upon his horns, ten diadems: and upon his heads, names of blasphemy. And the beast which I saw was like to a leopard: and his feet of a bear, and his mouth as the mouth of a lion. And the dragon gave him his own strength and great power. And I saw one of the heads as it were slain to death: and his death wound was healed. And all the earth was in admiration after the beast. And they adored the dragon which gave power to the beast, saying: Who is like the beast? And who shall be able to fight with him? And there was given to him a mouth speaking great things and blasphemies: and power was given him to do, two and forty months. And he opened his mouth unto blasphemies against God, to blaspheme his name and his tabernacle and them that dwell in heaven. And it was given unto him to make war with the saints and to overcome them. And the power was given him over every tribe and people and tongue and nation. And all that dwell upon earth adored him, whose names are not written in the

*book of life of the Lamb which was slain from the beginning of the world.
If any men have an ear, let him hear. He that shall lead into captivity shall
go into captivity: he that shall kill by the sword must be killed by the sword.
Here is the patience and the faith of the saints."*

She then read Revelations from the beginning up to Chapter
Thirteen, scanning the vivid pictorials once again, which told the story
in much the same way as it was inscribed. She wondered how accurate
the pictorials were. Were the illustrations only the monk's interpretation
of the verses or had he been instructed to paint them so by someone
with a more learned understanding of the material?

Flo could hardly imagine the days or weeks it must have taken
to complete a single page of the text. It had to have taken years to
complete the entire Bible, maybe even a lifetime. She had no way of
judging, but could visualize the monk sitting at a crude wooden desk,
his colored ink sets before him, creating this work of art under dim
candlelight, dank conditions and swelled fingers trying to perfect the
illustrations. Flo did not envy the man in the least.

She read on into Revelation Fourteen, but was startled once
again when she heard his voice, for the stillness of the library had been
interrupted as well as her thoughts.

"Jewish scholars have always stated that the war between good and
evil has been going on ever since the beginning of time; an invisible
battle, which up until this time has never been witnessed. The book
of Revelation was initially called the Book of Apocalypse, due to the
Latin and Greek start of the book. The first word of Revelation One in
Latin is Apocalypses. The words revelation and apocalypse are actually
interchangeable in English as far as their definition is concerned." He
paused and noted her interest before continuing. "Some scholars and
theologians would like you to believe that the final battle will be likened
to that of World War Two, a battle of men and armaments. I, for one,
had never really been sure up until this point, but I tend to agree with
the Jewish scholars now that Anhur has revealed his vision to us."

He noticed her confused look and sought to ease her mind.

"Almost all of the books which make up the Bible are historical
interpretations of the past. The book of Revelations is almost the only
one that deals with futuristic predictions. There are several others that

deal with visions and insights, such as the three books of Enoch and several others. Some have said the book of Revelations was a spinoff of the Old Testament Book of Daniel, though I'm not so sure of that either. There are similarities between them and it has been said but never proven that Revelations is merely an early Christian copy of Daniel, which is a Jewish text. Revelations was purportedly written around the year three hundred A.D." Again he paused and glanced at Flo with a brief smile. "I realize that you must be having a time of this, trying to make some sense out of the writing and the intended messages. Please don't become discouraged by all this"

Flo just shook her head, letting him continue uninterrupted.

"Now, I am not sure myself what the reasoning is behind some of the constant repetition in the book and I realize that it must seem confusing."

"That's an understatement if you ask me," Flo admitted. "But as I read, I'm beginning to understand why you're so concerned. This is where I have more questions than I have answers for, believe me... like I said earlier, I'll help if I can." She searched his face for some clue as to what she might say that would enlighten him. "I'm no scholar that's evident, but maybe if we start at the beginning, like you said earlier, it becomes all the more relevant to you and I. Correct me if I veer off for any reason, but the war between the angels began in heaven when Lucifer, the brightest and most respected of angels, sought to usurp the power that was God's. As I understand it, the symbol of his insurrection became the dragon himself that was cast down upon the earth. Prior to this though, the archangel Michel and his followers fought a raging battle in heaven with Lucifer and his followers to determine who justly ruled the heavens - its creator or Lucifer - an astute understudy. Does that sound consistent to you?"

"Yes, please go on," Monsignor Lorenzo invited.

"Michel struck a blow for the creator and decapitated one of the heads of the dragon, for which he was chastised by the Lord. He was laid in abeyance for his action. Lucifer and his cohorts were then cast to earth to rule the only divinity left at their disposal, the planet earth." She saw him nod his approval to her thoughts. "My question is, and don't think any less of me than you already do, but why wasn't the battle decided in heaven to begin with? If Michel indeed had the ability to lop off one of the eight heads of the dragon, why wasn't he allowed to finish the job up there?"

"Good question," the monsignor answered. "And it is one that I have thought about many times before. My thought is a rather simple one. As a young child learns from their parents through example, so are many acquired traits and habits. What is learned in infancy usually carries through into adulthood. An example was made of Lucifer as well, so that all who seek to challenge the divine authority of the creator are rejected. The rejected are no longer allowed the light of the divinity. This is why there are so many references in the Bible to being cast into darkness."

"Which is somewhat opposite in respect to the mantra of a born-again Christian, the saying, *I have seen the light of the Lord,*" Flo said.

"True, also you would agree I'm sure, in principle, that depravation of love or light or anything else for that matter, are powerful tools in their own regard. You only have to think of us humans in that respect to know that this is true. Let me give you a known example of what I am trying to say here." The monsignor paused a moment. "Lock a child in a closet for several months and the child becomes in essence emotionally deprived of the need for nurturing. Do it for a year and the child will become depraved as well? Now thinking in these terms, such as having had every possible comfiture a being could want for, the angels in this case, and imagine what happens when that is taken away from them. Do you see what I mean?"

"Yes, I do."

"We as humans are given this choice here on earth. Follow in the footsteps of righteousness and the light is yours, or as it refers to in Revelations, having your name written in the Book of the Lamb. Stray..., and the prospect of complete darkness is what you have to look forward to when your life ends. There are many analogies in the Bible that are sometimes literal and sometimes figurative. That is sometimes the trickiest thing to recognize when you are reading Revelations. Trust me; I have spent my life trying to discerning them. Let me use an example if you would."

Flo nodded, completely absorbed by what the monsignor was saying.

"When the beast, as you have read, rose out of the sea, he was said to have seven heads and ten horns. Do you remember the passage?"

Flo concurred.

"It is something that you read and possibly do not understand for its symbolism. Michael had lopped the eighth head off, as we have discussed previously. The red dragon is meant to represent evil, or the loss of God's light in that regard. The dragon is much more than that; it represents the temptations for failure of us newborn innocents here on earth. However, I feel there is much more to this than literal translation denotes. Each one of the heads represents one of the seven deadly sins, yet the Bible only states that blasphemy was written across the forehead of each one of the dragon's heads."

"What lead you to that conclusion?" Flo asked, trying to follow his line of thought.

"This symbolism did not occur to me until just a few days ago. It was something that until now I would have never considered until it became recently relevant. Were it not for Anhur, I probably wouldn't have given it a second thought." He held up his hand and stopped her from quizzing him, then continued. "It's strange sometimes, how one thought might bolster another, and it suddenly occurred to me that the recently deceased Pope Alexander knew the interpretation of this line all along, which is the reason why he used to use every one of the deadly sins as a reference in his weekly sermons. Like I said, the book of Revelations does not spell out any reference to the type of blasphemies. What else, I thought, could cause you to stray from the light were it not for all the deadly sins; greed, anger, sloth, gluttony, pride, lust and covetousness? The word deadly, in this case is referenced to what kills the soul and denies it the ability to achieve the light. This is the sole purpose of the demon, which rises out of the earth with the two horns of a lamb, which if you will, represents Lucifer, Beelzebub, or whatever name you wish to call him. He is the tempter of all who wish their name inscribed into the Book of Life. The devil, if you wish, avails us all of these temptations in the name of what we refer to as sins."

Flo was intrigued by the insight. "What about the eighth head, the one that was lopped off by the archangel Michael?"

"Good question! It is something that I have spent some time researching during the last week or so, and I came up with the sin of *fetishism*. The dictionary term today is somewhat different than how it was originally interpreted. It means literally to idolize your-self or idolize other gods other than the creator."

"That's interesting," Flo responded.

"This, I might add, is exactly what caused archangel Lucifer to be cast out of heaven to begin with. He thought he had risen above God. The Bible even states that he was the most favored of all angels in God's eyes. What other way was there for the Creator to seek retribution than to deny his most favored the light of eternity, if you will? He was truly guilty of fetishism."

"That makes sense. I think I'm not even going to ask how you came up with that one. I'll just have to take your word for it," Flo gently stated. "Still, there are several questions that have been nagging at me ever since the interview with Anhur. Why now?"

"That is a question I will not even bother to consider, as it's not a question of timing but one of pertinence!"

"Explain that if you would."

"Look around you at all the sorrow and pain being inflicted on one another, and that pretty much answers your question for you, doesn't it? I see that you are not readily convinced by the way you are looking questionably at me, so let me explain. Let's just take prejudice for instance. Even though it is not considered a deadly sin, let's just use it as a premise here in terms as it deals with ethnicity, which is just one of the many afflictions that pit one man against the other. I am sure you can think of many more. Think about South Africa as an example, if you would. The practice of Apartheid went on for close to sixty years, favoring the race of European origin over the native population. This is just one of many examples of worldwide injustices in that context. It was a struggle, if you recall, that took decades to right to a certain extent. It still has not been fully resolved to the satisfaction of many who live there, even to this day. The progress that has been made was a step in the right direction, but the lesson was not heeded by those who were informed of the grave injustices that had occurred.

"This same type of situation occurs in just about every nation of the world. Name me any nation that comes to mind and you will see a majority of people being persecuted for either their religious belief, the color of their skin, or their political or social affiliations, just to name a few. Never mind the class and caste systems that have been going on for millenniums. I could spend hours upon untold hours citing examples of social injustices alone. This is why it has become a question of pertinence."

"I see," she responded.

"You're a reporter and eminently qualified as well I might add. Surely you know what I am talking about."

"I believe I do."

"If you were to tell me you are not sometimes affected by the stories you write, I wouldn't believe you. I have seen the range of your emotions first hand. Please don't tell me you are not affected on a personal level every so often."

"Guilty as charged," she admitted, feeling the heat of a blush rush over her face.

"Don't you feel, some days more than others that the turmoil that surrounds us is raising to a crescendo?"

"Yes, for some time now."

"Were I to ask anyone else the same question that I just asked you, I am sure the answer would be the same no matter who you are. That is the truth of the matter. Who do you think is responsible for all this? I really need no answer from you on that. You know firsthand from what you read today. Let me quote just one line here, '*And they will adore the beast and the dragon and cling to its promises.*' Call it whatever you want - the beast, the dragon, the devil, Satan - we could again look into every religious belief and see the same semblance here. What better story do we have in scripture than the devil temping Jesus, '*prostrate yourself in my name and all this can be yours*', as the devil stretched his hands wide to show the kingdom he rules with impunity - earth."

"*Mine is the kingdom of heaven* was His answer," Flo responded, agreeing with his point.

"Right you are," Monsignor Lorenzo smiled. "So you see what I'm driving at here? Let's just use one other example. Were someone to ask most people what would make them happy, I'm willing to bet money would be the answer on everyone's lips. Their reasoning being, that this is a necessary means in order to acquire the comforts of this life, or in an effort to buy perceived happiness. Wouldn't you agree?"

"Yes."

"This is again another example of the same scenario that I spoke of earlier. Such is a temptation like all others we are faced with once again. The tempter leads us to believe that we will get rightful justification here on earth. Think about it… think about what the devil promised Jesus, '*all this I will give to you.*' Here's the catch though. Just sign over your soul in order to achieve the false sense of achievement he promises you here on earth and bask in the darkness for all perpetuity, like he does. The problem with that is we are striving in a false domain, one that is ruled by the barterer for the eternity of one's souls." He stopped shortly to let the point sink in. "You must agree that the key to happiness comes from within us, which is something you mentioned while we were in the desert. It's not at all influenced by any external force. We as a species actually derive more pleasure from doing *good deeds* for others than anything else. This is what the Bible and, for that matter, any other religious tome denotes. It is just one of the many things that enriches our lives and aids us in getting our names inscribed in the Book of Life."

Flo did not respond to this comment but allowed the silence of the room to shroud them once again as she gathered her thoughts. She finally spoke. "Why the Sahara Desert then?"

"My guess, and I'm not an anthropologist by any means, is because it was the preliminary point for all civilizations. The area at one time was not a desert at all, but a fertile area in all respects. Some of the oldest known civilizations started in that general area. The desert at times gives up some of the best clues to what I mean. From time to time, when the sands of the Sahara desert shift, areas that have been covered for centuries are exposed, allowing researchers a glimpse into its historical past. Some of these insights, if you will, are one, two, three, or more thousand years B.C. No one really knows for sure just when the area initially became populated. I have read that it once teemed with plant and animal life. There are glyphs etched into the sandstone of this area that attest to that very same fact. There are depictions of animals and trees and people that no longer survive the area.

"Now I suppose if this is true, again we must speculate as to when the dragon was cast down onto earth to begin with. There is no real timetable when all of this supposedly occurred. It has never really been dated anywhere that I have read, other than in a speculative manner. I am only assuming and I may be wrong once again, as many of us are..., who have no recorded description of our past after a certain point. This is to me, one of the most confusing points to consider.

"Revelations says, as you have read, that the dragon tormented the descendants of the woman with child. Are we to assume the author was talking about Mary? Many scholars would agree on that point yet once again, no name was given. Some would have you believe it is a metaphor for the start of Christianity, which is certainly possible. You have to remember one thing here. I can never refute anything outright unless I can prove it otherwise. The Catholic Church would have you believe the woman represents them and is meant as a means of comparison, surviving the torment the early Christians received in Rome as a fledging belief."

"Do you truly believe that?" she asked.

He looked quizzically at her. "I'm not sure, but it is the age-old struggle of good versus evil, a reminder to early Christians that perseverance will win out over persecution, but again we are speculating like everyone else about its true meaning. Suppose we are talking about only a metaphor here? This is another point to consider and another timetable to consider as well. Are you following me?"

Flo wondered about his question. "I am following you and see what you mean. You're right; there are no names, just a woman with child who was clothed by the sun, the moon at her feet. There is another possibility as you mentioned briefly before. Maybe it was the birth of mankind?"

"That is a possibility as well; if so, it brings us back to Eve and the Garden of Eden, which, according to the earliest testament, was the beginning of all creation. If that is the case, it would support the theory that man's first sin was one of temptation. Eve ate the fruit from the forbidden tree and then coaxed Adam to join her. The tempter in this case was the serpent, who according to many was no more than the devil in disguise." Monsignor Lorenzo stopped and caught himself. "Sorry, I'm getting a little sidetracked there, which is easy to do at times."

"I do it myself when I get deeply involved in research, so I know what you mean," Flo smiled in understanding.

"Anyway, every line in this book of Revelations can be interpreted to mean several different possible things at the same time. Only the author of this book knew for sure what the true intent was. The funniest part about that is that we aren't even really sure who the author is. All we have is a first name and nothing more. Some say that it is a collection of writings assembled by a man named John, and others say it is the writing of the Apostle John. No one is sure on that point either. All we really have is the name John, John who?" He shrugged. "I believe that this book was meant to be a timeless document that could be applied to all ages." He sighed heavily. "You know I have spent my entire life doing research on some of the very same subjects I have just touched on, but I have a confession to make." He chuckled. "I know a confession from a priest... this ought to be good, right... well, I have studied the book of Revelations in the past and had never ever thought that the book would come to life," he said, gazing somberly at her in the process. "Please don't look at me that way; it seems so judgmental... almost as if my creditability is waning, but truthfully, as much as I know, I really don't have all the answers."

"That's a scary thought," she said, smiling as she sought to bolster his spirit. "The fact you would confess any sort of ignorance or shortcoming on your part just shows me you are human like the rest of us. We all have a degree of uncertainty from time to time, otherwise as you said earlier, we would be devoid of feelings altogether. Rest assured I'll keep your confession between you and me." She noticed him smile. "Now if I remember correctly, that is called confidentiality of the penitent." She smiled while it was his turn to blush.

"What can I say/"

"At this point, nothing needs to be said, Monsignor Lorenzo." She laughed mirthlessly, watching as he followed suit. A minute later, she felt ready to proceed once again. "You asked for my insight into all this earlier, so let me begin. Let's suppose for a moment that the dragon was truly cast into the sea after he had been routed from heaven. I am only making literal assumptions here." She saw him nod.

"Now I am by no means a reliable source of information when it comes to all this, but let's just say that this dragon was thrown into the water off of the coast of Morocco, the west coast of Africa. Which, as you well know, is and has always been an area of known strife and turmoil, would you not agree?" He nodded once again. "Now as you and I both know; the book says that the beast came out of the sea. I am assuming that the beast and the dragon are one and the same, which I know you will concur with as well. So, that being the case here, and the devil or Satan or the dragon or beast whatever you want to call it was said to have control over the earth. Now, once again, if that is indeed true, then he also has the ability to change the physical conditions here on earth as well to suit his needs. Is that not a plausible assumption?"

"I believe that he can," Monsignor Lorenzo agreed.

"Since the northern section of Africa used to be a fertile area, as you so well put it, is it not possible that in order to rain strife upon its former inhabitants, that the beast changed the area into a desert to spite God and make war against the descendants of the woman? Create a void of water which humans need to survive and it becomes inhabitable. Let's consider for a moment here what the sudden loss of water has on plant and animal life - everything just shrivels up and dies. Better than that though, as the devil's plan seems to be evident, he wanted to make the area void of all life purposely. He now sets up an area of the world in which to do battle without detection. What better way is there than to turn the path of the battlefield into an arid desert? This drove the people away from their native land, resulting in hardship and discontent, which are tools the devil uses quite effectively, as you mentioned earlier." She paused, pleased that the monsignor appeared to be listening to her comments with rapt interest. "If this is a plausible theory and my geography serves me right, the Sahara desert is known for its oases' which are nothing more than underground rivers that make their way to the surface in different areas throughout the desert. I'm sure, if you asked Anhur, he'd be able to tell you the exact location of many of these oases' as I am sure that they are plotted on most maps of the desert too. The Scripture says that the dragon cast out water from its mouth to carry the woman away in a river, but the earth helped her out by swallowing up the water, which flowed out of his mouth. I think you get what I'm trying to say here?" She saw him nod. "Since you seem to agree with my line of thought, the Sahara indeed seems to be the area referenced in Revelations. Now, let us assume once again that the beast was cast into the sea on the northwest coast of Africa, as I mentioned earlier, and Anhur finally sights the age-old battle some thirty miles or so out of Asyut, Egypt. My question is this. Where are they headed and why? If we had a map of the Sahara, we might get a better idea of what I'm driving at here. Let's draw an imaginary straight line from West to East. That being the case, the battle should have progressed to an area just outside Cairo, not two-hundred miles to the south. Anhur said the fight is being lost by the so-called white side or in this case, the side of the good. Where is the battle headed for, as I am assuming that the white side is reeling in retreat? In doing so, is it diverting the line of attack away from somewhere?" She stopped for some sort of insight.

The monsignor smiled. "I am sure you are familiar with the term 'Armageddon,' which if you read further on into Chapter Sixteen, describes the final battle between the forces of good and evil. If you are right about the diversionary tactic, I believe they are going to be headed back in a northerly direction at some point in time." He paused for a moment and frowned. "The definition of the word, Armageddon might be of some interest to you. Its true meaning is cryptic, and it means *uncovering the veil*."

Flo sat stunned and speechless.

The priest continued. "The dictionary has taken the liberty to say the definition of the word Armageddon is the struggle between the forces of good and evil, but its literal cryptic translation is more relevant to us now, wouldn't you say?"

He waited for a response, though there was none forthcoming. Flo was still overwhelmed. "I will add one fact that is true as far as I know, and that is with the culmination of the final battle there is said to be a thousand-year respite of peace and tranquility before the final judgment day of all souls."

"Is this Armageddon a real place?"

"Yes, in one sense, no in another as to the actual location. I believe you are confusing the meaning here, like most others do. It is the ancient city of Megiddo, where Armageddon is supposedly going to take place. This seems to be the focal point that many scholars believe begins the end, the location where the final battle will occur."

"Then if what you say is true, they will have to change direction at some point in time, which will make it harder to locate them."

"I believe it just might."

Flo sought to change the disturbing subject for a moment. "Look, I must profess a degree of ignorance when it comes to what you have just said, and will just take your word for it now. I don't want to be rude, but if you don't mind, I'd like to get back to something that you pointed out earlier about the book of Revelations. That it is timeless and applicable for all ages."

"Yes, I believe I did say that."

"That being the case, is it possible that all of the natural calamities which befall man today are no more than the work of the beast, which seems to want to raise the level of uncertainty to the endmost degree? What I am talking about is volcanic eruptions, earthquakes, violent storms and the like?"

"I see what you are saying, and why of course it is, Ms Rinna. Everything encompassed within this realm is due to the works of the beast, wouldn't you say? There is no natural calamity that can't be attributed to the devil, in an effort to sabotage humanity. It is his domain, as we have said earlier."

"Which is my point. He seems to want it that way. Am I not right?"

"Yes, I seem to have indicated that earlier, in an indirect manner. You have to remember one thing and keep it in mind at all times; He feeds off of pain and suffering. That is how he likes it best. Any possible way he can trip you up, he will. It is something he is an expert at."

"My thoughts - correct me if I'm wrong here -It is with this ploy where he gathers his strength to fight, right?"

"Yes, it is," the monsignor agreed.

"Which brings me back to another thought," Flo stated, her voice rising with excitement. "Are not the Weeping Mary statues a warning sign … that the fight for the earth is being lost and she is giving us a sign of things to come, mourning her loss? Is she not the matron of this planet, if my memory serves me?"

"Yes she is. This is exactly what I needed to hear from you, a logical assessment of the current conditions. Please don't let me interrupt continue… continue, Ms. Rinna!"

Flo flushed. "If nothing else, I was always good at analyzing and assessing data, which was part of the reason I got such good grades in school. It has always been my mainstay whenever I investigate a story. Which leads me to one other thought, though it may be painful to you, it is what I feel brought us together to begin with. Allow me some leeway here, for I feel it is the reason why your mother disappeared to begin with, as well as countless others." She stopped in order to gauge his reaction but he was expressionless.

"Now, as Anhur so vehemently stated, the white side seemed to be losing, which is the side of the angels or the side of the good if you will. Now let us suppose the battle has been raging for millenniums. Maybe the legions of angels have dwindled to a point where there are not a sufficient number of them to wage the battle effectively any longer. The only sources left at their disposal are those who have their names inscribed in the Book of Lambs, or those about to be? Your mother…, being one of them." He started to say something but she waved him off. "The only way to stop from being defeated would be to collect those souls, living or dead, and utilize them to wage war against the beast." She searched his face for evidence that her assumption had some credibility.

"I had never thought about it in those terms, but it would explain why so many people have suddenly disappeared," he mused.

Flo continued anew. "These people would be those with their names written in the Book of Life as Revelations so states. If this is the truth of the matter, let me use my own metaphor here, if you will, it would be *the feast of angels*, feeding on those souls, utilizing any means at their disposal in order to win the battle. You know that the forces of evil have to be defeated in the end, and you, if I'm right, can finally ease your conscious mind that your mother had to be taken in order to win the battle in the end." She noticed he seemed to have an unseen burden lifted from his shoulders as his expression changed to one of silent glee.

"My only problem here, Monsignor Lorenzo is this," she concluded. "How in the world are we to aid in this process? Your mother's life should not have been taken in vain. There was purpose behind her disappearance, as well as the countless others that have left prematurely in order to hopefully make the final prophecy become truth. If what I am assuming has a ring of truth to it, my question to you is a rather simple one. What are we going to do about it?"

He abruptly shook his head an instant before he spoke. "I don't know."

CHAPTER 10

Opposing Forces

Washington D.C.

Luther Riggs, Director of the National Security Administration, was just as disgusted with his own shortcomings as he was with everyone else in the room. He had been screaming a litany of obscenities for the better half of an hour in hopes of reinstalling a measure of clarity of purpose. He had hoped this tactic would work, for he was looking for the true measure of subservience from every director in the room.

Surrounding him at the table were the directors and deputy directors of the CIA, FBI, and Homeland Security, as well as the Director of Foreign Affairs, who worked under the Attorney General, sitting in on this meeting out of necessity.

This hardly meant anything to Luther, who was hardly impressed by anyone of them. "I need you to find that woman no matter what the cost! Turn over every rock, look behind every bush and tree, nook and cranny this world has to offer and find her! Damn it, you had her location once, so find her again!"

Arthur Bremmington, director of the FBI, took offence with the constant haranguing and had finally had enough. It was not his fault the CIA could not find her when they knew her approximate location in Cairo, Egypt. "Director Riggs," he forcefully interjected. "I don't see what all the fuss is about. Haven't you already publicly denied any involvement with a cover up involving the missing person's fiasco? Unless the president has taken some affront to the situation, wouldn't the prudent thing to do is let it lie and allow it to die a silent death in due course?"

"Bremmington! If you had done your job when you had the chance, none of this would have happened in the first place!"

"Me? And exactly what do you mean by that?"

"Well let me see… where do I start?" Riggs said, wringing his hands in the process. "Now that you are the first one brave enough to offer your head on the platter, let's see here, you have her in the office of one of your assistant director's and she's nosing around trying to pry information out of your missing persons director and you do nothing! She practically waltzes in unannounced, asks a bunch of off-kilter questions and leaves before you even get a chance to detain her. Don't your assistant directors screen potential security risks before they occur? If you were not so busy playing house with your secretary, you might have some time to direct your subordinates properly. But no! Oh no, you sit in your ivory tower and let opportunity pass you by without the least bit of concern. When your man came to you with what you knew to be a threat to national security, did you bother to notify me? Better yet, did you bother to go after her before this whole mess became an international incident?"

This last accusation fired Bremmington's ire. "I believe you're the one with the problem here, Riggs," he snapped. "If your own subordinates had not dropped the ball to begin with, you would have known about the situation all along. I notified your department! There were five of your flunkies in my office when the information was made available to me! Not only that, they spent over two hours grilling my man and never bothered to inform you. So, who's really at fault here? Besides, who knew the pope had been kidnapped? For all we knew, it was a hoax. Do you have any idea how many times every year the Bureau chases down idiotic situations such as this? Take a wild guess, Riggs!"

Luther could have cared less what the director of the FBI had to deal with on a day-to-day basis and didn't give a rat's ass about the pope. He was glad the instigator was gone, though he wondered all along, who it was that was responsible for the clever handiwork to begin with. At this moment though, he was more concerned with saving face.

"Don't you for a minute question my leadership capabilities? What did you do to further the cause, may I ask?"

"I did what any good manager would have done," Bremmington shouted. "I fired my assistant director in charge of missing persons for mismanagement. What did you do?"

"If you are referring to my men, they are too highly qualified to just dismiss on a whim. They are on administrative leave as we speak, if you must know. My men are not as expendable as the flunkies assigned to run your departments!"

The FBI director was growing incensed. This had turned into a pissing contest, as he thought it might, but he was not about to be browbeaten in front of his colleagues. He forged ahead. "Let's get back to my original question, shall we? What are the concerns of the president? Maybe we should address them instead of seeing who has the bigger set here, Riggs."

"Did I say he had any?"

"You led us to believe he did or you would not have spent the last half hour berating us like little children. Furthermore, if you want to bring any more of my personal business to the table, maybe we could talk for a moment about yours?"

Bremmington knew more about Riggs that the man assumed about him, surely more than most of the timid directors who surrounded him. Riggs was no more than a raging queer as far as Bremmington was concerned, and he was not afraid of him either. If he was looking to cast stones, he had a fistful of them.

Luther Riggs was silent for some time as he thought about what the director of the FBI had said. He was not about to tip his hand on this one. If only they knew that this situation was much higher than the President of the United States, way higher than that. As far as he was concerned, the president was nothing more than a mere pawn in this game and there was much more at stake than this lowly director had a clue of. He knew he had to choose his words carefully. It was of the utmost importance that he did. The woman had to be silenced once and for all. That was what he had been instructed to do, and if he had to do it himself, he would. He would do anything he was told to do to protect the integrity of the Institution.

The Institution was the secret society whose motif was the abject symbol of an upside- down cross. His membership tattoo, an inverted cross, was etched into his skull right in the center of his forehead. He recalled the painful surgical procedure he had gone through as part of his initiation. The skin of his forehead had been sliced and peeled back like a banana skin in order to make the mark undetectable. Following the literal branding, his scalp had been restitched at the hairline, a painful reminder of his fealty, as it was done without anesthesiology. He put his index finger there momentarily to remind him of his intended purpose.

Their code of secrecy must be upheld at any cost. The Institution would not have survived all of these centuries had it not been for that. They preferred to work behind the scenes, and had total control of political and monetary power of the world and controlled it with ruthless authority. Luther knew the mere mention of the real name of the society would mean a guaranteed death sentence, so it went by a generic name amongst its members. He had witnessed past indiscretions by some of its former members foolish enough to break the rule of silence. He saw the result with his own eyes, the tortuous pain ... it had been more than enough to keep him in line.

He lied. "The president wants to avoid panic at all costs, and we can't have reporters running around spouting off inane thoughts and unsubstantiated facts or trying to incite the consciousness of the voting public. Look at what has already happened in Colorado. We have nut cases coming forward with ashes out of their fireplaces for crying out loud, claiming they're the ashes of the Senator's son, trying to claim their fifteen minutes of fame. Never mind fraudulently trying to collect the reward this distraught family has posted, hoping for their son's safe return. It's just not good politics not to do something about it. I'm sure all of you are well aware that the president will be running for re-election in two year's time. He can ill- afford to show his constituents that his administration can't handle this minor problem. It's a sign of weakness. I'm sure every one of you gentlemen will concur with these thoughts. The president's approval ratings are good and he intends to keep them that way. He's looking for your support on this matter. So, let's get back to the task at hand, shall we?" A murmur of approval rumbled around the table. "Now does anyone have any idea on where she might be?" Luther asked, striving for calm. No one answered. No one else wanted to voice an opinion on how Florence Rinna had presumably disappeared into thin air.

"Maybe we can force an answer to your dilemma out of the editor of the Post?" one of them suggested.

"That would be something I want to save as a last resort," Luther said, not that he hadn't already thought of that proposal. He knew numerous ways of forcefully obtaining the required information out of the man but the risk at this moment was too great. "Besides, there has already been too much public exposure as it is."

Luther looked in the direction of the Director for Homeland Security, Phillip Wisner, and his aim was to belittle everyone in the room for their incompetence. "Phil had you done as I had initially requested, you spineless idiot, maybe, just maybe, we wouldn't even be here today? How about it, Phil? Is there anything you have to say in your defense?"

The man squirmed in his chair, glancing from side to side looking for assistance. He latched onto Arthur Bremmington without saying a word, his forlorn eyes pleading for aid.

Luther bore down on him intent on making a fool out of the man. "I requested that you black out the editor's impromptu interviews and comments, yet you allowed him to spout off. I thought you told me you had complete control over the media?" The man hung his head and did not respond. He sighed loudly. "That's another reason why I said earlier that if you want something done right, you have to do it yourself." The man shrank further into the chair. "All right then, what do we really know, other than she was in Cairo at one point in time? Anyone have a clue to her whereabouts at this moment? This is a repetitious question, gentlemen, in case you're wondering?"

Arthur spoke once again. "You're the one tapping all of the editor's calls and supposedly eavesdropping on all his conversations, Luther. Maybe you should tell us?"

Luther was not about to let on that his department had failed on that point as well; someone privy to the inner workings of his department had coded all transatlantic calls generated to and from the editor's line. He had thought that that in of itself was an impossible feat considering NSA technical prowess, but he had been proven wrong.

He had issued a red letter of admonishment to that effect to all of his departments, but was not about to give Bremmington any more ammunition. The NSA was working around the clock trying to find the man responsible for just that. They didn't want to silence him as much as they wanted to hire him as a security advisor. Anyone capable of doing that was too much of a threat not to be reeled into the system. The funny thing was, all they could ascertain at this point was that the man seemed to be stationed here in the states and was protecting the reporter for some reason. His department had combed through her dossier and had yet to find anyone with the capability of doing just that. They were still working diligently in that respect, but would not give up until they found their man. It was priority one as far as he was concerned, as he continued to pressure his subordinates for a solution.

As far as the reporter was concerned, it was almost impossible to disappear without a trace in this day and age. He knew she had to have been coached to do so, but was still waiting for some electronic sign of her whereabouts. When that happened, he would be able to pinpoint her exact location and deal with the situation accordingly. He had his people standing by in event of her sudden reappearance. He didn't trust the CIA, and the possibility of failure was not an option. He answered the query with another lie. "As far as we can tell, she has not been in contact with him."

"Then how is she getting her stories to him, or do you know? Have you checked all other possible contacts?" Bremmington pressed.

"We have screened all of his mail, texts and phone messages on a continuous basis," Riggs replied. "The only other way we know of is through diplomatic pouch, which you are well aware, is off limits as far as the government is concerned. We can't randomly stop a courier to examine the contents of a briefcase, Arthur!"

"What about his web messaging?" Arthur retorted straight away, trying to corner his nemesis.

Luther began to smile; the permanent sneer on his face had all but been erased. Worldwide web messaging, they really didn't have a clue. The Institution invented it, for crying out loud, so they didn't have to bother sorting through the masses of paper now referred to as snail mail.

It was a lot easier to glean information they needed to know with just one push of a button. The hilarious thing about it all was how gullible John Q. Public really was. They bought the new technology hook, line and sinker. It wasn't invented for them, it was invented for us, he thought. The plus of it all was even better than the Institution had even dreamed. Now they could monitor almost any possible threat to the cause through their electronic transmissions.

The Institution thought of the computer as an extremely useful tool that could upset the global financial markets with just a few keystrokes. The best part of it all was no one even knew they were doing it. They had undercover people out in the field in key positions at central banks monitoring the financial system, just in case anyone stumbled onto their operation by accident.

This computer frenzy was not a boon to mankind, but a bust. They could manipulate anyone's fortunes instantly, if they dared not co-operate with the policies of the Institution. It was a useful tool, similar to a vise. Whenever a politician, or anyone else for that matter, failed to honor a simple request, all they had to do squeeze his accounts dry and make his credit cards useless, which was usually enough to convince them to act on their behalf. There was no longer any need for strong-arm tactics, the norm in the past.

The web! What a name. The Institution was the spider in the middle of that web and its vast networks were the strands of silk that made up the web. That was how the Institution had been modeled since the beginning. There were networks in every nation in the world. Since the invention of the Internet, networks of people had been eliminated, literally and figuratively. The Institution ran much more efficiently these days with just one stroke of a key. He finally returned to the question at hand and answered abruptly. "We have the editor's e-mails covered as well."

"Do you think she has a runner then?"

Luther was growing peeved with this line of questioning from the lowly director, but knew he had to have help on this one to succeed. "That has yet to be determined. Maybe I should be asking y'all that question?" He noticed that he had erred grammatically and felt the blood rush to his face. Whenever he felt the pressure, his backwoods Kentucky slang reared its ugly head.

The room was silent for several moments. He could tell that Arthur caught the error immediately, and had he been wanton to embarrass the man further, now was his chance. He didn't.

"We're watching the editor's every move," he said. "If the man so much as farts, we know about it. Between your men and ours, we're tripping over one another. Maybe you need to back your men off so we can do our job properly," Bremmington chided.

"That's totally out of the question! Anybody got anything else?" Luther snapped. The room went silent once again. He tried to soft-soap them. "Surely, gentlemen, there has to be. We have assembled here some of the finest policing and monitoring agencies in the world, yet you all sit mum when I ask for ideas." He examined every face at the table, He knew he had to produce results or else. He could figuratively picture his head lolling into a straw basket by the blade of a guillotine, the consequence of his inaction. The guillotine was only one of the tools the Institution used to use with aplomb as a silencing mechanism. He also knew that he probably wouldn't be that lucky if he failed. More than likely, he would be slowly tormented, having his body burnt to a crisp one excruciating square inch at a time. He hated pain, adversely, though he never grew tired of inflicting it if asked to do so. He grew to love his sadistic side almost as much as the pleasure he obtained from seducing innocent boys. He had been taught well.

Arthur Bremmington had had enough. "Why are we playing Where's Waldo? You're beginning to sound like the press, Riggs!"

Luther had a feeling that more damaging stories were in the offing if the woman wasn't found, for she seemed to have an uncanny knack for uncovering facts better left buried. "We're not!"

"Well, if that's the case, and we have covered every possible way she could be communicating with her editor other than diplomatic pouch, someone has to be helping her is all I can say. It seems like we're running around in circles chasing our tails on this one, Riggs. Like I said to begin with when this meeting convened, let's just wait a bit. Sooner or later, she'll turn up, and until then we're sitting here wasting time as far as I'm concerned."

The Director of Foreign affairs, David Cole, spoke for the first time. "I agree with Director Bremmington. I suggest we adjourn this meeting until something new develops."

Luther reluctantly agreed. Time though, was not something he had in abundance. Soon, the last key element of deception would be in place, or so he had been told. No one had to know what was coming and nothing or no one must stop it from occurring. That was why it was imperative that he find the girl. She was stirring up all sorts of religious righteousness without even realizing it. It was not the story of Jeremiah that bothered the Institution as much as its predecessor on the Weeping Madonna's. Prayer groups seemed to be forming all over the country, which was much more damaging than was at first realized. The Institution was more concerned about this turn of events than anything else, in a quandary such as this, that any more stories of turmoil would compound the problem of unintended religious fervor.

Within the grasp of the Institution was the final act of seduction. It was only a matter of time as far as the Institution was concerned, when the last vestiges of the innocents would be led to slaughter. Religious righteousness, my ass, he thought. Let them try to herald the message of the Almighty; as far as the Institution was concerned it was no more than an unheard plea of a ship floundering in the night. Soon the final trick was to be played upon humanity. They had their man in place and were just waiting for the right moment to unleash his golden tongue unto the rest of the innocents and finally convert the remainder of them once and for all to the side of Satan. Then the battle would be won once and for all, the final defeat of the remnants of the chosen ones.

As far as he could see, the plan the Institution had in place was foolproof. Undermine the economies of every nation in the world; add to that the promise of global mayhem and the Institution's job would be complete. Satan was already enacting his own form of revenge, casting his own biblical vials of injustice by causing global weather calamities at every turn.

The best way to corrupt the innocents was through science. They secretly funded research projects that brought to question every known assumption of truth in the Bible and like religious tomes in an all-out effort to confuse the masses. Agnosticism was a direct result of their efforts, and as of late, was making major inroads into mainstream society due to their constant diligence.

The Institution had even delighted in the fact that they were solely responsible for getting 'In God We Trust' removed from the United States currency. That was only one example of many that Luther could cite as the group tried to strike religious aspects from the social conscience of its people. He knew that the policies of the Institution were effective, for there had not been much opposition to the long-standing tradition. They had years ago triumphed in another arena, having successfully lobbied and struck prayer from the classroom. Historically though, their greatest achievement had been turning the Catholic Church against their own Knights of the Templar, which resulted in stagnating the further expansion of their religion into the Middle East and points beyond. Add to that their ability to splinter the church into segments of offshoots like the Lutherans and the Institution at one moment in time almost toppled the behemoth into manageable segments.

Still, their main fear was that the recent turn of events might destroy all that they had accomplished. The leader of the Institution, whom Luther once met, was a venerable sage known by the singular name, Detritus. He had expressed his apprehensions to his followers about these prayer groups. He was seemly concerned that this trend could become a worldwide occurrence, and knew the power of prayer might upset their plans in terms of the final deception. They couldn't afford to take a chance on this occurring.

Luther had heard many stories about their leader, Detritus. Rumor had it if anyone dared to look into his red eyes; they were immediately scorched from the inside out. When Luther met the man, he had been wearing sunglasses, so he was not sure how true this rumor was but only speculated as to the plausibility. He knew one thing for sure; the man was a true albino who for the most part disguised his colorless skin and huge disfigured head with a hooded robe. He had been also told that the man had alien-like qualities, among them abnormally huge eyes that bulged out of his skull. He had an oversized mouth that seemed to take up most of the bottom half of his face and his lips were as thin as the rest of his body. The memory of the man was enough to cause Luther to shudder.

Luther also heard that Detritus had the ability to speak or convey messages without the use of his lips, but could project thought into anyone standing close by as well as receive it. It was said that the man could receive projected thought from the netherworld as well. How much of this was fact, Luther wasn't sure, but the rumors abounded.

He knew though that Detritus had cared for the "Golden Tongue" ever since he was a baby. He had nurtured and schooled the child, who it was said was found wandering amongst the ruins of the ancient city of Aden amongst a pack of jackals.

When Luther heard this story, he was hard pressed to believe it, knowing enough about the natural scheme of things to know that the male jackal most likely would have eaten him because of his foreign smell. But then, he was taught not to question these purported facts but to accept them at face value. He knew all too well if this was a true fact, something with great power had to have protected the child from harm.

Luther heard yet another unlikely story about the baby, but could not prove that the child was the result of Satan's union with a human female. After the delivery, the distraught mother was asked who the father was but she would only say that she had been raped in her sleep by a ghoulish fiend, an Incubus. Of course, no one believed the woman and sought to have her committed. She escaped from the birthing clinic before that could be achieved and died of her own hand soon after the baby's birth. Luther had to wonder once again if the story had as much validity as it seemed to take on. He had always wondered which story was true about the man known only as the Golden Tongue.

Luther had met the Golden Tongue on one prior occasion. The orator was twenty-five years old at the time. The best description of the man that Luther could give was one of such exquisite looks that you could hardly take your eyes off of him. He had rounded child-like facial features that looked almost feminine in quality. The man's alluring blue eyes were impressive. Luther found it hard to describe the shade, having never seen anything like it before. He swore when you looked into the man's eyes that a spark of glitter exploded from them. He knew another fact; women would surround him en masse and swoon. He drew them like a magnet and every one of them tried to vie for just a solitary moment of his attention. When he spoke, his voice mesmerized you. Luther likened the encounter to entering a trance, the man's sotto voice both soothed and massaged the ear at the same time.

Some women became so desperate for his approval and attention that they literally tore off their clothes in a futile attempt to be noticed. Luther witnessed this unnatural event of women that seemly became turned on by just the sight of the man. Luther became instantly jealous of his extraordinary looks and his alluring charm. It was hard for him to believe how captivating the young man seemed to be.

Having been forewarned, he thought that he might be able to resist the man's allure, but found it almost impossible to do. He tried to shake off the feeling he was somehow being manipulated like everyone else who surrounded the Golden Tongue, but found himself, like them, lost in rapt attention. He did not think it possible that this might occur. He had scoffed at the idea when others mentioned their encounters with him, but now that it had happened, he began to wonder if this was merely an extension of the powers of their leader, Detritus. Or was it the allure of Satan himself? He was later told that he had been literally dragged away from the meeting in order to escape his sphere of influence. For that reason alone, he knew that the Golden Tongue would be the final seduction of humanity. No one would be exempt from his power of seduction.

*   *   *

Antoine had been assigned as the sole protector of the Minor family in Cairo for the last three weeks. It was a job that he grew to detest. It was not so much because of the old man, Anhur. He was no trouble at all because mostly the man just slept and prayed. Nor was it his grandson Sefu or his mother for that matter, but his eldest son, Badru who had become a thorn in his side. With his constant demands, which taxed his limited time and resources, Antoine knew that it was abject boredom that caused the son to take on the child-like qualities of a spoiled brat.

The entire family had been sequestered in a non-descript home on the east side of the city. It was an area carefully selected to least likely draw any attention or makes it easy for someone to locate them. Try as he might though, he could not appease Badru. As the days wore on, he became more like a festering sore than anything else.

In the beginning, Antoine shrugged off his constant demands as merely a readjustment to the situation that had befallen the family. He hadn't minded running to the market for a certain style of pistachios or pack of cigarettes, which could be expected. However, to appease Badru, he bought cartons of cigarettes. These usually lasted about a week before he had to replenish them. Then it became every fourth day, then every third day. Badru, he noticed, had one of those foul things hanging from his lips whenever he saw him. Antoine noticed that the man became more and more irritable too. He likened the man's behavior to that of a caged animal, pacing the living room floor like a tiger paced his cage, winging his worry beads to and fro like a mace, chanting obscure verses like a raging lunatic.

Antoine began to worry about the man's frame of mind more than anyone else in the family, who seemed to have adjusted to the circumstances with little discomfort. Once the man found that every whim of his imagination was to be provided for, the church picking up the tab for all these frivolities, he began to ask for more and more. First, it was a computer, and then it became every electronic device imaginable, even some things not readily available in a city of this size. He had been instructed to provide, but this was getting out of hand and he was no babysitter or go-for, for that matter.

Antoine had set up a singular means of communication with the family, a dedicated cell phone with only one number in the phone's directory - his. The phone began to ring constantly. The more he tried to ignore Badru's demands on his time the worse they got. When he began to get calls in the middle of the night, Antoine wondered what might right the situation. The off- hour calls were more than an annoyance, but were the last straw as far as he was concerned. He found his own temperament shortened by the constant haranguing. He did the only sensible thing left he could do and reported his concerns to the Vatican.

They were the same concerns he had voiced to the monsignor in private several days ago, right before he left for Rome, but either the priest thought them of little concern or else he had ignored them entirely. He wasn't sure which, but knew he was being slighted for his conscientiousness. This was reaffirmed when it took over a week to receive a response regarding his request for advice on what to do about the situation from his contact at the Vatican.

When he finally got the delayed response to his query, he was not expecting what happened next. The response came in a standard form letter but not with instructions he sought on how to solve the problem. Instead, the letter contained a curt form of admonishment for his lack of diligence. Toward the bottom of the letter were instructions for handing over the family to a papal representative who would assist them in their move to Italy.

There were no thanks for a job well done or anything else congratulatory for his efforts in finding the visionary in the first place. They surely had not even considered the effort he and his assistant had gone through to find the proverbial needle in the haystack to begin with. This annoyed him more than anything else did; it's not what they said, but what they didn't say that bothered Antoine the most. The more he thought about the structure of the letter, the madder he became. He felt used and unappreciated, for they never even bothered to explain the reason for the move to begin with, other than possibly hinting he was somehow incompetent.

This was not expressed on paper but even a dummy could read between the lines. It was that obvious to him. He furiously tore up the letter into tiny bits and cast them into the trash with a bit of finality attached to it. He then did what he should have done all along; he ignored the demands of Badru and waited for the emissary from Rome to arrive. He did not even inform the family of their impending move, leaving this as a surprise for the family. Let the next fool deal with the man, he thought. I'm washing my hands of the entire affair.

When the emissary arrived, Antoine thought that he was less than commiserative to his predicament and told him so. All he got in return was a cold shoulder. The emissary's only interest was to get the family on the plane with the least bit of discomfiture to all parties concerned. This attitude really bothered Antoine, as he had been sure he would be personally thanked for his efforts. When that did not happen, he finally decided he had had enough.

It was at that moment that he decided to broker Anhur's story to anyone who would pay. Once the family boarded on the plane, he discreetly made inquiries, hoping to sell the privileged information. He finally found someone who would pay dearly for the story. With his allegiance in check, the temptation of that large of a sum of money was too great for him to resist and he sold it.

CHAPTER 11

Megiddo

"What do you mean you don't know?" She said, shaking her head in disbelief. "You must have some idea on what to do here; you're the leading authority on such matters, are you not? Or have I been misinformed in some way?"

"Ms. Rinna, there are no guides or books that might deal with what we are up against. I'm not being a fatalist here but--"

She cut him off. "But what? You have to have some idea on how this is all going to unfold. Don't tell me that you haven't given the scenario the least bit of thought. I think I know you a little better than that, or am I wrong in assuming as much?"

"No, but you have to remember one thing," he replied patiently. "It has been written that the final battle has to come to pass in order to preclude the thousand years of peace. There's where the solution lies, as far as I'm concerned."

"Oh no its not, you're wrong, Monsignor," she stated forcefully. "Let me play devil's advocate here, no pun intended. You are of a mindset that the white side is winning or going to win. Let me be perfectly frank. This isn't a chess game, Monsignor, because they are not.... do you hear me.... *not* winning! You heard what Anhur said! We're dealing with the continuation of life here on this planet and the only way some of us are going to survive is by seeing to it that the side of righteousness wins. It's like I had told you earlier; people are being sacrificed daily for the good of others. That's the way I see it. The angels are soliciting reinforcements in an as-needed basis for now, but soon .... Very soon Monsignor, they will have to call in all the righteous souls in order to turn the tide. That's what I'm getting out of all this and I don't believe I'm wrong about that. What happens if the tide does not turn in our favor? Then what is written makes no sense at all, does it?" She tried to reign in her temper and took a deep, calming breath. "You asked me to give you an unbiased opinion earlier... and I...I am doing just that, but something has to be done." She desperately tried to lower her voice. "Look, in case you haven't noticed, I'm becoming a bit unnerved by all this and at this point, droll excuses are not going to work. Some sort of plan has to be put in place in order to turn things around. Don't you agree?"

"Yes," the monsignor replied. "But I am not so sure you are right when it comes to your assumption that planet will become void of habitation. That is an extreme thought, is it not?"

"Is it? The dinosaurs and for that matter, many species go extinct all the time," she said. "Maybe I'm wrong, maybe not, who's to know? You surely don't know for sure, but think about this for a moment. What if what was written could be altered somehow? Then what you purport then becomes moot in my book. I don't want to rewrite the facts as you know them, but everything that is written is not rule! You said it yourself earlier, that many of the known facts written herein are subjected to scrutiny. Didn't you say that, Monsignor?" She pointed to the open book that still lay before her.

"I did," he agreed, "Though it is constantly being challenged by others... not by me. There is where a measure of faith has to come into play; you have to believe at one point or another that what is written is essentially true."

"So you say," she retorted. "But mind you, as I pointed out earlier, we are not dealing with an opponent that fights fair. Queensbury rules don't apply here. He only fights to win and prove his point as well! You must remember that the great deceiver will do whatever it takes to win. You said it yourself, didn't you? We are talking about all the souls of the righteous here!"

The Monsignor could see what she was driving at and was somewhat amazed at her ability to do so effectively. He said nothing at first but just looked across the table, wondering about her; to him she was a study in contradiction, playing both sides of the story in order to prove a point.

What if she was right? What if anything done at this point was of no use? He knew another thing as well; if what she said were the truth of the matter, it would take the united effort on the part of all religions and all people of the world to combat this threat. The only way that he knew to do that was to expose the entire affair to the world and to see if his thought on the matter became the truth.

That would only happen if they could witness the raging battle with their own eyes, like she had stated earlier. Then out of the blue, he thought she said something that even he had not expected.

"You must use the power of prayer, Monsignor."

He had been looking right at her but had not noticed her lips moving. "Did you just say something?" he asked.

"No, why?" she said blankly. "As far as I can recall, you still haven't answered my question and I'm waiting."

He believed her, and thought maybe… just maybe, the mysticism of the angels had overcome him. At that moment, he decided on a course of action. "Look, I want you to go ahead and write this story. I told you what Pope Romanus said about the ramifications of your story, but I want you to disregard it for the moment. Can you do that?'

"Yes, but why the sudden change?"

"I have my reasons."

"Which are?"

"Let me just say I'm assuming at some point the Pope will have to concede and agree with our line of thought on the matter."

Flo felt he was being vague once more but did not press. "In order to write a convincing story, I'll need a little more insight on this city, Megiddo, before I can give the story my full attention."

"What do you want to know?"

"Please tell me everything that you know about Megiddo that might be relevant. Then I'll need some sort of reference material also. Can you arrange that?"

"Sure," he shrugged. "First turn to Chapter Sixteen and page down to verses fourteen through sixteen and read aloud what it says. This is the only pertinent reference to the city you will find in Revelations, though there are others in the Old Testament as well."

She did and read it out loud. *"For they are spirits of the devils, working signs: and they go forth unto the kings of the whole earth, to gather them to battle against the great day of the Almighty God. Behold, I come as a thief. Blessed is he who watches and keeps his garments, lest he walk naked, and they see his shame. And he shall gather them together into a place which in Hebrew is called Armageddon."*

Giuseppe nodded. "As I said earlier, the word Armageddon and Megiddo are interchangeable in this context. Let me give you some historical facts about the city so that you might better understand its strategic importance. At one time, the city lay at an intersection of two trade routes overlooking the valley of Jezreel in the northern area of Palestine, once known as Canaan. This area is now part of modern-day Israel. The city is said to be some five thousand years old, though it was last inhabited some twenty-three hundred years ago. Because of its strategic location, it became a city-state that had been laid under siege many times throughout its history. The Egyptians under Pharaoh Thutmose III defeated the fortress state and it is the first recorded battle in ancient times.

'Megiddo is referenced once again in the Old Testament Book of Kings. King Solomon fortified the cities of Megiddo, Hazor and Gezer. Sometime after the fortifications were completed, the area became known as Palestine, which was defeated by the Assyrians, who then controlled the area for some time. They appointed Megiddo the capital of one of their newly found provinces. Probably the most important aspect of the city is the fact that it was there in Megiddo that King Josiah of Judah was killed. He was one of the most important religious reformers of his time. His name is revered even to this day in terms of influential Jewish religious leaders.

'To give you a better understanding of why this religious man is so important, you should recall that when Moses died after the Israelites came to the Promised Land, Joshua became the next leader. He had assigned sections of the Promised Land to the twelve tribes of Israel and the Judeans settled in an area just south of city of Jerusalem. The Judeans ended up becoming the most powerful of all the twelve tribes. When the Assyrians conquered the area, the Judean tribe became part of the Assyrian empire. The Babylonians then went to war with the Assyrians and in a weakened state, the Assyrians asked Egypt for assistance in repelling the Babylonians.

'King Josiah of Judea was more interested in reuniting with Israel as part of the Promised Land and challenged the Egyptians under Pharaoh Necco to a battle, during which he was slain. This is why I believe the reasoning Revelations states the last battle will be fought there in Megiddo as the final battle as good triumphs over evil because of the religious significance of the location. I hope this explains the importance of Megiddo a little better and clarifies the passage you read."

"Not in its entirety," Flo stated. "Isn't there a reference to the second coming of Christ in the quote as well?"

"If there is nothing else I can say about you, Ms. Rinna, you don't miss a thing. Yes, there is also a reference to the great day of the almighty God, though in this context it means one of two things; either the total defeat of Satan and his armies or the arrival or second coming of Christ. This time though, He may walk among us and we will not even be aware of His presence."

"That was my take on the verse," she agreed. "I was just looking for verification of my thoughts. I have to explain something here, for I believe that at times you look at me as if I am confused. Hardly, a bit crazy, but aren't we all in one respect or another? In order for me to write a concise story, I usually study both sides of a story. In some respects, I'm my own worst enemy - or critic. In order for this piece to be insightful as well as enlightening, I have to have a feel for the story, if you know what I mean."

He nodded in agreement.

"However, I have a bit of a problem when it comes to the reasoning why you have changed your mind and want me to write this story, to begin with. I know that Pope Romanus has strictly forbid you or me from leaking any of this information without his approval, so why the sudden change of heart?"

"I just think that if you write this story the way you did your two previous stories, I would be in a better position to convince the Pontiff of our intent."

"At this point, it probably would be an interesting read and nothing more than that, unless you have made some progress in replicating the light. I'm afraid. I would have to agree with the Pope in this case. You must be able to back this type of a story with supporting evidence. Tell me truthfully, have you gotten anywhere in that regard?"

"Yes and no. I have made some discreet inquires into the matter, as I stated earlier, but to date, no one has firmly committed to the project."

"Who have you contacted up to this point?"

"There's the Institute of Optics in Orsay, France and a company in Zurich, Switzerland, whose name slips my mind at the present moment. Both of them have said that under the right conditions, they could possibly alter the blue light band throughout its spectrum but have no way of projecting it across a large area, such as a desert."

Maybe I can help in that respect. I have a close friend who has seemingly all the right connections. Maybe he can help us in this matter," she said trying to ease the priest's obvious look of despondency. "Otherwise, I believe that I'm just wasting my time writing a story that would never be published for lack of credibility."

"You have a point, Ms. Rinna."

"I realize that the pope's true intent is to limit the exposure to the facts by controlling who knows the truth about what is really going on, but I know this man, and know he would not divulge a word about what we know. I know he can help. But then again, it's not my call, but yours in this case. You're the one who's ultimately responsible," she murmured. "You tell me."

He said nothing for several moments and she waited patiently while he mulled over the dilemma. "Go ahead and call him, if you think he can aid our cause, for at this point I really have nothing to lose."

She studied his face for several moments and wondered if he was again holding back some important bit of information. She was getting that feeling again. When he looked away, she knew her assumption to be true for some unknown reason. "I'll call him and see what he says. I know he can help us through this." She fished through her purse, retrieved her cell phone, and dialed the number by rote. "Trey, I have a favor to ask."

*   *   *

Luther didn't really believe in red-letter days but could not believe his luck today. "I've got her now! I knew she couldn't hide forever!" he murmured.

His department had tapped into the mainframe monitoring her phone directory for ingoing and outgoing messages and the finally got an overseas hit. "Well, I'll be damned; she's in Rome of all places. I should have figured out she'd be there."

Rome was a big city and he knew they would have to triangulate her location to get a pinpoint fix on her, but unfortunately, she had not stayed on the line long enough for them to do that. For some reason, he believed she was lodged somewhere in Vatican City. Her last story about the Weeping Madonna's should have tipped him off to begin with. It would be easy enough to find her. All he had to do was make some arrangements and then dial her phone number.

They had taped her entire overseas conversation and repeatedly played it back for some hint to her location. The information was less than a day old but no matter; she could not hide any longer. He had her number. He laughed ruefully at his own pun. He wondered what she had been up to all this time, but that question became evident several hours later when he was given information about a supposedly farfetched yarn that had been bought from an overseas information broker based in Cairo.

Though the probability of the story being true never crossed his mind, Luther dialed the phone, hoping to be complimented for his astute diligence in handling the situation He never passed the information along. When he hung up, he could still hear Detritus's words ringing in his ears. "It's her life or yours. The solution should be evident to even a backwoods hick like you." He rubbed his forehead with nervous anxiety, hoping to ease the sense of depredation that now clouded his mind. He worried about the timetable as well; he had to have her in three days or else! This assignment he would handle alone. He trusted no one else with his own life at stake.

Why Detritus had given him only three days to complete the assignment had him wondering. No matter, he could bring her in on schedule, or so he believed. He opened the desk drawer and pulled out a small baggie of cocaine, followed by a straw. He needed to relax. After several minutes, he began to laugh out loud at the irony of the entire situation,

After his mind cleared, Luther surmised that the timetable had to have something to do with the much-anticipated debut of the Golden Tongue, whose religious show would be broadcast for the first time ever on the Christian Broadcasting station. He was sure that Detritus wanted no detrimental publicity that might possibly taint the message. He had watched a pre-taped copy of the show last evening and found that he was still mesmerized by the young man's voice. He took another snort and laughed mirthlessly at the obvious ignorance of what was about to transpire.

*   *   *

Monsignor Giuseppe Lorenzo could not help but notice the two of them as they sat in front of him. "Amore," he thought as he listened to them banter back and forth as if he wasn't even there. It was not what they said to one another as how they looked at one another that told the true story of their relationship. He was sure from what he had learned from Ms. Rinna that she had not yet weakened sufficiently to admit to what seemed self-evident. She was clearly in some state of love with Trey, though the Monsignor thought she was purposely evading the obvious.

"On a serious note here," Trey said, breaking into his ruminations. "You know, I thought I taught you better than that. Never leave a trail. You should have called me from a public phone or had sense enough to use someone else's phone, or at least called someone who could have relayed the message without drawing any attention to you or me. Snail mail would have sufficed in this instance. I'm not concerned here about me; I can take care of myself. It's you that I'm worried about. That's the problem with women," he scoffed. "No logical sense at all."

Flo bristled. "I'm sorry, I just got carried away. It won't happen again."

"That's an understatement, because at this point in time it's evident even to me that you haven't yet learned a thing, I taught you on how to hide in plain view!"

Flo sought to change the subject and appease him. "I'm not worried in the least now that you're here to protect me--"

He cut her off. "Damn straight about that, If there is a next time? You haven't got a clue here about the danger you're in, do you? I've have been covering your back ever since you left for Rome. That, I'm sure, is obviously something that has never occurred to you. Never, ever, under any circumstance, do you make direct contact with anyone you know? That was rule one in case it slipped your mind, and that includes your editor in this case!"

Flo flushed red, acknowledging her mistake with a silent nod of her head.

"Luckily for you I was able to intercept and scramble the call or the NSA would have already had you. According to them, you are a Code One security risk! Do you have any idea what that means?"

"No," She murmured.

"Terminate at any cost!"

Flo sobered immediately. "What? Why me?"

"I believe the British used to have the correct word for it. Sedition! Though I don't think the top levels of government issued the order. I believe the NSA is being manipulated by an outside source. They issued the order, but who's pulling the strings I have yet to determine."

Flo understood the implications of his statement and cursed her editor under her breath. "Okay, truce here," she suggested. "From now on, I will do exactly what you say. I concede you're the expert here."

"So, what is all this about anyway?"

Flo knew she would have to tell Trey what she had inadvertently gotten him into, but first she had to translate to the monsignor everything she had learned so far so that he fully understood the ramifications of the situation. When she finished, she noted the look of bewilderment in the priest's face and waited patiently for some sort of acknowledgement.

Trey grew impatient. "In for a penny, in for a pound. Come on, spill it, Flo. It's too late for remorse now."

"I don't think there is a translation for slang metaphors in Italian," she retorted.

"Well! Do something here," he snapped. "The day's burning away and I have to know in order to respond in kind."

"Whew! A bit of a nervous Nelly, aren't we? Besides, Monsignor Lorenzo has a fair grasp of the English language; it's just that his vocabulary isn't as extensive as ours. That's the only reason why I translated in the first place," she stated. She again spoke to the priest and finally got a nod of approval. "Where do you want me to start?"

"My apologies, "Trey said to the priest and then directed his gaze to Flo. "From the beginning would be helpful."

"It all started on my original trip to Rome to cover the purported death of Pope Alexander…"

Some two hours later, it was Trey's turn to react as he let out a low whistle. "This is a joke, right?"

"Hardly," Flo stated with emphasis. "I told the Monsignor you'd be able to help."

"In what capacity?"

"We need to know if you know of anyone who might replicate this blue light and be able to project it over a large area as well. I would have asked you over the phone, but it seemed too risky."

Trey considered. "You may want to translate this to the monsignor here; I will have to pull in some favors to get what you asked done. I believe the Massachusetts Institute of Technology is where we will probably have the best luck. I will have to ask my uncle, Dr. Kyle

Hanson, who is the director of the National Weather Service, to intervene on your behalf."

Trey left the room and returned several minutes later, sitting heavily in the chair.

"What?" Flo asked studying his face.

"It seems that the veil of secrecy you seem to be working under is not as hush-hush as you lead me to believe. When I phoned him, he was already aware of this blue bolt of light you are so bent on replicating."

"Can it be replicated?" the monsignor asked.

"My uncle seems to think it can, but he has already asked why anyone would want to in the first place."

"Did you ask him how long it might take to build such an instrument?' Flo asked.

"I did, but he didn't give me a definitive answer," Trey said, leaning back in the chair and putting his hands behind his head in the process.

Flo frowned.

"Look, I didn't tell him anything that might tip our hand, if that's what you're thinking," he said."If I said we needed it yesterday, he would have had to know all of the pertinent details"

"Did I say anything?" Flo replied

"It's the look you gave me. If you want my opinion here, I think you ought to publish the story in its entirety the way you just told it to me. I agree with the monsignor in this case that it would sway public sentiment if nothing else, and would probably aid your cause. What you really need here is a spin-doctor to give it enough credibility until we're able to replicate this light and see what this visionary supposedly saw. By the way, where is this Anhur you were referring to?"

"I believe he is still in Cairo," Flo replied. "At least, that's where I last saw him."

"Are you sure? His life is probably in danger," Trey frowned. "He must be protected at all costs."

Flo leaned toward the monsignor and directed the question to him. "He says the family arrived here in Rome as of yesterday, which is something that I was not aware of."

"I'd like to talk to him if it is at all possible. There is something else I'd like you to stress to the monsignor," Trey explained. "From what you have told me, he needs to convince the pope on what we have all agreed upon as well, that publishing the story is a must. I'm not sure how he's going to do this but it has to be done. By the way, have you even started writing this story yet?"

"Actually, I'm about halfway through. Still, it will probably take me some time to finish it and polish it."

"Well, you better get cracking then," Trey said with a smile.

Flo bristled at his audacity even though she knew he was taunting her. "I'm working on it, boss. You're beginning to sound just like my editor, and that's no compliment."

Trey chuckled at the implication. "We would probably work well together, if that's the case."

At this point Flo knew she was being baited and did not reply to the slight. She reached into her purse to retrieve the unfinished draft so that she could let Trey read it. Just then, her cell phone rang and she answered it out of habit.

Trey bolted out of his chair and snatched the phone out of her hand, disconnected the caller in the process. His lighting strike took less than two seconds to accomplish from the first ring. Flo reeled back in her chair in shock.

"Sorry, I had to," he said. "Since you last called me, have you used this cell phone?"

"No!"

"Has anyone else tried to call you until now?"

"No!"

"Good, look I have got to leave now. I'll catch up with the two of you later," Trey said, taking the phone with him.

"Where are you going…?" Flo tried to ask, but he had already out of the room.

After he left, Flo was shaken.

"What does your friend do for a living?"

"I… I really don't know for sure," she stammered. "He has never told me and he generally changes the subject whenever I ask him. I have a hunch he's an information specialist of some sort. I think he works for the government, but in what capacity I'm not sure. I know one thing. He seems to be well connected and I use him on occasion to provide me with information not readily available by any other means, if you know what I mean."

"I see. He seems to be highly educated."

"Yes, yes, he is…. I know that he graduated from Yale and played some football while he was there, but to hear him tell it, he was not talented enough to make the first team so he quit. He spent some time in the service, that much I know, but which branch I'm not sure of. Other than that, I really don't know that much about him."

"Do you trust him?"

"Yes, exclusively, why do you ask?"

"No particular reason, I was just making conversation," Monsignor Lorenzo commented. "It seems to have helped ease your nervousness about the entire situation. Look, I'm sorry I got you and your friend involved in all of this mess. It seems to me the more we delve into all of this, the more complicated it becomes for all of us. Maybe Pope Romanus was right after all. There is more to all this than meets the eye."

Flo wondered what he was driving at. "It anything, it's my fault for nosing around to begin with. No one's to blame here, and certainly not you. We did not set the wheels in motion to begin with, so let's forget about it, agreed?"

"Agreed," the monsignor nodded. "Will you be all right here alone for awhile? I have to leave for a while. There is something I need to attend to, but I will be back some time later."

"Sure, but I'm not going to stay in this conference room. I'll just walk back to the apartment and work on my story there. There is less of a tendency to be distracted."

*   *   *

The angels had gathered aloft the battlefield in an effort to regroup. Gabriel sensed the total disappointment of his war-worn leaders but did not know what words of encouragement, if any, he might transmit to the group that would help alleviate the state of depression that overwhelmed them. Gabriel knew one thing for sure; he was tired and weary and if he was, he was sure the other archangels felt the same. The battle had been raging for several millennia and holding back the armies of the Sons of Darkness seemed a futile endeavor. Their armies seemed to be expanding exponentially of late, and they were beginning to progress across the desert like a German panzer division. Gabriel was clueless on how to stop them. The closer they got to Megiddo, the more ground they were able to cover.

It was Ariel once again who lamented over their predicament, as he had begun to utilize his new-found voice recently. He'd become more critical of Gabriel's assessment of the ongoing situation. *You must send for Duma*, he transmitted with apparent authority, as he turned toward Michael for a nod of encouragement. He noticed though, none was forthcoming on this suggestion, for he sensed Michael knew the ramifications that sending for the Collector of Souls meant.

Only God can raise the dead to overwhelm them, he communicated with firm conviction. *It is not your or my call. He will enlighten us to when that might be necessary. It would be best if you held your thoughts to yourself at this juncture, for you know not the ramifications of what you are proposing, Ariel.*

Then petition him to break the first vial, Ariel pleaded. *Their armies grow stronger by the day and so does the beast. He feeds off of the human lust, and the slaughter of innocent life and you must divert them somehow.*

It is not for us to alter the course of the human condition, nor is it likely that Yahweh would look down upon us with favor were we to initiate anything such as breaking a vial. No, that is something that is irreprehensible to me, for once it has begun, there is no turning back.

Unleashing the plagues is not my idea of altering the human condition. Besides, unless you are totally unaware of your surroundings, enough has already been done in the name of Belial… for strife is rampant. Know this Ariel, the heat is building and the doors of hell have begun to open or have you not noticed?

I have, Ariel agreed. *But so have you. The doors are opening not only for the scourge of this earth, but also for you and me and the Sons of the Lamb. They are driving us toward the entrance to open them further; I feel the vacuum of the abyss grow stronger every day. Soon, very soon, Gabriel, you will have to petition the Almighty to aid us in some fashion whether you care to or not. The howl of the hole rings in my ears even now and we are still quite a way away. Other than that, maybe some sort of trickery might be useful? Maybe we can fake them out by using holograms of our troops?* Ariel saw the looks of contempt on that accord and changed tact. *How do you propose to bolster our ranks in order to push them back into the sea? Call for Duma, Gabriel, it's the sensible thing to do.*

Michel saw fit to intervene at this point. *I for one, will not be chastised ever again for something I felt strongly enough about in the first place. There is no place here for an emotional response and striking out on your own accord is not a wise path to take. It would do well for you, Ariel, to heed the message of our mission! Besides, trickery, smoke and mirrors or whatever you might want to design are his works not ours.*

Then, perhaps there might be another way of asking for assistance, the angel Lydius interjected. *Petition the woman, she has His ear.*

Once again, out of the question, Gabriel refused.

Marek interjected his thoughts. *If not, then it seems the wisest course of action is to let divinity rule and hope that the humans feel the heat as we do. I know they feel the insurgency of the planet; hopefully one day soon they will put the pieces of the puzzle together and see the true picture before it is too late and the doors to Hades swing wide.*

Ariel was still not satisfied. *Call in the Guardians then, there are enough of them to overwhelm the dragon at this point.*

They are councilors, not warriors! What do propose they do, talk the opposition to death? We need warriors at this point. Besides, if we were to do that, it would leave all of the humans vulnerable!

Some of the other angels chuckled at Gabriel's response.

Well, it is my opinion they don't use them anyway, they are hardly ever called upon by the humans in any capacity any longer, so why not utilize them to show a mass of force? Maybe it would cause the angel Lucifer to take notice and back off on his plan to enslave all of their souls? It's a thought that I feel you might want to consider, Gabriel, Ariel said.

Look, we are not bound here, nor are we bound to alter the natural course of man's fate. It is up to them to do what they see fit. It is their right to use their free will in any way they choose. We are not here to intervene in any way. We are here to fight the battle, and it is their choice which side they wish to join. We cannot, nor will we, interfere in their choices. If they wish to abet Satan at the cost of the eternal light, so be it. I forbid you to interfere at this point, Ariel.

That is not my intent, nor would I intercede without approval of the group, Ariel objected. *It is my opinion that you at least have to consider all of the options available at your disposal as I mentioned previously, before we get driven any closer to the gates. At least petition for all of the living good souls to be taken at once so that we might have a formidable force in which to combat the Sons of Darkness. Otherwise, I believe we will be totally annihilated before we can get the gates closed again.*

Again, I will not intervene with their destiny, Gabriel refused. *We have been told that we were to only take what souls were needed to keep from being overrun. I will not circumvent a direct order and drive them back toward the sea for your benefit, Ariel!*

At least allow us to vote on the proposals that have been set forth, Ariel pleaded. *Look below at the mass of carnage that rests below your feet, Gabriel, and tell me we can go on like this indefinitely.*

Gabriel did look down and tears welled up in his eyes over the losses they had endured this day. Bodies lay strewn all over the sand below them. He knew Ariel was justly concerned about the slaughter, but his hands were tied and there was nothing he could or would do about them. *I cannot allow the group to even vote on the proposals, for you know as well as I do, He knows and sees all. He is aware of the outcome and we are not privy to such thoughts as those, Ariel.*

Michael forced a conclusion to their thoughts. *Amen to that, Brother Gabriel!*

Marek seconded the motion by drawing his blood-soaked sword once again and pointing it toward the battlefield below them. He abruptly left the company of the other angels to join in the battle once more.

CHAPTER 12

Enlightenment

Trey knew there was only a limited amount of time left before he would have to power up the phone again. At first, he thought about putting the phone on a train headed out of Rome but first he had to know who was looking for Flo. He assumed that the caller knew the woman, but would not be smart enough to know that he would attempt to triangulate their position just as they were trying to triangulate hers. His main focus was to make it less than obvious that he was on to them. He'd been able to thwart their earlier efforts and now had the advantage of surprise on his side. He drove south out of Rome as quickly as possible, following a road that paralleled the old Roman aqueduct, which still stood almost intact, even after some two thousand years. He marveled at the size and the soundness of the structure as he searched for a suitable area in which to ambush whoever was looking for Florence.

"Come on here!" he said. He glanced at his watch in a moment of frustration. It had been fifteen minutes since that first call and he wanted to be sure that no suspicions were aroused. He almost drove past a suitable location, but jammed on the brakes hard enough to make the tires cry. He threw the car into reverse as soon as his forward motion had stopped, causing the car to lurch and squeal in reverse simultaneously. Backing up and stopping in front of the old stone church, he looked up and smiled at the open belfry, a perfect location in which to observe the archway of the aqueduct that sat at the intersection of two roads.

He thought this to be a perfect location and swung the car around, parking it under the arch directly across from the church. He got out, opened the trunk and removed a valise. Then, he reached into his pocket and powered up the cell phone. He keyed the number of the weather service and knew the phone would stay open until it was disconnected or the battery died. This would give them ample time to pinpoint the exact location of the phone. He then opened the passenger door to place it on the floor between the front seat and the passenger side door. Perfect! Anyone who saw it lying there would think it fell out of her purse. He left the door to the vehicle unlocked, then hustled across the street to the church, valise in hand.

Luckily, the front door to the aged church was not locked and he silently stepped inside, carefully listening for signs of human activity. Fortunately, for him, no one seemed to be inside as he carefully scanned the interior. He made his way up the center aisle of the church, looking for access to the belfry. The church was cool and dank and smelled like a combination of candle wax and musk. He made his way onto the apse and found a door to his left that led to the rear of the church.

He found the worn stone stairway behind the sacristy and made his way up the stairs to a door that led to the belfry. He found that door unlocked too, which surprised him. With a shrug, he opened the door and glanced inside the small room. He realized he had to stoop in order to move around, but it was the perfect viewing location to watch for vehicles emerging from underneath the arch of the aqueduct. He was less than two hundred yards from his vehicle but the stone arch of the belfry was low enough so that he would not be readily noticed.

He sat down, opened his valise and removed the Glock, tucking it in his waistband. He then began to assemble the sharpshooter's rifle stored in thick foam compartments. He could assemble the rifle in pitch darkness, if necessary, after years of practice. He heard the two halves decisively click together and then screwed the silencer onto the barrel. Once he was satisfied everything was assembled correctly, he installed the scope and loaded the rifle. In one fluid motion, he raised and sighted it. The target area beneath the ancient aqueduct and the area surrounding his vehicle seemed only feet away under magnification of the scope. Trey knew at this point it would depend on how many people showed up whether or not he would use the gun in order to thwart their efforts.

The ex-CIA operative hated this game of hurry up and wait; it reminded him of the reason why he had quit the service in the first place and started his own company two years ago. He hated waiting for anyone or anything, a quirk of his for sure, feeling he had little precious time to waste, and sitting around waiting for something to happen was not one of them.

Once his company was established, he had hired several men to perform the tedious stakeouts. He enjoyed intel-gathering without the burden of being in the field. Still there were times such as these where he had no other option, but it still pained him to do so. He was more adroit to the complexities of the computer and found it more advantageous to his line of work than wearing out the seat of his pants.

He felt that while working for the CIA he had been underutilized, but nevertheless sometimes missed the comradeship of department employees. He wished that the department had ceded to his request to come in from the field, for he would have never have quit had he been allowed to do so.

Trey was thankful for the training the department had given him, for it proved invaluable once he started his own business. The contacts he had secured were useful in expanding his fledging business. Most people never fully realized what an expansive enterprise intelligence gathering was; a multibillion-dollar business that kept expanding every year. Trey figured at the rate at which his small company was growing, it would be only be a short matter of time before he could retire, if he so wished.

Trey noticed a white van pull up next to his rented car a half hour later. At first, no one got out of the vehicle. He watched the van through his scope and wondered how many men were inside, but could not tell with the way it was parked. All he saw was the rear of the windowless van. Then, the driver's-side door slowly opened and Trey watched a man slowly exit the vehicle. He could not see his face at first; it was not until he walked around the front of the van and began to peer into the window of the rented car that Trey saw his face, one that he did not recognize. Trey also noticed the transponder in the man's hand but waited for several more moments to see if anyone else joined him. When no one else got out, he began to wonder why they would send only one man to kidnap the reporter and risk losing her through insufficient manpower.

He shot out the rear passenger-side tire. The shot was inaudible. The man, now searching the car, appeared startled by the noise of escaping air. He backed out of the car and looked around. Trey was sure that if anyone else were in the van, they would have gotten out at this point. No one did. Then he noticed the man finally turn in the direction of the church and look around, pulling his suit coat off to the side. He spied the gun in the man's waistband.

Trey left the rifle in the belfry and headed down the stairs, making his way to the entrance of the church as fast as he could. On his way upstairs, he had locked the side door so he knew there was only one way in. If he had this figured right, whoever was after Florence would assume she was inside the church. He had his back up against the locked side of the double door when it opened. The man's gun appeared first but Trey waited. It seemed like an eternity before the man stepped any further into the entrance. Trey heard him mutter and saw the gun shake. He heard the man curse the Lord's name with increasing regularity as if gathering the courage to enter. When the man's shoulder finally appeared, he struck. Hitting the man in the collarbone, he saw the gun drop as he wheeled the man's arm around behind his back and placed the Glock behind his ear. "The best course of action for you is to have a seat" he said, forcing the man down into a nearby pew. He reached inside the vest pocket of his coat and removed the billfold, flipping it open in the process. Trey let out a slow whistle while he increased the pressure on the barrel of the gun.

"Where is she, and who are you?" Luther demanded.

"At this point, I would think it would probably be best if I asked the questions, don't you think?"

"Suit your self," Luther sneered. "But I think you're in over your head on this one."

"I'll be the judge of that. Besides how would you know if I'm working alone or not? My thought is you're guessing or hoping, one or the other. You're a long way from home aren't you, Director Luther Riggs?"

"Hardly."

Trey heard the resentment in the director's voice and thought for several seconds. "Suppose you tell me what would bring the Director of the NSA to Rome to do what any number of field agents might do at a moment's notice. Don't you also think it's unwise and a bit dangerous to go solo on a kidnapping assignment to boot?"

"No comment, you shit."

"At this point it probably would be a wise idea if you explained yourself, don't you think, Director Riggs?"

"I had to find the girl," Riggs muttered. "She could be in danger. There are people who want her dead and I wanted to warn her."

Trey doubted the answer and snickered. He doubled the pressure, knowing the man had to feel a major headache coming on. "That's mighty chivalrous of you, Director, but there's a little more to all this than what you're telling me. We'd be curious to know who you're really working for. It's certainly not the president, because at this point, he could care less what a lowly reporter had to say."

"And how would you know?"

"My recollection is that he is strong proponent of all the amendments to the constitution to begin with, which was one of his platforms for election, if I recall."

"Look ease off, will ya?" Luther sneered. "I have a proposition to offer. Give me the girl and I'll give you anything you want. You name it; money, prestige, fame, you name it, you got it. How does five million dollars sound to you?"

"And where would you get your hands on that much money?" Trey asked. "Besides, why in the world would she be worth that much money to anyone?" He jammed the gun into Luther's skull, hoping to entice a more detailed explanation.

"Damn it, stop that. I have connections, like I said," Riggs said, voice rising in fear. "You name it. Anything you could dream of is yours for the asking. The institution will take care of you. Just take me to the girl and I'll get you anything you want."

"That's never going to happen, so you had better get that out of your head," Trey said. "Besides, you'll never find her, not as long as I'm alive."

"I'll bet if I hung around the Vatican long enough, I'd see her sooner or later," Riggs disagreed. "You know we're going to win when this is all over."

Riggs' last statement stuck a raw chord with Trey, now that he knew Anhur's story. He sensed the evil of the man and knocked him out with the butt of his handgun.

Trey slipped the man's billfold into his jacket pocket and retrieved the rifle. He flattened the other three tires before leaving, knowing he would have to move Flo in order to ensure her safety. If the director knew, so would others.

Several days later, Monsignor Giuseppe Lorenzo was doing his best trying to convince the pontiff that the money that he was requesting would be well spent if it could prove without a doubt that the visionary was telling the truth.

"Giuseppe, we are talking about an initial request for three million dollars?" the pontiff said, voice rising in dismay.

"But wouldn't it be worth it if it proved without a doubt that the odds are not stacked in our favor any longer? Look, you read my report, tell me I'm off base and I'll drop the whole matter and go back to my research. Besides... you asked me to check into this anomaly to begin with and now it just seems to me that you no longer feel it is necessary to pursue the matter any further. Sweeping the entire matter under the rug will not make it go away, Your Eminence."

"I didn't say that. I am curious and want to know the truth as well as you, but you're proposing the launching of a satellite to boot. How much are you really asking for here, just to prove a theory?"

"A theory, Your Eminence? I would hardy call it that. Proof of scripture would be a more accurate statement. Besides, if money seems to be the issue here, allow me to print the woman's story and you can read it. Besides, it's not as if the story isn't pretty much public knowledge at this point. Once the device is ready to launch, it will be an impossibility to keep the situation secret any longer. Besides, like I said earlier, we're talking about the light of angels here!" The Monsignor noticed the Pope scowl. "I am sure that the international community will assist us in our quest for the truth. Not to mention any other Christian-based faiths that wish to ascertain their validity once and for all."

"It is possible you might convince some groups to donate out of curiosity, but answer this question Monsignor, how much are we really talking about here?"

Giuseppe knew the former financial secretary was about to suffer a bout of apoplexy over the sum. "Fifty million give or take," he replied, doing his best not to cringe himself. "It's not that the church can't afford it, and I feel the money would be well spent in this instance."

The Pope was wordless for some time and the Monsignor began to succumb to the incessant motion of the man's fingers while he waited for a reply. He pressed. "I was also told that the same result might be possible with an unmanned drone, but at this point, they are still working on this method of scanning as well, which could be a considerable amount less than the original estimate."

"With the use of this drone as you mentioned, how much would it be then?"

"Just around twenty million, which I'm told is reasonable."

"Twenty million is a reasonable sum; have you no concept of finance or monetary value?"

"Most likely not," Giuseppe admitted. "But then again, it is not my area of expertise. Regardless, this idea is the only way to obtain proof positive in this case. I would hate to think of the alternative were we to stand by and do nothing."

The pope sighed heavily. "Have the woman print the story then, but there are a few conditions which I will require you to adhere to, Monsignor Lorenzo! First, I want some assurance that the satellite or drone or whatever they utilize is operational before you print the story. Second, I want to lessen the impact of the story with an actual sighting of the battle so that the church cannot be accused of sensationalism. Are we perfectly clear on this point, Monsignor? Lastly, we will see if you are right in this instance and we get some monetary assistance. I want you to assign someone to that task now."

"Yes, Your Eminence!"

"Are you happy now that I have finally capitulated? If there is one thing I can say about you at this point, you are tenacious."

Giuseppe smiled briefly at the compliment but was pressed to broach another subject that concerned him.

"Giuseppe, is there something else you wish to discuss?" the pope asked. "I can tell by the look on your face that there is more. I would have thought you would be jumping up and down with glee by now. You have been after me for weeks to approve your proposal."

"There is."

"Well, tell me by all means, while you have me in an agreeable state."

Giuseppe removed a piece of folded paper from his pocket and passed it across the desk to the pope. He watched as the pope unfolded the paper and then saw red infuse his face. He knew from his reaction that the pope was well aware of what the symbol meant. "Have ever heard the name Detritus before?" The pope said nothing, as if in silent invitation for Giuseppe to continue.

"He is the tormentor, the robber who hung on the left side of Jesus as he was crucified on the cross on Golgotha, the hill of the skulls. He joined in with the soldiers, scribes and Pharisees as they challenged Jesus to save himself in light of his constant persecution. The Apostle Luke best described his true nature when he said, *'If you are Christ, the king of the Jews save yourself and us.'* You, I am sure, are well aware of the amount of torment Jesus had to endure prior to his death. Detritus seems to be the man solely responsible for the religious insurrection which surrounds us even to this day." The monsignor noticed the look of puzzlement on the pope's face. "Not the original man, mind you, the name has been utilized ever since that time. He is the leader of a group that goes by the name of the Institution. No one is sure of the real name of the group, which I'm sure you are aware of. We have done some research on the group. The Institution dates back to Jesus' death.

Several days ago, one of his agents tried to kidnap the reporter but his efforts were thwarted, for the time being."

"Thwarted by whom, if I may ask?"

"She has a friend who joined us several days ago. He has been invaluable in assisting us in our quest for the truth. His name is Trey and without him we would not have progressed as far as we have. For safety's sake, the couple is not staying within the confines of the Vatican any longer. We have moved them to a monastery outside Rome with Anhur and his family. I talked to the head of security and he assured me that some of the Swiss Guard would be assigned to patrol the monastery, incognito of course. I am sure that Detritus will not give up looking for the woman in hopes of squashing the story before it becomes public knowledge. I, for one have no intent of carrying any innocent blood on my hands. I don't think I could live with myself if that were to happen. I have grown quite fond of the two of them."

"Wise decision," the pope mused. "I don't want any blood on my hands either."

Giuseppe frowned. "But what bothers me most is that after discussing the situation in depth, we still are not sure how he came to know of our intent. There has to have been something we missed along the way for the Institution to become so well informed of our plans. I am sure that he will redouble his efforts to find the woman at this point."

"I believe you're right," the pope agreed. "Though you seem skeptical, don't question your abilities, Giuseppe. I trust you will do what is right and necessary. Know this; the threat is real, as I forewarned you some time ago if I recall. Be careful. Is there anything else I should know about?"

"There is one other matter which I am sure you will want to be appraised of."

"Which is?"

"I mentioned it some time ago, before you were elected pope, but we never really had the time to discuss it further. It is something that has been preying on my mind for some time now, but I believe it's altogether relevant to the current situation at hand. Some time ago, you unfortunately chastised me for mentioning and questioning the content of the third letter at Fatima." Giuseppe raised his hands in hopes of staving off any criticism. "Bear with me on this," he requested. After a moment, the pope nodded. "You forewarned me earlier, but I must insist whoever interpreted the third letter seems to have gotten it all wrong. I believe that the third letter refers to…. and let me explain my thoughts fully on why I feel that I am correct before you discount my thoughts once again. Now, I certainly mean no disrespect and I hope that you allow me to continue."

"Everyone is entitled to their own opinion, as long as it does not contradict church dogma. I will allow you to continue."

"It doesn't."

"Then by all means continue, Giuseppe."

The monsignor slid the third letter of Fatima across the table to the Pope, hoping that he would read along. "You are well aware, I am sure, that the three letters have been sequestered since 1917, when the Virgin Mary appeared before Sister Lucia dos Santos in Fatima, Spain, until a viable explanation could be ascertained from their contents. I believe it was Blessed John the Twenty-Third, who late in the 1960s released the first two, letters to the faithful as a goodwill measure. The third, and I am sure the most important letter, was not released until some sort of event could be tied to its content, and that was the wounding of John Paul II in 1981. Before he was shot, the church never could come up with any way of explaining the third letter of Fatima, so from the late 1960s until the late 1980s the letter was sealed in a vault awaiting some valid explanation. Allow me to read it aloud, if you don't mind, and I am sure you will see what I do. Its true meaning only becomes evident at this moment in time."

Giuseppe received the pope's nod and proceeded to read;

"I write in obedience to you, my God who commands me to do so through his Excellency the Bishop of Leiria and through your Most Holy Mother and mine.

After the two parts which I have already explained, at the left of Our Lady and a little above, we saw an Angel with a flaming sword in his left hand; flashing, it gave out flames that looked as though they would set the world on fire; but they died out in contact with the splendor that Our Lady radiated toward him with her right hand: pointing to the earth with his right hand, the angel cried out in a loud voice:, 'Penance, penance, penance!'. And we saw in an immense light that is God: 'something similar to how people appear in a mirror when they pass in front of it', a Bishop dressed in White 'we had the impression that it was the Holy Father'. Other Bishops, Priests, men and women Religious going up a steep mountain, at the top of which there was a big Cross of rough-hewn trunks as of a cork-tree with the bark; before reaching there the Holy Father passed through a big city half in ruins and half trembling with a halting step, afflicted with pain and sorrow, he prayed for the souls of the corpses he met along the way; having reached the top of the mountain, on his knees at the foot of the big Cross he was killed by a group of soldiers who fired bullets and arrows at him, and in the same way there died one after another the Bishops, Priests, men and women Religious, and various lay people and of different ranks and positions. Beneath the two arms of the Cross there were two Angels each with a crystal aspersorium in his hand, in which they gathered up the blood of the Martyrs and with it sprinkled the souls that were making their way to God."

Giuseppe paused for several moments to let the content of the letter sink in. "I myself believe that this prophecy has yet to be fulfilled. It was easy to explain away the letter with the wounding of John Paul II, but I totally disagree with the findings. This letter is very similar to Revelations as far as its true meaning is concerned, and I am afraid the intent of the letter concerns you." Giuseppe saw Pope Romanus pale before he spoke.

"Why on earth would you think this concerns me?" he asked, pushing the paper away.

"Think about it for a moment. The battle is progressing toward Megiddo. That and the fact that the Angel of Death is foretelling the demise of mankind unless they repent is something that you and I cannot ignore. You read my synopsis of what I thought might happen; that coupled with the fact there is a wooden cross on the hill of Megiddo and has been there for quite some time is no coincidence." Giuseppe saw something in the pope's demeanor that demanded further explanation. The pope was in a defensive posture, arms crossed across his chest, something that Giuseppe had never seen before. "You are the bishop in white for all intents and purposes; something that I have always perceived about you."

"Why do you say that?"

"I don't know," Giuseppe replied honestly. "It may be just because of your partiality for wearing white gowns whenever we met. That and your white brows and pale skin, I don't know, and I pray I am wrong in this case. Nevertheless, think about it for a moment. The white gown denotes purity and is the official color of the papacy as the true representative of Christ here on earth. The letter states that Sister Santos thought it was a pope as well. That is why I believe the wounding of John Paul conveniently explained away the true intent of the letter."

"Possibly, but he was a pope as well."

"Yes, but there is more to this than just that point," Giuseppe continued. "If you tie the true meaning of the letter with that of Revelations Sixteen, you will see there is no coincidence. I have taken the liberty of discussing this point with both Flo and Trey and they agree with me. There seems to be only one thing that bothers me though. I am not sure of the outcome."

"What do you mean by that?"

Giuseppe detailed the discussion he had with Florence about the possibility of the Legions of Angels losing the battle. "It was something that I never thought of, and it never occurred to me."

"Let's pray that they don't lose!" the Pope said with a degree of finality.

"My thoughts, though more people seem to be disappearing by the day, which is why I possibly think she might be right."

"Giuseppe, there are times when you must rely on the Creator to intervene when he feels it is necessary. Now may be that moment."

"I hope you're right. But you also know that in the end, it will be your responsibility to shoulder, not anyone else's."

"I am fully aware of that Giuseppe and I have prayed for divine intervention every single day since this all started."

CHAPTER 13

The Golden Tongue

Kansas City, Kansas

The time was right and the void was apparent. So many calamities had befallen humanity that they were more than ready for an assured voice, the voice of hope. The masses were disillusioned with the lame excuses the leaders of the world had to offer and they were hungry for any new word that might ease their troubled minds.

The emcee stood off to the left side of stage prodding the auditorium audience to 'Give it up for Ahriman,' but there was no need. The din of the crowd roared their approval of his message as all eyes were on the man in center stage in the white linen suit. The silver microphone glistened in his left hand as his arms rose above his head, almost as if he were signaling a touchdown or field goal. This gesture would become his trademark. The oddest part of the gesture was that both his thumbs were turned downward toward the ground in a most unnatural way, though no one seemed to notice the obscure implication other than his mentor, Detritus, who stood just off stage watching his prodigy with approval.

This had been the first real exposure of his powers of persuasion, and success seemed imminent for the thirty-year-old orator with the shock of snow-white hair. Some people who attended the show would later relate the experience to others as one of the most profound they had ever witnessed, describing the man as a luminescent white figure who seemed to float about the stage like a specter. Mostly though, they described the experience as mesmerizing. Word would spread quickly that someone had finally arrived to lead them through the mass chaos of this life.

What was most unusual about the first public appearance of Ahriman was the crowd reluctantly left only after the stage lights had been dimmed and the police had been called in to assist in the process of dispersing the crowd. The group was still calling out in unison for the orator's encore long after he had left the premises.

Ahriman's popularity increased with each assembly, so much so that he quickly gained a following of people who made the journey with him from city to city, enthralled by his charisma. Not since the early 1960s, with the arrival of the Beatles, had such a mania progressed as quickly. By his third public appearance, the media was enthralled with him. The word spread and calls poured in with offers to syndicate his show. His first nationally broadcast show was a raving success. Now came calls from all over the world with demands on his time, yet Detritus felt that the fervor of the man's message had not yet reached everyone here in the States. Until that was accomplished, he felt it a waste of time to take the message internationally.

Ahriman was oblivious to the publicity and accolades he was receiving for his message. He portrayed himself as a humble man with humble intent. His message was painfully simple at first; 'Use conscious thought.' The message had a definite religious undertone to it, which was the intent. Ahriman was instructed to bring the message to the people in dibbles and dabs, which worked well in the beginning. Then the message got a bit more complex with the first of many predictions, which entailed the future uniting of all nations and nationalities in a common cause to combat the inequalities that existed in society. The message had drawn the interest of many who wished to quell the seething unrest brewing due to the hardships people around the earth now faced.

There were detractors however, who scoffed at the idea as being an impossible undertaking, an unachievable idea that had no chance of success, especially by an unknown entity. Ahriman's agent, a man named Marcus, would only smile when asked about Ahriman's critics and would not comment other than to say, "Just wait, you will see with your own eyes the sparkling revelations in store for us all." Ahriman never granted interviews for any reason. He had been discouraged from doing so, less chance of giving away the true intent of the message.

Detritus had taken a page from history when he first instructed Ahriman what to say and do. He had used the rise of Hitler as his prime example on how to brainwash the masses without them being any the wiser. He likened Hitler's rise to that of a symphony, which began with a lone instrument playing a solo piece, which was then united with a section of musicians at a time until the entire orchestra played in unison. The octaves of the piece then built into a crescendo at the finish, united in a singular cause.

However, it wasn't the music being played that concerned Detritus as much as the silence which followed the last lingering note. This end time is what concerned him; when only the resonance of the piece still rang in the ear out of memory. This is how Detritus wanted the end of days to conclude, in complete silence. He wanted the end to finish in a complete void, the void of God.

The messenger, as Ahriman was sometimes called by the press, began a slow and methodical procedure of heralding in all of his naysayers by addressing their doubts of his true intent in every one of his sermons. He was a brilliant orator who had a knack for silencing the contradictory tone of the detractors, which up until this time seemed to be political in nature due to his voice. Soon his critics were muted as more people came to believe that he was a true sage of sorts.

The major religions here in the United States had not even bothered to address their concerns about the man and his message other than an occasional comment that he was nothing more than a storefront preacher and a flash in the pan who would soon fade into oblivion once his promises proved to be unachievable. They secretly feared only one thing about the man; the losses of their own flocks and the revenue they provided if they criticized him. So, it was best to remain mum and not fight the rising fad, but better to turn ones back on his viable ideas, just in case they never blossomed into reality and left you looking like a fool.

Surprisingly however, just the opposite of what religious leaders thought had occurred. Ahriman did not fade away as some had predicted, but grew in popularity as more people came to see him to witness with their own eyes what all the uproar was about. Soon it became evident even to his detractors that he converted more people to believe in his message that, 'Anything is possible with perseverance.' It soon became evident even to the religious leaders that the man was no fluke. They misjudged the messenger and his message and the effect he had on people in general, for soon his name was on everyone's lips.

The politicians whole-heartedly embraced the man as a visionary of sorts in an effort to show the people they were smart enough to know a good thing when they saw it. Basically, they were riding on the coat tails of a rising star, some in hopes of bolstering their flagging careers, others in hopes of reeling in a rising threat to the political machine that had squashed individual thought and action for so long through fear and intimidation.

Detritus was no fool, however. He knew what was about to happen and he schooled his liege in what to say: "Apathy is the tool politicians give to the beleaguered. Hope is the wellspring of humanity!" The message was heralded by the press as insightful and enlightening, yet there really wasn't anything new about the message. It was the messenger, not the message, that was important here, and many failed to realize it.

When the man was officially invited to the White House for a private meeting with the president, most political analysts agreed on one point; that Republican and Democratic parties alike wanted the man in their corner. Each party would do anything to show that the messenger was in their corner and favored one over the other. Nothing could or would be farther from the truth. This country, as far as Detritus was concerned, was just a staging area for the rest of the world only because other nations still held the United States in such high esteem because of the lingering thought that it was still the land of opportunity.

Once the photo of the President embracing Ahriman made the front page of major newspapers with the caption, 'President Embrace's Radical New Ideas,' Detritus knew it was time to take the message international. He had patiently waited for this moment and relished the thought of finally accomplishing a lifelong dream.

What better place to do so than make the first stop Berlin, Germany. No one thought about the similarities of past and the present and no connection between the two was made. It was here that Ahriman launched his first public attack against organized religion, focusing on the negative effect religion had on society as a whole. No one expected the message to be taken almost verbatim from one of Hitler's early lectures, pronounced with such verve that no one sought to question the motive behind the message. The Messenger had truly arrived and unquestionably convinced the awaiting German audience that there was truth in his words. About all that was reported about the lecture, due to selective censuring, was that the religious leaders of the world had better take notice that they were not fulfilling the needs of their flocks.

Of greater media interest, however, seemed to be the masses fighting to touch the sleeve of the Golden One's jacket in hopes of being led out of the quagmire they had brought unto themselves. It was reported that just by touching the sleeve of his left arm, ones could feel a sense of salvation and their fortunes would be enhanced.

The news of this revelation left many wondering if the Messiah had been reborn and walked among them once more, performing miracles to back his wise testament. Many began to speculate as much, which made Detritus smile all the more. This gave Detritus the idea to instruct Ahriman to stage some startling revelation on stage to show proof positive that he had mystical power s for healing and that he could heal entire groups of people at one time.

The latest message Ahriman promised the people, 'Salvation from their miseries.' This was nothing more than a fragment of the real message being fed to the people piecemeal. Only Detritus knew the entire verse, which he had taught and preached to Ahriman during his childhood years, '*The golden tongue will promise them salvation from their miseries, provide comfort for their consciousness, not unlike the wrecker's light, and they will follow his lead while true salvation, like the ship, is dashed on the rocks of false promises.*

The Institution had devoted its entire existence to undermining and disrupting all known religions of the world through propaganda and other tools, pitting one religion against another in an effort to totally confuse the beliefs of the people. This was being brought about in very subtle, yet effective way by the Messenger. He had been schooled thoroughly.

With the Berlin proclamation, some of his detractors began to question the Messenger's real intent. They sought out some of the most enlightened of men to see if any of them concurred with the message. Most of them did not. Those that were persuaded to publicly voice their opposition to the Messenger were soon sought out and chastised in the name of their opposition. Then some of them disappeared, while others heard of their disappearances went into hiding in fear of their lives. It was soon understood that any criticism voiced against the Golden Tongue was dealt with swiftly.

However, a funny thing happened in regard to Ahriman's initial promise of uniting all nations under a common cause; world leaders began to embrace some of the ideas of the Golden Tongue. Slowly, as the tour progressed though its fifty-nation capital city tour, the nation's leaders began to address some of the issues that bothered those most, and solutions began to be found. No one had expected these results, which were thought impossible up to this point in time. This bolstered the popularity and integrity of Messenger once again.

It was not until the attacks on organized religion became more evident did any religious leader feel it necessary to counter the rising tide of insurgency. Pope Romanus, who happened to be on a tour of his own and was in Manila at the time, made a brief comment to the effect that the Anti-Christ walked among the people of the earth. This set off a string of protests from allies of the Messenger against the Catholic Church and its policies.

The Golden Tongue countered the allegation with a pointed comment in rebuttal, pointing out that several religions of the world were stodgy and out of touch with the realities of the present day situation. Though he made no mention of any religion specifically, he did make mention of how Rome and Mecca appeared out of touch with reality and may as well join hands unto a common cause. This comment caused a firestorm to develop between the two religions; outwardly as far as either religion was concerned, nothing could be further from the truth. Secretly though, they had identified their nemesis and had been discussing ways to rid themselves of the menace that was believed to be the anti-Christ.

Radicals within the Muslim religion called for the Messenger's head, though mainstream Muslim leaders would not comment one way or the other. The Catholic Church refused to even acknowledge the slight, choosing instead to ignore the pestilence for the time being.

This somewhat bothered Detritus, who sought to increase the friction between the two and raise the level of religious unrest? He knew he was taking a chance by stepping up the attack against the two major religions and that he could possibly lose his speaker. Doing so might run the risk of destroying everything he had accomplished so far, but it was a chance he was willing to take. After all, the meteoric rise in Ahriman's popularity made him almost untouchable at this point. Nevertheless, Detritus took no chances though and quadrupled the security around his star, just in case.

One of the last cities on the Messenger's tour was Manila. Because the Pope had made his comments there some weeks earlier, the Golden Tongue was figuratively run out of town. Many of the Ahriman's detractors had tried to make Manila the final front in which to confront the man. Thousands of people thronged into the streets and fighting broke out between the two opposing forces. Posted signs incited the followers of the Messenger. "Crucify the Anti-Christ!" Marcus, his agent, thought it wiser to cancel the appearance rather than risk the man's life. This was a wise decision, for the streets were awash in blood and it took the Philippine army three days to clear the streets.

Pope Romanus was appalled by the massacre in Manila and called together his circle of eight, as well as the entire College of Cardinals. They were in constant session to try and find a solution to the rising unrest that had befallen them. No one had any viable solution to the problem as of yet, but something had to be done and they had to react quickly to the situation. Acting quickly was something that was hard, if not impossible, for the church to achieve in the past.

Some of the cardinals, dissatisfied with Pope Romanus and his apparent lack of verve, began to call for the pope's head. They were hoping that he would voluntarily step down in hopes of alleviating rising dissent within the church. They cited an obscure canon law meant to dissolve the authority of a corrupt pope and hoped to persuade the majority of the College of Cardinals to agree with their line of thought. This was not to be.

As far as the majority of cardinals were concerned, they concurred with the pope's assessment of the situation. The Anti-Christ had arrived. The Pope, they argued, was in fact the unquestionable authority of Christ on earth, and many insightful cardinals thought that overturning the authority of Pope Romanus fed right into the growing dissent that surrounded them. Their intent was to quell the religious insurgency by some other means. An all- out effort was made to increase diplomatic relations with not only Muslim, Jewish, and Buddhist faiths but all others as well in order to counter the message of insurgency the Golden Tongue spewed out with increasing regularity.

Some of the Catholic Church's efforts began to bear fruit, as more non-catholic church leaders began to brainstorm their ideas on how to effectively stave off the rising tide. The promise of a united front against the threat became more evident as the days passed.

A secret commission of religious heads was formed to try and piece together all of Ahriman's messages in an effort to understand his intent. Was Pope Romanus right in calling the man the true Anti-Christ? Many of the commissioners began to think so. The problem was the issue of countering the menace in such a way as to discredit him before he became too strong to do otherwise.

Secretly, Pope Romanus began to see what was all too evident to Monsignor Lorenzo in the first place; the end of days was approaching, yet he was too stubborn to admit as much to his protégé. He went only so far as to approve the fifty-million-dollar request in hopes that it might speed up the process of finding a solution to their problem of light spectrum intensification. He hoped when the time came that Monsignor Lorenzo knew what to do. It was a lot to ask of the young man, but he also knew that it had become a team effort at this point and not the responsibility of one man to bear on his own. He had been secretly advised that some of America's brightest minds had united together at MIT in a singular cause to solve the dilemma. He vigilantly prayed that a breakthrough was only days away.

Detritus, on the other hand, had begun to unite world political leaders to counter the religious might. He knew one thing for sure, and that was that politics and religion was like oil and water - they never mixed. He had to strengthen his position in any way he felt necessary. He knew if he had the political machine on his side, it would become a lot easier to counter any threat that might arise from his religious opposition. He also had his spies in place and knew what strategies were being discussed from his opposition. The vestiges of the old network served him well, as he continued to counter the opposition before they even spoke out.

All this turmoil served to strengthen the forces of darkness and they continued to march on. More people began to disappear as well, almost epidemic in proportion. The pleas for government assistance with this problem went unheeded, as usual. The only benefit to the entire dilemma seemed to be the increased popularity of television shows with titles such as, "Lost," and "Missing." More people called into the show's producers in hopes of getting their love one's featured on their shows. These shows, which were initially limited to American audiences, received worldwide syndication. Just about every nation on the planet had aped the shows in an effort to aid their viewing audiences in finding an answer for their missing loved ones.

More statues of the Virgin Mary began to bleed and no one had a clear-cut answer as to why. It caused one learned observer to comment, "The Virgin is crying tears of sorrow for the demise of her domain and for humanity as well!"

In conjunction with that, people began to step forward with proclamations that they had had encounters with angels. This baffled religious and scientific communities alike and the tabloids had a field day with it all. A proclamation in one of them stated that potable water had been tainted with a hallucinatory drug of some sort. The sardonic remarks of these tabloids however were not good enough to convince anyone with an ounce of sense otherwise. Everyone began to sense something was about to happen and it did.

The minor reconstruction of the Coptic Church in Asyut had been completed and no one expected what was now a nightly event once again, as it had happened many years ago. The Virgin Mary appeared over the top of the triad of towers once more and no one could explain that either. More astounding than that was the same figure appeared over the most sacred of mosques in Mecca and it sent the Muslim community reeling.

All of these revelations in a singular form were enough for one to take pause, but along with these enlightening revelations came increased torment. The rate of tragic weather calamities was on the rise. Incidents of earthly tremors occurred almost on a weekly basis. No one could explain that either. Some of the tabloids were quick to exploit that angle stating, 'the earth was wobbling so much it was about to leave orbit and head out to another solar system altogether.'

People began to panic and they turned to Ahriman the Messenger for hope.

CHAPTER 14

Anhur and the Desert

"You can't just launch a drone on foreign soil without permission. For all the Egyptian government knows, it's a threat against them and could lead to an all-out war, Monsignor Lorenzo. Use some common sense here... someone should have thought to ask permission before we went through with this plan to build this thing to begin with," Trey vehemently stated.

Flo sought to temper the man a bit. "Of all people, Trey, where do get off accusing the monsignor here of incompetence? Besides, you were brought in as a technical advisor were you not?"

"Hardly," he replied. "I came here of my own volition to protect you, if you recall. Besides, I don't recall having the authority to negotiate with foreign governments. What do you want me to do, Flo? Dial the phone and ask to speak to the president of Egypt? I'll tell you one thing; you'd never get through, so why ask me?"

"The least you could have done was to mention the fact," she complained. "Why leave it to the last minute before you mention something as important as that? You're the man with all the connections; I can only assume something as trivial as that would be a piece of cake for you, Trey."

Monsignor Lorenzo sought to ease the tension between the couple. "We are a sovereign state and country. Let me talk to our diplomatic corps and see what we can do about the issue."

"What if we can't get permission to use the drone? What will happen then?" Flo asked.

"Plan B, I suppose. We'll have to wait and see if what they have accomplished can be modified for a satellite, though according to my uncle, the farther they are away from the earth's surface, the worse the resolution becomes," Trey said succinctly. "The only benefit to a satellite as far as I can see is that there would be no need to ask permission from the Egyptian government. They don't own the atmosphere."

"I'll see what I can do," the monsignor said.

"While you're at it, you may as well ask for permission for a compliment of at least twenty people and the equipment necessary to support them. I have a feeling we're going to have a convoy out in the desert before this is all through."

"Why do we need so many people?"

"Monsignor, my thought is that this is the least number of people we could field to accomplish this assignment effectively. You add it up and let me know if you think I'm being excessive. Two technicians to run the drone, at least four of the scientists that developed it to begin with, the two engineers that built it, in case we have any design flaws that need correction, a refueling team of at least four people, which could double for a launching team, two statisticians, two cartographers and the four of us."

What's a cartographer?" the priest asked.

"A mapmaker," he replied. "We're going to have to not only plot a grid, but map the area. The only reason there are just two of them is that they will have the benefit of a tracking satellite."

"Which four are you talking about? There are only three of us in the room."

"Monsignor, you surely can't go out in the desert without Anhur. He's the key to this whole operation. Without him we'd only be guessing at the proper color."

"I guess you're right, excuse me. I just wasn't thinking is all. Have you talked to him? Is he willing to go back?"

"Yes I have and he said he was. He mentioned that he was homesick and couldn't wait to return. He also felt it necessary to prove once and for all he was telling the truth," Trey replied. Flo was perplexed by the statement. "In addition to all your other abilities, Trey, are you fluent in Arabic?"

Trey never answered her.

"I never doubted the story once we realized the scope of his vision. Did you, Ms. Rinna?" the priest said offhand.

"To tell you the truth, at the time I was a bit skeptical, until we had some time to discuss the complexities of his vision. I hope for just one thing, that we are able to find the ongoing battle once again."

"You and me both," Trey replied. "It's an immense area to cover and I highly doubt the battle is going to still be in the exact same location you pinpointed over two months ago. I'm glad you had the presence of mind to get a GPS sighting. At least we have a starting point. My only worry is finding it at all after all this time. Frankly, I'm a bit worried. What if the artificial light doesn't work, then what? Dr. Hanson never said he was one-hundred percent sure about the results. The only thing he said was, 'Anything can and probably will go wrong in an unforgiving climate such as that,' and I believe him."

"What about a wave of optimism at this point, Trey?" Flo scolded. "It's the least we can do to bolster the flagging spirits of everyone concerned. Think positive, Trey."

"I hope that's all it takes, but we will know in a few days, won't we?"

Trey noticed the monsignor smile faintly, and when he spoke, there was a note of optimism in his voice.

"Three days is all? You never said as much."

Trey was still trying to adjust to the sporadic bursts of English from the priest. "I thought I did." Trey noticed Flo's eyebrows arch and realized he hadn't. "I'm told the equipment is going to be packaged for shipment in the next day or so. The only question I have at this point is where to ship it? One other thing, Monsignor, you might want to inform the Egyptian government of our true intent. My thought is that it would be much wiser to tell them the facts behind the request to begin with."

"Do you think that is wise? What if they say no?"

"Let's just say this; I think certain arm-twisting tactics could be utilized by our government if need be. Not though any official channels mind you, but in a clandestine manner. I think some officials readily agree with your synopsis of the situation."

Trey noticed the priest smile broadly as he replied.

"Then I think it's time we printed Ms. Rinna's story, don't you?"

"Yeah, I believe so," Trey shrugged. "It couldn't hurt at this point."

The two men looked at Flo.

"It's about time, isn't it?" she nodded.

"I'm afraid so," the two men said in unison, causing the three of them to chuckle together.

The story, which was released two days later through United Press International, caused an immediate furor over religious righteousness. The four-page article was printed in its entirety by most of the major publications. Most of those who commented on the article thought it to be one of the most thorough and insightful pieces ever written. However, there were those who scoffed at the very idea and thought the content was ludicrous at best and not fit for even the slimiest of tabloids much less a major publication. Nevertheless, comments such as these did not deter the facts and the accolades were abundant.

Flo's editor at the Washington Post was mad as hell at his star reporter for sending the story through the wire service without his approval. Publically, he abruptly fired her for doing so, but later recanted when asked why he would want to fire a possible Pulitzer candidate. He couldn't wait for her return so he could personally dress her down behind closed doors for her breach of protocol.

When the follow-up article secretly made it onto his desk the next day, he was all smiles once more, though he still hadn't the faintest clue as to where she might be when he published it.

Actually, she was sitting in an airport hanger in Cairo along with Trey and Anhur waiting for the special delivery to arrive. The article was explosive and had changed the Egyptian government's mind about refusing them permission. No arm twisting had been necessary, which came as a surprise to not only Trey but most who thought the opposite decision was a sure bet. The only stipulation the government made was that the group be assisted at all times by a company of soldiers, to protect their own interests, of course.

Detritus was incensed when he read the article, a major setback to forwarding his plans. He only wished that he had made Luther's death a bit more painful and damned the incompetence of the man once again. When he read the follow-up article the next day, he was beside himself, wondering what on earth had happened that something as damaging as this had virtually slipped by him without notice. It was not as if he hadn't been apprised of the situation from the start, but it was his inability to do anything to stop it from becoming public knowledge. The web had failed him for the first time and there was no excuse for it as far as he was concerned.

He called out to his master for more devastation and his plea was heeded once more. It snowed in the Caribbean that day in October, and in the Fiji islands, something that had never occurred before. It was similar in effect to that snowy day of late August in New York; the effect of the anomaly was devastating to its inhabitants, who were ill prepared for nature's cantankerous onslaught. Along with that, the ring of fire erupted once more, sending out a one-hundred-and-fifty-foot tsunami, which made it all the way across the Pacific swamping the San Francisco Bay Bridge.

Trey learned of Luther's death, knowing that no one would readily come after Flo now, but decided against telling her. He knew her explosive articles had made her almost untouchable, besides that he hardly left her side. He had his own personal reasons for protecting her.

As they sat in the hanger, Flo suddenly felt alone, wondering what would become of them all if they were not successful. "Trey, why do you think the Monsignor begged out of joining us at the start of all this?"

"I don't know, you seem to know him better than I do," Trey replied. "Maybe he has become skeptical of the possible results. I really don't have a clue why he didn't join us; he never said anything to me. Did he say anything to you?"

"He was evasive, that's for sure, but it wasn't anything that I haven't noticed in the past. Prior to now, I could usually shame him

into explaining himself. That's what worries me; I would have thought
he would have been the first one on the charter this morning."

"Maybe he has more pressing issues to tend to, Flo."

"Let's be honest here. What would be more pressing of an issue
than validating what he has been a staunch proponent of to begin with?
Right from the start, even when I had my doubts, he was unswayable
in his beliefs. I'm wondering, as I have been for some time now, if he
knows more than he's telling us."

"Have you asked him?"

"I hinted as much."

"So have I, but a lot of good that has done me," Trey responded.
He leaned over and kissed her gently on the cheek.

Flo flushed from the spontaneous act. "Let's be serious for a
moment, shall we?"

"I am, but press on if you must! Did you ask him outright or
did you just expect him to tell you everything he knew right from the
start?"

"I don't know, I suppose I did."

"We're talking about a level of trust here, Flo."

"I trust him. I just assumed that he would--"

Trey cut her off. "If it's solely an issue of mutual trust, you're as
leery as they come."

"Are we talking about the same thing here, Trey?"

"You're an extremely educated woman," he shrugged. "You figure
it out."

"Look, I've been hurt before and I have to be sure is all," she
defended herself. "Sometimes a girl has to do whatever is necessary to
protect her best interests."

"Whatever," Trey said, frowning. "Maybe the whole issue here
has to do with a leap of faith, which is something I'm sure you're not
ready to make, and maybe he's not either. The only way I know of
accomplishing that is to believe in what you're being told is the truth,
and to have faith in the person as well. Maybe he thought you were just

after a story and nothing more. Maybe you haven't earned his trust as of yet. I know I haven't earned yours for some odd reason I've yet to fully understand."

Flo was quiet for some time and did not respond. She understood what he was driving at on both fronts yet did not want to admit that he may be right. She fumed for some time, fully understanding that he knew more about her than she thought possible. She got up and started to walk toward the opposite side of the hanger.

Trey called after her. "That's a responsible answer to a direct question. Maybe he feels the same way I do," Trey surmised her answer to his question when she never turned back.

Trey, disgusted with his ability to convince her otherwise, returned to the issue at hand, turning toward Anhur and asking him once more if he could identify the light if he saw it again. He was assured of as much and then began to discuss the secrets of surviving alone in the desert. By the time Anhur had finished speaking with him, the cargo plane had landed.

Flo surveyed the runway, thinking about what she had been told about herself. In the final analysis, she knew Trey was right, but was glad the plane arrived to delay her answer. A distraction was what she was hoping for and she was glad it appeared. It was a lot easier than dealing with their current goals. Personal issues could wait another day. She watched the plane touchdown, landing on only one set of rear wheels at first before it leveled out on the remaining rear wheels and then the front. She wondered if that was normal and then thought the payload must have shifted in flight. The plane turned and headed toward the hanger. By the time it was abreast of the hanger door, a company of soldiers appeared out of nowhere and surrounded the plane. Flo had not even been aware of the military presence until that moment and wondered how long they had been there.

Moments later the rear cargo door opened and a group of people emerged to exit the ramp. She turned to inform Trey of the arrival only to see him standing next to her. His appearance startled her momentarily and she wondered how long he had been standing there. She tried not to show any outward sign of her surprised reaction but watched as Trey stepped forward to greet the new arrivals.

"Uncle Kyle, how are you, and how was the trip?"

"I'm fine and the trip was uneventful, which is something to be thankful for. Trey, you look fit and ready, as usual."

"Trey then turned toward Flo. "I'd like you to meet Florence Rinna, our media specialist for the group. Flo, this is my uncle, Dr. Kyle Hanson, head of the National Weather Service and the man solely responsible for us all being together today."

Dr. Hanson smiled broadly. "Your name has preceded you Ms. Rinna. It's a pleasure to rub shoulders with a celebrity every once in awhile."

Flo blushed as they shook hands, surprised by the older man's firm grip. "My pleasure Likewise, Trey has told me so much about you that I somehow feel we are already old friends."

"I'd like you to meet the rest of the group," Hanson gestured to the group gathering behind him. "Dr. Charles Palmer, head of oceanographic research and a good friend of mine. Dr. David Newman, head of research at MIT, and his two fellow engineers, Abraham Walker, and Yin Tse Chee, the two men who built the light refraction energizer, as they have dubbed our little experiment." He went on to introduce the rest of the entourage and then excused him self from the rest of the group. He took Flo and Trey off to one side, asking her politely but pointedly if she truly believed what she had written about outside influences intervening in worldwide weather conditions.

"Of course, I do," she replied. "But more than that, there are many other factors I considered before I decided to add this to the story. I believe once we locate what we're looking for, your questions will answer themselves, Dr. Hanson."

"I hope your right," he stated flatly, then changed to direction of the conversation to something less serious in nature.

Within the hour the convoy of trucks was headed south in a precise military fashion toward the city of Asyut. An Egyptian troop carrier led the way and another took up the rear, Egyptian flags at all four corners of the vehicles slapping time to the speedy movement. They had the remainder of the day to make it to the GPS location and the following day to set up the equipment. There would be no testing of the device until the following evening; everyone concerned had agreed that the device could only be effectively used at nighttime, the sun a hindrance to the effectiveness of the device.

Trey decided to separate himself from Flo. He wanted to give her time to think seriously about their relationship and in what direction it was headed. He opted to ride with the trio of MIT specialists who had banded together for obvious reasons. He wanted to know more about the theory regarding the machine they had developed and any glitches they thought might develop with its usage.

By late afternoon, they had arrived in Asyut and turned east into the desert. They did not stop but pressed on, hoping to make it to their destination with enough time to set up camp and get a good night's rest. Everyone was aware that it would be a hectic day tomorrow, but by this time, Trey was glad the army had decided to tag along, sure that they would assist them in expediting the process.

The following evening, they were ready for the first test. All eyes turned toward Anhur, who by this time realized that this entire experiment relied on only one thing - his memory. Flo was worried that because of his age, he might not remember anything with exacting detail, but after the first pass with the drone, he said only one thing.

"Make it a sharper blue."

On the succeeding passes, the light became more defined and Flo noticed Anhur begin to smile with a sense of satisfaction. She began to change her mind about the man at this point and thought that they may succeed after all. Unfortunately, this was also when the first of many problems with the design began to surface. It took two more nights for the engineers and scientists to get back to the point where Anhur was satisfied with the results to begin with. After several more passes, the man began to beam with joy, jumping around and erupting into compliments to the engineers and technicians in staccato bursts.

Once Anhur was satisfied with the color and before the next pass of the drone, he returned to the exact spot he had seen the armies to begin with. He peered over the lip of the valley, hoping to see the sight once again. Everyone followed him and stood alongside the man who now squatted down, peering intently into the valley below. No one said a word while the silence and darkness of the valley below encompassed them all.

Suddenly, out in the distance, Flo saw the drone as it left an azure blue haze on the desert floor. The only problem she saw with the entire operation was the speed of the drone. It approached too swiftly. She knew it would take an eagle's eye to see what Anhur had clearly seen in the split second the light passed over the valley. She wasn't the only one who thought as much. Dr Hanson spoke up.

"Is there any way we can slow down the drone? It's going way too fast to be a useful tool to us, Dr. Newman."

"I'm afraid not," he replied. "If we slow it down too much, the techs have informed me earlier, it will just fall out of the sky."

"How about increasing the altitude of the drone? Along with increasing the signal, wouldn't that help us see the valley better?"

"We can try raising the altitude, but increasing the signal may burn out the generator."

The drone passed over the valley for the second time and Anhur let out a moan of dissatisfaction. "There is nothing there!"

"Let's try it one more time at a higher altitude," Dr. Hanson suggested. "I'm sure it will work."

The next pass spread the beam wider, but once again, no one saw anything.

"Increase the signal, Dr. Newman, or else we are just wasting our time out here. You have to realize if it came from space, it had to be extremely bright to begin with."

The next time through, the light was blinding to the naked eye after the darkness of night, though this time around a voice called out? Flo could just make out Trey's figure right before he disappeared into the valley below.

"Try it once more, I thought I saw something!" he shouted.

On the final pass of the night, several others finally saw what Trey had. He was on the opposite side of the object marking the spot when the drone passed. He left his shoe in the exact location, as others had now seen it as well. It was a sword, half buried in the sand.

Anhur whooped with joy at the confirmation, for he saw it too. Many of the others risked the steep decent to join Trey. With flashlights in hand and with thoughts of discovery on their minds, they circled his shoe but there was nothing there. Utter disappointment overwhelmed them. They spent some time discussing the anomaly and decided to leave a marker there until morning.

Several team members could not stand the suspense of it all and decided to wait there until first light. They were disappointed to see there wasn't anything to be found under natural light either, and had they bothered to ask Anhur, he could have told them, for he had tried the exact same thing on his first sighting.

Later that day when everyone gathered for a recap meeting, the gloom was evident. Some of the members were ready to throw in the towel on the entire affair when informed there was nothing to be seen along the desert floor by day. It was Dr. Parker who rose to the occasion once more.

"I believe it's a raving success! Just because you can't see it with the naked eye doesn't mean it isn't there. Think about it for several moments will you, but think along the lines of a parallel universe if you will, one that we have a window into with the use of this light generator."

A voice from the back of the room spoke. "I concur, Dr. Palmer. We were never supposed to see anything with the naked eye in the first place. God never meant us to. It was only after we just about destroyed our own destiny that he allowed Anhur to see what has been going on for millennia, the battle for our salvation."

Most of the people did not recognize the voice, but Flo just smiled; she knew he had finally arrived.

"I'd like to personally thank everyone in the room for all the hard work you have done," the voice continued. "It's commendable on any level and I believe we can continue on from here now that we have the first clue. This is where Ms. Rinna comes in, for she was the first one to recognize what was painfully unapparent to me at the time. We have to pick up the trail from here. Somewhere between here and Megiddo, we will find what Anhur discovered in the first place. It is a daunting task due to the area we must cover in this wide expanse of desert, but it is one I believe we will surmount. I also concur with Dr. Hanson on one very important aspect regarding the speed at which the drone travels, it limits our ability to see. We need a way of effectively harnessing the light to our advantage. This particular issue I will leave in more skillful hands, for I am sure you gentlemen will find a better answer to this than anything I might suggest."

The priest had made his way to the front of the tent. "For those of you who do not know who I am, I'm Monsignor Giuseppe Lorenzo, a religious historian and proctor to the Vatican library and an adviser to Pope Romanus, who funded this research project. I am sure, were he here today, he would tell you with heartfelt conviction, thank you for a job well done."

The group applauded the priest's vote of confidence and began to tackle the issue as the priest walked back down the aisle and out of the tent. Flo followed him out.

"Well stated, Monsignor. I doubt that anyone could have expressed their thoughts with any more conviction than you. When did you get here?"

"To tell you the truth, late last evening, while everyone was busy testing the drone."

"Why didn't you step forward?"

"I saw no need," he shrugged. "Everything seemed to be under control and there was nothing I could have done to assist anyway."

"So you saw the partially buried sword in the valley?"

"No, but remember one thing Ms. Rinna, and then you will know why I never bothered to look at it. There is a quote you might want to remember about all this. '*And they will leave signs in the desert*,' which should answer your question as to why I never bothered to show up until now. I knew there would be something out there in the first place, Ms. Rinna."

Once again, Flo was amazed by the man. "Could I ask you a question on a personal note and get an honest answer from you?"

"Sure."

"Do you think I am suffering from a lack of conviction?" She noticed his brows knit, which seemed to answer the question.

"I believe only you can answer that honestly. Why would you ask that?"

"I was told once that it sometimes takes a leap of faith to convince yourself that you can trust someone or something explicitly enough to truly believe and rise above the negativity that surrounds the human condition and weighs it down. Do you believe this to be true?"

"Why, yes I do," he replied. "Sometimes the hardest thing you'll ever do is convince yourself. I believe we both have been doing just that ever since we began to tackle this issue, don't you?"

Flo was silent for several moments, nervously twirling her hair. "I believe I have and never realized it. Yes... yes, I have, haven't I?" she mumbled painfully.

By mid-afternoon a solution had been found to slow the light beam down. The designers decided to mount the light generator on a helicopter. It was also agreed that the search pattern would fan out in a hundred- and eighty-degree radius if nothing were found in a direct western heading. The cartographers informed them if they could find three items in succession; they could plot the likely direction of travel. This seemed to lift everyone's spirits, for it would make it easier to follow the path with plotted information to go by. It was also decided that spotters would be placed on board trucks and spaced so that the likelihood of missing a clue would be lessened. The only question raised at this point was what they were specifically looking for. This question was bantered about for some time until Dr. Newman settled the issue.

"Anything that is visible as a reflection to the blue luminance! Anything else is to be considered a false indicator because it is most likely visible under natural light."

Dr. Hanson then rose and addressed the assembly. "The reflection of the sun's rays off of the desert floor can burn the retina of the eye. This eye damage causes the mind to compensate and see images that aren't really there, such as a mirage for example." He gazed around the group gathered around him. "From now on, everyone who is awake during the day, and in the sun, is required to wear sunglasses."

When they were finally ready to proceed, tracking the movement of the otherworldly armies was not as difficult as assumed for the first five or so miles, until they lost the trail. As Flo had presumed, it had turned, but in which direction it was hard to tell. There was some argument concerning this setback. Some thought it would be a slight curve toward the north east while others thought it would veer sharply by a flanking maneuver.

It took some time to realize that the movement of the armies was in a zigzag pattern. This was the point where the Egyptian commander Enzo had decided to lend his expertise in field maneuvers to the endeavor. Up to this point, he mostly sat idly by with his troops, laughing at the inane antics of the group, for he never fully understood the scope of the operation. It was not until Anhur explained what they were trying to find and got him intimately involved that he reluctantly stepped forward with curiosity. It then became obvious to all that the pattern was explainable due to the fact that the forces of white were trying with all their might to turn their opposition to the southeast, away from its intended direction, while they retreated. The pattern was somewhat hard to track in the beginning but soon became evident with the aid of the satellite and computer plotting.

The only problem now was trying to figure the rate of travel. Some of the men even suggested they pull up and position the group in the area of Megiddo, but no one was sure at this point from which direction the armies would arrive. Monsignor Lorenzo finally squashed that idea, arguing that the whole intent was to film the actual battle in progress and if they erred in their assumption, it would be too late to correct the error. The idea was tabled and they continued to follow the trail, which now proceeded in a true northerly direction, following the Nile.

Somewhere between Asyut and Al Minya, the battle crossed the Nile and headed in the direction of Mount Sinai.

They were in the middle of the Arabian Desert when it was finally deduced that in order for the armies to cross the Suez gulf, they would have crossed at the narrowest point of passage. That location was in the area of Ra's Gharib. Too much time was being wasted following the trail. The Monsignor finally realized what the tacticians were driving at, a logical premise and finally relented. He gave them permission to cross the gulf to expedite the search, using only the helicopter on the opposite side in order to hopefully locate the battle.

Anhur demanded that he be included in the search crew. He had for some reason shown excessive signs of fatigue. Members of the group begged him to drop out, for his job was apparently finished as far as everyone in the group was concerned. He had done his part and no one faulted him if he decided to return to Rome to his family. He however, vehemently denied his failing health and demanded to accompany them.

"It is my wish to look once more upon a sight that no man before me has ever seen with a human eye! Allah has commanded it to be and you cannot deny me."

No one could, or would, argue his point, and relented.

It was while they flew on the opposite side of the Gulf that they picked up the trail once again. Anhur sighted the first real evidence of a battle, a partially decomposed corpse. The find was astounding in its own right as the pilot radioed the location to the rest of the group.

That morning as the light of dawn broke once again, the helicopter landed five miles inland, where it would again wait for darkness to resume their search. That morning, Anhur felt the first pangs of death. He drifted in and out of reality and Trey knew that he did not have much longer to live. Once, when he woke for the umpteenth time, he pointed and spoke at the same time.

"They are not far away from here, only ten or twelve miles in that direction."

Trey could not help not feel for the man who thought he would not make it into the night. It was with that bit of believable information that the helicopter flew back to retrieve those who had made it all possible to begin with, leaving Trey with Anhur resting comfortably inside a tent. No one doubted the visionary at this point. By late afternoon, the helicopter had returned. What surprised Trey the most was that as the sun fell; the man began to rally once again. Most of those who had seen him this morning could not believe his resilience.

Once the sun had set, everyone boarded the helicopter, but this time they did not light up the signal generator right away. They flew in the direction Anhur had pointed to for close to twelve miles when Anhur shouted over the din of the rotors.

"Here!"

The helicopter pulled up and began to circle. Once the generator was charged and the switch thrown, the group in the chopper witnessed something that everyone supposed they would never in a million years see - a battle raging below them.

Anhur was the first to comment on the sighting.

"Allah be Praised!" he shouted, and then slumped over.

The Monsignor, who was nearest to him, silently thanked the man for his perseverance as a single tear rolled off his cheek. He reached over and closed Anhur's eyes with his fingertips, muttering a quiet prayer as he did so. The rest of the group was too mesmerized with what they witnessed below them to notice the final exchange.

CHAPTER 15

Unveiling the Truth

As soon as Anhur passed away, the monsignor noticed a presence standing next to him. The image had the semblance of a face with a permanent scowl and the figure was as Anhur had so vividly described months earlier. It was one of the most beautiful, yet ugly, figures Giuseppe had ever laid eyes on. The best way Giuseppe could describe the angel was illogically, as rotten decay. The Monsignor turned away from the sight and spoke its name almost as if he had been instructed to do so. "Duma, why?"

"It is necessary that I take him, for he is needed immediately!"

The Monsignor, who thought he was the lone witness to the event, soon realized that all who were on board witnessed the faint presence. He surmised the reason why they had seen the angel was due to the reflection of the blue light off the surface of the desert floor, which surrounded them with a hazy blue effervescence. The Monsignor turned back toward the angel and spoke. "Do what you must!"

There was no reply, only a blue haze where the angel once stood. Giuseppe also realized one other feature about Duma; he had no wings as Anhur had denoted. He now knew why the early artists had added the feature to early depictions in order to mask the vulgarity of the figure. Giuseppe looked back at the others only to see the last vestiges of horror- stricken faces staring back at him. At that exact moment, he knew this was all real.

Several moments later, the copter began to pitch from side to side, as if the pilot thought it necessary to dodge the figure of yet another angel who hovered in front of the windshield. The angel looked like a hardened warrior to the Monsignor, its drawn sword dripping with black blood and pointing down to the battle below. The angel shouted at the pilot.

"Ignore the vision!" Giuseppe called out. "It will do us no harm; just steady the helicopter, lest we crash!"

Moments later, he saw his first demon as it flew right through one bay door and out the other in an effort to evade yet another pursuing angel who had stopped short of the open bay door. His eyes naturally followed the dark shadow of the demon, which escaped the light and disappeared into the darkness.

He heard Flo scream and looked over to see her grasping at Trey in a petrified manner. Trey encompassed her in his arms as she buried her head into his chest in an effort to escape the sights that surrounded them. Surprisingly, this was the first time he had witnessed any sort of outward affection between the two of them. He turned away from the couple to check on the other occupants, who other than looking startled, showed no other outward signs of distress. He looked forward once more only to see that the angel no longer reflected in the windshield.

This was his first chance to look down and witness the raging battle below. What surprised him most was that it was a two-dimensional battle. Opposing forces flew through the air in multidirectional flight, soaring and diving to elude death. This scene somehow reminded him of vultures circling and diving on their prey. He saw the demons swooping down onto the field and hacking at the ground troops while the angels tried to fight them off. He realized he was in a state of shock and disbelief, his mind painfully refusing to believe what he was seeing was real. He found he could not look away, but watched the aerial battle for several moments longer before he turned his attention to what looked like a conventional battlefield of opposing forces on the ground.

At first, it was hard for him to adjust to the ever-moving position of the helicopter, but soon he began to focus on just one spot in order to see the raging battle with better lucidity. Under the influence of the bright blue light, he found that if he squinted, he could witness the carnage below with abject clarity.

"My God, she was right, we are losing!" He turned away from the sight and looked at Flo.

Something drew his eyes back to the scene. An object of some sort had caught his attention, something that he had glimpsed upon for just a split-second. Just off to one side of the withering light, it stood there. The figure was hard to discern at first, but then his eyes recognized something his mind did not want to comprehend. "It can't be true," he mumbled. The creature stood on its stump-like two rear legs; it's back angled in a defensive posture. Its seven heads oscillated like the movements of a snake. There was a crown perched atop each and every one of the heads, and they glistened in the blue light. The light affected the crowns and blazed from blue to pure red. The dragon engaged no less than two dozen warriors at the same time, striking at them with lightning movements of its heads. The monsignor watched as one of the warriors fell out of synchronization with the moments of the multiple heads. He was immediately caught and ingested by the raging beast. With lightning movement, the beast retreated several steps and seemed to roar in defiance before reengaging the warriors once more. The dragon seemed to immediately increase in size with each repast.

"My God, it's feeding on their souls!"

Monsignor Lorenzo noticed another thing about the beast that he had trouble comprehending. He saw the remainder of an eighth head, a stump which rose just above the creature's left shoulder. It had been amputated by the Archangel Michael's sword. The stump had never truly healed even after all this time and oozed a greenish-black fluid that slowly seeped down its front shoulder and onto the sand.

He saw the dragon back off once again, another warrior clenched between its jaws. This time it did not consume the soldier but suddenly dropped the warrior onto the sand. All seven heads looked upward at the same time, straight at Monsignor Lorenzo. He felt a tug at his soul and made a hasty sign of the cross to ward off the influence he felt he was now under, kissing the cross that hung around his neck. He felt the screams of protest from the beast, a reaction to his denial of its purported reign.

The monsignor quickly turned away from the sight in an effort to escape the beast's influence and shouted at the top of his lungs. "We need to leave this place of evil!"

He bent forward onto his hands on his knees to fight off an instantaneous need to vomit. He found his senses numbed and silently swore to never look down upon the scene again. Then, he felt an arm encompass him and turned to see Dr. Hanson trying to console his withering spirit. The pilot, who heard the screams, turned in his seat to see what the commotion was about. The doctor calmly spoke. "Veer away from the battle and kill the lights!"

He was reproached in unison by the remainder of the occupants, who seemed to have fallen into a trace-like state from viewing the scene below.

"Do what I say!" he demanded. "I'm in charge now and I want you to kill the lights!" The pilot obeyed and darkness encompassed the group once more. The priest found his senses once again and turned to Dr. Hanson. "Is there any way we can film this?"

Dr. Hanson turned to Dr. Newman and repeated the question.

"Yes!" Newman shouted over the rotor noise. "But the cameras are on one of the trucks en-route. I presumed if we did find what we were looking for a permanent record of the event would be required, so we built a special camera that filters blue light into the visible light spectrum as it films."

"Remarkable, Dr. Newman!" Hanson complimented him. "I would have never thought to do so myself."

"It just comes with the territory I guess, though I believe you are being modest. You would have done the same were you in my shoes."

Giuseppe listened to the dialog and smiled ambiguously at the fortunate news. "His Excellency would want to know…" Then darkness surrounded him and he slumped to the floor before he could finish the sentence. He felt the doctor catch him on the way down, laying him carefully on the metal deck.

Giuseppe woke several minutes later, confused. As his eyes focused, he saw several faces scrutinizing his every reaction. The smell of sulphur registered in his mind and he violently shook his head to escape the putrid scent. He heard a voice.

"That should do the trick."

He did not recognize it. He suddenly felt queasy, his stomach rolled and he stifled an expulsion once again, only to feel his throat blaze in return. "Get me up," he pleaded meekly. Once in a seated position, he felt the helicopter quickly descending. The helicopter alit several moments later with a jarring effect. No one moved, nor did they say anything. The group was motionless and the rotors had completely stopped before anyone even made an effort to disembark. Giuseppe sensed the group was somewhat afraid to leave the sanctity of the helicopter bay. He turned once again toward Trey and Flo, only to notice Trey trying fruitlessly to pry his hands from the death grip with which she held his. He saw Trey's troubled look as he bodily picked her up as if she were weightless, and watched him step down out of the bay door into the night.

He could not help but feel for Flo, whom he knew had been traumatized by the sight they had all witnessed. This he thought proved only one thing to him, something he had thought she had lacked all the while, faith. The reasoning was altogether simple. She had been questioning her faith from the moment he met her.

After Trey had left, the rest of the group followed suit. In the break of dawn light, he glanced at his watch for the first time. They had been airborne for well over three hours. "Impossible," he said out loud as he looked at the body of Anhur the Minor once again. His corpse nothing more than a grey dust, but the priest could not help but admire the figure all the same.

No one slept, but instead gathered to relate their experiences. The whole scenario took on a highly religious aspect even though the priest knew this group was multi-denominational. Giuseppe opted to remain silent the whole time, intent on listening to the witnesses' own interpretation of what they had seen. In the end, he surmised that no two recollections of the event were duplicated.

Flo left Trey's side for the first time and made her way to where he was seated. "How are you feeling?" he asked.

"I really couldn't say at this point, but the best word that comes to mind is traumatized."

"I believe that would be an accurate description, but traumatized or not, you know you have to write about your experience in order to make some sense of it all, don't you?"

"I know… you are right, but I don't know how I will be able to at this point in time."

"You know, there was something a young lady once told me that struck a chord, and I'll quote her to you if I must. She told me this; 'write while it is fresh in your mind or you will lose the perspective the subject matter demands'." He took her hand. "I'll let you in on a secret. She is one heck of a writer. If you want, I could give you her name. It might help you decide whether you can draw up the courage to do what she seems to do so well."

"I don't know…"

"Yes, but I do know. I also know that this experience must be told to the rest, just like Anhur had done. He gave his life to prove his vision. You are not even asked to give that."

"I suppose, when you put it in that perspective, it only requires the gumption to do so, doesn't it?"

"Like I said earlier, it takes courage to face your foibles head on, if you follow what I'm trying to say. Besides, it would be better if there were some sort of personal slant to the story when it is finally filmed and broadcast to the world. People would have a better understanding of what they are looking at and might better comprehend the gravity of the situation. You have been with this from the start and there is no better person to give the rest of us the proper explanation of the possible end result. From what I heard earlier from the group, it is only a matter of two weeks at best before this whole revelation comes to pass, unless we do something to assist. You have been right all along. We are losing, but I still hold out the hope that mankind can change the situation. I know that seems to be a tall order, but we will have some help if I have this figured right. I know at times I seem to be altruistic, but believe me when I say this; I'd have it no other way."

Once again, Flo was amazed by the man. "Let me ask you one question before I do what seems so evident to you. How did you achieve such an unveering attitude?"

"Actually, that is a three-part answer which I hope you will spend some time contemplating. Trust yourself, for it is in your heart to do so. Trust your fellow man, for there is some goodness in everyone. Above all, trust in God, for he lights your way. This is my mantra, the same one that guides me each and every day. You would do well to wear it like a badge of courage, Ms. Rinna." Giuseppe squeezed her hand once more, then got up and left. He had suddenly grown weary of the whole experience.

He was awakened at dusk to the roar of heavy trucks and the bleating of camels. At first, his mind did not at first register the strange sounds of the animals, for they were foreign to him. He smelled their musk though, which had permeated the tent. He peeled back the flap of his tent only to witness the backside of one directly in front of him. It was in the process of relieving itself, which partially explained the smell. He suddenly had an instant fear for the animals, reasoning that what you don't know will hurt you. He wondered if he should risk leaving the safety of the tent, but by this time could stand the smell no longer and decided to chance it.

The entire camp seemed to be in an uproar over the intrusion of the Bedouins, who had followed the convoy of trucks to their location. The commander of the Egyptian army seemed to delight in making the situation worse by goading the Bedouin leader on. The Monsignor stood watching it intensify and wished Anhur was still alive; he seemed to be the only one who could dampen the commander's reckless attitude. He did not notice Trey's presence beside him until he spoke.

"There seems to be some dispute over why we are on their lands without permission. The commander is telling the Bedouins in no uncertain terms that he has the full authority of the Egyptian Government and does not need their permission to gain access their lands. The Bedouin leader is in the process of telling the commander that he is violating a signed pact in doing so. I won't bother to tell you what they are saying now; suffice to say it is quite offensive in nature," Trey said.

"I see, but what are we going to do about this predicament?" the priest asked.

"Shhh…" Trey said. "I believe they are asking for money at this point and the commander is telling them they will be lucky to escape with their lives and that we are on an official business matter and he won't be blackmailed by the son of a dog. They're posturing at this point. I believe the Bedouins are just after some supplies. But it's not important. I was sent to get you and need your advice." He took the Monsignor by the elbow and escorted him away from the altercation, just in case it developed into something worse.

"What seems to be the problem?"

"Well, since you funded this project and actually have the final say, I was wondering if you would do me a favor."

"Just ask," Giuseppe said.

"Well, now that the photography equipment is here, the group would like your input on the list of likely candidates to assist on this evening's filming flight? I realize that Flo has been with you from the start of all this and she is vehement that she be included on the roster, but I'm worried about her. I don't know what you said to her earlier, but it is my opinion that she is not in the frame of mind to endure another round of enlightenment. I wish you would either exclude her from the list or make up some excuse on why she needs to stay behind. I believe she has seen enough already. You saw how she reacted last night; I expect more of the same."

"You really do care a lot about her I see, to concern yourself about her welfare?"

"There's more to it than that I'm afraid," Trey said. "I'm in love with her, have been since the moment I saw her. I just never had the guts to tell her how I felt?"

"I see," Giuseppe said. "Well, I can't fault you on your choice. I will say one thing, which I hope might ease your mind a bit. I believe she loves you too but is afraid to admit it. I believe when the time is right, you will get her to agree that you both feel the same way about each other." Giuseppe smiled. "As far as me talking her out of going tonight, I wonder? She's a hard one to convince at times, but I'll see what I can do. If she puts up too much of a fuss though, I'll have no other choice but to cede to her wishes. Let me try and convince her otherwise because I believe you may be right."

"Thanks, Monsignor, I couldn't ask any more from you than that."

The flight lifted off without Flo, with seven observers on board along with the pilot; Trey and Kyle Hanson, Dr. Parker, Dr. Newman and Commander Enzo, who insisted on going after talk about the discovery had spread though the camp. "It's the least you can do for me, priest, now that I have run off those Bedouin curs," Enzo had said. "You should have let me dispose of them in my own way, instead of intervening; I'm sure they will be back when their free supplies run out."

The monsignor wasn't about to argue with the man again and ceded readily. The way he looked at it, there had been one death associated with the discovery already. He was not about to add others to the list.

When the helicopter arrived at the same location as the initial discovery, there was nothing to be seen, as they now expected. Having already plotted the probable location of the battle today, they moved forward on a northeast heading and found the battle a short time later

The only ones who had not seen the conflict thus far were the commander, who seemed enthralled by the sighting, and one of the technicians who came aboard to film the event. The monsignor knew what to expect the second time around, but still was disturbed by the ramifications of it all. The only thing different this time from the initial flight was their approach. They were flying much lower in order to utilize the full effect of the light. This time, Giuseppe witnessed the raging battle for quite some time without it affecting him. He saw the faces of the warriors quite clearly at this altitude and tried to remain objective. He knew the battle was the struggle for the essence of man, the battle to save souls from damnation.

After flying for some time, he spoke. "I have not seen the beast yet! Let me know when any of you spot him," he called out to the group. He heard a few murmured responses, but kept his eyes pinned on the battle below.

Then he saw her, once again shocked by the sight of her, thinking after all this time she would have faded from his memory like his father had. His mother - no, she was no longer his mother, but a warrior fighting for God. She wielded a sword and fought furiously on the front line. He called out to her by her Christian name. "Donna!" His heart wept for her predicament and he bit his lip in order to stifle the sudden rise of emotions that overwhelmed him. "Jesus, give her the strength to carry on," he prayed and then shouted her name at the top of his lungs with all the emotion a son could muster for the love of a mother. "Donna....to your left!"

The beast had appeared out of nowhere and Giuseppe could see it stomping its way toward her. He knew his mother had somehow heard him, for she turned at the last moment to avoid being eaten. The beast roared in disapproval of the near miss. All seven mouths of the beast were agape. Then, the monsignor thought he heard a voice.

"Give me your soul and I will spare hers."

Suddenly the warrior archangel Marek appeared in front of him, bloodied from battle.

"Deny the beast the satisfaction, and do not fall prey to his false promises."

"But I must!"

"The great deceiver would rather have your soul than hers. Your destiny has yet to be fulfilled!" Marek said, then flew down to assist her.

Giuseppe looked on with saddened heart, as the beast had the semblance of his mother in its jaws, carefully pursing her with his lips while it waited for an answer.

No, I cannot capitulate!" the priest shouted, yet subconsciously he had already agreed in principle. It was at the exact moment of the voiced denial that the Archangel Marek struck at the beast's neck from behind with the hilt of his sword. This caused the beast to react to the blinding maneuver by opening his mouth and letting his mother fall. She, however never hit the ground. She was scooped up by the angel and raised aloft of the beast. Giuseppe saw the angel taunt the beast with his sword, beckoning it to come closer. It never did, but instead shrieked with all seven of its heads, a horrifying sound that deafened the priest. He looked at the others and realized they knew nothing of what occurred between him and the angel Marek, nor did they realize that the foreign sound they heard was the shriek of the seven-headed beast. For some reason, Monsignor Lorenzo alone seemed aware of exactly what had produced the sound.

Giuseppe sat heavily onto the bay floor; he heard no more, his world was suddenly silent, knowing he was being punished for his breach of faith. Were it not for the angel, he would have readily succumbed to the temptation to save his mother, and probably would have paid for his misjudgment with his eternal life.

Trey sat a short distance away next to the cameraman. Other than viewing the miniature screen, he really never looked below the entire time the blue light was on. He had apparently seen enough the night before to satisfy his curiosity. Instead, he kept a watchful eye on the rest of the group. When the Monsignor slumped to the floor, he made his way over to him and sat next to him, sensing something amiss.

"Are you all right, Monsignor?"

The priest did not answer. Trey asked the question again, still no answer. He shook his shoulder in an effort to draw a response. The priest turned slowly toward him; a look of profound disapprobation evident by his ever-whitening features. He repeated the question for the third time and noticed the priest's facial features change somewhat as it became evident the priest had finally recognized him. Trey began to worry as the priest pointed to his ears and then grabbed his lobes, violently shaking them in the process. Trey finally understood what the man was trying to convey. He surmised the unnatural sound he had heard earlier must have affected the priest in some inordinate way. He watched as the priest removed a slip of paper and pen from his vestment and began to write, but could not read the note which was written in Italian. He took the note and stuffed it in his pocket, knowing Flo could translate its meaning later. He no longer tried to ask the priest anything, but instead hoped that in due time his hearing would return of its own accord.

Upon their return to the camp, a meeting was called in an effort to discern what had happened to the priest. No one was quite sure what had happened to cause the priest to go deaf. Flo was visibly distraught over his condition, but gathered the nerve to chair the question and answers session,

"What did you see?" she asked pointedly, demanding answers in turn of every member of the flight. No one was exempt from her probing demeanor, for she knew that without the Monsignor, there was probably little hope of finding a solution. "Trey, you saw him slump into a seated position. Was there anything that you saw or heard prior to this, other than the strange sound that all of you seemed to hear, that might have led you to believe he was in distress?"

"Look, we've been over this a dozen times already," he said. "There's nothing more to add. You're beating a dead horse at this point and I see no reason to continue any further."

Even the fearless Enzo, the Egyptian commander, was beginning to waver under her constant haranguing.

"Wait!"

Trey reached into his shirt pocket and removed the note the monsignor had penned in the chopper from his pocket, rather meekly. He handed it to her.

"He did write this," he explained. "I'd forgotten about until this very moment. Look Flo, everyone in this room is concerned for his welfare. No one questions his viability at this point, but I think you need to back off a bit and let us address some other concerns that have come to light."

"Such as?"

"If we decide to return for further filming, are we likely to endanger anyone else who decides to volunteer to further study the revelation? You know the Monsignor is not totally incapacitated, he is altogether normal in most respects except for his hearing. You've been with him all the while. You, of all people, know what he had in mind right from the start. The way I look at it, you'll just have to be his voice from now on, just translate what he writes on paper and we will do as he says. That's about as simple of an explanation that I can come up with to solve this."

The rest of the group murmured their approval to the suggestion and waited for her to answer. She read the note and did not reply to the proposal.

"Well, what does it say?" Dr. Hanson demanded.

"He wants the film to be broadcast to the world," she replied. "He would like for us to continue filming and tracking the battle… that's the gist of the note." She rose abruptly from her chair. "I have to see him." She rushed out of the room before anyone could say another word, heading in the direction of the monsignor's quarters. Trey followed her out. He knew there was no way he was letting her out of his sights in her condition. That and he wanted to know what was really written in the note. He knew there was more to the note than what she had admitted to telling the rest. Trey hung back as the two of them sat together. Flo gave the monsignor one of her writing tablets and asked for a concise explanation into his loss of hearing. The Monsignor, though, would not comply other than to say he had brought the punishment upon himself.

"Turn your attention to the task at hand; we are just beginning to realize the implications of everything that has been shown us."

CHAPTER 16

The Conflict

The film was broadcast the following day along with Flo's hastily written article, a brief summation of her first article along with a descriptive narration on what she had witnessed the evening before. This was the first astounding event in months, and upstaged the Golden Tongue's meteoritic rise to world power and his call for a new world order.

The copy stole the front page of every major publication worldwide and the fact the article was proven on film made everyone, stop and wonder.

For the first time in their lives, some people began to realize what the enlightened few had been stating all along might possibly be the truth.

"Repent, the end is near!"

The Media didn't even have to sensationalize the event - it stood on its own merit. The world seemed to grind to a halt for the first time anyone could remember and nothing else seemed to matter as the original filming of the event ran on a continuous basis across the airwaves. The inordinate event was the only topic that seemed to be on everyone's mind. Many speculated as to the true meaning of the sighting, but few knew what to do to halt the progression toward Megiddo, as Flo had so stated in her article. She had even posed an open challenge to all concerned to recommend a possible solution to the crisis.

That evening, church bells tolled in every town, city, state and country worldwide and people flocked en masse to every church, mosque, synagogue and temple, seeking to make some sense of it all. They left offerings and prayed for redemption. The coffers of every one of these religious buildings were overstuffed with donations of silver and gold, many thinking they could buy their way into salvation with monetary recompense. Some entered but never left the confines of these buildings from that day forward, thinking they would be protected from the obvious by the walls of the edifices and the sanctified ground upon which they stood.

Everyone who sought the true meaning behind the sighting turned to their respective religious leaders for answers to the almost unbelievable sight, but there were no answers. At least not in the beginning, for the religious leaders were just as stunned with the revelation as the masses were.

The film caused many to turn to their scriptures for answers. Religious tomes of all denominations were sold out within hours of the first broadcast, and many turned to violence to obtain a copy of their holy books. In response to the overwhelming demand, the presses began to endlessly churn out the tomes, to no avail. A lucrative black market instantly sprouted.

By the following morning, panic set in as people thronged to famed religious sites hoping for some sort of sign of their redemption. The entire wailing wall in Jerusalem became no less than ten people deep at all times. Lourdes was swamped by pilgrims, many of them turned back by force in order to preserve the grounds. In Mecca, the population of the holy city quadrupled in a day's time, and the same could be said of Vatican City. People forced their way into all of these holy arenas in order to bolster their rectitude.

Some people who thought all was lost and saw no redemption for their stained souls turned to suicide as an avenue of escape, while still others took it upon themselves to act as judge and jury, sacrificing not only themselves but their entire families as well in the name of God. This was not an isolated event either; it was happening all over the world. Some picked strange or more innovative ways in which to take their own lives or the lives of their loved ones. One man even nailed his entire family to crosses in hope of staving off the inevitable with his sacrifice.

The sighting worked on the minds of some of even the crazier ones, who took insanity to the streets, indiscriminately killing at random. There no longer seemed to be any deterring reason why they could not act out their aggressions on others. After all, there didn't seem to be much time left now, and retribution in the legal sense was the least of their worries. Incidents of personal assault rose exponentially in all forms, and it was all the police could do to stop the vicious onslaught on unsuspecting citizens. Martial law had to be proclaimed in some countries, preempting all out mania.

The day of the broadcast, film crews of every major news station in the world headed to Egypt hoping to get some exclusive footage of the ongoing battle. Once there, many were disappointed to learn that the sighting, which was visible to the naked eye under the influence of the blue light, was actually not recordable with conventional filming equipment. This baffled the media experts and some began to question whether this was a staged event as the Golden Tongue had quickly proclaimed.

"It's nothing more than a hologram, meant by some to draw many of the errant flock back into the fold."

Many reporters began to echo the statement Ahriman had proclaimed, seeing there was nothing to view but endless sand. Ahriman had become the master of ruse and lied for obvious reasons. He had been upstaged. He was trying to squash the tide of religious fervor before it had a chance to take hold and sweep everyone up in to a frenzied fervor. Detritus had warned him from the beginning that something like this would be the only thing that could truly de-stabilize their efforts in winning the final battle of deception. Many people, now confused, did not know where to turn. No one found instantaneous answers or solutions and people reeled.

Three days after the initial broadcast, an announcement was made. There would be an international meeting of distinguished religious leaders of every faith in an effort to discuss and study the phenomena. On the agenda were three primary issues in which the group was set to address. The first point of contention was to find a common ground between all religions so they could explain to their followers in detail what it was that they were really looking at when they viewed the battle, coined TEOD or The End of Days by the press.

The second major issue was what to do to turn the tide of events in favor of the angels, or the side of righteousness as many believed it to be, and to discuss what the future may hold for the world if they lost the struggle.

The third major point of concern had to do with Ahriman, and what could be done about his increasingly slanderous behavior toward all religions in general. He was being dubbed the anti-Christ on a more frequent basis by most religious leaders finally were convinced of his corruptive influence. Many now citing that, the Martyrs of Manila may have been on to something with the name long before the man began to show his true intent.

When Detritus heard of the impending meeting, he counseled Ahriman to do the same with the political leaders of the world to counter the implied threat to their domain. This meeting was scheduled to take place at the United Nations building, with not only registered nations but all nations, including the ones who had been excluded from attending up until this time. His intent was threefold as well.

The first issue at hand was to unite all nations in agreement in order to issue a proclamation. He hoped to discredit the sighting of the TEOD in it's entirely by forwarding expert testimony to prove his claim. He would encourage politicians to stand behind his slanderous lie, forcing most of the predominant world leaders to condemn the sighting as false.

The second major issue he wanted to address was what might be done to quell the religious uprising that had occurred as a result of the TEOD filming. The people had taken the streets back from their respective governmental bodies. He wanted to know what possible steps might be taken to bring order back to society in general.

The third issue dealt with trade and commerce, which had, for obvious reasons, totally stopped. The loss of commerce devastated the financial markets and if it went on much longer would serve to drive most of the debt-ridden governments onto insolvency. Detritus had Ahriman add this point to the discussions, not because he cared one iota about the markets, but to show that Ahriman sought to look out for the best interests of governments he meant to represent.

Many outside observers noted that the stage was being set on two world fronts, pitting church against state and white against black armies respectively. None of the experts was quite sure what to do about either problem, for there seemed to be no obvious solutions to the ensuing power struggle.

There was the third front, which was even less obvious to those who chose to study the problem - an increase in religious fervor and more calls to the On High to intervene. This elicited more wrath from the devil himself and the planet began to churn. More calamities befell men in the form of increasingly severe weather patterns. There was not a day that passed since the TEOD became visible that a least one hurricane or earthquake or one eruption did not occur. The ring of fire was truly ablaze at this point and no one dared make a prediction on how or when it might stop. Hundreds of thousands of people were affected daily by this increasing insurgency and thousands upon thousands were dying. The screams of the lost and dying could no longer be ignored by either church or state and no one nation was exempt. Some religious experts decidedly went out on a limb and ventured to say that the vials associated with the book of Revelations had begun to pour and there was no way of stopping the impended doom that the breaking of those vials had begun.

When some reporters found that there was no story to be had filming the TEOD, they focused their attention on the original participants of the excursion, doing interviews and trying to get a personal slant on the people involved. This in turn brought instant notoriety to every member of the group. Calls came in from all over the globe, hoping that any one member of the group could add some positive perspective to the entire ordeal.

The only one who really had any in-depth knowledge of the situation other than Flo could not even comment due to his impediment, and that was the Monsignor, who had made his presence conveniently scarce. He had slid into a state of depression over his own lack of faith in this instance and remembered all too well what the then-Bishop Alvito had warned him of some time prior. "Pray your eyes and ears will be open when the time comes," he had said. Giuseppe experienced a newfound respect for the man, and wished he could talk to him once again, if only to thank him for his insight into his character. Unfortunately, the cardinal had passed on right before the group had left for Egypt, another reason he had come to the desert later than the others, having staying back to attend the funeral.

He did, however, allow Flo to speak in his stead. He knew from this point forward, unless something changed, that she would be the one everyone would turn to for answers. It would be though her voice that would continue to be viable to all concerned, just as Trey had noted.

Flo tried, but began to doubt her abilities once again. The camp was in a complete turmoil ever since the reporters had begun to arrive and it was getting worse as the days progressed. She was plagued by reporters every time she left her tent. Trey, who now had become her shadow, had to fend them off in order to protect her. They found creative ways to escape the exposure, whenever they left their tent to see the monsignor, often using the camouflage of Bedouin garb to get around unnoticed.

After three days of constant upheaval, Doctors Hanson and Palmer had seen enough and decided to leave the fray while they still could, returning to Washington. There was much more to it than that though, because they had been subpoenaed to appear in front of a State Department inquest looking into the entire affair.

Trey and Flo were subpoenaed also, but she refused to leave the monsignor for a legal nuisance. The monsignor had expressed his wish to return to Rome in order to speak to the Pope and she planned to be there. She did, however, make a suggestion.

"Trey, why don't you accompany your uncle to the states? You have a thorough understanding of what's going on here and will be able to explain the situation better than anyone else might."

Trey was furious with her suggestion. "You have to be kidding, right? Just because we have gained a bit of notoriety doesn't mean you or I will be exempt from harm. Think about this for a moment. If every one of us were suddenly silenced, all that we have done in this case would be to concoct some idiotic story and make it believable and the whole affair disappears right into thin air, just like it never happened to begin with. No. I'm not going anywhere and you aren't going anywhere alone either. If you say we're going to Rome, then Rome it is, besides whether you would like to believe it or not, you need me, more now than you ever needed anyone in your entire life, and not just to watch your back either! This is no game--"

Flo caught him off guard, hugging and then kissing him freely for the first time to keep him from saying anything more. "You're right," she whispered. "I do need you, but never wanted to admit it before now."

"Damned right you do, as much as I need you and that seems to be something we finally agree on--"

She smothered his voice with a kiss once again.

Dr. Newton from M.I.T. decided to stay on to supervise the filming. He had expressed an interest in doing so right from the start. He wanted to follow the battle right to the walls of the ancient city. By the time most of the original crew had left, there were at least one hundred specialists from all over the world there to take their place. Most of them were sent by their respective countries in order to authenticate or disprove the discovery once and for all.

Monsignor Giuseppe Lorenzo was examined by the Vatican medical staff, but only after he had been persuaded to do so. Flo insisted on the check-up and would not take no for an answer. The medical staff could not find anything physically wrong with his ears. He still had not told her the real reason for the handicap, though she was aware that he did tell the pope as much in an extended letter he had written on the return trip.

When the trio met with the pope, he was visibly troubled and irritable from lack of sleep. He did not extend his usual courtesies, which seemed perfectly understandable under the current circumstances to Flo.

"Is it true that there could possibly be only two weeks before they reach Megiddo?" he asked, looking at the monsignor, Flo and Trey from across the desk.

"In theory, yes," Flo said. "Unless something happens to drastically alter the future course of events, we see no other outcome. I would like to sit here and tell you otherwise, but at this point I believe it's just wishful thinking."

"Did you discuss possible remedial solutions with the Monsignor prior to him losing his hearing?"

"I did, though other than him coming up with a singular solution at one point, no other remedy could be found to delay the inevitable. Look, Your Excellency, I don't have to tell you the reasons why I think it is unlikely that anyone can slow down what seems to be a likely ending to all this. The degradation of society, the lack of moral values and loss of faith seem to have all played a part in strengthening the armies of darkness and there seems to be little time left to correct these misdirected values." She paused for a moment. "That is…unless we can unite all religious organizations immediately and do it in such a way that we can achieve a singular voice where everyone stands behind a central figure to put up a final stand against Lucifer and his minions."

The pope said nothing for several moments. "So, what was it that Monsignor Lorenzo came up with as a possible solution?"

Flo glanced at the monsignor, who gestured for her to continue. "That, I'm afraid is a rather simple answer, but when he said it, it seemed like an abstract thought, like it had been mysteriously interjected into our conversation. At one point he thought that I had mentioned it, but I didn't."

"Well, what did he say, Ms. Rinna?" the pope asked edgily.

"Use the power of prayer!"

The Pope looked at the monsignor at this point. "It's a powerful tool in any arena. How did he ascertain that?'

"That was my thought. When, at a later date, I asked him how he had come up with this, he said one other thing that struck me as odd. He said, and I quote, 'Sometimes we are guided in our efforts to find solutions to complex problems.' So I asked him in what context he arrived at the solution. He said, 'I must have been guided by the angels.'" She frowned. "Do you think that is possible?"

"I most certainly do. Why do you ask?"

318

"Have you ever seen an angel up close?"

"No, I can't say that I have."

"I have, and they scared me half to death. How could something so adjectively ugly find a place in God's realm is beyond me."

"Describe to me what you saw, if you would, Ms. Rinna."

"I don't know if you'll believe me but they certainly are not chubby little babes with wings. They're the opposite of everything I thought to be true. I'm afraid the religious artists had it all wrong right from the start. Their facial features have left a lasting impression on me. They looked as if they were sculpted with grey modeling clay by a deranged artist of some sort with a penchant for gouged valleys and sharp peaks. They also had hideously sunken yellow eyes. I had always thought that anything that came from heaven had to delight the senses in one way or another. I was always taught that the closer you came to the right hand of God, the more perfect your features and your soul seemingly became. It was a misconception on my part, having been taught that to look upon an angel was to look at something that was perfect in all respects. The demons I saw were much more alluring to the eye, but as the monsignor said, that is all part of the act of temptation to begin with."

Flo got no response from the Pontiff, so she waited. When no response was forthcoming, she continued. "You know, ever since we left Egypt, hordes upon hordes of people have flocked into the desert in order to get a look at an incredible sight. You have to ask yourself a question. Are they just curious or do they truly believe in what they are seeing? These people, like most of the others, I think, are trying to make sense of it all. But I asked the same question they are now asking some time ago. Why now? The monsignor answered the question for me and I feel his response is something that needs to be addressed to all concerned. But unless we do that in a judicious manner, I'm fear the worst."

"Then the three of you will have to accompany me when I leave for the conference tomorrow," the pope stated matter of factly. "Besides, who could better explain what needs to be said than the three of you?"

"No one, I guess," Flo commiserated, "But there is one question I have to ask before I agree."

"Which is?" the pope asked gruffly.

"You and the monsignor seem to have been in constant contact ever since this whole thing started, is that not true?"

"Yes, I was the one who initially asked him to look into this matter to begin with. Why do you ask?"

"Well, I knew that much already, but as much as I know about this entire situation, there is one point which seems to bother me. You and he seem to know how this is all going to turn out. Don't you?"

"The monsignor seems to be the only one who can answer that, if you ask me."

"Was he speculating in your opinion, or does he have some idea that you thought might be feasible?"

"I really don't know where you are going with this, but to answer your question, yes… he did have, but to be perfectly honest with you, there are going to have to be several things that have to happen before this scenario of his becomes a reality. All I can to tell you is this; I don't deal in the realm of speculative reasoning or theories for that matter, Ms. Rinna. I don't have the time for it. Unless there is something tangible you wish to point out, you're wasting my time. I would suggest that you might better ask the Monsignor what he had in mind."

Flo sensed the pontiff was just as evasive as the monsignor seemed to be, but she let it drop.

The invisible armies had just about reached the border of Israel by that evening. The government of Israel had issued a proclamation denying anyone other than the citizens of their country access to its borders.

This in turn caused an international incident both inside and outside of its borders. Both Muslim and the Jewish factions of the country took to the streets in protest of the government's edict.

The Muslim states in the Middle East united for the first time in protest of the edict and warned Israel if they did not freely open their borders, they would call for the total annihilation of the state of Israel.

The twelve tribes of Israel had finally united in a just cause and vented their wrath on the state, threatening war.

The religious community within the country took control of the streets and assaulted the government buildings, as Israeli soldiers, torn between duty and belief, stood idly by for the first time anyone could remember and let buildings burn.

Still the government would not capitulate, but instead sent out stern warnings to anyone who cared to take heed that they would use nuclear force if necessary to repel any assault on their borders. Tensions raised and for the first time in its history, the United States, a formerly staunch ally of the state of Israel, refused to come to their assistance, leaving the door open for the annihilation of the state. The U.S. also responded in a manner that shocked surrounding Muslim states, stating in a curt response that any use of nuclear weapons would be dealt with in swift measure. Many observers construed this to mean that the United States would annihilate the Jewish state themselves if they failed to capitulate.

The U.S. government instead pleaded with both sides to use some common sense for once, considering the extenuating circumstances, begging the state of Israel to rescind its edict before there was no country left to call their own.

Radical groups within the Middle East brought their influence to bear and urged their religious leaders and governments as well in their respective nations to issue an all-out Fatwa against the state of Israel. The Fatwa was sought to unite all of the nations under a just cause and send their armies out at once to end the evil occupation and restore all the lands that were once considered Palestinian, which included Megiddo.

"It is the fundamental right of all world governments to rule within their domains with absolute authority over all of their constituents in order to protect their leaders and their policies, written to benefit the people under their jurisdiction, for the good of all," stated the Golden Tongue. "No one individual or group should be allowed to interfere with the policies and decision-making processes of any legislative government for a singular purpose. Nor should any group be allowed to use its influence to sway governmental policies for the good of the few or the one. Many of our world government's today are practicing partiality in order to lessen the impact of a few unbridled voices, which seem to sway public opinion in their favor. Most of the constitutions of law and order are, for the most part, based on the premise that all of its individual citizens are granted equal rights.

"It is my opinion that the governments of these countries should use whatever force necessary to squash any behavior that is counter-productive to its constitutional rights, Such actions serve to stifle anarchy which might result from individual groups who, in the name of God or the creator or any such other religious being, seeks to diffuse the power of the governmental bodies in which they reside. I call out to every world government to side with the government of Israel in order to enforce the right of its government to dissuade the minority of peoples for the good of all. Also, I might add that it is the right of any free government to protect its own borders without interference from other counties. This includes denying free access for the sake of fulfilling a quest of uncertain origin and to protect imminent domain.

"There should be no such thing as the separation of church and state, which breeds civil disobedience in the name of religious fervor. Furthermore, it is the intent of this meeting to establish guidelines which allow the governments of these nations to punish its non-conforming citizens without fear of recourse from the group as a whole."

The Golden Tongue completed his opening statement to thunderous applause.

"Furthermore, the perpetrated hoax in which we are now exposed, should and will be exposed for what it truly is; a figment of certain religious groups trying to reinforce their power and justify their existence in the name of Jesus or whatever religious deity they name. Do not be fooled by such trickery, for it only serves to feed the few who think that their way is the only way. I intend to do something here that has never been done before. I will prove to you what indeed has been the real lie for centuries. That is that the core belief systems of all of these groups are tainted by the devil himself."

The opening address then delved into what would later be called an affirmation proclamation, which was heralded as one of the most sweeping lectures on the rights of state over religious freedom anyone had ever heard before. It was delivered in such a convincing way that by the time Ahriman completed his speech, the proclamation was seconded for a vote, which surprised even the most casual onlooker. When it passed unconditionally, since the United Nations, as a rule, could never agree on anything, much less sweeping world reform on something as sensitive as religious rights, which until this day had never even been broached, everyone was astounded.

When select representatives of their perspective nations were asked why they had obviously voted for a referendum that countered their own constitutions, the reporters received pretty much a stock response.

"I can't tell you for sure why. I guess we were caught up in the moment."

Detritus smiled when he heard their responses.

In the meantime, the religious assembly met in Bern, Switzerland. The Pope arrived with his entourage but took a back seat to other major religious leaders who presented themselves at the meeting. There was some tact involved in doing so. First off, the pontiff wanted to gauge the sincerity of the group and their intent. He also wanted them to see that everyone had an equal voice, which was not to be influenced by the number of followers each leader had. After all, he was smart enough to see that if anyone were upstaged at this point in time, they would never be able to come to any sort of agreement whatsoever.

Secondly, he decided, against the wishes of the College of Cardinals, not to even address the other religious leaders unless he was specifically asked to do so. He opted instead to have a statement read on his behalf, prepared by Monsignor Lorenzo, concerning the truth about the revelation, which would be presented by Ms. Rinna. The College balked at the very thought of the idea.

He knew he was gambling a bit by allowing a layperson take a forum that truly belonged to a man of the cloth, but like she had said, who at this point was more immanently qualified to do so other than her?

His council of (now) seven had informed him that the woman had as much face and name recognition as he had and what better way to show all concerned a complete trust and belief than letting her speak on behalf of the Catholic Church. A compromise was struck. The Monsignor was to begin the two-hour dissertation, with Flo taking over midway to finish the reading, thus allowing her to field any questions the group might have.

When Flo originally read the prepared document, she was amazed by its accuracy. It seemed to her as she read it in its entirety that she had been transported back to the origin of the quest. The vivid detail in which the document was written seemed almost altruistic in nature. There was no mention of the Catholic Church and what it had gone though to reveal the sighting. The document only stated facts backed by scripture - not just any scripture, but the scriptures of all known religions. Flo, who up until this moment had never seen any of the Monsignor's writing, could hardly believe what she was reading. There was no question in her mind that he was a far better writer than she could ever claim to be. She was mesmerized by his writing style right from the start, for when she began to read the document, she never put it down until she had completely finished it. He had even given her credit in the final lines of the document, which she never had a hand in and wanted struck from the final page. The monsignor though, would not concede, writing furiously that without her none of this would have become a reality and that they probably would still be wandering aimlessly in the desert.

Flo's presentation of the second half of his document had a dramatic impact on the religious leaders in the room. Trey sat nearby in complete awe of Flo's capabilities. He could not help but admire her all the more, but his were not biased thoughts either. He gazed around the room only to find just about everyone who attended also held in rapt attention by her voice and convictions.

No one up until this time really had any idea how the discovery was made in the first place, and just the idea that something as innocuous as a single beam of light from space could somehow be a dire warning to humanity of its impending doom made them listen. That and the fact that it took a concerted effort of both the scientific and religious communities with a common goal in mind to find answers that seemed improbable and unlikely right from the start.

There was sterling praise for Anhur and his tenacity, which brought a rousing applause from not only the Muslims gathered there but by all who came to recognize that the visionary had crossed religious boundaries in order to assure that world knew of his vision.

When the dissertation was finished, everyone stood and applauded. Flo would not accept the accolades alone, but grabbed the Monsignor and brought him to his feet to accept what she rightfully thought was his to begin with. The priest did not have a clue as to what was going on, but when he stood, Flo noticed a single tear roll down his cheek. The sight reminded her of Cairo and the Weeping Madonna.

It seemed like eons had passed since she first laid eyes on the miraculous sight and she felt suddenly weary from all that they had to endure right from the start. She felt as if she could no longer go on, but when she felt a hand support her back, she turned and felt she could endure. Trey had made his way up to the podium at the request of the Pontiff and whispered in her ear.

"One day things will change, just you wait and see."

She suddenly felt better about their chances, only because he instilled a measure of confidence in her once again. She knew he believed in her and was proud of her accomplishments. At the moment, it seemed to be the only thing that mattered to her.

Once the applause had faded, the first question was one that she had expected.

"What solution, if any, were you able to come up with that might aid us in our hour of need?" one of the elders asked.

She felt it necessary that the Pope answer that question and deferred it to him. He stood and looked around the room for several moments in order that the group might measure his level of sincerity.

"Just as God utilizes his angels as a means of communication, we the religious know when tidings are sent and by whom. The message was quite clear and it was something that utilizes me only as a vessel to convey. I will quote the exact words, as there are no others. Use the power of prayer."

The pope immediately sat down once again. The room grew and remained silent. The only sound was that of the rush of reporters leaving in unison to convey the message. The funny thing about most statements such as these was that generally after the impact wore off many, under normal circumstances, would rise to refute such a statement. This time, no one did, nor did anyone ask another question. They all silently filed out of the room, ending the assembly for the day.

The only other comments that pope did make out came at the end of the second day, when he backed the Muslim call, denouncing Israel for not opening its doors to all who wished to enter. He cited that the city of Jerusalem was the site where many of today's religions were initially based to begin with. He deplored the use of an artificial boundary as a means of denying what was essentially a religious right of all so inclined to cross. "How can tens of thousands of people be intuitively wrong when it comes to witnessing this TEOD, as everyone seems to want to call it?" he questioned. "I for one would readily join them in order to prove to anyone who doubts that this is nothing short of a miraculous revelation, and should be addressed as such."

This is exactly what most of the denizens of the Middle East wanted to hear as the pressure on Israel continued to build. By the time the battle finally crossed the border into Israel, the government had capitulated, which seemed to stave off what was considered inevitable otherwise an all-out war.

After the first day of the Synod had concluded and the news spread that there was a possible solution to all the turmoil, a strange thing occurred. People could be seen on street corners, in elevators or places where it was never normal to see it before, praying.

What was once thought of as a private act now became commonplace wherever one looked. It took less than a day for many of the trend-setters to pick up on the latest vogue idea and run with it. Prayer parties became the rage for some, but for most others it became a beacon of light in which some saw a possible way out of the continued conflagration that weighed them down. What once was a weekly ritual now became a continuous occurrence in all religious institutions. As the voices of the fervent wafted up into the heavens, the battle momentarily stalled.

Nevertheless, to give the devil his due, with this increased fervor, a maelstrom befell the planet that no one had ever witnessed before in the history of mankind. Midway through the third day of the two meetings, the wind began to blow unabated.

This event was conveniently ignored by the meeting of nations, where many of the political leaders began to believe that the TEOD was no more than a hoax. To prove the point, there was a demonstration of a man who seemed to magically appear to stand next to the Golden Tongue. When Ahriman slung his arm through the image, it wavered like a distorted picture. Ahriman made no comment, but only watched as the figure began to walk from the podium and into the aisle between circular rows of desks that surrounded the podium. The man had a blue aura that surrounded him, somewhat similar to the artificial light used to illuminate the battle. After walking the length of the aisle, the figure faded into oblivion.

Ahriman spoke only after the blue light had faded. "Judge what you have witnessed for yourselves in this matter. Was it real or was it a hologram? This is the answer you must decide upon. I will give no further comment on the matter. There is something that I would like to leave you all with, which may not seem relevant at this moment but will come to pass shortly. A scourge will encompass the earth and wash away the supposed righteousness. Just watch and see!"

And so it did. The wind increasingly howled and at speeds never seen before now. The clouds darkened and world seemed to be obscured from the light of day. The seas raged as a result, which made it impossible for even the largest of ships to make way. Entire coastlines of countries were washed away by surging tides. People who could, fled inland, others who were not able to were taken and swallowed in watery graves.

Communications became a problem as towers toppled and buildings fell from the persistent onslaught of wind and rain. It now became a luxury to have lights, as electrical utilities began to fail under the strain of downed wires. This in turn caused the electrical grids to collapse. These were not isolated events, but commonplace occurrences in every corner of the globe. Then the earth began to shake.

Ahriman laughed mirthlessly when asked by a reporter about the increasing manifestation during a proceeding lecture to some fifty thousand. "Why ask me? Ask those who appeal to a non-existent God for answers. Their prayers are nothing more than failed invocations. Why don't you go and ask the uninformed masses who turn their heads to the heavens in hopes of being rescued from an uncompromising savior, if there is one?"

"But are they not asking for help?" another reporter asked.

"All you have to do is ask me and I will end your strife. Follow me. I will show you true salvation as it was intended to be!"

Many who were once doubtful listened in earnest and began to follow him en masse wherever he went, while others were still leery.

"What would you have us to do?" they asked him.

"Align yourself behind me and I will show you the way!"

"How?" they asked

"Swear your allegiance to me and listen. I will show you peace and ease your sorrows!" More people joined behind Ahriman.

"How will you ease our strife?" others asked.

"I will show you what truly might have been done were you not misguided right from the start," he replied. "I will show you what I do, and can do. I will put an end to the turmoil that the almighty has bestowed on you rightful sinners. Come to me and follow in my footsteps!"

More heeded the man's word, while still others were not as sure.

"Can you give us some sort of sign so we know you word is true?' the unsure asked.

"I will reduce the tremors of the earth and you will be able to walk unencumbered once again," Ahriman said. "Then will you believe?"

"Yes," more of them said as they turned to him for salvation from the tempest.

Still some questioned his abilities. "What good would it do to stop the tremors and quakes if the wind would still just bowl us over like matchsticks?"

"At some point in time you will have to decide what you truly believe in," he replied. "What is a tangible promise of a new world order that produces results and what is only an implied promise that has no basis? This is what you must decide on your own and only then will you understand where your allegiance rightfully rests."

After the tremors abated, more misguided souls turned to him for guidance, denouncing their religious affiliations in the process. The human condition was stratifying as a result and religious righteousness began to wane in favor of the new world order.

The battle between light and darkness marched ahead once again, and those who had chosen to follow the progression of the TEOD were hard put to keep up with its increasing speed.

Some of the angels began to cry out in despair, as the howling of the abyss had now made it almost impossible to communicate. Still, Gabriel would not relent. *"Stay the course that He has chosen! He will reveal His intentions when the moment calls for Him to do so. Strike any insincere thought of defeat from your minds!"* However, at this point even Gabriel could not hear their responses as the howling of the abyss was just too great.

The archangel Ariel had brought Duma, the angel of death to Gabriel's side, so that he might finally agree, but Gabriel only shook his head, denying the request once again.

CHAPTER 17

The X Factor

The tremors of misfortune began to abate as Ahriman had predicted they would, and so came the call to those who had converted to the new world order to rise and repel the forces of religious righteousness.

Ahriman knew that the forces that backed him were increasing; he felt the energy, the surge of power from their tainted souls and the newfound control he had over them, and he radiated even more. He felt as if every word he spoke would one day be interpreted as the new scripture for future generations. He called out to his followers that his recorded word would now be referred as the Future Testament, though this slight was meant for all Bible-based religions in general and was meant to drive the final wedge to split the newfound religious unity in two, it had the opposite effect.

Now the religious took a page out of the book of the Illuminati and began to secretly meet in order to find a way to undermine the Antichrist. They had finally figured out that every move they made was somehow known to Ahriman. The religious leaders of the world finally stood united to derive a way of undermining this ominous threat. They had found a common thread that united all religions of the world and proclaimed war against the Antichrist and his penchant for undermining their religious deities, and the right to practice their beliefs in an unabated manner.

There had already been several attempts to assassinate Ahriman, but they had failed miserably. Detritus used these failed attempts to bolster the resolve of his newfound followers. He spoke through Ahriman once again. "Would you rather they nail me to a cross to prove my morality, or will you stand with me and pave a new way into the future? A future, if you can visualize it, with the absence of malice and disenchantment. A future that sets aside the frailties of the human condition for one where we all stand as equals to one another without the religious consciousness that alters our perceptions and feeds our inadequacies with prejudice."

Once again, Detritus had torn a page out of scripture, altered it to suit his needs and used it to convince his followers that he was the righteousness of the world. Still, it was felt that even that was not enough to persuade the masses to turn the tide against the Sons of the Lamb. Ahriman called out once again for the nations of the world to denounce the spectacle of the TEOD as a fraud.

However, as Ahriman was doing so, the top scientists of the world, closely monitoring the progression of the battle, forwarded a theory that seemed to explain what actually was being seen on film. The theory was that there was most likely a parallel universe that closely assimilated Earth's and had to some degree, an effect Earth's humanity.

Ahriman, but more importantly, Detritus, was stunned by the theory, wondering how the scientists could be discredited. He accused major religious communities but more especially the Catholic Church of bribing scientists to forward what he considered utter non-sense. He demanded proof that no coercion had taken place.

Many religious leaders disagreed with the conclusions drawn by the scientific communities, especially with respect to the parallel universe theory. They would rather have thought the correct conclusions to be that the spiritual and real world were interwoven with one another. Nevertheless, even with this difference in opinion, a new alignment began to take place between the scientists and the religious leaders uniting for the first time to prove what was now undeniable to most people who sought to question the sighting.

Other related facts began to surface. It was Dr. Hanson and other leading weather specialists who first noticed something odd about the abnormal change in wind patterns, now that they were sustained for an inordinate amount of time. Instead of crossing the globe in known circular patterns due to variations in high- and low-pressure systems, they now became unidirectional. The patterns and variations thereof began to point toward the Middle East. To be more precise, they pointed directly at Megiddo. There was no viable explanation for this to happen, and for that reason many scientists began to wonder if an outside force could affect something as complex as weather patterns.

Even more astounding than that, satellites orbiting the Earth began to pick up a vortex pattern as it surrounded the ancient city of Megiddo. This in turn led the scientists to believe that a vacuum of sorts was being generated. The only thing that this anomaly could be compared to was something that only happened in outer space - a black hole. The oddest thing about this scenario was that the data could not be readily substantiated. When scientific teams went to Megiddo to verify their satellite data with ground-sensing equipment, the results were inconclusive. While this did not prove the event was not occurring, it left the scientists wondering if what they saw via satellite was in actually a reality.

It finally took an astute scientist who chose to study the background of the TEOD films to note that the battle was now being waged under the influence of abnormally high wind conditions. These newfound winds led more scientists to believe that a vortex of sorts was definitely occurring. They also plotted the direction of the battle, which at this point ran parallel to these winds. This was no coincidence in the minds of the enlightened few, who implored other scientists to continue studying the phenomena. They believed they would then draw the same conclusion.

If that wasn't enough to convince the skeptics, it was also found that the magnetic field that encompassed the earth had collapsed in the area of Megiddo. There were only two other areas that had been known to exhibit this sort of characteristic on a continuous basis, found off of the coast of East Africa where three continental plates converged. The other one was located off the coast of South America, where there was no viable explanation for the magnetic field collapse.

Many scientists in the field of Paleomagnetism refused to acknowledge the religious aspect and began to proclaim that a shift in the magnetic poles of the earth was occurring, which they had determined had happened on five prior occasions throughout earth's history. With this shift in magnetism, it was assumed that the magma within the earth's core also shifted, causing numerous volcanoes to erupt due to the unequal subsurface pressure and magma shifting. This would easily explain the sudden weather changes and were, as some scientists proclaimed, not the result of one man's call for wrath to reign.

The argument about this line of thought was debated for a number of days, but no one could refute the undeniable fact that it all pointed to one area of the globe. Several scientists within the group went further out on the limb and proclaimed the change in magnetic flux had a direct correlation to the alignment of all of the planets within the solar system, which was scheduled to occur on the twenty-first of December. This fact weighed heavily on the minds of the scientists as well as many anthropologists who still believed that this alignment was the key factor in the conclusion of the Mayan calendar. The Mayans had called this day the end of times, for no other reason than the event had never occurred during the era in which they reigned. They were known to be premier astrologists, coupled with research and astute studies of the stars and the effect they had on their lives and livelihood. Therefore, when they could not explain this anomaly of planetary alignment, the Mayans chose to give the gods of their underworld their due and called it, the Day of Reckoning.

These ideas bolstered the religious might and caused many church leaders to further denounce Ahriman as the Antichrist as a fake and a charlatan, calling out for one of their own to rid the planet of this impudent menace.

Along with that, many religious scholars began to unearth supporting evidence to back the claim that the Jewish scholars had it right all along. The final battle was approaching and it would not be fought with men and armaments of a tangible nature, but would be fought and determined by what was being witnessed now. This event was now being interpreted in not only the codex's of the Bible but in the Dead Sea scrolls. To add further proof, some scholars turned to the book of *Centuries* written by Nostradamus, the physician and astrologer, and his quatrains of future predictions for collaboration. The same information was said to be found there. These proofs were immediately discounted by Ahriman as nothing more than a scheme to prove a theory to a non-existent event.

Still, an around the clock vigil was kept by many as they watched the march toward Armageddon. Tensions seem to rise with each passing day as many took heed once again to the visionary Anhur's words, which seemed to ring out with truth.

"You must testify!"

The fervor of religious righteousness rose to a fevered pitch. More people took to the streets, banners in hand to proclaim that the tide could be turned and the minions of Satan could be defeated by the Sons of the Lamb. Along with this event, many took to the streets in prayer processions that grew to be miles long. This added further tension to the situation, which in turn caused more protesters to confront one another. Riots became commonplace. As more people seemed to align them- selves with one side or the other, it soon became evident that some sort of way to determine who was who was needed.

In an instant, black and white armbands began to appear. Those who chose not to wear them in public were scrutinized by both sides. Still others felt the arm bands were not a true indicator of the severity of the issue and many of the religious began to wear crosses or other religious symbols openly around their necks. It became apparent to both sides that if you chose to wander into the streets portraying your affiliation, you might not ever return.

Many didn't.

Detritus did not take these subtle shifts in stride but began do as Hitler did to the Jews during World War Two. He called for the extermination of all who chose to affiliate themselves with a known religion. In order to achieve this, he knew he had to be sanctioned by all world governments to do so. Many nations readily sided with Ahriman. Their economies were in a shamble, their currencies useless and there was constant unrest in their streets. They were powerless to control what had become all-out mayhem. The only method of exchange within these countries was gold and silver, but more important than that were foodstuffs.

Whole nations were literally starving to death due to the calamities that befell them. Third world countries were affected the most and this is where Detritus decided to concentrate his efforts and implement his plan of mass eradication first. He was well aware of the fact that the countries that were better off would not readily complain about the loss of citizens from third world countries. He knew that they had never risen to the defense of tyrannical leaders such as Pol Pot or Idi Amin and weren't likely to do so with this much turmoil surrounding them.

Most nations were no longer worried so much about their borders as much as they worried about their dwindling food supplies. Foreign aid from well-to-do nations to those nations less fortunate seemed to cease, as it now became an issue of have or have-not. The countries that still had adequate supplies utilized their armies to protect these valuable commodities not only from the possibility of theft from their own people, but to keep other nations from knowing the extent of their supplies.

It was in this arena that Detritus felt he could exert the most pressure. He used his influence of his alliances with politicians to allow them to only give to those who swore their allegiance to the new world order in an effort to starve out the resistors to his cause. This ploy seemed to work, and many more of the disenfranchised began to switch sides in order to eat.

The religious hierarchy protested vehemently about the policy of stratification based on religious belief, but most of all it was Pope Romanus who became the most vocal opponent to this policy. He maligned such heads of state, accusing them of spiritual annihilation. He was able to convince several of the better off countries to desist in this practice for the time being.

Monsignor Giuseppe Lorenzo had returned to Milan almost immediately after his return from the religious convention, expressing his desire to return to the Duomo of Milan, the only place he felt comfortable. Pope Romanus tried with all his might to dissuade the man from going, but also knew why he was going and could not fault him on his decision. He agreed to let Giuseppe go for several days, hoping that he could sort out his breach of faith in that short amount of time. Still, he had reservations about his absence, knowing he needed every one of his remaining councilors at his side in order to sort through the calamities that befell him. The pope also knew that time was running out for all of the faithful unless something could be done posthaste. Still, considering what Giuseppe had accomplished for far, Pope Romanus could not deny the request. No one other than him really knew what had happened to the Monsignor's hearing to begin with.

The two of them had had a lengthy but awkward discussion on paper about the Monsignor's predicament, though no real headway had been made in convincing the man that he had not breached his allegiance with God.

His most convincing argument and the one that the Pope could not refute was that if there was no breach in his vows as a priest and more so as a man of faith, his hearing would have already returned. Deep down in his heart, the Pope knew this to be true, but tried to dissuade the thought for the sake of not only Giuseppe's well-being, but because he was indispensable at this moment in time.

More so, the pope thought that with time, Giuseppe might receive absolution for his breach of faith through his deeds. The Pope, who tried to prove his point, performed the rite of Absolution on the man. He let him leave only after he swore, he would turn right around and join him in the fight for their salvation if his hearing returned.

Due to the deteriorating conditions within Italy, the pope thought it best that Giuseppe not travel alone, especially with the white collar around his neck, which he refused to remove. At this point, the collar had become a bull's-eye of sorts and the pope feared for the younger man's life.

The monsignor had expressed a desire to make a lone pilgrimage to the Duomo, but the pope, recognizing his deteriorating condition, would not allow it. To him, Giuseppe looked pale and gaunt and in dire need of a meal. The pope surmised what others hadn't; the man seemed to be fasting his way into oblivion. He refused any sort of nourishment, even when the pope ordered him to eat. In his present condition, the pope knew that man had not eaten since his confrontation with the dragon, even though he fell short of admitting as much. The only thing the monsignor had done to sustain his well-being was to sip water on occasion. With all this in mind, the pope refused to let him go solo and asked Flo and Trey to accompany him. He lent them the use of his jet for expediency and safety's sake, praying that some sort of intervention might take place and he would soon return.

*   *   *

Flo had been asked by her editor to return to the site of the revelation and continue to forward her enlightening articles on the advancing catastrophe. For the sake of her friend the monsignor, she refused to do so, but readily agreed to accompany the monsignor to the Duomo when asked. Trey, who would not leave her side at this point under no condition, went with her.

The monsignor, artful at masking his depressed condition, acted as if nothing had occurred at all. He planned to leave the two of them to wander through the streets of Milan while he took refuge inside the cathedral.

On the flight North, Flo broached the subject of the Antichrist. "Do you believe this man Ahriman to be the true Antichrist, Monsignor, or do you believe him to be an imposter?" she first asked and then wrote the question down.

"Think about his name for a moment, will you?' he wrote.

"In what regard…? Other than it is an uncommon name, I really don't follow your point."

The priest asked for a larger pad of paper and began to write his retort in a furious manner. This action unnerved Flo, who suddenly felt as if she had once again angered the man.

She read his note to Trey. "I believe you still haven't caught on yet. Even after all this time, I should think that you would have all ready known the answer to this question, but seeing as you seem to be clueless, once again I shall endeavor to enlighten you one last time." She glanced at the monsignor and spoke to Trey. "The name, Ahriman, is underlined three times." She paused a moment and then continued. "The name Ahriman is a derivative or alternate name for the evil God, Angra Mainyu, which traces its roots to the ancient Persian religion of Zoroastrianism. Most scholars who have studied this ancient religion in depth have concluded the name Ahriman is the embodiment of all things that we consider evil. This evil God has a counterpart if you will, a ying and yang of sorts, as it deals with the basic concepts of this religion. The Ahura Mazda or the good god is its counterpart.

'This Angra Mainyu, or Ahriman, is said to have developed demonic spirits, which are represented by afflictions to the human condition represented as pain, suffering and death, which if you haven't noticed, is what is what is happening to humanity at this very moment in time.

'Moreover, some of the gods of this religion are even found in Hindu texts as well. And, to enlighten you even further because it is such an ancient religion, some scholars have noted that the basis for Judaic and Christian based religions trace their roots of origin to Zoroastrianism. Whether or not this is true, I cannot tell you for sure, but there are woven into modern day religions the traces of many ancient religions.

'The religion of fire, as Zoroastrianism is called, is still practiced in some areas of the world and its priests go by the name of Magi. I am sure you get the correlation here; the Magi crossed the desert following the star of Bethlehem to bring gifts to the baby Jesus. Like I said some time ago, there are many correlations available to us if we bother to look at them objectively."

Flo turned toward the monsignor when she finished reading but he was fast asleep, or pretending to be. She turned toward Trey. "Was he trying to say that the gifts of myrrh, frankincense and gold from the Magi were most likely an analogy for the passing of certain beliefs from one religion to another?"

Trey had her re-read the monsignor's written reply one more time, and then nodded. "I believe that is exactly what he was trying to tell you."

"You know, sometimes this subject of religious origins is all too confusing for someone like me," she said slowly. "You could spend a lifetime researching something as complex as this subject seems to be and never be absolutely sure of the conclusions you draw."

"Now I think you get some idea of what make the monsignor tick, don't you?"

Flo never answered, lost in thought.

The battle raged on unabated and seemed to grow in intensity the closer the battling warriors neared the ancient city. The filming of the event grew more dramatic, but now it was nearly impossible to discern the lines of defense or for that matter get a clear picture of what exactly was going on. Some scientists began to wonder if the blowing sand from the surface winds was interfering with their ability to see the battle clearly, somehow diffusing the blue-white light. An argument ensued as to what was really happening at this point.

"The interference is not caused by sands which are visible to the naked eye, or sands we can feel pelting our faces, but by sands that are only visible under the influence of the light." Dr. Newman from MIT said.

"What's the difference?" one of his detractors asked.

"The difference is relatively easy to explain," he replied. "We are using the latest technology available to filter out any interference from external sources; light, dirt or in this case, sand, as you purport."

"I don't believe you," the detractor stated. "Either that or your equipment is faulty. Would you have me believe we are losing the picture to the opposite side because of what is going on in a dimension we have no control over?"

"That's exactly what I've been trying to tell you all this time, and from all the recent observations that have been forwarded, I would have thought you might have drawn the same conclusion that I have. Two days ago, we brought out the latest signal generator, which has twice the power. The camera has twice the resolution and the picture still isn't any clearer!"

"I find all this hard to believe."

Dr. Newman grew tired of the inane questions. "The vortex the satellite sees is what my camera sees as well!"

"That's impossible, and you know it!"

"Well, if you can come up with a better answer to the problem, you had better let me know. As far as I can tell, both dimensions seem to be merging with one another the closer we get to Megiddo. Unless you can come up with something more tangible, I've got work to do."

"Again, I'm trying to tell you that it is impossible for two unlike dimensions to intersect!" the detractor argued.

Dr. Newman stopped and turned to face him. "But that is where you are wrong, my friend. It is possible if you add something to the equation that you refuse to acknowledge - the X-factor."

"Well, you had better enlighten me, for I haven't a clue what you mean by the X- factor."

"It's rather easy to equate as far as I'm concerned," Dr. Newman shrugged. "The X-factor is intervention from the hand of God."

*   *   *

Once again some of the angels were asking for the exact same thing,

"Gabriel, you led us to believe at some point in time, when the truth became inevitable to the humans, that we would finally get some assistance to defeat the dragon!"

"Ariel, once again, you wish to alter the fate of man by interfering. I must once again ask you to cease, as this is not your call to make."

"Gabriel, both Michael and you know that due to what has happened to mankind, there are legions of Guardians at your disposal; utilize them before it's too late!"

"I cannot and will not honor your request! Not until only one of us is left standing. Only then will the lone survivor petition the Almighty for assistance. Let us pray it never comes to that point. Listen to reason here, some headway has been made. The battle stalls at times."

"I agree that it does, but then it lurches forward once again at an ever-quickening pace. You and Michael, better than all the rest, know what that means. Don't pretend you are naïve enough not to know what is transpiring here. We are drawn closer by the day."

"That Ariel, is none of your concern, remember that."

Marek had drawn his sword in defense of his leader, using a show of force in order to diffuse the situation, but Michael ordered him to stand down.

Ariel made one final petition. *"Then call out for the rest of the chosen ones and make a last stand before it is too late. I know if we had a few more legions, we could turn the tide and drive them back to the sea."*

The howling wind however, carried the plea towards the abyss.

CHAPTER 18

Terminus

The Duomo of Milan stood in shambles. From the piazza, Flo could make out many of the spires that once adorned the roofline, now scattered into thousands of pieces strewn around the periphery of the building. Many more of them were broken and hung precariously from the edges of the roof. She noticed many of the statues that once fit snugly into their alcoves were either broken or missing. She scanned the entire piazza and noticed that some of the surrounding buildings had collapsed and lay in mounds of rubble. No one was on the piazza, deserted except for the pigeons that could not fly due to a thick coat of dust that had coated their feathers like tar.

The monsignor stood frozen on the top step of the Metro. He had not moved for quite some time. Tears streamed down his cheeks, yet his face was expressionless.

Flo knew he was crushed by the sight of it all and moved to console him. She wrapped her hand around his waist and hugged him gently. He did not react, but stood looking up at the aged edifice as if he had lost his only friend. She recalled what he had once told her about the events that led him to his calling, and knew this was the place he had so affectionately described.

She coaxed him into movement, pulling him forward with her arm. He did not resist and they rose and traversed the piazza almost halfway before he began to resist. He stopped and turned to his right. He looked up and Flo noticed him looking at what looked like a giant television screen turned upside down, hanging precariously by only one stanchion. As they stood there, a slight aftershock from the earthquake sent tremors through the piazza. The screen came crashing to the ground, a plume of dust rising in its place. She noticed the monsignor smile momentarily and then turned away as if dismissing the entire event as inconsequential.

Before they proceeded to the entrance of the Duomo, Flo saw the caution tape encircling the front of the church. The entire south wall had broken away, leaving a visible gap to the interior. Its two massive gothic oak doors were splintered and the archway of the doors had been compressed by the shift in the cathedral walls.

The monsignor disengaged himself from her and began to walk toward the smaller door to the left. Flo watched him walk away. She turned to Trey. "What does this remind you of?"

"I really can't tell you at this point, other than to say it is a tragedy."

"It is that, but more than that it reminds me of the Catholic Church itself," she said, her voice somber. "It's crumbing around us and we are hard pressed to do anything about it." By this time, the monsignor had reached the door and was trying to force his way in. "Trey, go and give him a hand. He means to get into that cathedral one way or another."

The two men were able to force the door open wide enough where they could pass through. What surprised Flo when she entered, other than the size and grandeur of the building, was that there were people inside. With the door open, Flo noticed that no one made an effort to leave, though her original thought when she entered was that they had been trapped. It soon became apparent that was not the case.

The monsignor scribbled a note in English to Flo.

'Leave me.'

Flo refused, shaking her head vehemently. She felt Trey's hand on her shoulder as the monsignor made his way up the center aisle towards the altar.

"Leave him be," Trey suggested. "He needs the time alone without distraction. If you don't understand that, then I don't think you know him all that well. If it is any consolation to you, we won't wander too far away, just in case."

"I know, but I'm worried."

"Don't be."

Flo watched as the monsignor stopped in front of the altar and knelt on the marble floor. This is where he stayed, immobile like a statue.

It was late afternoon before Flo stirred; she had fallen asleep against Trey's shoulder, seated in one of the last pews of the cathedral. Her eyes immediately sought the monsignor, who remained in the position they had left him. "How long can anyone stand to be in that position for an extended period of time?"

"I don't believe you understand his level of conviction, Flo," Trey said with a sigh. "Come on let's go and try and find something to eat. I'm starving."

"What if he's not here when we return?"

"Trust me for once, he's not going to go anywhere," Trey reassured her. "You had to have seen the look on his face when he was first afflicted. That tells the story in a nutshell. I won't say anything more."

"Do you think it is safe to leave?"

"Safe enough," Trey said patting his armpit in the process. "I didn't come here unprepared; we have an advantage of sorts."

When they returned to the cathedral after eating, the sun had fallen and the only sources of illumination were the candles on either side of the altar. Flo had to strain her eyes in order to see the darkened outline of the priest before the altar. He had not moved. "How long do you think he's going to stay there, Trey?"

"It is my thought that he will remain there for as long as he can endure."

"Do you think we ought to move closer to him, just in case?"

"No, I don't," he shook his head. "We'll just keep an eagle eye on him and wait. He has all the time in the world, and he deserves it. He'll let us know when it's time, until then we'll just be patient." He turned to her. "Can you do that?"

Flo was miffed by the remark but did not comment.

It was not until the wee hours of the morning that Trey finally noticed the priest move; his left arm had come up first and then his right and it looked as if the man was invoking God in some manner that Trey could not hear. "Flo, wake up!" He nudged her shoulder in the process.

"What time is it?'

"It's almost daybreak."

Flo, who was still gathering her wits about her, spoke groggily. "How do you know?"

"The early morning light is just starting to diffuse the colors of the stained-glass windows."

Trey noticed the priest had finally turned his head and seemed to looking in their direction. He then saw the priest beckoned them ever so slowly. Trey had to admire the man; he had stayed in one position for over twenty hours, a feat he knew he could not replicate.

When they reached his side, he asked for assistance in rising. He and Flo guided him arm-in-arm to the first pew, where Flo gave him a bottle of water on which he sipped gingerly. She also offered him some bread she had saved from dinner the night before. He nibbled on it for several moments and then stuffed the rest of it in his vestment pocket, waving them away in the process.

They retreated once again to the back of the cathedral. Trey's only comment was, "It's your turn." He was fast asleep moments later.

It was mid afternoon when he was woken by an incessant jab to the ribs. He turned to find Flo pressing her elbow into his side. "What's going on?"

"He calling for us once again," she explained. "He sat for no more than twenty minutes and then walked to the altar and placed the bread I gave him on it and then kneeled there once again. He hasn't moved since. I felt so sorry for him that I started to cry, but he just about staggered to the altar. I wanted to assist him, but then I remembered what you told me."

When they approached him, Flo gasped and shook her head at the sight of him. His hair had turned snow white and he looked ten years older.

"Impossible," Trey remarked, but when he looked into the monsignor's eyes, he saw the look of determination shining in them once again. "Flo, ask him a question."

Flo turned to Trey, befuddled by the request.

"Go ahead and ask him anything."

When she did, the monsignor answered her promptly. Trey turned to the altar to see a white lily lying there amongst the dust and debris, where the bread once lay.

Impossible, he thought, lilies do not bloom this time of the year!

Again in Rome, they tried to catch up on events that had transpired in their three-day absence. By the time they were briefed on the latest developments, it was hard to believe the battle had progressed this far and even harder to believe what the scientists had come up with. Even more incredible still was what was happening around the globe there seemed to be total mayhem.

"What else can happen?" Flo said dejectedly.

"That depends," Trey replied. "I'm beginning to believe the pot is boiling. What fascinates me at this point though is why more and more people seem to be drawn toward the fire."

"What do you mean by that?"

"Here, read this," he said, extending the latest report from Israel. "The battle is no less than twenty miles from Megiddo, but what amazes me is the sheer number of people gathering to witness the event."

Flo read it, disbelieving. "Did I read this right? There are close to two million people headed for the city?"

"No, you read it wrong," Trey shook his head. "There are two million already there and the numbers are increasing by ten percent a day. If you do the math, and if what my uncle tells me about the time line proves to be true - that there are seven days or less until the battle reaches its destination - you're looking at over three million people standing around waiting and praying for something of epic proportions to happen."

Flo shook her head in wonder.

"Add to that number the people Ahriman has directed to the site to counter the viable threat, and you can just about double that figure. The way I figure it, that's enough people to ring the ancient city fifty deep. I don't care what your editor wants at this point. You're crazy if you think it will be safe to go back there under any circumstance."

"I hear you loud and clear, don't preach, not now anyway," Flo frowned. "Let's think about this for a moment."

"Write from here," he urged. "Your editor hasn't a clue where you are anyway. At least until we hear from the monsignor."

"I suppose you're right."

"You know I am," he said. "Just let common sense prevail for now."

*   *   *

When the monsignor walked into the room for his meeting with the council of seven, he heard the gasps of surprise. Though he hadn't bothered to look into a mirror, he knew his outward appearance had radically changed. What surprised him most was the look on the pontiff's face. It was a look he had never witnessed before in his life, and when the Pope made the sign of the cross, he had a feeling the pope already knew something mystical had occurred. When the pope spoke though, he acted as if everything was normal. He gestured him to have a seat opposite of him and tried to make him feel like his prodigal son returning home after an extended absence. The monsignor sat slowly, unsure if he had the energy to make it though the meeting.

The pope said a prayer over the group before he turned to one his council.

"Bring the monsignor up to speed here. I would like a full report from every one of you, and don't leave anything out." He turned to his right and spoke anew. "Monsignor Sforza, please begin."

It took close to two hours before the group had divulged all of its information.

"Well, what do you think, Monsignor Lorenzo?" the pope asked

"Do you want me to be truthful?" Giuseppe asked his voice again strong and sure.

"Why, of course I do," the pope assured him. "I would have it no other way."

"It's not what I think that matters any longer; it's what you must do that matters from this point forward. Like the shepherd who gathers his sheep unto his fold, you must gather every one of the religious leaders and all the high priests of every known denomination together under that fold. Then, you march into Megiddo. At the precise moment that you confront Satan and his cohorts, it will be through the power of prayer from all who remain who fear retribution that you will have the energy to defeat him. This, I warn you, must occur at the moment of confrontation or all will be lost."

The pope's face drained of color.

"I have given this dilemma my utmost consideration," Giuseppe continued. "This you must do without Ahriman even having a clue about what it is you intend to do. Let me stress here that the matter of secrecy is of the utmost importance. If a word of what we are planning to do reaches his ears, I am afraid there is no hope for us, for he will do everything in his power to prevent us from prevailing."

Uproar ensued in the room. The pope raised his hand to silence the group, though one of them spoke up.

"How do you come to that conclusion, Monsignor Lorenzo?"

"Because it is written in the third letter of Fatima, the true forecast of future events. Never mind, there is no other viable explanation other than the letter to guide us. Pope Romanus knows the reasoning behind my thoughts. I believe he is in a better position than I am to explain to you what I mean."

The pope paled even more.

"We have five days to accomplish this task, so I believe we haven't a moment to lose, is that not correct, your Excellency?"

"Yes," he said in an almost inaudible voice. "I pray to the Lord that you are right, Giuseppe!"

"You know I am," Giuseppe replied somberly. "He has told me as much. Besides it's our Lady who still sheds her tears of blood for all of humanity and the world in which they occupy."

When the three of them met once again, it was Trey who had the greatest reaction to what was discussed. "What do you mean, we're going to Megiddo? Monsignor, that's nothing short of suicide."

"It's providence that leads us down the path of righteousness," he said. "Have no apprehensions. Know this. You will feel His hand upon your shoulder and He will stand among us. Don't fear what you weren't meant to comprehend, just do as He directs us to do."

"Are you positive?" Flo asked.

The monsignor slid two copies of the Fatima letter across the table. "Read this, and then the both of you will understand. I have an apology to make. This is something that I have felt would come to pass for quite some time. To be totally honest, I withheld it from the both of you for altruistic reasons, but more so I owe you an apology, Ms. Rinna. I never thought you were correct in your assumptions, which was my mistake."

Flo picked up her copy and read it. When she had finished, she spoke. "I guess this not only explains your guarded behavior, but it also explains what must happen in the end, I suppose."

"There is no other recourse," the monsignor said.

"If that's the case, what can we do to help?" Trey commented.

It was the twentieth of December. The battle stalled one mile from the center of the city of Megiddo and stayed there for an entire day. It was no longer possible to film the event, and those who were not there were deprived of witnessing the events as they unfolded.

The wind had suddenly stopped, which caught everyone off guard. Those standing a distance away from the battle were able to witness the planetary alignment. Only the planet Venus had to move just a fraction to form a perfect alignment. News of this event made its way by word-of-mouth to the front of the crowd and people began to radiate fear of what was about to transpire. The mood of the crowd became somber and chaste; this heightened their fears as many began to call out for redemption.

That night, a lightning storm of epic proportions erupted in the heavens. Lightning streaked across the sky, leaving hundreds of momentary tentacles etched into the darkness. This continued unabated for hours on end and lit the night unto day. The oddest thing about this occurrence was with all of this lightning, it still did not rain. Not a drop fell from the sky nor did the temperature vary either.

A dead stillness encompassed the crowd.

This caused the level of anxiety among the observers to rise even further. Many became scared and ran away from the site, sending waves of panic throughout the crowd. Still others were not deterred by the sight but prayed all the louder. They kept a vigil, knowing something of dramatic proportions was about to happen.

In the interim, between the lightning strikes, the ground began to shake once again. Only this time many fissures began to form, opening the earth almost a foot wide in places. Some of the crowd began to moan in protest over their predicament and once again, some of them began to run away, fearing for their lives. Still others denounced the Creator for abandoning them. They were cast into these fissures, which seem to momentarily open wider to allow them to pass, never to be seen again.

Some of the crowd was literally trapped on islands that formed from these cracks. They screamed for assistance and some good Samaritans began to utilize whatever means necessary to improvise a means of spanning these fissures to save them. Some even began to use their own bodies as human bridges, risking certain death by their acts of heroism. For all those who chose to run from impending disaster, ten more moved forward to take their place, inextricably drawn forward to close the gaps that had been opened by unbelievers.

The religious leaders of the world had managed to make it to a pre-designated staging area at the rear of the crowd. Trey volunteered to scout the front of the crowd when they arrived in order to inform the pope and the others of the conditions that might befall them. He did not return that night, nor did he return early the following morning when the wind once again rose to such a fury that it was almost impossible to see ten feet in front of your face.

"Monsignor, do you think he is lost, or maybe worse, has been killed?" Flo asked, fearing Trey would not return.

"He will return," the monsignor reassured her. "You must give him time. Have faith in him for once, it is something that you lack and needs to be addressed from this moment forward, else wise I believe you will not make it through this day unscathed. Do you understand what I mean when I say this, Ms. Rinna?"

"I do, I do, but that does not make me less of a person to show some sort of emotion for him. I am concerned for him and I love him, but most of all I am concerned for all of us."

"Many of us will not survive the day," the monsignor stated. "That much I am sure of. With that in mind you must steel your reserves and keep the faith, especially now in the hour of his need."

Flo understood the double-entendre once again and hugged the man. She felt nothing but skin and bone, but did not relinquish her grasp for some time, her windblown hair now a mask that covered the monsignor's face.

It was some time later, about mid-morning, when Trey finally made it back to the group. Flo ran to him when she saw him and gathered him in her arms. He looked drawn, covered in dust. She wiped his face with a scarf that covered hers and searched his face in order to judge the severity of the news. "How bad is it?" she asked.

"Bad enough for me to rush back here as fast as humanly possible in order to inform the rest."

"What do you mean?' the monsignor asked, joining them.

"It would probably be better if I explained what I saw to all concerned," Trey said. "That way they will have a better understanding what we are up against."

However, when the monsignor spread his arms to indicate all the leaders, Trey realized what he was asking.

"There are thousands of religious here, Trey. I believe what you are asking is a near impossibility under these conditions," Flo said, looking to the monsignor for some sort of acknowledgement to her assessment.

"Well then, maybe the heads of the churches will do."

When they had gathered around him, Trey began to recount the sights that he saw; the people, the fissures, their moods and the conditions they were about to face. "But the most incredible event of all was something that I find almost hard to believe, something that I've never witnessed before. As soon as the first light broke over the horizon, the wind began to howl. I was so used to the intensity of it that when it occurred again, I never gave it a second thought, other than it had returned with unabated fury. I was making my way up toward the front of the crowd, sidestepping confrontations from what I assumed to be Ahriman's followers and those who have come to pray, when I heard a howling noise somewhat similar to a freight train. I looked ahead to see how far I had to go when I saw a wall of dust spin into what looked like a giant tornado. To be truthful, it wasn't exactly a tornado either; but a spinning cloud of dust that rose just high enough to obscure anyone's ability to see the city of Megiddo from that point forward. To be perfectly honest I have never seen anything quite like this before. I did not advance any further, but stayed back, just in case the funnel had the ability to sweep anyone away. I noticed people who were no more than several feet away from the wall were not affected by it. Then one man gathered the courage to try and pass though the cloud to get to the other side. He was lifted and carried by this funnel, if you will, up and away, thrown into the crowd some forty feet away. Several more people tried the same thing and the same thing happened to them. This is apparently the vortex that my uncle spoke about. I tried to make my way off to one side to see if it was just occurring in front of us. As I did so, so did the crowd, who began to look for an alternate entrance to the city."

"Did you find another way in?" one of the church leaders asked.

No, I didn't. Though to be honest, it would have taken the better part of the day fighting the shifting crowds, to circle the city. I can only assume that it goes all the way around the city, which would explain the circular motion that you can see but cannot feel until you come in contact with it."

What else did you see?" Flo asked.

"It's not so much what I saw from that point forward, but the feeling I got from this circular cloud. It just felt ominous!"

"What are we going to do?" another religious leader asked.

"We will do as we have intended to do all along," the monsignor stated firmly. "We will march to the front of the crowd."

"How are we going to pass though a barrier that seems to be impregnable?" still another leader asked.

"We will worry about that minor detail when we get there," the monsignor shrugged.

"Then who will lead us?"

It was the Pope who stepped forward and tried to instill a note of confidence into the group. "I will, and my College of Cardinals will follow right behind me. One of us is bound to make it through, allowing all others to pass. All you have to do is to follow my staff; it will lead us to where we need to be."

The monsignor smiled at this point, knowing his mentor had willingly taken charge and accepted his fate without question. He had expected nothing less.

Flo turned to Trey and whispered in his ear. "What do you think awaits us on the other side?"

"I haven't got a clue."

The pope gathered the College of Cardinals behind him, witnessed the look of apprehension to downright fear on some of them as he spoke. "We must pray for our redemption!"

He began to walk toward the front of the crowd, while the religious leaders followed in tow. Several men from the crowd joined him on either side, forming a wedge.

"Clear a path!" they said as they procession began to inch forward ever so slowly at first. Soon, the crowd began to give way and the procession continued to proceed forward in a slow but deliberate manner.

When the crowd began to push to either side, some members of the new world order cursed the group. Some of them began to spit on them. Still others began to hurl food or whatever they could find in their direction, and many of the religious become plastered in the vile consequence of their detractors. Some of the priests were bleeding, having been struck by flying objects. The righteous within the crowd tried to set up a human barrier between the leaders and their detractors.

The followers of Ahriman tried to disrupt the procession at various intervals, but the group held fast as more of their supporters stepped forward to assist them, opening a clear path for the procession.

As they approached closer to the wall, it became evident to many that it was as Trey had described; an ominous sight and one that seemed impenetrable.

The pontiff stopped just a foot from the raging turmoil.

He paused for several seconds and Flo wondered what he intended to do. She and Trey were off to his right. She saw him lift his staff above his head and heard his incantation.

"In His name, the commander of heaven and earth, the light of all and the creator of everything we come to know, I command as His representative that you open up a way."

He struck the vortex with his staff and it opened up into a view Flo wished never to set eyes upon again.

There, in front of her, the battle raged on; the Sons of the Lamb and the sons of Satan fighting for their lives.

Moments after he struck the vortex, two angels appeared on either side of the opening, holding it open. They seemed to have made an arch with the use of their outstretched arms, allowing only the religious within the procession to pass.

As soon as Flo passed the threshold of the opening, her ears were assaulted by the noise of battle. True as the scientists had predicted, the two dimensions had collided and she could see, hear and feel the clashes of swords. She looked up to see the angels swarming the battlefield, giving chase to the demons who tried desperately to escape their swords. The battle seemed to have turned, though there were less Sons of the Lamb on the field.

She noticed the pope stop from time to time, praying over one or another of those fallen, seemly oblivious to the carnage that surrounded him and the attempts on his life. He began to falter in step as he proceeded. The monsignor grabbed his arm to aid him.

The few angels that were left began to intervene, beating back all who sought the life of Pope Romanus. Flo turned to see some of the other religious leaders felled by those who opposed them. She desperately clung to Trey as he made himself a shield to protect her with his body. She suddenly noticed he had a sword in his right hand and it was covered in blood. She did not know when or where he had acquired it, but she knew he was intent on using it in her defense.

They had progressed nearly a half a mile into the fray and stood now near the initial line of defense of the city. She saw the base of Mount Megiddo from her vantage point and could barely make out the cross atop of it. She knew from what she had read and researched after acquiring the third letter of Fatima that this was their intended destination.

The line of defense fell back as they progressed. As they reached the base of the mount, she feared the pope could go no further. She heard Monsignor Lorenzo coaxing the pope into movement. One of the Muslim leaders stepped forward, along with a Jewish Rabbi, both assisting him. The monsignor, himself in a weakened state, gladly stepped aside to allow the two clergy to assist him.

They had just made the first step onto the incline when suddenly the brightest light Flo had ever witnessed flashed in front of them, the same blue-white light that Anhur had so vividly described. She was sure that her eyesight should have failed her by the visual onslaught, but to her surprise, it didn't.

She looked up to see what she was sure was a hallucination; a vision of the most beautiful woman anyone could ever imagine. She knew words could hardly give an accurate description of what she saw, as the woman floated above them, radiating in beauty and light.

The Virgin Mary floated above them and as she did so, she outstretched her arms in such a manner that Flo had the impression she was holding something of great weight.

Suddenly, to the left and above her right shoulder an angel appeared. In his left hand he held a flaming sword, which he pointed it to those below him.

She heard the Monsignor's voice. "Duma, the collector of souls!"

The angel screamed in rage, "Penance, penance, penance!"

Flo turned to look behind her. The clashing of swords ceased for a moment and the battle stopped momentarily. She could not believe that words alone could alter anything, much less a raging battle. When she turned again toward Our Lady, she saw the flames from Dumas's sword ignite the ground near her. She felt the heat as it singed the hair on her arm and the scent of burning flesh wafted through the air. She turned to see the body of one of Satan's minion's burn into the soil that surrounded him.

She turned once again to the vision and saw the woman quench the sword of the angel, knowing if she hadn't, he would have rid the scourge of Lucifer through fire, one soldier at a time. Once the flame of the sword was quenched, the battle began to rage once more.

The Pope continued to climb with assistance. They reached the top of the flattened mount to gaze at the cross before them. The Virgin Mary now hovered well above the cross. When Flo looked beneath it, she saw the pope had stumbled and fell prostrate in front of the cross. He finally made it to his knees with assistance, but no further than that. Something seemed to be holding him down. Flo looked up at the cross once again to see a sight and wished she had never been born.

There, in front of the cross, stood Ahriman. Slight to his rear stood a man in cloaked garb. Flo saw a red light emitted from his eyes and had to turn away. She looked back at Ahriman, who then spoke with such eloquence that Flo felt it hard to resist him.

"Give their souls unto me."

The pope replied in such a forceful manner that the dry soil floated around his face. "Never!" Several of his minions advanced and stabbed him with their swords. Flo watched in shock as the pope collapsed onto the ground. She screamed out in anguish. As she did so, her voice distracted Trey. The monsignor grabbed the sword out of his hand and advanced on Ahriman with lightning speed, driving the sword up and into his heart until only the hilt was visible.

"Detritus," the monsignor said. "How does it feel now that you had to give up your son as well in an effort to save the souls of the ones you were sworn to take?"

Detritus, whose eyes flashed bright red, raised his arm and lowered his hood. Flo found it almost impossible to comprehend his features; the evil incarnate atop of the man's head were the horns of a lamb and he roared out in anguish at the loss of his son. He tried to answer the challenge but his voice was tenuous at first. Gathering his strength, flames shot out of his mouth instead of words.

The monsignor taunted him once again. "It is a high price to pay for the sin of fetishism, Lucifer. Now what will you do? Your son is slain and your kingdom is crumbling around you!"

"I shall destroy you, like all others who dare oppose me!"

"Before you try to do that, answer one question," the monsignor challenged. "Do you want us to nail your son to this cross? I can think of no better symbolism!"

Detritus roared out in defiance once again. The dragon appeared behind him. Flo could not believe the size of the creature, its heads lolling from side to side, deciding whom to strike first.

The Monsignor was not daunted by the sight of the beast. Flo heard his voice once again.

"Why is it that you cannot do your own bidding?" he chided. "Must you always draw your strength from the beast, which exemplifies the evil you enjoy?"

Enraged, Detritus grabbed the priest and tried to shake the life out of him while his minions began to indiscriminately slaughter the religious leaders on the mount.

Trey rushed forward to assist the monsignor but was batted away by the beast. Then, out of nowhere, legions upon legions of angels appeared and clouded the air.

It was the Archangel Gabriel who swooped down, lopped off the head of Satan with his sword and held it high as an offering to Our Lady, as the monsignor collapsed on the ground.

Our Lady smiled at the offering and vanished.

In her place, two more angels appeared, carrying crystal vases. They settled on the arms of the cross. The vases looked as if they were filled to capacity with blood - the blood of the faithful.

Flo watched the legion of angels descend on the beast and hack it into a thousand pieces. All at once, a deep hole opened up in the ground in front of the cross. Flo saw the boiling magma at the bottom of it, and all she could think about when she saw it was that it reminded her of her thoughts and expectations of Hell. It was written as such.

The angels tossed the remains of the Ahriman, Detritus and the beast into the hole as towering flames erupted from within.

She turned away from the sight to shield her face from the heat and flames, only to see the wall of dust fall on the horizon, allowing those who had subscribed to see what would prove to be inevitable while still another legion of angels descended onto the field of battle slaying all the opponents to His will and ended the reign once and for all.

Then, the sky grew black and a sense of trepidation washed over her once again. Flo's first thought was the sky had darkened by what looked like a plague of locusts approaching the city, but then she realized it was the scarred and blackened souls of the lost as they made their way into the hole of fire.

The start of a new beginning...

9 798893 912395